Deadly
Aim

Also by Patricia H. Rushford
in Large Print:

Desperate Measures
A Haunting Refrain
Now I Lay Me Down to Sleep
Red Sky in Mourning

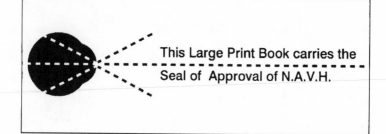

This Large Print Book carries the
Seal of Approval of N.A.V.H.

An Angel Delaney Mystery
Book 1

Deadly
Aim

Patricia H. Rushford

Thorndike Press • Waterville, Maine

Published in 2005 by arrangement with Baker Book House.

Thorndike Press® Large Print Christian Mystery.

The tree indicium is a trademark of Thorndike Press.

The text of this Large Print edition is unabridged.
Other aspects of the book may vary from the original edition.

Set in 16 pt. Plantin by Elena Picard.

Printed in the United States on permanent paper.

Library of Congress Cataloging-in-Publication Data

Rushford, Patricia H.
    Deadly aim / by Patricia H. Rushford.
      p. cm. — (An Angel Delaney mystery ; bk. 1)
    (Thorndike Press large print Christian mystery)
    ISBN 0-7862-7283-X (lg. print : hc : alk. paper)
    1. Police shootings — Fiction. 2. Policewomen — Fiction.
    3. Large type books. I. Title. II. Thorndike Press large
print Christian mystery series.
PS3568.U7274D39 2005
    813′.54—dc22
                                   2004025066

To Travis, my partner in crime

As the Founder/CEO of NAVH, the only national health agency solely devoted to those who, although not totally blind, have an eye disease which could lead to serious visual impairment, I am pleased to recognize Thorndike Press* as one of the leading publishers in the large print field.

Founded in 1954 in San Francisco to prepare large print textbooks for partially seeing children, NAVH became the pioneer and standard setting agency in the preparation of large type.

Today, those publishers who meet our standards carry the prestigious "Seal of Approval" indicating high quality large print. We are delighted that Thorndike Press is one of the publishers whose titles meet these standards. We are also pleased to recognize the significant contribution Thorndike Press is making in this important and growing field.

Lorraine H. Marchi, L.H.D.
Founder/CEO
NAVH

* Thorndike Press encompasses the following imprints: Thorndike, Wheeler, Walker and Large Print Press.

ONE

Mist rolled gray and thick over the small coastal town of Sunset Cove, Oregon. Perfect weather for what needed to be done. Ordinarily he left it up to his manager to oversee the operations. But not tonight. Well, morning actually. It was nearly 3:00 a.m.

Though he'd worked with the same crew for over a year, he didn't trust them, any of them. He'd gotten word that one of his dealers was skimming — and worse, stealing controlled drugs from local pharmacies. Of course, most dealers skimmed a little, but J.J. was getting far too greedy, even thinking about setting up his own business. He should know better than to pull a stunt like that. Nobody double-crossed Duke and got away with it.

Duke. Humph. A rich name for a rich dude. That's all they knew about him, and that's all he wanted them to know. Not even his manager knew who he really was or what he did.

He rolled his thick shoulders and massaged his neck muscles through his black turtleneck. He'd had a rough week. Not that it mattered, of course. For him, one day faded into another. But it wouldn't always be like that. Two more years and he'd retire, at least from his day job.

Catching a glimpse of his reflection in the window, Duke smiled. To look at him, no one would suspect that he was anything but an upstanding citizen.

He left the window, moving silently to his closet, where he took the polished wooden case off the shelf. Opening it, he lifted his .45-caliber semiautomatic pistol out of its velvet-lined case, shoved in a magazine from his stockpile, and slipped the gun into his holster. He then lifted the silencer out of the case and dropped it into his right pocket.

His lips curled in a sneer. These babies were rare, and the government kept close tabs on who had them. Not his though. The previous owner was six feet under. When Duke was sixteen years old, after years of abuse, he'd finally gotten the upper hand over his father. And he'd been lucky enough to stash the silencer and the gun before the cops had shown up.

Duke looked down at the gun. He could've skipped the silencer. Sunset Cove's finest would be too far away from the docks to hear anything, and most of the residents would be asleep. But he wanted the added insurance.

He donned a drab olive rain slicker and jammed his feet into iron-toed work boots. The jacket stretched tight across his shoulders as he tied the laces.

Ten minutes later he entered the condemned brick building and made his way to the far end, through what had once been an office, and out to the dock. The old dock rocked and moaned in protest as he moved into the darker shadows of the building, where J.J. wouldn't be able to see him. While he waited, Duke watched the lights across the bay and up the hill where Sunset Cove's wealthiest residents lived. *Some day.*

He sniffled and used the back of his hand to wipe his nose — blasted fog always made his nose run. He didn't like having to be out here in the open and so close to where the drugs were stored. Didn't like having to deal with these punks on a personal level.

But Duke couldn't help chuckling quietly to himself. J.J. would think he was coming up in the world. Maybe, if the kid believed in God, he would be going up. Doubtful though. The guy had done time for messing up his girlfriend's face with a knife, among other things. J.J. wasn't exactly what you'd call religious. But then neither was Duke.

Duke stiffened when he heard the pilings groan. He drew the .45 out of his holster, attached the silencer, and released the safety.

"Don't come any farther," Duke warned, lowering his voice to the familiar growl he used when he talked to these punks. His godfather imitation.

"Uh — okay."

The kid sounded nervous. Good.

"Word come down you wanted to see me. What's happenin'?"

Duke liked watching the kid squirm, just like he'd enjoyed watching his father plead with him. Too bad. He had the upper hand and intended to keep it.

"Somethin' wrong?" J.J. reached inside his jacket.

Duke tensed, then relaxed, when J.J. pulled out a pack of cigarettes. "You tell me."

J.J.'s hands shook as he held the lighter to his face. The whites of his eyes glowed yellow. "This don't sound so good." He took a drag and blew smoke out of his nose. "Somebody been rattin' on me. Cause if they have —"

"You got the money from last night's take?"

"Yeah." He lifted a pack off his shoulders. "Seventy-five hundred."

"That's all?"

"Hey, man, what're you saying?" J.J. set the bag on the dock and took a step away from it.

"The usual take for a weekend night is ten grand," Duke reminded him.

"You thinking I kept some of the money? Cause if you thinking that, you'd be wrong, man."

Duke stepped out of the shadows.

J.J.'s startled gaze went from the gun to Duke's face. "You set me up, man. You're the . . ."

The look on J.J.'s face escalated to terror, then froze as a bullet tore into his chest.

TWO

"Can I buy you a cup of coffee?" Angel Delaney said as she looked over at her partner. She and Eric Mason had been driving around in their squad car for over an hour, and she needed to stretch.

Eric was one of those TDH kind of guys. Tall, dark, and handsome. He was a little shy and a little full of himself too. But then, why shouldn't he be? His thick brown hair always settled in perfect order, no matter which way the wind blew. He had long lashes that framed his eyes and a smile that made a girl's toes curl. Broad shoulders, tapered waist, slim hips — men spent hours at the gym carving out muscles like his. Had circumstances been different, Angel might have been interested, but she made it a point not to date any of her fellow officers.

Eric glanced at his watch, then lifted his

blue gaze to Angel's and winked. "Throw in one of those cinnamon rolls with the cream cheese frosting, and you got a deal."

"You're on." Angel flashed him a grin and unfastened her seat belt. Before she could open the door, the radio crackled and a dispatch operator broke through.

"Two-eleven in progress, Bergman's Pharmacy, Fifth and Washington."

A robbery. In unison, they groaned and whipped back into their seats and fastened their belts. Angel flipped on the siren as Eric responded to the call. He peeled out of their parking place and headed north.

Traffic was light in Sunset Cove on that Sunday morning. Most of the town's eleven thousand citizens were either in church, at home reading their morning papers, or making their way to the beach. At the moment, Angel would've given anything to be jogging along the shoreline rather than racing to a robbery.

A familiar uneasiness seeped into her veins, and her heart raced with anticipation as it often did when she and Eric responded to a call. What would they find this time?

She'd moved back to the Oregon coast a little over a year ago to escape the crime-ridden streets of Bay City, Florida, a suburb south of Fort Myers. She'd grown up in Sunset Cove, but like a lot of kids, she couldn't wait to leave home. Her first move took her to Portland State, where she earned a degree in criminal justice. She then moved to Florida, and after three years and a lot of heartache she'd come back. But even in the short time she'd been gone, her hometown had changed dramatically; it wasn't at all the sleepy beach town she'd left. The crime rate — especially drug-related crimes — had tripled from what it had been.

"You okay?" Eric asked.

She tossed him a questioning look. "Sure. Why wouldn't I be?"

He shrugged. "You look a little nervous."

Angel shook her head. "I'm fine." She looked out the passenger side window and swallowed back the lump in her throat. *Four years on the street. You should be used to it by now.* No matter how many times she told herself that, the anxiety she felt en route to a crime scene never seemed to fade. Angel had heard other officers talk about the fight or flight response. An odd mix of excitement and fear pumped the body full of adrenaline. Then the body went into autopilot mode, taking whatever steps were needed to ensure its safety and the safety of others. It was a normal reaction, even for police officers. Still, she didn't like to show it, or accept it — not around fellow officers, especially her father.

Angel tried to focus on the storefronts that stretched along the five-block area nostalgically referred to as "Old Town." Most of the downtown area had been built in the early 1900s. The place had become run-down, but in recent years remodeling and updating had helped restore it to its former glory, as had the city's beautification projects. Gardens, window boxes, and hanging planters invited tourists and shoppers to browse, and the crocuses, daffodils, and hyacinths were just coming into bloom.

The town was quiet now; the shops didn't open until 10:00. Maybe the call had been a mistake — or a prank. Eric pulled up in front of Bergman's Pharmacy and slammed on the brakes. The store was situated at the end of the street — an old brick building that separated the newly refurbished and the ready-to-be-demolished.

Angel cut the siren, then released her seat belt and opened the door. The rat-tat-tat of automatic weapons shattered the fragile spring morning. The store window exploded, spraying shards of glass onto the sidewalk and street.

"Get down!" Eric yelled.

The world shifted into slow motion. Everything except her heart, which rammed into overdrive. She raised her arm and ducked back into the car to escape the storm of crystal shards. A bullet thunked into a hanging basket overhead. The basket creaked as it swayed, straining the three chains that suspended it. Terror pinned Angel against the seat, jerking her back to the shooting at the Bay City day care. For what seemed an eternity, she couldn't move. She forced herself to breathe and tried talking herself out of the panic.

Don't think about it. You're okay. They didn't hit you. You can do this.

Eric bolted out of the car. Using his open door as a shield, he called for backup. Angel knew that before long the street would be swarming with flashing lights. But in the meantime, they were faced with an active shooting situation. They would have to go in — and soon.

Angel crawled across the seat over the console and slid out the driver's side. She hunkered down beside Eric. "Great way to spend a Sunday morning." She hoped her voice didn't reveal the panic still pumping through her veins.

"Humph." Eric leveled a steady gaze on her, then reached out to touch her forehead.

She flinched. "What are you doing?"

"You're bleeding. Looks like you caught a piece of glass."

"Must not be too bad. It doesn't hurt." At least it hadn't until he'd mentioned it.

Eric retrieved a tissue from the box behind the driver's seat and handed it to her.

"Thanks." She dabbed at the wound and stuck the tissue in her pocket, not bothering to look at it.

Sirens broke the stillness, and while Eric tried to call the store owner, two squad cars pulled up, blocking the street. One was a county sheriff's vehicle, the other police.

"What have we got?" Nick Caldwell, a fellow officer and friend, exited his car and positioned himself beside Angel. Nick was tall, probably six foot four, thin but muscular. He was six years her senior and had been her oldest brother's best friend. When they were kids Nick had practically lived at the Delaney house.

Bo Williams, the deputy sheriff and ex-linebacker with the University of Oregon

Ducks, joined them. Bo still looked the part of a football player — six feet tall, heavyset, with wide shoulders and a mean expression.

"A war zone," Angel answered. "Automatic weapons. We'll need to get in there. Someone inside made the 911 call. There may be victims."

"Can't establish contact with the store," Eric clipped his cell phone to his belt. "No one is answering."

Mike Rawlings, another officer with the Sunset Cove police department, tore up on his bike and jumped off, taking cover with the others. Angel filled him in.

"Let's move. Eric, you and I can go in the front. Mike and Bo, cover the alley. Nick, direct things out here — set up the perimeters and contact the Oregon State Police for air support. We could use more officers. We may need them."

"You giving the orders now?" Nick asked.

"Yeah, you got a problem with that?"

"I'll let you know." Nick's face cracked in a patronizing smile.

"Hey, I got a problem with it, Delaney." Mike frowned. "Why don't you stay out here? I'll go in with Eric."

Angel bristled. The comment carried a

silent message. *Let the men handle it.*

"Ease off, Mike," Nick said.

Mike looked like he was about to argue the point, but he didn't. He and Bo separated and took off down the street to cover the alley. Staying low, Eric sprinted across the sidewalk. Glass crunched under his feet.

Angel followed a few steps behind. Her heart hammered as the panic set in again. Weapons drawn, she and Eric flung open the front door and stepped inside.

Silence. An uneasy silence that affected her more intensely than the gunfire and the shattered window.

Eric moved forward.

Someone moaned from behind the counter.

Eric spotted him first. "Looks like somebody used the poor guy for target practice." He dropped down and felt for a pulse.

Angel stared at the older man's blood-soaked lab coat. "Is he . . . ?"

"He's alive. Barely." Eric got to his feet. "I'll call it in."

The old man gasped and tried to sit up. "Billy . . ."

"Take it easy, Mr. Bergman." Eric knelt beside him and eased him back down. "An ambulance is on the way."

Angel peered into the cracked ceiling mirror above their heads, trying to spot movement in the aisles. "Think they're still here?"

"I doubt it, but we'd better have a look around just in case."

Her gaze locked on the violet blue eyes staring at her through the shattered mirror. A stream of blood ran from a small cut on her forehead down to her eyebrow. Angel looked away, forcing her attention to the bullet-riddled shelves behind the counter.

They wouldn't have to do an inventory to tell what was missing. The gang had pulled off a number of burglaries up and down the coast over the last couple of months, most of them pharmacies. Word was they'd moved up from L.A., thinking to find easy pickings in small towns like Sunset Cove. According to Mike, who worked with troubled youths, they'd been recruiting local kids as well.

She heard a shuffling sound. "Looks like someone decided to hang around."

Eric frowned. "Let's hope it's a customer or maybe a clerk."

"Too early for that. Maybe the scumbags aren't finished yet. I'll have a look."

"Angel." Eric grabbed her arm as she

moved away from him. "I have to stay with Bergman. As soon as the paramedics get here, I'll have Nick help me carry him out to them. I'll get with you as soon as I can. In the meantime, watch your back."

"Right." She swallowed hard. Chasing these guys was the last thing she wanted to do, but backing out wasn't an option. Though she couldn't quite make out what they were saying, she heard Eric talking with someone on his radio. She crept down a middle aisle, past the dozens of cold remedies and pain relievers. At the end of the aisle, she leaned forward. The business end of an assault weapon protruded from a cosmetic display four aisles down. She jerked back. *Get hold of yourself. You can do this.*

"Police!" she yelled. "Put your weapon on the floor and come out with your hands up."

"Don't shoot," a small voice squeaked. "I'm comin' out. Jus' don't shoot me."

"Put the gun on the floor and slide it toward me."

A dark hand, no larger than her own, appeared from behind an end display of baby products. The hand lowered the gun to the floor.

"Come out where I can see you. Hands on your head."

A kid in camouflage fatigues with a black bandana tied around his head stepped clear of the shelving.

"Billy?" Angel kept her gun trained on the boy. She'd collared him a couple weeks ago for shoplifting a package of gum from the minimart off 22nd Street. Had the gang recruited him? Bergman had said his name. Could Billy have been responsible for all this? It didn't seem likely.

"I . . . put my gun down." Billy raised his hands.

"Smart move." Angel started toward him then stopped.

A movement to his left caught her eye. *He isn't alone.*

She dove back into the aisle just as two armed men jumped in front of Billy, waving their guns back and forth like twin Rambos. A barrage of bullets pelted the metal shelves and the floor where she'd been standing.

He'd set her up. She scrunched into a ball and covered her ears. *No! Not again.*

The shooting stopped. Angel raised her head, relieved none of the officers had been there to see her cower.

Eric came up behind her, his gun drawn. "You okay?"

Angel nodded, stunned and embarrassed

by her reaction to the gunfire. "Yeah. Fine." She looked beyond Eric toward the storefront. "Bergman?"

"Medics are with him. It's not looking good."

Angel jumped up when the back door to the pharmacy banged shut and shooting erupted in the alley. Angel cringed. Mike and Bo's handguns were no match for the high-powered automatics these guys were toting. She just hoped they wouldn't try any heroics.

"Nick, we need you back here." Mike's voice came over the two-way radio on Eric's belt.

"Come on, Angel." Eric headed for the door. "Our guys are going to need all the help they can get." He spoke into his lapel mike. "We're coming out."

Angel stood behind Eric as he eased open the door. The shooting had stopped. Stepping into the alley, she spotted the three gang members as they disappeared around the corner at the end of the alley with Mike, Bo, and Nick in hot pursuit.

"Let's go!" Eric sprinted after them.

Angel ran a few feet, then hesitated when she noticed an empty squad car blocking the alley — the car her father usually drove. Angel's stomach lurched.

Her father was too old to be running after these guys.

By the time Angel hit Main Street, she could see no sign of the other officers or the robbery suspects. She was about to turn back when Billy poked his head out of a condemned building not twenty feet from where she stood. She caught a glimpse of the weapon he'd been carrying earlier. Retrieved no doubt when his buddies came to his rescue.

"Billy." Angel drew her gun. "Hold it right there."

Billy raised his hands as if to comply, then ducked back inside.

Angel followed him into the abandoned structure. She moved slowly beside the rough concrete wall, her eyes taking a while to adjust to the darkness. Beams of dusty light squeezed in through filthy windows of the once thriving cannery. The air was stifling; the stench of stale smoke and urine almost made her vomit. Apparently, it hadn't been abandoned by everybody. Were the others hiding in here as well? She scanned the area but saw no one.

Footsteps pounded on the stairs. Angel turned on her lapel mike and radioed her position. "I just followed one of them into the old cannery." She hesitated before stepping away from the wall into the open. She would have to go some twenty feet across the grimy concrete floor to get to the stairs. Twenty feet that seemed like a mile. Scanning the area, she saw no one. If she didn't move fast, he'd get away. Angel ran to the stairs and with her weapon clutched in both hands began to climb. At the fifth step she paused.

The footsteps had stopped. She dragged in a ragged breath to ease the dread rising in her chest. Was she walking into another trap? Should she go down and wait for backup? *No. You can handle this. He's just a kid.* She crouched low and, with the metal railing at her back, moved up three more steps.

"Billy!" Her stern voice echoed off the walls. "Give yourself up. You know you can't get away. Maybe we can cut a deal."

"No!" Billy yelled, and seconds later he dove past her, slamming her against the railing and nearly propelling her over it.

Angel grabbed the rail to steady herself and lunged after him. "Stop! Stop or I'll shoot!"

Billy paused at the bottom. His frightened gaze fastened on hers. "I didn't do nothin'." He stood there motionless for a moment, then raised his gun.

THREE

Aim for body mass. The repetitive voice from her instructors at the police academy jammed into her brain. She'd done it nearly every day on the shooting range.

No! This isn't a target. He's just a kid.

But he has a gun. It's either him or me. Angel aimed and fired. A bullet tore into Billy's shoulder. He twisted and staggered back. His eyes widened.

Another gunshot splintered the silence. Then another.

Angel froze. Billy's gun clattered to the concrete floor with an oddly hollow sound. He moaned and reached for her, then dropped on top of his gun.

Angel stared at him, then at her own weapon.

Oh, Angel, a voice in her head cried. *What have you done?* She holstered her Glock, as if burying it would hide the truth. Her knees buckled. She grabbed the railing and forced herself to move toward Billy's limp form.

When she reached the boy, she radioed in her position using her lapel mike and asked for an ambulance. Pulling off her jacket, she pressed it to his wounds. Blood pumped like a small geyser, and Angel knew she must have hit an artery. The dark burgundy pool beneath him spread to her knees and soaked into her slacks.

"C'mon, Billy. You're gonna be okay. Stay with me."

In the dim light she studied the boy's face. Only moments before, Billy had been involved in an armed robbery. Now he looked like a sleeping child.

"Hang on!" She shook him. "Listen — the sirens. You can hear them. We'll get you to the hospital."

A gurgling sound came from his throat. Blood oozed from his mouth.

"No!" Angel gasped. A wild hysteria erupted in the pit of her stomach. "You can't die!"

God, don't let him die. Please.

"Angel?" The voice sounded as if it was coming from a deep well. "You in here?" A bright light streamed into the warehouse, then disappeared again as someone came in and let the heavy door close behind him.

Nick hunkered down beside her, looking from Billy to Angel and back again. "What happened?"

Angel concentrated on keeping her voice steady as she explained.

Eric dropped down beside her and felt Billy's carotid artery for a pulse. "He's dead."

Angel shook her head. "He can't be." She raised her eyes to meet Eric's. "He wasn't supposed to die."

"Angel . . ." Nick wrapped an arm around her shoulders.

She shrugged it off. "Don't."

The door jerked open again as the EMTs arrived. Angel felt cold as she let Nick lead her outside, where officers were already securing the scene. She ducked under the yellow tape and sank into the seat of a squad car parked at the curb.

Nick poured a cup of coffee from the thermos he kept in the backseat. When she didn't take it, he wrapped her hands around the cup and lifted it to her mouth. "Come on, Angel. Don't take it so hard. Hey, I know it's rough. The first time always is. But the kid didn't give you a choice. It could be you lying in there."

Eric crouched down next to the car

door. "Nick's right, partner. It's part of the job."

Angel shook her head, not trusting herself to talk. She couldn't count the number of times she'd fired at a human-shaped target. One, two, three, four, five shots without blinking. Sometimes during practice, she had tried to imagine what it would be like to shoot a real person, but all the practice in the world couldn't have prepared her for the real thing. She had just killed another human being. A child. Billy had committed a crime, but he didn't deserve to die.

"Did you get any of the others?" Angel asked.

"We lost them." Eric folded his arms and leaned against the car. "I stopped looking when I heard the shots."

Angel stared into the coffee. She heard Mike and Bo come up, and Eric explained the situation. Both offered their support.

Then Nick extended his hand toward her. "Uh . . . it's just routine, Angel, but you know the drill. I need your duty weapon and magazine."

Angel nodded and handed her gun to him. The police would enter her weapon as evidence. The guys in the crime lab would check it against the bullets in the kid's body. Bullets she had fired. Then internal affairs would investigate, as they always did when an officer used deadly force. And she'd be put on administrative leave. She shuddered and pushed the thought to the back of her mind.

When Nick gave her a replacement, she frowned, wondering how he'd gotten one so fast.

"It's mine. I had an extra one in the trunk," he explained.

"Thank you." She shoved it into her holster.

The replacement was a way of maintaining normalcy by letting her know she had taken appropriate action. Angel only wished she could believe that. If it had been up to her, she'd give the weapon back and . . .

No, you have to stop thinking like that. You're a police officer. Weapons are part of the package.

Nick, who served not only as sergeant but also as their union rep, hunkered down in front of her. "I called in for a lawyer, Angel. He'll try to get here today."

She nodded. It was all part of a prearranged plan for situations like this. Officers paid their 1.5 percent in union dues and got representation if and when they needed it. And it looked like she was going to need it.

Nick rested his hand on her knee. "Would you like me to take you back to the station?" he asked. "You might want to get cleaned up. The, uh, lab is going to want your uniform too." He glanced down at her bloodstained slacks and the jacket she'd bunched up and set on the floor of the car. "And we're going to need a urine sample — you can take care of that at the station."

"I'm heading back that way," Eric said. "I can take her."

Angel shifted her gaze from Nick to Eric. "Thanks," she said to Nick. "But if it's all the same to you, I'll ride back with Eric." She needed the familiarity of the patrol car and Eric's presence.

"Sure." Nick patted her knee and stood. "Eric, if you're leaving, I'll need to take a look at your weapon as well."

"Sure." Eric took out his weapon and handed it to Nick. "Since when did you get so efficient?"

"Since I've been working with Detective Riley from the Oregon State Police. He's thorough. And he'll be handling the investigation. We have a call in to him right now." Nick checked the magazine and handed the weapon back to Eric. "Thanks."

Looking up at Nick, Angel asked, "Are you sure you don't need me to stick around?"

He shook his head. "We pretty much know what went down. You can give your statement later. The crime lab guys will go over everything."

Crime scene. Detective. Investigation. The words weren't new to her. She'd used them herself numerous times. But now they felt like knives cutting into whatever reserve she had left. She was going to be investigated. What would Dad think? Her stomach twisted at the thought of facing him. Her father had been a police officer for over forty years.

Angel frowned. She'd seen his car at the scene, so where was he now and why hadn't he been with the other officers?

Her heart thudded as her mind reeled with possibilities. Had he been hurt? Called away?

"Have any of you seen my dad?"

None of them had.

FOUR

Callen Riley scooped up a load of paint on his brush and, with his left hand gripping the gutter, reached for the far corner of the fascia. Another hour and he'd be finished with the trim.

A siren pierced the crisp sunny morning and seemed to be coming from downtown Sunset Cove. Not a welcome sound at any time, but especially not now. He tried to ignore it — tried to convince himself it was just a traffic stop. Anything serious and dispatch would page him. Until they did, he wasn't going anywhere.

He'd been waiting the entire weekend for a clear day so he could work on the exterior of his beach house. This was supposed to be vacation time for him. His supervisor in Portland had insisted he take a few days off to move into his new place. Tomorrow he'd start working officially with the other law enforcement agencies in Lincoln County.

Tomorrow, not today. Even so, he mentally prepared himself. His weapon, a .40 caliber, was tucked in its holster hanging on a hook in the back of his closet, covered by his official Oregon State Police jacket.

Standing on the upper rung of his extension ladder, Callen glanced down at his sister as she opened the sliding glass door and backed onto the deck.

"No, Mutt, stay," Kathleen ordered. "You can't come out here. Go see the girls. A white dog and blue paint are not a good mix."

Callen's rambunctious white pup yipped an objection and stuck his black nose out the door. She gently moved him back in with her bare foot, closing off his escape route.

"Ready for a break?" Kath set two steaming cups on the low wooden table between two white Adirondack chairs.

He was, and the coffee smelled great, but he didn't want to stop painting. Nothing, not even the enticing aroma of his favorite coffee, would deter him. "Not yet, but you go ahead."

"Honestly, you've been at it since 7:00." Kath brushed a hand through her red hair and settled onto one of the chairs. "I thought you were moving to the beach to slow down."

"It's supposed to rain tomorrow, and I want to get the trim finished." Callen leaned back to admire the paint job. The blue trim looked almost too bright against the weathered gray siding.

"You don't think the blue is too bright?" Kath cocked her head in a scrutinizing pose as she sipped at her steaming drink.

"Nope. It'll be fine when it dries." Even if the paint was too bright, he wouldn't admit it to Kath. As the older sibling, she had the very irritating habit of pointing out his faults and trying to fix them. Besides, he'd seen the color combination on several houses up the coast and decided he'd use it if and when he ever got his own place at the coast. And now that he had it, he intended to do exactly what he wanted. The three-bedroom house sat on a piece of beachfront property, on a bluff only a few blocks from downtown Sunset Cove. The town was on a beautification kick, and he'd gotten a great deal. Even so, the view had cost him plenty. But it was worth every cent.

"How's the kitchen coming?" Callen dipped the brush into the paint can.

Kathleen and her girls had come down from Portland on Friday to help him move in. They'd worked all weekend, painting and wallpapering as well as unpacking his kitchen boxes and putting things away. He'd rearrange everything to his liking later, but for now he was happy to get stuff into the cupboards and out of sight.

"Great. I love it. You did good, Callen. The grapes on the wallpaper trim make it look like an Italian villa. I can't believe how well it matches the tiles and the pottery you bought."

He let the compliment slide off. People, even in his own family, always seemed surprised at his artistic nature. Just because a guy was a cop didn't mean he couldn't be creative.

A glob of paint dropped from his brush and spattered on the plastic drop cloth he'd laid over the shrubs. He ignored it and went on painting the eaves in front of him.

A rapid burst of what sounded like distant gunfire disrupted his thoughts.

"Is that what I think it is?" Kath threw him a worried look.

He shook his head. "Can't be. Not here in Sunset Cove." He sucked in a deep breath, knowing as soon as the words left his mouth that they weren't quite true. In recent years, the crime rate in coastal areas had mushroomed. Callen debated whether or not to check it out.

"Well, if it is gunfire, I suppose that means you'll be going to work?"

"Maybe." Sirens again. Curiosity almost pulled him away, but he knew dispatch would page him if he was needed. His beeper was on the kitchen counter, where he could easily hear it. Normally he kept the beeper clipped to his belt, but he hadn't wanted to get paint on it.

"So, little bro, think you're going to like it here?" Kath took a sip of coffee and let her gaze linger on the rolling surf. He paused and glanced in the same direction, spotting a surfboarder paddling out past the breakers.

"Already do." He couldn't help but smile. The house was almost ready. It had taken six months of weekends and days off to remodel and clean up — the house had more than lived up to its reputation as a fixer upper. Since it needed a roof, he'd torn the old one off and added a dormer to the former one-story cabin, ending up with a great master suite and an extra bathroom. It had also needed new electrical wiring throughout, some new plumbing, and sheetrock in places where mold had taken over the walls.

"I'm insanely jealous, you know." Kath crossed her jean-clad legs and gazed out at the water, now a perfect blue as it reflected a cloudless sky. "I'd love to live on the coast."

Callen gave her a smug grin. As a kid, he'd enjoyed making her jealous, and still did. "You and Stan and the girls can stay here anytime."

"I know." She sighed, and her gray-green gaze settled on him. "But it's not the same. If we didn't have to be near the airport for Stan's job . . ." She let the comment fade, a wistful expression on her face.

"You'd still live in Portland," Callen teased. "You wouldn't be able to stand being in a small town like this, and you know it. There aren't any shopping malls. No Nordstrom stores. You'd never make it. Neither would the girls."

Kath reached over and swatted his leg. "I'll have you know I can go for at least a week without going to Nordie's." She grinned. "But you're right. We're all hopelessly addicted. Speaking of the girls . . ." She checked her watch and frowned. "They should be up by now."

Callen chuckled. "Darn right. I would've

had them up and working their tails off by 7:00."

"Sure you would."

Callen's nieces, Ashley, eleven, and Jenna, thirteen, were sleeping late because it was the weekend and they'd been up until 1:00 watching some chick flick with their mother. Callen had gone to bed early.

He thought he heard another spattering of gunshots. Callen put the lid on the paint can and started down the ladder. Beeper or no, he had to see what was going on. He tapped the lid down tight and set the paint on the deck, then wiped his hands on the rag he'd tucked into his back pocket. He shoved open the door and nearly tripped over Mutt as the white patch of fur raced for the open door and freedom. "Mutt, get back here!"

The phone rang. The dog kept running, and Kath took off after him. Callen snatched up the receiver from the wall phone. "Yeah?"

"Detective Riley?" It was the dispatch operator.

"Speaking."

"We have an officer involved in a shooting at Sixth and Main. Please hold for Officer Caldwell."

Callen recognized the name. He'd met

Nick Caldwell and his boss, Joe Brady, several weeks before when he'd gotten called in on the Kelsey case. Jim Kelsey was still missing, and it was beginning to look as if the wife had killed him.

Almost immediately, Caldwell came on the line. "Detective Riley, this is Nick Caldwell. We paged you, but you didn't respond."

Callen apologized and looked around on the counter for his beeper but couldn't find it. "What's up?"

"We're going to need you on this one. I know this is your weekend to move in, but we have a major problem here." Caldwell filled him in on the pharmacy robbery, and as he spoke, Callen's level of guilt escalated. He should have responded to the gunfire sooner. "We went after the shooters," Caldwell continued, "and Officer Delaney cornered one of them, a kid about twelve. She had to use deadly force."

Groaning inwardly, Callen brushed his fingers through his hair and tipped his head back. *This was not on my to-do list.* But to Caldwell, he said, "I'm on my way." He hung up and glared at his sister, who was leaning on the counter with Mutt squirming in her arms and whining to be put down.

"You have to go in, right?" She rubbed Mutt's tummy and received a wet kiss for her efforts.

"Where's my beeper? I left it on the counter this morning."

Kath bit her lower lip and frowned. "I don't know, unless. . . . Oh, my goodness. I bet it got put in with the other kitchen stuff." She opened one of the drawers, fished around, and finally pulled it out. "Callen, I'm so sorry. I didn't look at it closely. I must've thought it was a timer or something." She looked stricken. "They've been paging you, haven't they?"

"Don't worry about it," he grumbled, grabbing the pager and clipping it to his belt. Paint or no paint, he should've had it on him. Going to the closet, he lifted his shoulder holster and gun from its hook, expertly slipping it on. As he put on his jacket and opened the door, he said, "It's okay, Kath. I doubt I could have made a difference anyway."

Once in his car, an unmarked Crown Victoria, Callen hit the switch to turn on his lights, burning rubber in an effort to make up for the time he'd lost. It took him all of three minutes to reach the scene.

Officer Delaney was sitting in one of the patrol cars when he pulled into the parking lot in front of the old cannery warehouse. It wasn't hard to pick her out, since she was the only woman around. She looked in his direction, then tipped her head down to stare into the cup of coffee in her hands. Something about her demeanor and the glazed look in her eyes squeezed his heart. For the first time since leaving the house, Callen wondered if things would have been different if he'd responded when he heard the first barrage of gunfire.

Nick Caldwell and another uniformed officer stood next to her, and when Caldwell saw Callen, he hurried toward him.

"Detective, Officer Mason was just going to take Angel back to the station. Do you need to talk to her first?"

Callen shook his head. "We can give her some time to pull herself together. My main concern is making sure the weapons are all checked, and I'd like to do a gunshot residue test on all of the officers involved."

"You got it," Nick said. "I already told her we needed a urine specimen, and I collected Angel's weapon and bagged it. She fired three shots into the victim. Several of us got shots off at the pharmacy. I think Eric and I are the only ones who didn't fire." He pointed to a squad car. "Eric's the one getting into the car with Angel."

Callen opened his trunk and secured the GSR kit. "We'll check him first, then the others."

After introducing himself to Angel and Eric, Callen turned to Eric. "I'll need to check your weapon."

"Sure." The officer produced his duty gun, confirming what Caldwell had said about him not firing. He had a full magazine. "Nick said you were thorough," Eric said when Callen handed the .40-caliber Glock back to him.

"I try to be. I'd like to do a GSR test too."

Eric frowned. "What's that?"

Callen wasn't surprised at the question; most officers didn't know about the procedure. The Oregon state lab was one of a dozen or so places in the country that had the equipment for GSR. He produced a sterile swab from his kit. "I do a swab of each officer's hands and send it to the lab, where they test for gunshot residues."

"Interesting." Eric nodded and offered his right hand.

Callen dipped the swab in a bottle of sterile water and rubbed Eric's hand with it, then placed it in a paper envelope.

Glancing over at Nick, he said, "I'd like you to get the other guys lined up, and we'll do them all at once."

He went around to the passenger side of the squad car and tested Angel as well. Her hand flinched as the swab went across it. Callen made the mistake of looking at her and got caught up in the depth of her violet blue eyes. Beautiful eyes.

Words got stuck in his throat, and he cleared it. "Caldwell said you were going back to the station," he managed to say. "That's a good idea." Best to remove her from the scene as soon as possible, before the media descended on them. He'd need to talk to her eventually, but his interview could wait. For the moment he'd get statements from the other officers at the scene.

Callen hated situations in which an officer had to use deadly force, and this one sounded bad. Shooting a kid — the media would have a field day. He frowned as he watched the squad car drive away.

Angel Delaney. What kind of name is that for a cop?

FIVE

On the way back to the station, Angel reminded herself she'd done the right thing. *These things happen,* she told herself again and again.

"Anything I can do to help?" Eric asked.

She offered him a weary smile. "I was just thinking."

"What about?"

"I — I could've sworn I only fired one shot."

"So?"

"There were at least three shots fired."

"That's what I heard." Eric frowned. "You're saying someone else shot the kid?"

"I don't know." Angel glanced at him. "You're thinking that's not possible, aren't you? That Billy and I were alone in the building."

"What I'm thinking doesn't matter. You know what went down. If you say somebody else was there, I believe you, but . . ." Eric hesitated and glanced in the rearview mirror as they approached city hall. The police station was housed in the north half of the building. Since Sunset Cove was a small town, and since they only had fourteen officers in the entire department, they didn't have a lot of the perks of a big city.

"But?" Angel folded her arms.

"Just be sure you have your facts straight, that's all. You were pretty shook up back there. It's possible that you blocked it out. It happens. I remember my first time. I was nervous — I can tell you that. This guy came at me with a knife. I had to shoot." He frowned. "Craziest thing. I thought I only fired once. Turned out I'd cranked six bullets into the guy."

Angel had heard similar stories before. She'd been trained to fire in succession at body mass. Had she done that? Apparently, but she remembered having second thoughts. She didn't tell Eric how she'd hesitated, how she almost hadn't fired at all. Her weapon, a semiautomatic, had a hair-trigger response. Was Eric right? Had she blocked it out?

She closed her eyes, trying to remember, but all she could see was the blood pumping out of Billy's wound and the color seeping out of his face. She stared at her red-streaked hands and blood-soaked pants. Would the stains ever come out?

"I'm not the only one that's happened to," Eric went on. "Talk to anyone who's had to use deadly force and they'll tell you the same thing."

"I suppose . . ."

"Angel." Eric settled a hand on her shoulder, his blue eyes filled with empathy. "You did the right thing back there. The kid was bad news. All I'm saying is, it doesn't matter if you fired one shot or three — or if you emptied your gun. You did what you had to do."

Angel nodded. "I guess I did." But his reassurance did nothing to ease her anguish.

Eric dropped her off at the back entrance of the historical red brick building, promising to check up on her later. Angel headed straight for the women's locker room, where she stripped off the bloodied uniform and placed it into a plastic bag. Once the crime lab techs finished examining the clothes, they would dispose of them. She'd have to get another uniform. But there would be plenty of time to do that while she was on administrative leave, waiting for the investigation to end.

She stepped into the steaming shower, letting the hot water pound against her skin and watching the swirls of soap pour into the drain. Her throat clogged with sobs she tried to stop.

He had a gun. I did what I had to do, Angel reminded herself again. She turned off the shower, dried off, and made her way across the tile floor to her locker. She pulled out her off-duty uniform — a pair of running shoes, jeans, a T-shirt, and a sweatshirt. She dressed quickly, blaming her chills on the coolness of the room.

Angel decided to write out the report while it was fresh in her mind. She wanted to get it down and get it over with as soon as possible. She took the uniform to the temporary evidence lockers, opened an empty one with her key, stuffed the bag inside, then signed it in along with the locker number. She put a tag on the locker to let other officers know it was in use.

In the report room, Angel poured herself a cup of coffee, picked up the forms, and settled herself at a table. Thankfully, no one else was around, partly because it was Sunday and partly because all the available officers were at the crime scene.

She'd only written a few words when her boss, Joe Brady, Sunset Cove's police chief, ambled into the room. "Nick told me I'd find you here." Joe was a big man with a stomach badly in need of toning. He wore a suit and tie — church clothes.

"I'm sorry you had to come in. I know how important Sunday mornings are to you."

He set a plastic collection bottle on the table in front of her. "Why don't you take care of this now, if you can. When you're through I'd like you to come into my office." He leaned over, resting his hands on the back of the chair across from her.

"Sure. No problem." Angel grabbed the bottle and hurried to the women's rest room. Giving urine samples wasn't all that unusual. The department did random drug testing on all of their officers from time to time. But this was different and humiliating.

She washed her hands and took the specimen with her into Joe's office, where she set it on his desk and sat in a chair across from him. She clenched her hands to keep them from shaking. Then, maintaining more control than she thought possible, she told him what had happened.

She thought about telling him the same thing she'd told Eric — that she'd fired only once — but like Eric had said, she needed to have her facts straight first. And she just plain didn't know what the facts were. Her magazine would show how many shots she'd actually fired, and Nick had that sealed in an evidence bag.

Joe leaned back in his chair, then let it bounce forward. "Sounds like you followed procedure. We'll probably hit a few rough spots dealing with the press on this one, with him being a kid and all. But I don't foresee any problems."

Angel felt a thread of relief weave in and out between the tension. "Good." She pushed herself out of the chair and headed for the door. She had her hand on the knob when Joe's cell phone rang.

While he listened to the caller, his lips formed a tight, thin line. He held up his hand for Angel to wait. "I see. Right. Thanks for the call." Joe looked up at Angel, then pulled his gaze away. "You might want to sit back down."

"What's wrong?" she asked as she eased back into the chair.

Joe rose and walked over to the window.

"Joe?"

Stuffing his hands into his pockets, he turned around to face her. His hazel eyes held hints of anger and accusation. "He was only twelve years old. Did you know that?"

"I . . . yes. I met him a couple weeks ago." Angel gripped the arms of the chair. "He had a gun, Joe. I followed procedure."

"For your sake, I hope that's the case." He ran a hand across his balding head.

Angel frowned. "I don't understand."

"It was a toy gun, Delaney. The kid was carrying a stinkin' toy gun."

SIX

They'd find J.J.'s body soon. Duke raised his foot and set it on the rear bumper of his car and bent over to tie his shoelace. The cops were still swarming all over the place, looking in every nook and cranny for the men who pulled off the robbery. A futile effort — those kids would be long gone by now. There were a lot of places to hide in Sunset Cove.

Duke was plenty steamed about the robbery. Those idiots were supposed to keep a low profile, not hit the local establishments with guns blazing. He had expected petty theft, but not armed robbery — not gunning down an innocent old man.

Things were getting out of control. An icy trickle of fear ran down the back of his neck. If these guys weren't careful, they could blow the entire business apart, just like they'd shattered that window at the pharmacy.

Since he'd eliminated J.J., he would have to find a replacement and quick. He needed someone with as much street smarts and pull as J.J. He'd met several potential dealers through the Dragon's Den over the weekend. He sneered. The saps who ran the place had set up the teen club to help kids who'd gone down the wrong road. They hoped the kids would somehow find God and turn their lives around. Fat chance. The kids came in to shoot pool and hang out and eat, not to be rehabilitated. Their "safe" weekend dances were safe all right — safe for the kids to pop designer drugs.

Maybe he'd go to the club tonight, play a little pool and pick out his new contact. It wouldn't be hard. All he had to do was keep his eyes open for the one guy the others looked up to. There was always a pecking order. He had a hunch the highest guy in that pecking order was the one who'd set up the pharmacy hit.

Duke knew just how to bring him into the business. Money would interest him initially, but keeping him would require something more compelling. The threat of being turned over to the cops might do it. His main man would make the initial contact and bring him in.

He rubbed his eyes, feeling the grit from too many hours on the street. Maybe he was getting too old for this business. His mother had always warned him about burning the candle at both ends. Maybe she'd been right, 'cause he was sure feeling the heat.

SEVEN

Angel went quiet at the news about the kid's gun. She sat stiffly in the chair, staring out the window, her eyes fixed on a cherry tree coming into bloom. Her dark hair hung in damp ringlets that dripped water down her back. She wished she could think of something to say. She hoped Joe would tell her it would work out okay, but they both knew the opposite was true.

"What now?" She turned to him, knowing her eyes and voice betrayed her, making her sound vulnerable and afraid.

"I'll have to put you on administrative leave."

She nodded. He was going to have to find an officer to replace her. Unfortunately, there was no money in their already overextended budget.

"I suppose you'll want my key to the evidence lockers," Angel said.

He nodded, and she removed the key from her key chain and set it next to the urine sample.

Joe pulled open the top side drawer of his desk and moved papers aside — probably thinking he'd have been better off not hiring Angel in the first place. She knew he'd hired her as a favor to her father. Frank Delaney had asked Joe to offer her a job after one of their guys had been killed in a domestic violence case a little over a year ago. The police chief had done it as a favor, but Angel had been more than qualified.

And she'd proven herself, especially with her negotiation skills in domestic violence cases. She could take care of herself. She could and would get through this.

Apparently finding what he'd been looking for, Joe pulled a card out of a banded pack. "I want you to see a psychologist. Dr. Campbell has worked with officers in the past."

"I don't need —"

"No is not an option," Joe snapped. "Seeing a shrink in a case like this is standard protocol, and you know it."

She did, but she didn't like it.

"Call. The sooner the better."

Angel took the card.

"You'll make an appointment?"

"Yes."

"You shouldn't be alone," Joe said. "Do you need someone to give you a ride home?"

"That won't be necessary." She looked him in the eye. "I'm fine."

"You don't look fine."

She sucked in a deep breath and squared her shoulders. "How do you expect me to look? I just shot a —" The words caught in her throat, and she ducked her head.

"Look, Angel, I don't mean to seem hard-nosed about this, but I know what can happen in cases like this. One guy I worked with in Portland a few years back accidentally killed another officer. Took it so hard he committed suicide. I don't want that happening to you. You need support. Family."

Her spine went rigid as he spoke. "I'm not going to kill myself."

"Good. Now go home."

"I'd like to finish my report first." She started for the door.

"You don't need to write this up. Your statement will be in Detective Riley's report." Joe cleared his throat.

She looked back at him. "Did you want something else?"

"No, I'm just . . . I'm sorry this happened to you." For a moment he looked sympathetic.

"Thanks." Angel raised her chin a notch.

"Uh, if you need to talk about it . . ."

Joe's comment faded as she closed the door.

She turned back, thinking she should go back and apologize, but through the window she saw him picking up the phone. She hurried past the receptionist's desk and steeled herself against the tears that would come if she didn't get away from the police station fast. She would not cry — not in front of Joe, not in front of anyone. She balled up the paperwork she'd started and threw it in the trash, then headed for the locker room, where she gathered personal items from her locker. A book she'd never opened. A brush, hair bands, an extra pair of tennis shoes. The small black notebook she kept in her uniform pocket.

Brandy Owens came into the locker room. Her replacement? Brandy was the only other woman police officer in Sunset Cove.

"Hey, Angel, what's up?"

Hadn't she heard yet? Good. The last thing Angel needed was more sympathy.

Brandy frowned as Angel grabbed her

stash of candy bars off the top shelf and dumped them into her duffle bag. Brandy had large blue eyes and kept her tan even after a long winter; Angel suspected she spent some time each week either lathering on the sunless tanning lotion or lounging in a tanning bed. Her blonde hair was woven in a neat French braid that reached the middle of her back. "You cleaning out your locker?" she asked.

"Yeah."

Brandy glanced at her own and grimaced. "Not a bad idea. Except I'm afraid of what I might find in there." She hesitated. "Are you sick or something? Joe called and asked me to come in today but didn't say why."

Angel gulped and choked back the thick mass forming in the back of her throat. "Something like that." She mustered up a smile. "I'm out of here." She hurried away before Brandy could ask any more questions. She wasn't ready to talk to her or anyone else. She needed time alone to think. No, not to think. Angel didn't know what she needed; she only knew she had to get away.

As she walked out of the building, she had the foreboding sense she was leaving for the last time. *That's crazy. You'll be back. As soon as the details are cleared up and the crime scene investigators determine what happened. You were doing your job. You'll be back to work in no time.*

EIGHT

Angel made her way through the parking lot to her rebuilt 1972 Corvette. Luke's car, really. She'd just taken it over when he left. An old ache made its way into her heart again as thoughts of her brother overtook her own problems. He was the oldest of the five Delaney kids. Dad's favorite. At least he had been until he disappeared. He'd graduated from Harvard Law School with honors then joined a prestigious law firm in Portland. Four years ago, he'd gone on a business trip and never came back. He'd sent a note telling the family not to worry. The note read like a will. In it he'd asked Angel to take care of his car.

Tears rimmed her eyes. She brushed them away with the palm of her hand. This was not the time to be thinking about Luke. She slid behind the wheel, pushed the key into the ignition, and twisted it, bringing the engine to life. Lowering the windows, she reached for the door, but Nick grabbed hold of the frame before she could shut it.

"What are you doing here?" Angel turned away, pretending to be looking for something in the glove box. When she finally looked back, he was still there, resting his arms on the door.

"You gonna be okay?" His concerned gaze leveled on hers as if daring her to lie.

"Why wouldn't I be?" She avoided looking him in the eye, hoping he wouldn't press her. It wouldn't take much for her to fall apart.

He shrugged. "You were pretty shook up back there. I thought —"

"I'm fine, Nick. I'm going home."

"Uh, did you hear about the kid's weapon?"

"Unfortunately, yes." She ran a hand through her damp curls.

He nodded and straightened. "Want me to follow you?"

"I'm perfectly capable of driving myself home." Her tone was sharper than she'd intended.

He raised his hands in surrender. "Okay."

"Nick . . . look, I'm sorry. I know you're

trying to help, but I'm okay. Really."

"I understand. If you need me, I'll —"

"I know. You'll be there." Like he always was. Only she didn't want his help or anyone else's. She wanted to be left alone.

Nick closed the car door and tapped the roof with the palm of his hand. "I'll check on you later."

"Sure." Angel started to back out when she remembered the replacement gun Nick had given her. "Um — Nick, do you want your gun back?"

"No. It can wait until you get yours back. I have three more at home."

"Okay, thanks."

An hour later Angel stood under a hot shower in her apartment, scrubbing Billy's blood from under her fingernails with a brush. Even though she'd washed every trace of blood away, she lathered her body with fruit-scented soap over and over until the water went cold. She slammed her palm against the faucet to shut it off, then stepped out of the shower and rubbed herself down.

Shivering, she pulled on warm sweats and towel-dried her hair. Black as midnight, it curled in loose ringlets and reached two inches below her shoulders if she straightened it out. Tears had turned her mascara to smoky gray smudges, adding depth to the shadows forming under her eyes. She turned away from the mirror and the accusing gaze that stared back at her. Had she really killed a twelve-year-old boy? Had his weapon really been a toy? It didn't seem possible. How could she have made a mistake like that?

This can't be happening. It's a dream, right? Please, God, tell me it's a dream.

Angel didn't get an answer, but then, she hadn't expected to. God wasn't paying much attention to her these days — if he ever had. His indifference had come through loud and clear with Luke's disappearance, and even more so with Dani's death. A little over a year ago, her best friend, Dani Ortega, had been shot and killed while they had been trying to save the children in a day care center.

Angel blinked away the fresh onslaught of tears. God had been as silent then as he was now.

Still chilled to the bone, she went to the kitchen and heated a cup of water in the microwave. She paced across the clammy linoleum floor while she waited, rubbing her arms to warm them. Her apartment was one of those cookie-cutter places, long and narrow with not nearly enough light. There was a closet on the left of the entryway, and her bedroom was off to the right. The hallway opened into the kitchen, left, which melted into the living room with a breakfast bar in between. In the far left corner of the living room was an angled wall with a shelf for her television set and stereo. Under it was a gas fireplace.

She wandered into the living room to the sliding glass door and miniature patio. Pushing the heavy door open, she stepped outside. She had a view of the ocean, though sometimes she wondered why she'd bothered. The weather was often gray in Oregon, with the ocean and fog melding into an obscure mass. At times like that, she actually missed Florida. Today though, the sky was clear, the temperature in the high sixties. All up and down the beach, Angel could see people taking advantage of the pleasant spring day. Below her a couple walked along the shoreline, stopping to examine something they'd found in the sand.

The microwave beeped, letting her know the water was hot. She stood on the deck a while longer, her hands gripping the rail. A cool breeze ruffled her hair, and she inhaled deeply of the moist salt air. She'd read somewhere that deep breathing relieved stress. It didn't.

Her teeth were chattering when she came back inside. Going to her fireplace, Angel switched on the gas and stared into the flames. The beeper sounded again.

"Okay, okay. I'm coming." Angel wandered back into the kitchen and dropped a chamomile tea bag into the steaming water, then swirled and dunked. Giving the spent bag a final squeeze, she set it on the little ceramic tea bag holder her mother had made in an art class several years ago.

Angel took her drink to the sofa and curled up under a cream cable-knit afghan. Her mother, Anna, had made that too. Angel warmed her hands on the cup, almost wishing her mother was there now, cooking up her spicy chicken noodle soup. She'd dish up a steaming hot bowl and bring it to Angel on a tray. *"Eat up, honey. It's good for you. It'll make you feel better."*

A tear slid down her cheek, followed by another. And another. "Not even your soup will make this better, Ma."

Her mother would be getting home from church about now. She'd be bustling around in that huge Italian kitchen of hers, getting lunch and making preparations for dinner. Sunday dinners at home had been one of the things Angel missed most when she'd lived in Bay City. And home had been a haven for her when she'd come back from Florida. She'd stayed six months, licking her wounds, trying to get over Dani's death. Trying not to blame herself. Not a day went by that she didn't wonder what she could have done differently, wishing she had run into that day care ahead of Dani.

Then you'd be dead.

Maybe that wouldn't be so bad. I wouldn't have been there today. I wouldn't have fired at that boy.

Billy. She wondered if her dad knew about him yet. He probably did. He'd been there. She'd forgotten that until now. She'd meant to check with dispatch and find out why he hadn't been at the scene with the others. He must've been called away. She couldn't imagine Frank Delaney staying on the sidelines or not showing up when something like an officer shooting involving his daughter was going down. Unless he'd been hurt.

The phone rang. Angel glanced at it and turned back to her tea. She wasn't ready to talk to anyone yet and wondered if she ever would be. After three rings the answering machine picked up.

"Angel." The rough voice belonged to her father.

Angel blew out a sigh of relief. He was safe, which meant he'd gone to another call.

"Just heard about your run-in with the gang. Joe said you brought one of 'em down and that you were taking it pretty hard." Her dad hesitated, then added, "Don't. You hear me? The streets are better off without punks like that."

"He had a toy gun, Dad," she muttered into her drink. Chances are, since he'd talked to Joe, he already knew about the gun. Angel thought briefly about picking up the receiver, but she couldn't trust herself to talk. Especially not to her father. Frank Delaney was a veteran police officer, crusty and tough. He would be okay with the shooting, he just wouldn't understand why it was tearing her inside out. Angel had never told him about Dani and how her world had collapsed, how she almost hadn't come out on the other side of the darkness, and how sometimes she felt like she was still there.

Her father didn't tolerate weakness in any of his kids. Well, that wasn't exactly true; he expected some weakness in her, a girl, but she'd proven over and over that she could be as tough as any of his sons.

"Call me." He hesitated. "Oh, by the way, your mother wants you to come for dinner."

The machine clicked off. She was about to unplug the phone when it rang again. She got up to answer it. Her hand shook as she reached for the receiver, then stopped. It was probably her mother, the last person she wanted to talk to. "Sorry, Ma. I just can't . . ."

After the answering machine beep came a male voice. "Hi, honey," Brandon Lafferty crooned.

Had Brandon already heard? Probably not. The news programs wouldn't start until 5:00, and Brandon's plans for Sunday mornings usually included golf or tennis with his father and brother at the country club. "Just wanted to remind you about tonight. Pick you up at 6:00. I thought we'd have dinner at Maxwell's. . . . Love you."

"Oh no," Angel groaned. She'd forgotten all about their date. The last thing she felt like doing was going to a restaurant, especially one like Maxwell's. The restaurant sat atop the three-story Smith building and gave diners a perfect view of the beach. Normally she enjoyed eating there, but not today. *Please not today.*

Angel reached for the phone to call him back and even punched in the number. But then she hung up. She couldn't say why; maybe she just needed to do something other than think about the shooting. And Brandon would provide a good diversion.

She was just about to sit down on the couch when the phone rang again. This time she gave up and answered.

"Angel, honey. It's your mother."

"I know." Angel rolled her eyes. For some strange reason, her mother always felt compelled to preface every phone conversation with her identity.

"Your father told me what happened. I'm so sorry. It's a terrible thing, honey, even if you were just doing your job like he said. You shouldn't be alone, sweetheart."

"I'm okay, Ma. It's not a big deal."

"Since when is shooting someone not a big deal?"

"You want me to feel worse than I already do?" Angel rubbed at the beginnings of a headache. "Ma, please. I don't want to talk about it, all right? I feel bad. And I'm really sorry all this happened."

"Of course you are." She paused. "Listen, sweetheart, I made a chocolate cake this morning before church. Your favorite. I'm bringing some over." With the change in subjects came a change in tone. Angel had never been able to figure out how her mother could make the switch so abruptly. Nothing seemed to bother her, at least not for very long.

"You don't have to do that." *In fact, please don't.* But she couldn't bring herself to say this. She loved her mother's chocolate cake.

"Of course, I don't, but it's what mothers do. I'm coming, no argument." She hung up.

Angel thought seriously about leaving. She didn't want to deal with her mother on top of everything else. Ma was the kind of woman who'd love you to death if you let her. Which was one of the reasons Angel had moved into her own place. Now that her kids had grown up, Anna spent most of her time taking care of other people. But she had loved having Angel come back to what she called her empty nest. She still thought of Angel as her baby girl and probably always would.

When Angel had decided it was time to move into her own place again, her mother objected.

"Stay, Angel. We have plenty of room."

"It isn't right, my living at home anymore," Angel told her. But she hadn't dared tell the real reason — she felt smothered. It wasn't easy trying to fit back into the home she'd grown up in. There were too many memories, too much confusion; and instead of treating Angel like the adult she'd become, her parents acted as though she had never left home.

Angel, too, found herself reverting back to adolescence, back to a time when life was simpler, where burglaries, assaults, child abuse, and murders were light-years away. For a while it felt good to be cared for, but after six months she couldn't handle it anymore. "You and Dad have raised your kids," she told them. "You deserve some time alone."

"And what would I do with more time?" Anna had asked. "The last thing I need is to be alone."

"But you have Dad, and Tim's kids." Anna adored her grandchildren. But with five kids, she'd expected to have more than two, and she rarely missed an opportunity to let all of them know about it.

Anna waved her hand. "Your father doesn't need me. And Tim and Susan are taking the kids to the new day care at the hospital. Please stay," she pleaded. "It will give us time to get to know each other."

"What do you mean? I already know you."

Anna moved her head from side to side and settled her dark brown gaze on Angel. "Oh, honey. You don't know me at all."

What did you mean, Ma? How could I not know you?

A gentle knock sounded on the door, pulling Angel from her musings. She tried to ignore it, but whoever it was put a key in the lock.

Startled, Angel bounced to her feet. "Who's there?"

The door swung open. Her mother's salt-and-pepper hair barely showed above two large paper grocery bags. She was still wearing church clothes — a floral-print, knee-length dress and black heels — and was carrying an oversized black purse. Her slender legs looked like those of a much younger woman.

"Hi, honey, it's just me."

Angel glanced at the phone, then started toward the door. "How did you get here so fast?"

"I was in the neighborhood." She'd apparently used her new cell phone — the one she swore she would never buy.

Angel bit her tongue to keep from saying something she'd regret. She wished she had never given her mother the key to her apartment. Anna had insisted the family have a key in case of an emergency. Did the shooting constitute an emergency? Apparently.

Angel took the grocery bags and set them on the counter, sniffing appreciatively. Whatever was in those bags smelled wonderful. If she were the least bit honest with herself, she'd admit that deep down she was glad her mother had come.

"Oh, sweetheart!" Anna deposited her purse on the kitchen counter, then hurried to Angel's side. "You look terrible. Are you running a fever?" Her hand automatically went to Angel's forehead.

Angel ducked and brushed her mother's hand away. "I'm not sick, Ma. I just . . ." *Shot and killed a kid.* She couldn't finish the thought, not aloud at any rate.

Anna wore an injured expression on her face, the one that said, *I'm your mother, Angel. Don't push me away.*

Angel ignored the look and peeked into the bags. "What's all this?"

"You'll see." Her mother smiled, her hurt apparently swallowed up in the pleasure she took in feeding her only daughter.

Angel pulled out a bag of cookies. She opened it and inhaled deeply before snagging one. "Grandma's oatmeal chocolate chip?"

"Of course."

Angel closed her eyes for a moment, savoring the moist, chewy morsel. "Mmm," she said, trying to talk around the cookie. "These are so good."

"Don't talk with your mouth full," Anna scolded, though obviously pleased with Angel's response.

Angel shoved the rest of the cookie into her mouth and reached for a quart-sized plastic container. "Soup?"

"Chicken noodle." Anna ran water in the sink and washed and dried her hands on the towel hanging from the refrigerator handle.

In the other bag Angel found a chocolate cake and a container of icing. "You didn't have to do all this."

"Of course I did." Anna wrapped an arm around Angel's shoulders. "You're my baby. Besides, it was no trouble."

Angel resisted the urge to step into her mother's embrace and be enveloped in the comfort she knew those arms would bring. She'd stopped needing her mother's comfort years ago. Running to Mommy with every little hurt wasn't something Dad appreciated, so she'd quickly learned to tend to her own scrapes and bruises.

Anna let her arms drop. She covered the awkward moment by saying, "Where do you keep your pans?" Not really needing an answer, since she'd been the one to organize the kitchen, she opened the cupboard next to the stove and took out a saucepan. "I'll heat up your soup. Maybe you could put icing on the cake. Didn't have time to do that. I'd just gotten home from church when your father called."

"You didn't have to come," Angel said again.

Anna opened the lid on the soup container. "I know." Dumping the still-frozen soup into the pan, she turned on the front burner. "You want to be independent and on your own. You think you don't need anybody — especially me." The hurt look was back. "But honey, we all need looking after now and then. I can't imagine what it must feel like to . . . to do what you did today. I only know it can't feel good."

Angel swallowed the new lump forming in her throat and looked away.

"There are times," her mother went on, "no matter how grown up we are, that we need someone to look after us. That's all I'm doing, honey. Looking after you." She pulled a wooden spoon out of the plastic utensil holder next to the stove and poked at the frozen soup, then added a little water and stirred.

Angel rubbed her forehead. Why was it that just being around her mother for more than a few minutes turned her back into a kid? She had no energy left for arguing with the woman. And what would it accomplish, anyway? More hurt feelings?

You'll never be able to change your mother, and if you could, would you want to? Besides, who's to say she isn't right?

The food looked and smelled great. Angel opened another small plastic container filled with gooey chocolate frosting and pulled a butter knife out of the utensil drawer.

"What? You aren't going to argue with me?" Anna set the spoon on the ceramic spoon rest.

"Would it do any good?" The corners of Angel's mouth turned up in a reluctant smile.

"Probably not." She leaned over and kissed Angel's cheek. "Sometimes your mama does know what's best."

Angel dumped the entire container of frosting onto the middle of the cake and began spreading across the surface while her mother cut into a crusty loaf of French bread. The warm sourdough scent made her mouth water. "Did you bake bread this morning too? I'm going to have to start calling you Martha."

Anna chuckled. "I'm not that efficient. I picked it up at the bakery on my way over."

Angel made one more pass over the glazed cake. Then, making sure she had ample frosting on the knife, she licked it clean. She stuck the knife in the sink, thinking she should probably finish helping her mother, but any energy she'd had seemed to drain right down her legs, leaving them weak and shaky. Angel managed to make it to the sofa, where she collapsed and closed her eyes.

"Your lunch is ready," Anna said a few minutes later. She had set a place for one at the counter, complete with a place mat and a vase full of cut flowers.

Angel padded into the kitchen and leaned over and smelled the flowers. "These are nice. Thanks."

"I picked those up at the market too." Anna slipped her purse strap over her shoulder. "Enjoy. I'll see you later."

"You're not staying to eat with me?" Angel surprised herself with the question.

"Can't. Have to get home and fix dinner. Tim and Susan are coming over with the kids tonight. I promised Tim I'd make pot roast."

"Yum."

"You can come too. There's always room."

"I don't know. I don't feel much like going anywhere. Brandon wants to take me out to dinner, but . . ."

"Good. You should go. It will do you good to get out."

Angel braced herself for the Brandon lecture — the one where her mother told her she and Brandon should get married and have babies. But the lecture didn't come. Instead, Anna gave her a peck on the cheek, waved a good-bye from the door, and left.

"You're slipping, Ma," Angel said to the closed door.

So she gave herself the lecture while she ate. She had known Brandon Lafferty since high school, and they had dated off and on since then. Brandon had been her best boy friend without actually being her boyfriend. Everyone thought they'd get married, but Brandon went off to law school and Angel became a cop and moved to Florida. When Angel came back to Sunset Cove, they picked up where they had left off. While Brandon clearly wanted their relationship to progress, marriage and babies seemed as far off to Angel as it had back in high school.

She turned back to the soup and dipped in her spoon. It smelled and tasted like it always did. The onions, garlic, chicken, carrots, and celery, with Ma's favorite spices — cilantro, basil, and a pinch of chili peppers — warmed her inside and out. The fragrant aroma calmed her nerves but unfortunately brought on another rush of tears that rolled down her cheeks and dripped into the broth. Dipping into her pocket, she dug out a slightly used tissue, wiped her eyes, and blew her nose. When she'd finished the soup, she devoured an oversized piece of cake and felt much better.

Angel put away the leftovers, rinsed her dishes, then wandered over to the sofa, where she stuffed a cushion under her head, stretched out under her afghan, and closed her eyes.

Sometime later she woke to a dinging sound, and after a few seconds realized there was someone at her door.

"Angel? Are you in there? Come on, open it up. It's me."

Angel yawned and groaned at the same time. Her mother must've called Tim. "Hang on, I'm coming."

Her head felt like it had been used as a target in a rock-throwing contest. She had a serious pain behind her eyes.

When she opened the door, Tim brushed past her. "Mom told me what happened. Are you okay?"

"Yeah." She rubbed her forehead and frowned. "I guess." She looked at her brother. Tim was thirty-five, five-ten, and had hazel eyes and sandy brown hair with a touch of copper. He favored the Irish side of the family, while she leaned toward the Italian. He must've come straight from church, as he was still wearing his clerical collar and black shirt and slacks. Ordinarily on a Sunday afternoon, he'd wear something more laid-back.

"Why are you here?" Angel rested her hands on her hips, not caring that she was being obnoxious.

Tim ignored her surliness and wrapped his arms around her. "I'm sorry, sis."

She relented and hugged him back, clamping her lips together to stop the pesky tears.

"How can I help?"

She pulled away. "I guess you could pray. Maybe God will listen to you. I sure don't seem to be getting anywhere lately."

"He's listening. He always is."

"Yeah. Whatever." She didn't want to talk about God. But something inside welled up like a pot of boiling water. "Why, Tim? Why did I have to be the one to shoot that boy? Why did he have to die?" She pushed at his chest when he reached out to comfort her again.

Her brother ran a finger inside his clerical collar and opened his mouth to speak, but she didn't give him the chance. "I'll tell you why. Because God doesn't care."

Tim lowered himself into the recliner while she paced back and forth and went on raving. "I don't need your help, or God's, or Ma's for that matter. I just need you all to go away and quit acting like I committed some sort of heinous crime. I was doing my job."

She stopped in front of him, suddenly feeling like an idiot.

He looked up at her. "Are you through?"

"No." She turned away from him and went to stand in front of the patio doors. *What's gotten into you? You're losing your grip.* She took a deep breath and let it out slowly. "Yes." She walked back toward him, her gaze glued to the floor. "I'm sorry. That was uncalled for."

"Yes, it was, but I'll let it slide this time. You're upset, and that's understandable. I wish I had an answer for you, Angel. All I know is that God is there for you. He loves you, and if you'll let him, he'll bring you through this."

I wish I could believe you. She folded her arms. "I don't see how. A twelve-year-old boy is dead because of me."

"Would you like me to pray with you?"

"No. What's the point?" She hitched herself up on the bar stool at the counter.

Tim shook his head. "I've seen a lot of people struggle with their faith — especially in times of trouble. A child dies and they ask why. They blame God. It's a normal reaction, I guess. But I just never expected it from you. You were always the strong one when we were growing up. You were the one who never wanted to miss Sunday school. You memorized all of the Bible verses and, man, Angel, I remember when we'd go on vacation — you'd spend the entire trip singing Jesus songs and driving us all crazy."

She shrugged her shoulders. "Yeah, well, things change." She didn't want to be reminded of how things used to be. She'd seen too much evil and too many prayers go unanswered in the past few years. She'd come to realize that God — if there even was a God — existed outside of reality, watching creation's demise and doing nothing about it.

But Tim wouldn't let her get off that easily. "Remember when I was in the hospital for so long after the accident?" he asked.

"Of course." He had nearly killed himself as a teenager. Like a lot of kids, he'd plunged headlong into booze and partying. He'd been the only survivor of a car accident in which four of his friends had died. At first, the pain had been so great that he'd wanted to die too. Not only had he lost his friends, he'd lost a leg as well.

"You know what kept me going, Angel? Prayers. Your prayers. You came to see me every day, and you kept telling me that God was going to make it all better."

A smile tugged at the corners of her mouth. "I also told you to quit feeling sorry for yourself and get your lazy carcass out of bed."

"That too." Tim got out of the chair and walked toward her. He'd made a full recovery and had been fitted with an artificial leg. "The point is, God answered our prayers. He made everything more than all right. God used that accident in a number of ways to give me a better life than I had before. I never touched a drop of alcohol after that night. And I met Susan. She was a candy striper, remember?"

"I remember Peter and Paul threatening to steal her from you if you didn't shape up." Tim had married Susan six years later. She'd become a nurse, he the pastor of St. Matthew's Church.

"You're avoiding the issue."

"What do you want me to say, Tim? You want me to agree with you — to say that God is going to make everything right? I can say it, but I still don't believe it."

"You're obviously too upset to think clearly."

"Because I disagree with you? You have your faith, and that's fine, but don't push it down my throat."

He glowered at her. "Some things never change. You are still the most infuriating, stubborn, and obnoxious sister a guy could have. When you come to your senses, call me. In the meantime, I'll be praying for you."

Tim turned around and left, pulling the door shut behind him with a resounding thud.

Oh, that was good. Your big brother offers his help, and you attack him. What's wrong with you? He was just trying to be helpful.

But he didn't have to be so pious about it. She pinched the bridge of her nose. In a way, she wished she could go back to the faith she'd had as a child, but that wasn't possible. As she'd told Tim, too many things had happened to convince her that God could not be who she had once thought him to be. How could a God of love allow such despicable things to happen? Dani had believed in God. Dani was dead.

A chill shuddered through her. Something akin to stage fright weakened her knees and gripped her around the chest, making it hard to breathe.

You're overreacting. Snap out of it. She glanced at the clock. Brandon would be here soon, and she needed to get ready. The two of them would have a cozy, quiet dinner. They'd talk about his work and his family. Maybe after dinner they would come back to her apartment and relax in front of the fire. Or maybe they'd walk on the beach in the moonlight.

She rubbed her hands down her face. "I'm not ready for this."

Maybe not, but it sure beats being alone and thinking about that kid.

NINE

Callen walked from the entry of the old cannery to the north corner, where he took a left and headed down the hill to the waterfront. He couldn't say for certain what prompted him to go down to the marina. Maybe he just needed to put some distance between himself and the crime scene — and the media. With two crime scenes to deal with, the place had turned into a three-ring circus.

It could have been nostalgia that brought him to the docks. He'd come here often as a kid and watched as the boats came in with their holds full of salmon to be cleaned, packed, and shipped to distributors. The condemned warehouse had once been a thriving cannery where boats could come right up to the private dock, but the dock was fenced off now to keep the public from injuring themselves on the rotting wood. The place had been empty for over ten years; laws protecting salmon had put a strain on the entire industry.

While he walked toward the water, Callen thought about the deadly force incident. Something about the shooting didn't ring true, but he couldn't say why. According to the officers involved, the gunmen had had an arsenal. So what on earth was the boy doing with a toy gun? Regardless of the reports he'd heard, he couldn't seem to tie the woman he'd seen with the action. Worse, he couldn't get the image of Angel Delaney out of his head. Sitting in that patrol car, she'd looked like a kid fresh out of college — her eyes wide and innocent and almost desperate. She wasn't beautiful like Karen had been, but cute. She had that all-American girl look a guy couldn't help but appreciate.

He pushed the image of her aside, pulling back into focus the job at hand. He had no time for women. After his wife's death he'd decided not to get involved seriously with anyone again. He still hadn't gotten over Karen or the child he'd never know.

Get your act together, Riley, he chastised. *This is not the time to be licking your wounds. You have a job to do.*

He'd spent hours that day checking out

both crime scenes and making sure he had crime lab people working at both locations. With two crime scenes to cover, he'd had to call his supervisor to send out two crime lab crews. Each team was made up of a scientist and a lab tech or assistant. Since the crime lab folks didn't work weekends, they'd be on overtime.

He'd put the first team from Lincoln City on the officer-involved shooting, and the second from Newport on the pharmacy. While he was waiting for the teams to get there, he questioned the various officers who'd responded to the armed robbery at the pharmacy and the ensuing chase.

The suspects had fled on foot, but Callen suspected they'd had a vehicle waiting for them not far away. Or maybe they had a preplanned meeting place. Which posed another question — what was the kid doing in the warehouse alone while his buddies were hotfooting it to the getaway vehicle?

Maybe the boy hadn't been alone. And if not, why hadn't his cohorts moved in to protect him? Had they all gone into the old warehouse and out the other side? With it being a condemned building, all entrances should have been boarded up, but since when did that stop anyone? Maybe they'd escaped by boat. Callen paused to jot the notation down in his notebook. He'd ask the other officers about that possibility and bring it up when he questioned Delaney.

Callen's gaze wandered over the wharf and bay. Here in the downtown area, rocky cliffs held back the ocean, leaving a wide opening, about a hundred feet, that served as an entryway into the cove. The cove provided a perfect place for fishermen to moor their boats and bring in their catch for processing.

He wandered down one of the piers, where a man was hosing down his charter boat. Large red letters on the bow read REEF CHARTERS. The guy wore a red-and-black flannel shirt with faded jeans and knee-high rubber boots — typical fishing apparel.

"This yours?" Callen asked as he approached the vessel.

Blue eyes warily looked him up and down. "Yep."

Callen pulled his ID out of his left jacket pocket. "Detective Callen Riley. I'm with the Oregon State Police. We're investigating a burglary."

The fisherman glanced at the badge then turned back to his task. A stream of water shot from the nozzle, hitting the deck full force. The wind picked up some of the spray and tossed it in Callen's direction.

He stepped back.

"Sorry about that." The fisherman turned the nozzle on the hose to shut it off.

"No problem. Mind if I ask you a few questions?"

"Nope."

Despite the man's lined face, Callen judged him to be in his thirties, already a crusty fisherman.

"Uh — name's Dean Jenkins." The fisherman jumped onto the dock, setting it to rocking so hard that Callen had to grab hold of a nearby piling to keep from toppling. He set his legs apart to maintain his balance.

"How long have you been here today?" Callen asked.

"Depends. I came out around 4:00 this morning. Took a couple guys out bottom fishing. We all got our limits and came in. Been in for about an hour."

"Did you see or hear anything unusual around here this morning?"

Jenkins frowned then turned the nozzle back on, moving the stream of water back and forth across the dock, where the morning's catch had apparently been gutted and cleaned.

"Nope. Why're you asking?"

Callen used the back of his arm to wipe perspiration off his forehead. Even though the temperature was only in the high sixties, the sun was baking him through his jacket and sweatshirt.

"There was an armed robbery at the pharmacy up the street around 9:00 this morning."

"Sorry. We were still out past the breakers then." Jenkins turned off the water at the spigot and began wrapping the hose in loops around a hook protruding from the piling. "Anybody hurt?"

"Mr. Bergman was injured, and we have one fatality." Callen withheld the boy's name and the circumstances.

Jenkins frowned and shook his head. "Too bad. You might want to talk to the guy who owns that rig across the way." Jenkins pointed to a thirty-foot sailboat on the next dock over. "The owner lives aboard. Fellow by the name of Jake Ensley. Better do it quick though. He's just passing through on his way to Victoria."

"Thanks."

Callen walked back up to the main dock. Coming up the ramp, he noticed what looked like a person lying inside the fence and directly behind the abandoned cannery. His system went on alert. He ducked beside a dumpster, checking the area. From his vantage point, he couldn't tell if the guy was dead or just sleeping off the remnants of cheap booze.

There didn't seem to be anyone around, so he hurried back the way he'd come and stopped at the fence. Whoever it was didn't appear to be moving. Looked like a corpse to him — especially considering the dark stain on the bleached wood next to the body. The stain could be wine, but experience told him otherwise. He had to check it out before calling for another crime lab team.

Using his cell phone, he notified dispatch and asked to be connected with Nick Caldwell. While he waited, he looked for a way around the fence. The only way he could see to get in other than to cut off the lock was to swim.

He told Nick what he'd seen and asked him to bring cutters to deal with the lock. "I don't see any easy way in here," he said. "The building is boarded up."

"Copy," Nick said. "But we don't have to go through the gate. Come on up to the front of the cannery. There's a place on the far west end where the boards are loose that will give us direct access."

Minutes later the three men squeezed through an opening that should have been boarded up to prevent trespassers from entering a dangerous area.

The rickety dock groaned and swayed with their weight as they walked the twenty or so feet to the body. Nick emerged from the building and joined them.

Callen hunkered down to get a better look. A kid, eighteen maybe. "He's dead." He glanced up at the two grim faces.

Nick frowned and motioned toward the body. "The kid looks familiar."

"Could he be one of the gang members from the pharmacy?" Eric asked. "Maybe we wounded one of them."

Callen shook his head. "This guy was shot at close range."

"You can tell that just looking at him?" Eric gave him a skeptical look.

"There's stippling on his face." He pointed to the small red dots on the skin. "It's caused by the powder exploding from the gun barrel in bullet projections and landing on and burning the skin. You only see that in shootings six feet and closer."

Eric looked impressed. Nick seemed anxious to get moving.

Callen let out a long breath and called his supervisor to okay another lab team. It was going to be a very long day.

TEN

Angel's doorbell rang promptly at 6:00. When she opened the door, Brandon was standing there in his charcoal gray suit, looking like the lawyer he was. He had thick, sandy brown hair, gray-blue eyes, and a killer smile. He turned that smile on her now as he handed her a bouquet of roses with baby's breath and ferns. "Picked these up on my way over."

Angel's breath caught as he pulled her into his arms for a kiss. "You look gorgeous," he said when they came up for air.

"Thanks." She'd taken pains to wear something feminine. Normally she'd have settled for a casual sweater and khaki pants, but tonight she'd dressed in a sleeveless black dress and topped it with a long-sleeved blouse that shimmered in iridescent shades of purple and teal as she moved. "Why don't you come in for a minute while I put these in water?" The delicate pink roses were just opening. Soft fragrant petals tickled her nose when she buried her face in the blooms. "This was really nice of you."

"Perfect roses for a perfect lady." He came up behind her, and with his hands on her shoulders, nuzzled her neck.

Angel shrugged out of his embrace and set the flowers on the table. "What a line. I'll bet you say that to all the girls."

He chuckled. "Only those named Angel. And I only know one Angel." His arms came round her again, pulling her close and bending down for another kiss. She stretched up on her toes and wrapped her arms around his neck, thinking how perfectly they fit together, she at five-four and he at five-eleven.

At the moment Angel couldn't imagine why she and Brandon hadn't married. She liked being with him. Felt comfortable around him — most of the time.

And he brings me roses.

He released her and sighed as he checked his watch. "Much as I'd like to just stay here and keep doing what we're doing, I'm starving."

"So you're telling me your stomach takes precedence over me." She managed a smile.

"You got it." Brandon turned her around and steered her toward the door.

They were on their way out when Angel's neighbor, Rob Landis, reached out and snatched up his newspaper. "Hey, guys. How's it going?" He didn't seem the least bit embarrassed about being caught in his ribbed tank undershirt and boxer shorts. Turning to Angel, he said, "Saw you on the news tonight. Well, not you, they put a picture up. You, uh . . . doing okay? I mean, hey, tragic mistake. But the kid was bad news, right?"

Angel wasn't certain how to respond. She was tempted to walk away without commenting, but that would be rude. Rob and his wife, Brenda, had helped Angel move into her apartment.

"Yeah." Angel glanced at Brandon. "Terrible mistake. But you do what you have to do. I'll talk to you later; we're just going out."

"Sure. Have fun. Hey, want me to record this stuff for you? It's not every day you get that kind of news coverage."

"You don't have to do that. I'll catch it later." Or not. How could the man be so blasé about something so horrendous?

"Okay. Think I'll record it anyway."

Brandon took her arm as they walked

down the steps. "What's he talking about?"

"Long story. I'll tell you later." As they reached the landing, her heart dropped to the vicinity of her knees. "Oh, no," she groaned. "I should have known."

The media had found her.

There were no newspapers or television and radio stations in Sunset Cove. Most of these people had come in from Portland. No doubt the entire state, maybe the entire country, would know about her involvement in Billy's death after tonight. She hadn't thought about the far-reaching effects of the shooting until now. She thought seriously about going back inside and curling up under the covers.

Cameras flashed and whirred as Brandon and Angel approached his car. The press had apparently been hanging around the parking lot, waiting for her to appear. Brandon unfortunately had parked his shiny black Lexus beside her Corvette. "We'd like to ask you a few questions," several reporters asked simultaneously.

"No comment." Angel flinched when someone stuffed a microphone in her face.

"You killed a child, Ms. Delaney." The woman's voice had an accusatory edge. "What do you have to say to his parents?"

The unfair accusation cut deep. Angel

stopped and glared at the reporter. "That *child* was a gang member. He had a gun."

She bit her lip. *Not a smart move. It won't do any good to antagonize the press.* "I'm sorry it happened. I was only doing my job."

"You don't have to defend yourself to these people, Angel." Brandon pressed closer to her and in a low voice added, "It might be better if you don't say anything at all."

He lifted his arm to protect her and pushed through the mob to his car, then opened the passenger side door and guided her inside. Relieved, she sank into the comfortable leather seats, strapping herself in. The press swarmed around the car like yellow jackets around a garbage can.

Brandon ducked into the car and shut his door. "I'm sorry, Angel. I saw them milling around when I came in, but I had no idea they were after you." His jaw tightened as he maneuvered the car between what had to be twenty people. "If I'd known, I would've parked on the street and hustled you out the back."

Angel bit her lip, wondering what he was thinking. "I should've realized they'd come after me as soon as they found out about the shooting." She looked back. The press was already disbanding, getting into their cars and vans.

Brandon drove around until they were certain none of the vultures had followed them, then he headed for the restaurant. Once they'd been seated, handed menus, and ordered drinks, he leaned forward, arms on the cloth-covered table. "Want to tell me about it?"

"No." She sighed. "But after all you've just been through, you deserve an answer."

"Darn right. If I hadn't been there to rescue you, they'd have picked your bones clean by now."

Angel chuckled despite her sour mood. "I wouldn't go that far. I could've handled them on my own. But thanks." The lights had dimmed, and in the candle's glow, Angel recounted the day's events until the waiter came to take their order. They both ordered the salmon special with Caesar salads. When the waiter left, Brandon sat there a moment, staring at the flowers in the center of the table.

Angel felt a moment's fear while she waited for his response. Would he tell her he couldn't afford to be connected with her?

"Not that it's any consolation," he finally said, "but it sounds like you did the right thing." He reached across the table to take her hand.

She relaxed. She should have known Brandon wouldn't send her packing. His parents would, but Brandon wasn't like them — most of the time. "I guess. I don't know. I keep wondering if I reacted too quickly. I honestly thought he was going to fire his weapon."

Not a weapon. A toy. Angel rubbed her forehead, trying to ease away the beginnings of another headache. She took a sip of tea and lifted her gaze to Brandon's. "Why would he do that? Earlier in the pharmacy he acted like he was going to give himself up, but maybe that was a ruse to get me to let my guard down so his buddies could have a clear shot at me."

Brandon shrugged. "I guess we'll never know, unless he forgot his gun wasn't real."

"How could he not know?"

"Got me. If he wasn't so young, I might suspect that he wanted you to shoot him."

"Suicide by cop?" Angel knew of several situations in which people had forced a confrontation with an officer, hoping they would be killed.

The waiter eyed her warily as he placed a bread basket on the table and refilled their water glasses. She was going to have to get used to those sidelong glances and wary looks. No matter where she went, people would wonder.

When their waiter left, Angel lifted the warm linen cloth lining the basket and withdrew a rosemary herb roll. "I'm in real trouble here, aren't I? Even if I was following police procedure, the press is going to fry me."

"Not necessarily. Most people are sympathetic with the police where known criminals are concerned. From what you've told me, the kid was a gang member."

Angel didn't see it that way. There was little or nothing right about what she'd done. "Brandon, if . . ." She set her bread on the plate and glanced down at her folded napkin.

"If?"

"The union is supposed to provide a lawyer, but I'm not sure I feel comfortable with someone I don't know. If I need legal advice . . ."

Brandon reached for her hand. "I'll be there for you. Count on it."

She smiled. "I'm sorry to spoil our dinner with this stuff."

"I wanted to hear about it."

"Thanks." She drew in a deep breath.

"You know what I really want?"

"What's that?"

"I'd like to forget about Billy Dean Hart-well for now. Let's have a nice dinner and talk about something totally unrelated."

"Good idea." Brandon tore his roll in half and slathered butter on it before taking a bite. "When we're finished eating I have a surprise for you." A mischievous grin lifted the corners of his mouth and lit up his eyes.

"Can you give me a hint?"

"Nope."

The waiter brought their salads and re-filled their water glasses again.

"So what do you want to talk about?" Brandon asked.

"You."

Brandon talked briefly about his work, not going into much detail. Being the junior partner in the law firm, he got many of the cases his father and older brother, Carl, passed on. The business had been started by Brandon's great-grandfather. Unlike most law firms, which either specialized in criminal law or corporate law, they covered all types of cases. Brandon handled a lot of bankruptcies and divorces but hoped some day to move into criminal cases.

"Have you heard about the Kelsey case?" Brandon asked.

"Who hasn't? Are you representing her?" Michelle Kelsey was the primary suspect in her husband's disappearance.

"Yeah." His grin reminded Angel of a kid with a giant Snickers bar.

"I hope you get her off, Brandon. Scum like Jim Kelsey deserve what they get. I don't blame her for killing him."

"I'm not just going for an acquittal. Michelle says she didn't do it, and I believe her."

"You can't be serious." Angel reached for her glass of iced tea. "There were witnesses at the restaurant who said they'd been arguing. And she'd bought a gun a week before he disappeared."

"All circumstantial evidence," Brandon argued. "There's no body, remember, and no way to prove he's dead."

"Her gun had been fired recently." Angel tore her roll in quarters and set them aside.

"She says she'd used it for target practice."

"Right — and she used her husband as the target." Angel reported what she'd heard about the case secondhand. Though she knew the Kelseys, she hadn't been involved with the investigation.

"She's not a killer. She's a victim." Brandon's hand pressed into a fist.

"Brandon, I'm on her side. I've seen her bruises more times than I care to remember. I must've been called out to their place at least three times since I've been here, and she never pressed charges."

"She wanted out, and he wouldn't let her go."

Angel nodded. "Which makes for a good motive. Michelle felt trapped and did the only thing she could to get out of it. Kelsey was the worst kind of abuser. He brainwashed her into believing he had a right to slap her around whenever he felt like it."

Brandon frowned. "Yeah. The guy was a piece of work, but she didn't kill him."

"The evidence says otherwise." Angel leaned back while the waiter took her salad plate and replaced it with the main course.

"The evidence doesn't prove a thing," Brandon insisted.

Angel sighed and waited for the waiter to leave, then leaned forward and met his intense gaze. "Has anyone ever told you that you'd make a great lawyer?"

He laughed. "I'm sorry. I feel strongly about this one."

"You know what?" Angel straightened.

"I hope I'm wrong. Go for it. This will be a high-profile case for you. Congratulations. How did you end up with it, anyway? This is the kind of thing your father would take or at least hand off to Carl."

"Actually, Michelle — uh, Mrs. Kelsey was already my client. She'd come to me wanting to start divorce proceedings. So when her husband disappeared and she realized the police suspected her of killing him, she wanted to retain me as her lawyer."

"Divorce? She came to you? No offense, but . . . you guys aren't exactly cheap. I doubt her husband would have put out money for it."

"You've got that right," Brandon snorted. "And she has money. She's been secretly putting it away for a few years now in her own account, for an emergency. She also came into some money through an inheritance — an aunt or something. She managed to keep it from her husband."

"So Michelle was planning to get a divorce? Too bad Jim's not around. I'd have liked to see the guy squirm." She scooped up some garlic mashed potatoes on her fork. "On the other hand, maybe it's a good thing he isn't. He might've ended up killing her."

She closed her eyes and let the warm potatoes linger on her tongue, enjoying the blend of butter, cream, and garlic. Maxwell's made the best garlic mashed potatoes on the coast — except for her mother's, of course.

They ate in silence for a while, and Angel savored every bite. Sometimes she wished she could cook, but that talent hadn't been passed down from mother to daughter. Not that Ma hadn't tried to teach her. Angel hadn't wanted to learn any more about homemaking skills than she had to. She'd gotten by so far, but she cringed at the thought of being married and having to come up with meals on a daily basis. Brandon was accustomed to eating well. The family had a housekeeper and cook, and he still lived at home — something she couldn't understand. Of course, she might not have minded either, if her parents had the Lafferty house, with its six thousand square feet of living space, plus a full-time maid, gardener, and chef. What would Brandon expect in a wife? Would he want them to live in his parents' home? Could he afford domestic help? He'd have to if he married Angel.

She brushed the pesky thoughts aside. She had no intention of getting married to

Brandon or anyone else for a very long time. Her life was too unsettled — and after today, even more so.

Angel concentrated on the food. The salmon was as delicious as it was beautiful. Grilled to melt-in-your-mouth perfection, then topped with a light blackberry sauce. The vegetables — beans, asparagus, broccoli, and carrots — had been grilled and served in a citrus marinade.

"How's your family?" Brandon asked. "This dinner reminds me of something your mother would cook up. Her baked salmon is the best."

Angel had to agree. "They're the same as always. Dad talks about retiring, but I doubt he'll leave until they kick him out. Ma is busy with church stuff. And she's still volunteering with Meals on Wheels. Did I tell you that now she's doing hospital visits as well? The woman never quits. She sews for Tim's girls and knits and quilts. I don't know where she finds the time to do it all." Angel picked up her glass. "Do you know she came by the house today, after . . ." The lump came back to clog her throat, and she fought a wave of tears.

"Angel . . ." Brandon's face was wearing that helpless male look.

She excused herself to go to the rest

room. By the time she had used the facilities and washed her hands, the tears were well under control. At least she hoped so. When she got back to the table, the busgirl was taking away their empty plates.

When the waiter came with the check, Brandon handed him a credit card. A few minutes later, they were walking out to the car. Angel had actually enjoyed dinner and was glad she'd decided to go. She'd managed to put the shooting out of her mind for a little while at least.

Instead of taking her to her apartment, Brandon headed north on Highway 101.

"Where are we going?"

"You'll see."

Angel closed her eyes and leaned back, thankful for any diversion that would keep her from dealing with Billy's death.

ELEVEN

When they reached the outskirts of the city, Brandon made a right, taking them east along Vista View Terrace. The road meandered into the hills and through Sunset Cove's most prestigious neighborhoods. From their vantage point, the bay looked like a huge bowl with openings at each end. To the west it narrowed and curved where it met the ocean. To the east the hills separated just enough to allow the Ilchee River access. They drove past a number of elegant homes perched on the hillside, overlooking the cove.

"We're not going to your place, are we?" Angel asked. The last thing she wanted to do was face his parents.

He took hold of her hand. "You don't have to worry about Mom and Dad. They wouldn't let this kind of thing affect the way they feel about you."

Probably not, Angel mused. She'd never

gotten the impression they cared that much about her anyway. Somehow she doubted they'd appreciate their son bringing home a . . .

Angel quickly turned her attention back to the road.

Brandon's home, mansion actually, was located on Sunset Drive in an upscale housing development. Brandon answered her question by going past his street.

As they drove, Angel glimpsed some spectacular views of the bay and ocean between homes. Finally Brandon slowed and turned into Bayside Drive, which took them down the hill closer to the water. "I hope we're not going to a party. I'm not in the mood."

"Nope. Just you and me." He smiled at her again, his eyes twinkling.

"What are you up to?" She couldn't help smiling back, finding his excitement contagious.

"You'll find out soon enough. We're here."

Brandon pulled into the driveway of a home that looked like it belonged on the cover of *Coastal Living* magazine. The lawn, what she could see of it, sloped down to the water's edge.

"Who lives here?"

"No one at the moment."

"Then what? Is it for sale?"

"Come on. I want to show you around."

"Are you thinking of buying it?"

Brandon turned off the engine and reached for her hand. Raising it to his lips, he kissed it then pulled her closer, brushing a kiss against her cheek and lips. "I might be. Let's go inside."

"Shouldn't you have a realtor show it to you?"

"I already made arrangements." He got out of the car and came around to open her door. Holding her hand, he led her toward the entrance — a covered tile patio and large double doors, both framing beveled glass ovals.

"Come on, Brandon. Why are you being so secretive? Why are we here?"

"You'll know soon enough."

He stopped and turned her toward him. Cupping her face in his hands, he lifted her head, forcing her to look into his eyes. "I love you, Angel."

"I . . ." Before she could finish, Brandon kissed her again. Angel was glad he hadn't let her finish. He thought she was going to say "I love you too," but she wasn't; she'd never been able to say it. She definitely cared for him, maybe loved him in a way; she just wasn't certain it was the kind of love that would sustain them in a permanent relationship.

Brandon released her. "Let's go inside." His key easily fit in the lock, as though he'd been opening the door for some time.

"Belongs to a friend of yours, doesn't it?"

"In a way." He laughed. "Come on. You have to see this."

The alarm system beeped when they entered. Brandon punched a series of numbers into the panel near the door and closed it. He turned on the entry light, revealing a magnificent tiled floor in cream-colored shades. He took her coat and tossed it on the curved banister that wound up wide carpeted stairs, then grabbed her hand, pulling her to the great room. Light from the entry flowed into the spacious living area. A huge kitchen with granite counters was off to the right. The kitchen alone was almost as big as her entire apartment. "Wow. My mother would love this kitchen."

"Yeah, she would. Can't you see her making one of her great pasta dishes in here?"

She nodded her head. "This place is awesome. But it's so big and elegant and . . ." *Expensive*. But then, cost probably wasn't an issue. He was, after all, a Lafferty.

To the left was a living area with a three-sided fireplace and a built-in large-screen television and stereo system. There was no furniture, but Angel could picture two sofas and two chairs with ottomans. They'd have to be natural — maybe white or cream, with colorful pictures on the wall and accent pillows. Or maybe something informal like rattan with tropical prints.

Brandon left her in the center of the room and went to click on a switch at the far wall. The huge fireplace burst into flames. He came around and stood behind her then directed her toward the sliding glass doors. There were five sets, actually, spanning the entire front of the house. All of the doors opened to a deck, offering an unobstructed view of the river. The alarm beeped again as he opened one of the sliding glass doors and stepped outside. "Come here. You have to see this."

As they stepped away from the house, the light dimmed, allowing her to see the inky black water and the lights of homes surrounding the bay. Several boats moved along the waterway, one of them the popular stern-wheeler that took guests out for dinner cruises.

"What do you think?" He took hold of her hand.

"Oh, Brandon. It's beautiful."

"I've always wanted to live in a place on the bay."

So he was thinking of buying it. "Then you should, Brandon. This is nice."

"Do you really like it?"

Angel shrugged. "Sure. Who wouldn't? I haven't seen the rest of the house, but I'm sure it's great."

"Well, the rest of the place is nice. But the view is my favorite part — and the fact that it's so close to the water. You can't see it very well right now, but there's a dock and a motorboat."

"So are you going to buy it?"

Brandon wrapped his arms around her. "I already did." He kissed her again and drew her back inside. "I want you to see the rest of it."

Angel had enjoyed the evening, but the day's events were taking their toll on her. She was exhausted. Even so, she dutifully followed Brandon up the stairs, making appropriate comments as he showed her the oversized bathroom with a Jacuzzi tub and shower for two. She was mildly impressed with the huge his-and-her walk-in closets and the bedroom that looked like it could easily accommodate fifty kids on a sleep over. She liked the balcony that overlooked the living room and kitchen below and the two bedrooms and baths that would make a wonderful guest suite.

"It's really nice, Brandon, but I'm getting tired. Can we go now?"

Brandon looked disappointed. "I'm sorry. I was so excited, I forgot — after all you've gone through today, you must be wiped out. We can go in a minute. I have something really important to tell you first."

Angel rubbed the back of her neck. He was buying the house and wanted her to be excited for him. It wasn't so much to ask. "It's really a great house, Brandon."

"I'm glad you think so, honey. Because . . ." He hesitated, drawing her into the circle of his arms again. "Because I bought it for us."

"Us?"

"Marry me. It's time, don't you think? We've known each other since high school. I want you to be my wife. I want to start a family."

Angel pulled away from him. She was speechless for a moment, her mind not able to process the words. Finally she managed to string some together. "You can't be serious. A guy doesn't go out and buy a house like this, then ask his girlfriend to marry him. What happens if I don't want to get married?"

"I . . ." Brandon stared at her, openmouthed. "The minute I saw it, I knew it was for us. I love this place. I thought you would too."

"I do, but that's beside the point. Buying a house is something couples do together. I'm not ready for this. I don't want to get married."

"Look," he soothed. "You're upset about what happened today, that's understandable. Just think about it for a while."

Angel tried to calm down but couldn't keep the edge out of her voice. "It's not about the shooting. I don't *want* to get married. I don't *want* children, and I don't *want* this house." She walked out and sank onto the front porch step, cradling her head in her hands.

She heard the door opening and a series of beeps as Brandon set the alarm. She'd hurt him, but she honestly didn't know what to say. She still couldn't believe he'd buy a house for them without her input. Granted, it was a beautiful place. And she had been dating him exclusively for the past year. But how dare he assume so much?

Brandon sat down next to her. "Angel . . ."

"Don't say anything, please. Just take me home."

"But —"

"I don't want to hear it. I don't want to know why you did it. I just want to go home."

"Okay." His voice sounded scratchy.

Angel sighed. Brandon loved her. She knew that. But did she love him? *"He's a good man, Angel,"* Ma had often said. *"You could do worse."*

Well, he could be a prince for all she cared. She just wasn't ready.

They didn't say a word to each other as Brandon drove back to town and into the parking lot of her apartment complex. The members of the press had apparently given up for the night. At least there were none around that she could see.

Brandon got out and came around to open the car door for her, but she'd already gotten out. When they reached her apartment, he pressed a hand to her shoulder, turning her toward him. "Angel."

She reached up to cover his mouth. "Don't, please. I know you meant well, but . . . maybe it is the shooting. Maybe. . . . I don't know. All I know is that I can't get married right now. I'm not ready, and I may never be ready. I'm sorry."

Brandon avoided her gaze. He didn't reach for her or kiss her good night as he usually did. But then, why would he? He waited for her to open the door and step inside, then turned and hurried down the stairs and got into his car. Angel waited in the doorway and watched until his taillights disappeared around the corner.

She could almost hear her mother's scolding voice. *Angel Delaney, what have you done?*

TWELVE

It was after 9:00 when Callen got back to his house. Kath and the girls had gone back to Portland hours ago and had left a note on the counter. He rubbed Mutt's head as he read it.

Sorry you couldn't make it back before we left. We cleaned up the place and left dinner in the fridge. Hugs and kisses, Kath, Jenna, and Ashley.

Callen smiled at their thoughtfulness and set the squirmy dog on the floor. Mutt took off running, snatched up a rubber duck, and settled into a game of duck versus dog. If the squealing was any indication, Mutt was winning.

Callen chuckled at the dog's antics as he opened the refrigerator. Not much in it except for the stuff Kath had left him — a plate of deep-fried chicken, potato salad, and overcooked green beans — all apparently purchased at the grocery store deli down the street. He grimaced. This kind of food was one of the reasons he'd learned to cook. Not that he was a health-food nut or anything. He just appreciated food done right. Hopefully he'd be able to get to a health-food store soon, or at least to a market that had a health-food department.

He ignored the chicken dinner and pulled out the bag of raw vegetables he'd brought with him from Portland. Downing a full-size dinner at this time of night would probably give him heartburn anyway. After pouring a glass of milk, he went outside on the deck and set his food on the glass-topped patio table. He'd found a huge sale on patio furniture last fall and had gone all out. This was the first time he'd used it.

He then pulled on his jacket and brought Mutt outside, substituting the squealing duck for a rawhide bone. Once the dog was settled, Callen sat down on one chair and put his feet up on the other.

Munching on a spear of celery, he let himself enjoy his pleasant surroundings. It was a bit nippy for an outdoor meal, but he wasn't about to let a little thing like cooler temperatures and Northwest drizzle spoil his dinner. Once he got established here, he'd invite some of the law enforcement officers over for a barbeque. Though he seldom ate red meat, for them he'd do big, juicy T-bones and baked potatoes, maybe corn on the cob, and a salad or two — one with salad greens and another with homemade bow-tie pasta, feta cheese, tomatoes, and his special balsamic vinaigrette.

So far he liked the people he worked with. Nick and Eric had been especially helpful and didn't seem to resent his coming into their territory. Part of that, Callen suspected, was that their superior, Joe Brady, had high respect and appreciation for the Oregon State Police.

Investigations always went better when all the law enforcement agencies worked together. He wondered briefly how Angel Delaney would be to work with. Eric and Nick had nothing but praise for her; both went out of their way to assure him that she was a good cop. "Small but mighty," Eric had said.

"If she says she was forced to shoot, then she was. I have no doubt," Nick had told him.

Mike Rawlings had been a little less flattering. "Seems like a nice kid. She did her job."

Bo Williams, the deputy sheriff, didn't

123

have much to say. He liked her okay, but thought she was too small to be a cop. Though Bo didn't say it in so many words, Callen suspected he didn't approve of having women on the force.

He sighed. Deputy Williams didn't seem to like him much either. Maybe the guy was naturally touchy and ill-tempered.

When he caught himself eating too fast, he stopped and deliberately slowed down. He'd been trying to overcome his bad habits. Eating too fast was one of them.

Karen had put him on the healthy eating kick. She'd insisted on buying everything organic and had become a strict vegetarian, saying nutrition and the right supplements were the only way she could build up her immune system to battle the cancer. She had juiced four times a day, eaten no red meat. But in the end, cancer emerged the victor. Maybe if she'd started sooner. Maybe if she'd taken the chemotherapy. But with the pregnancy she'd opted not to.

After she died Callen hadn't cared if he ate or not. Finally, when he came to his senses, he adopted his healthy lifestyle primarily because she would have wanted it.

He put his fork down. The ache in his chest had come back along with the thickness in his throat. He hoped someday he'd be able to think about her without feeling like his insides were being ripped apart.

Callen tipped his head back. The night was dark and clear, and the moon spread a silvery, shimmering path across the water. He was going to like it here. He just wished Karen and the baby could have been there to share it with him.

When he finished eating, he piled his dishes in the dishwasher, wiped off the counter, and headed to the bathroom for a much-needed shower. He couldn't remember a time when he'd been wearier. Stepping in front of the mirror brought renewed concerns. Had he really looked that bad all day? Of course, he'd been painting when he left that morning, and when you got called in, you basically went as you were. A smile tugged at the corners of his mouth. No wonder he'd gotten some strange looks. He cocked an eyebrow and peered at the bright blue streaks highlighting his dark brown hair. He showered, and after finally getting the latex paint out of his hair, he went to bed.

Sleep should have come easily. Instead, his mind churned with the day's events and the questions surrounding them. How had the young man ended up on a pier behind the cannery, the same building where Angel Delaney felt she had to use deadly force against a twelve-year-old?

At first Eric had suggested J.J. might have been one of the gang members who'd been wounded in the gunfight at the pharmacy, but Callen had ruled that out almost immediately. The medical examiner put the time of death around 3:30 a.m. There had been no ID on the kid's body, but his fingerprints were on file. John James Monroe, nicknamed J.J., was a known felon with a criminal record in California. He'd been picked up for theft, dealing, and pimping, just to name a few. Judging from the ecstasy they found in his pocket, Callen figured the kid had brought his old habits with him. His best guess at the moment was that J.J. had been shot in a drug deal gone bad.

The victim in the officer-involved shooting, however, was a different story. Billy Dean Hartwell had no criminal record, except for a shoplifting incident. They found drugs in his pocket as well. Insulin.

Delaney had some hard questions to answer. He'd called her around dinnertime and left a message on her answering machine. Callen glanced at the green lighted numbers on the radio alarm. Ten o'clock.

Too late to call now. He'd try again in the morning.

His list of things to do scrolled through his brain, making sleep impossible. He finally gave up and threw his covers off and headed for the living room, where he turned on the television set. And there was Angel and some preppy looking guy surrounded by reporters clamoring for answers.

"Police officer kills a twelve-year-old boy, details at 11:00," the news anchor reported.

"Great." He ran a hand through his hair. "How did those turkeys find her?" Someone must have leaked her name.

Callen pulled his notebook out of the pocket of the jacket he'd hung in the closet. He'd written Officer Delaney's number in it. He dialed, but again no answer. "Officer Delaney," he said after the beep, "this is Detective Callen Riley with the Oregon State Police. I'm sorry I couldn't get back to you today. It's probably too late to warn you, but somehow the media got hold of your name. I'd hoped to keep them away from you for another day or so. Also, I'd like to set up a time to talk with you. You can reach me on my cell phone." He gave her the number and hung up, wondering where she might be and if she was all right.

Needing to get some sleep, he turned off the set and went back to his bedroom. He opened the window and stretched out on the bed, listening to the waves crashing on the shore. As his eyelids drooped, he concentrated on the ocean sounds and said a prayer for Angel Delaney and the family of the boy she'd killed.

THIRTEEN

At 10:45 Angel turned on the television and tried to get interested in the brainless sitcom with its canned laugh tracks. During a commercial break, the newscaster gave a plug for their feature story of the day: "Police officer kills twelve-year-old boy, details at 11:00."

A shot of her and Brandon filled the screen. She looked haggard, the annoyance with the reporters evident on her face. She wished she'd been friendlier. Maybe the press would've been more empathetic — maybe not. Then the camera cut away to an attractive black woman with dark burgundy hair and a colorful dress. In the background the reporter continued to talk. "We'll talk with the victim's family and —"

Angel clicked to another channel, where a woman at a sewing machine was teaching her TV audience how to make velvet gift bags. Angel watched the woman sew up a seam, then realized she would probably never sew a gift bag or anything else. She turned off the set and got ready for bed.

It was then she noticed the blinking light on her answering machine. Both messages were from Callen Riley, the Oregon State Police detective. In the first one, he said he wanted to interview her so he could get her version of the story. Angel didn't want to be interviewed. "Humph. Like you have a choice," she muttered to herself.

In the second message he apologized for the media invasion. "Too late, but thanks," Angel answered the recorded voice while she slipped into her cotton knit pajamas. He had a pleasant voice and sounded as though he really cared. Maybe the interview with him wouldn't be too bad.

Though Angel didn't want a recap of the shooting or the press version of what happened, she couldn't help but turn the news back on at 11:00. She wanted to hear what Billy's family had to say; she would have to talk with them at some point. She also wanted to know how the pharmacist was doing. She curled up on the sofa, wrapped the afghan around her shoulders, and tucked her feet beside her.

As Angel suspected, the burglary and shooting incident topped the news program. "Gang members allegedly broke into a drugstore early this morning in Sunset Cove," a news anchor reported. "In recent months gang activity and drug use has infiltrated the normally peaceful community on the central Oregon coast. Police tell us the gangs apparently have come in from the L.A. area and have recruited youth here in Sunset Cove."

The camera cut away to Joe Brady. "In recent years we've managed to keep gang activity to a minimum. We're doing our best to find those responsible."

"Chief Brady, can you comment on what happened today? We understand that one of your officers shot and killed a twelve-year-old boy."

"I'm not at liberty to comment at this time. We should have a full report in a day or two."

"You said the gang has been recruiting youth in the area. Isn't twelve a bit young?"

"Unfortunately, no." Joe ran a hand over his balding head.

"Then you believe the victim was a gang member."

"We're looking into it. What I can tell you is that the entire department is working hard to apprehend these criminals."

"There you have it, Kelley," the reporter said. "We'll report the details as they develop."

The anchor turned to face the camera. "In what police are calling an unrelated incident, another body was found in Sunset Cove today. Police are withholding information pending notification of family."

Angel uncurled herself and pressed the button on the remote to increase the sound. "Another body?" For once she wished the media had more information. She hated being out of the loop. She thought about calling dispatch and having them put her through to one of the officers on duty, then decided against it. She'd wait until morning and talk to Eric or Nick, or maybe even Joe.

"I've just been told we have some new information on the Sunset Cove shootings." The anchor's comments brought Angel's attention back to the news. "Donna Middlewood is on the scene in Sunset Bay with Officer Eric Mason."

"Eric?" Angel frowned. "What's going on?"

The anchor continued. "Donna, I understand you are just outside Officer Delaney's apartment, is that right?"

"That's right, Kelley. Eric is with the

Sunset Cove Police Department and is, in fact, Officer Angel Delaney's partner. Eric, I understand you and your partner responded to the robbery. Can you tell us what happened?" She tipped the mike toward Eric.

"I don't believe this." Angel went down the hallway to her door and peered through the window blinds to the parking lot below. Eric was leaning against his car, arms folded, still in uniform. She frowned as anger flared up inside her. "What are you doing in front of my place talking to a reporter?" She'd thought all the reporters had left.

It didn't take long to come up with an answer. They must've found out Eric was her partner and followed him. Angel went back to the living room and watched the live interview.

"I don't know what I can tell you. You guys usually seem to know more than we do," Eric said.

"What happened that led up to the shooting?"

"Look, I'm not the person you want to talk to about the investigation." He offered the reporter one of his devastating smiles, and Angel could almost see her swoon.

"Were you with Officer Delaney when she shot the boy?"

His smile faded to a frown. "I think I know where you're headed here. And I'm not buying into it. The kid had a gun. He was a threat."

"We understand it was a toy gun."

Eric ran a hand through his thick hair and glanced around as if looking for someone to rescue him. "It doesn't matter if it was a toy or not. When officers perceive a threat, they react. She had to stop him."

"But he was a child."

"He was involved in a robbery. Hey, I'd have done the same thing. That's all I have to say."

"What about the other shooting? Can you give us any information on the victim or what may have happened?"

He took a step back. "Sorry. I have nothing more to say."

The reporter thanked him. "Back to you, Kelley."

"Thanks, Donna." The anchor turned back to her notes. "The owner of the pharmacy, Gerald Bergman, is listed in critical condition after being shot in the chest and stomach. And as we've heard, the tragic events didn't end there. One of the officers shot and killed a young boy. His family is asking why."

Because he aimed a gun at me.

The doorbell rang. Probably Eric. Angel debated whether or not to let him in. She had mixed feelings about him talking to the reporter. It seemed disloyal in a way. She had to admit, though, that he'd done a better job with the media than she had. Finally, she relented and opened the door.

Eric leaned against the door frame. "I was in the neighborhood and saw your lights on. Thought I'd stop and see if you needed anything."

"Come on in." She closed the door and went back to the sofa. "They're talking to Billy's family."

Eric settled on the couch and watched it with her. "Are you sure you want to see this?"

She shushed him.

It was another reporter, a man; Angel missed his name and didn't recognize him as one of the regulars. "We spoke with the boy's family minutes ago, and they've been kind enough to talk with us."

Eric folded his arms across his chest. "Humph, these reporters just don't know when to quit."

"Quiet. I want to hear this." Angel clicked up the volume.

"Mrs. Hartwell," the reporter began, "we've been told that your son was a gang member. It that true?"

"No." His mother shook her head, burying her face in her hands. "Billy was a good boy."

"How do you explain the fact that he was in the store at the time of the robbery — the robbery, I might add, that has seriously injured the owner, Mr. Bergman?"

Mrs. Hartwell dabbed at her eyes. "It was my fault. I sent him to the store this morning to pick up a prescription for his grandma. She's diabetic and had run out of insulin. I called Mr. Bergman at home, and he told me not to worry. He said he'd go in early and let my boy in. My boy wasn't there to steal anything. I don't understand how the officer could make a mistake like that. Billy Dean didn't do anything wrong."

That can't be true. Angel stared at the set, unable to believe what she'd heard.

"We've been told that the officer mistook his gun for the real thing," the reporter went on, "and that he was threatening to fire at her."

The woman was crying in earnest now. "I'm sorry, I just can't do this."

A stern-looking man settled a long-fingered hand on Mrs. Hartwell's shoulder.

"It's all right, Mavis." The camera focused in on him. Tall and thin, he wore his black hair cropped close to his head and had on a business suit. "I'll answer the questions. I'm Billy's uncle, Ray Broadman." Turning to face the camera he said, "It's clear to me that what we have here is a case of outright prejudice. Officer Delaney saw an opportunity to kill a black boy and did so."

Angel stared openmouthed at the television screen. "I can't believe he said that."

"The guy's nuts, Angel." Eric touched her shoulder.

"I need to hear this." She leaned forward, and Eric's hand dropped away.

"Billy was at the wrong place at the wrong time," the man continued. "Like his mama says. He was a good boy. Do you want to know what was in his pocket when that woman killed him? His grandmother's prescription and a candy bar — bought and paid for. He even had the receipt. Billy was not a thief. His so-called weapon was a birthday present. You know how boys are, always playing Rambo and GI Joe."

"So you're accusing the officer of being racist?" the reporter asked.

"What other explanation can there be? Officer Delaney claims she was doing her job. She might think killing a black boy isn't a big deal, but she is dead wrong. I've already talked to a lawyer. Officer Delaney is going to pay for what she's done, make no mistake about that. If the state of Oregon won't bring her down for killing that boy, the black community will."

The anchor closed the segment by showing footage of Angel and Brandon. "The officer responsible for Billy's death refused to give us a statement other than to say she was sorry it happened. Is this another case of police brutality? Of excessive force? A racial incident? It's still too soon to tell."

A picture of Billy flashed on the screen. An adorable boy with a smile as big as Texas.

The reporter continued. "What happened to Billy Dean Hartwell? Was he an innocent bystander as his family says, or was he a gang member? Sources on the street tell us that Billy was not in any way affiliated with the gang that has been operating in the area. We'll bring you the latest news on this case as it's made available."

Angel turned off the set and sat there in stunned disbelief. Billy had gone to the pharmacy for medication. Had she been mistaken all along in counting him as one of the gang members? He'd come out from hiding and looked scared and acted like he was giving up. She had assumed that he'd lured her out in the open so his pals could get a clean shot at her. Maybe he was coming to her for help, and the shooters took advantage of the situation. Angel stared into the fireplace, trying to assemble this new information.

Billy had made a purchase, but that didn't change the fact that he'd run from her in that building, or that he'd raised his gun as if to shoot at her. Or had he? Maybe he'd started to raise his hands in surrender. Had she been so frightened, so fearful for her life, that she'd misread his intent?

"Don't pay any attention to them, Angel."

She jumped at the sound of her partner's voice. "Eric, I forgot you were there. What did you say?"

"The guy's a nutcase. Don't listen to him."

She slumped back against the seat and folded her arms. "What if he's right? What if Billy wasn't involved with the break-in? What if the kid was innocent?"

"Come on, you know better."

"They're taking me to court. You heard him. I could be tied up in court for months. I don't have that kind of money."

"What about your lawyer friend? Maybe he'll defend you. He probably doesn't do charity cases, but maybe he'll make an exception."

Angel didn't respond. Of course, Brandon would represent her — and for nothing. Wouldn't he? She leaned forward, resting her elbows on her knees and her head in her hands. Her lower lip trembled and a sob escaped her throat. "What am I going to do, Eric?"

He reached over and rubbed her shoulder. "Quit punishing yourself. You know what went down, so don't let this guy or those reporters get to you. The media is into sensationalism. They blow everything out of proportion. Seems like every time a cop has to use deadly force, the media is on it like maggots on a rotting corpse."

Angel grimaced at his analogy. "You're right about that." Rising from the sofa, she adjusted the tie on her robe, wrapping it more securely around her.

"I should go." Eric stood too, as if anxious to leave. She didn't blame him. He wasn't used to seeing her this way — so close to the edge.

She walked him to the door. "Thanks for coming by — and for the pep talk."

"No problem." He turned back, filling the doorway with his large frame. "There's no way the grand jury's going to indict you. Trust me on that."

"I hope you're right."

After saying good-bye and closing and bolting the door, she leaned against it, wishing she could be as sure about all of this as Eric seemed to be.

As she headed to her bedroom, the phone began ringing. *Who'd be calling this late?* She walked down the hall, planning to answer it, but in the end she went back to the sofa and let the machine do what she'd bought it to do.

"Hi, Angel," Brandon said after the beep. "Must be sleeping, huh? Listen, I'm sorry about tonight. It wasn't fair of me to buy the house without talking to you first. It's just that the place was available and there were already several people interested in it. I felt I had to move fast. The proposal still stands, but no pressure, okay? I didn't realize how serious your situation was until I saw it on the news tonight. My timing wasn't the greatest, was it?"

"No, it wasn't," Angel muttered, her annoyance with him reappearing.

"I just wanted to apologize and tell you I love you."

Angel didn't want his apology or his declaration of love, she just wanted to be left alone. She wanted peace of mind. She wanted to believe like Eric that everything would be okay. She turned off the lights, curled up under the afghan, and sat there for a long time, staring into the darkness, listening to the steady pounding of the waves. Sometime around midnight, she made her way to her bedroom and crawled into bed. Sleep came in snatches as images of Billy Dean Hartwell invaded her mind. Images of him raising his toy gun and laughing like a child at play. Images of her, pulling the trigger.

FOURTEEN

The phone woke Angel at 7:00 the next morning. Her head still hurt. She refused to open her eyes. After three rings the answering machine picked up and said, "Hi, this is Angel, please leave a message at the beep."

"Angel?"

She groaned into her pillow. "Dad, it's too early."

"You still in bed? Come on, now. I know you can hear me." He sighed. "You know how I hate to talk into these things, but I got something to say."

"Well, say it." Angel mumbled but made no move to get out of bed.

"Don't let those yahoos get to you, Angel. I saw that idiot bad-mouthing you on television last night. He's trying to make a racial case out of this. Ain't gonna happen if I have anything to say about it.

Already talked to the guys in the department, and they are all on your side. Mike says he can't believe the guy would go that far. Says he's going to try to talk to him. Just wanted you to know that." He hesitated again. "I wish you'd answer your cussed phone. I don't like talking to a machine." After another long pause he hung up.

Angel opened her eyes then closed them again. *Coward. You should've talked to him.*

She crawled out of bed and shuffled barefoot to the kitchen. Still half asleep, she poured water into the coffeemaker, scooped coffee into the filter, and hit the on button.

The phone rang again, and again she relied on the machine to intervene. This time it was Joe. Angel picked up as soon as she recognized his voice. "Hi, Joe. I'm here." She pressed the stop button on the machine to end the recording. "Sorry."

"How are you doing, Delaney?"

Terrible. "Okay, I guess."

"You watch the news last night?"

"Yeah." *And I'm still reeling. I feel like I've fallen into a black hole and someone put the top on.*

"Look, I hate to ask, but I need you to come in. Normally I'd give you a few days before we do a formal questioning, but this Broadman guy is stirring things up royally. I got a call from the mayor this morning, and he got a call from the governor before he contacted me. They want this mess cleared up yesterday."

"I don't know what I can do about it."

"You can cooperate. Give us your statement. We should have a report from the crime lab in Portland by Tuesday or Wednesday. This thing is taking top priority. Have you made an appointment with the shrink yet?"

"No. The office wouldn't even be open yet." Her tone sounded defiant, and she quickly added, "I'll do it today." *But I don't want to. I know it's protocol, but I'm afraid to go and to talk. I'm afraid I'll fall apart.*

"Good."

"Joe?" Angel bit her lip, not sure she really wanted to know any more, yet feeling that she needed to.

"Yeah?"

"On television last night, I heard that another body had been found."

"That's right." Joe paused for a moment, and she wondered if he'd tell her about it. He cleared his throat and went on. "We're not disclosing much to the media yet, so keep the info under your hat. Detective

Riley spotted a body out on the pier behind the old cannery where you cornered the kid. No connection to the burglary or your situation that we can see. They found drugs on him. The victim was a known dealer out of L.A. — probably involved with the gang."

"Have you identified him yet?"

"Name's John James Monroe. Goes by the name of J.J. Ever hear of him?"

"No, doesn't ring a bell. Um — one more thing. The family says Billy wasn't a gang member. Is that true? He was at the pharmacy, and I assumed . . ."

"Don't second-guess yourself on this, Delaney. Besides, it's not me you have to convince. When can you get here?"

She glanced at the clock on the microwave. "In an hour."

"Good. Your union lawyer will be here too — he called this morning to get your home number. Detective Riley with OSP will be here as well. Hopefully, we'll have everything cleared up in a few days."

"I hope so."

Just before hanging up, he made an attempt to reassure her, saying he was on her side.

Angel wished she could believe him, but his job was on the line as well as hers. Joe might be loyal to his officers, but she had no doubt he'd sacrifice her to the wolves if things got too hot. He'd never said as much, but she suspected that if he hadn't had to fill his quota of female officers, he'd never have hired her.

Why am I even thinking about whether or not he'll support me? It isn't going to come to that. I fired at the kid because I had to. He was a threat.

No, he wasn't. The voice was almost audible in its intensity.

Yes, he was. I had no choice.

Angel pushed aside the internal arguments and finished her coffee as she dressed and got ready to go to the police station. She was about to walk out the door when she remembered the psychologist. Better at least make the appointment before Joe got on her case again.

"Oh yes, Miss Delaney," the receptionist said after Angel had introduced herself. "We've been expecting your call."

"Why's that?" She knew why. Apparently Joe was checking up on her. The knowledge didn't improve her mood.

"Um, Mr. Brady said you'd be calling. He just explained the circumstances."

"I see." How much had Joe said?

"Dr. Campbell has an opening this afternoon at 2:00. Could you come in then?"

"Sure," Angel told the receptionist. "The sooner the better." *Might as well get it over with.* She was obligated to make one visit to the counselor, then she was off the hook. With the appointment made, she hung up.

You may need to go longer. The thought was invasive and sounded too much like her mother.

"I don't need counseling," she argued aloud. "It would make me look weak to the other officers — especially to Dad."

This has hit you hard. Besides that, you're still struggling with Dani's death.

"Dani's death has nothing to do with this. I'll be fine." She paused with her hand on the doorknob. "As long as I quit talking to myself."

She took a deep breath to brace herself for an attack by the multitudes of media. But they weren't there. Too early, she guessed, or maybe her news was already getting old. One could only hope.

Angel got to the station at 8:30 sharp. Joe greeted her as though this were an ordinary briefing on an ordinary day as he ushered her into the interrogation room — the same room she herself had used to question witnesses. The room was filled by the rectangular wooden table and six chairs. A pitcher of water and several glasses sat in the center of the scarred table.

The two men Joe had told her about were already seated, and both stood as she and Joe came in. Angel recognized the OSP officer immediately. Yesterday he'd arrived on the scene unshaven and wearing scrubby looking, paint-splattered jeans and a sweatshirt. He'd even had streaks of blue paint in his hair. Today he wore a tie, and under his tweed jacket she could see the familiar outline of his holster.

He cleans up well. She turned from his assessing gaze and focused her attention on the lawyer.

"Officer Delaney." The other man introduced himself as Randy Grover and reached across the table to shake her hand. "I'm sorry I didn't make it down here yesterday. I live in Portland, and there was no way I could get here before 6:00." The lawyer, an average looking man with a stocky build, wore glasses and had a bald spot on top of his head, similar to Joe's, though not as pronounced. He smiled and shook her hand, but his eyes told Angel that she wasn't high on his priority list.

"It's okay. I don't think your being here

sooner would have made a difference."

Randy Grover sat down, opened his briefcase, and removed a legal pad and pen. With pen poised above the pad, he looked up at them as if to say, *Let's get on with it.*

"Officer Delaney." The guy from the Oregon State Police came around to where she stood to shake her hand. "Detective Callen Riley." His hand felt warm, firm, and strangely comforting. "This is a tough time for you." His statement echoed the concern and understanding she read in his face. His eyes, a gentle sea green, searched hers, forcing her to look away for fear he'd see too much or look too deep.

She needed air. She gulped back a surge of panic that nearly made her bolt for the door. She might've run if her legs hadn't gone all rubbery on her. Her voice caught on the thank you she muttered to Detective Riley as she slipped into the chair he pulled out for her.

"I was hoping we could wait a day or two for the formal statement," Riley said, glancing at Joe then returning his gaze to her. "If you're not up to this today, we can postpone it."

Neither Joe nor the lawyer commented. Grover looked like he had other things to do. Joe leaned against the wall, his expression unreadable. In her earlier conversation with him, he'd left no doubt as to his opinion.

She glanced up at Riley. "Thanks, but I'm okay with it. We're all here, so I might as well get it over with."

Detective Riley nodded. "All right, if you're sure."

She nodded. *I'm not. I may never be, but I don't seem to have much choice.*

Riley produced a tape recorder from his open briefcase and set it on the table in front of her. The lawyer had a smaller one of his own. Angel gulped back another wave of panic.

"We'll try to make this as easy as possible on you." Riley's soothing voice washed over her.

Easy? How could it ever be easy? Already the hard wooden chair hurt her rear, and she shifted to find a comfortable position.

Detective Riley poured a glass of water and set it in front of her. From the counter behind him he snagged a box of tissues. When she frowned at his actions, he murmured, "Just in case."

His kindness was almost her undoing. There was such a thing as being too nice. Angel closed her eyes for a moment, pushing her emotions back. She needed to be objective and to tell her side of the story. "I'm ready."

Detective Riley and the lawyer punched the record buttons on their machines. Riley began by giving his name and the date, and listed the others present in the room, then asked her if she was aware that she was being recorded.

"Yes," she answered. Obviously she was, but Oregon state law required officers to inform the party being recorded.

"Officer Delaney, this is a criminal review of the shooting, not an internal affairs investigation. It is not required that you submit to this interview."

"Wait a second." Randy Grover turned to Angel. "Are you sure you want to do this?"

She hauled in a ragged breath. *No, I'm not sure of anything. I want it all to go away, but it won't.* "I want to get it over with. This is as good a time as any."

The lawyer leaned back, willing to let it go. She'd seen some lawyers blow long and hard at this point. Grover seemed to have other things on his mind.

Angel glanced over toward the door, where Joe was still standing, then at the lawyer sitting opposite her, and finally to the detective, who sat at the narrow side of the table just to her left. Her heart hammered so loudly she felt certain they'd catch it on the tape. "Go ahead. Do you want me to start with the burglary?"

"Way before that," Riley said. "Start at the beginning of the day from the time you got out of bed. Work your way up to the shooting. Be sure to include any prescription drugs you take, alcohol consumption, amount of sleep, that sort of thing."

Drugs? Alcohol? What was he thinking? "I don't take anything, and I would never drink before I went to work."

Riley nodded. "Just take your time and give as many details as possible."

She cleared her throat then took a sip of water from the glass to moisten her dry mouth. She set the glass down and rested both arms on the table. Staring at the water glass, she began talking.

Starting early on made the telling easier, until she got to the actual shooting. She emphasized that she had yelled at the boy to stop. "He did stop, and I thought he was going to give himself up, but then he turned around and raised his weapon. He pointed the barrel right at me. I know now it was a toy, but I had no idea then. The gun looked real, and I felt I had no choice

153

but to fire or be killed."

"Were you in fear for your life?" Riley asked. He'd been leaning back, the way a disinterested high school kid might slouch in class. Only he seemed anything but disinterested. He'd listened to the entire account with his gaze fastened on her.

"Yes." She rubbed her forehead and took another drink of water. "I truly believed he was going to shoot me. When he raised his gun, I . . . I fired." Angel licked her lips, shoving away images of Billy's face, the blood. She couldn't let herself think about that. Not now.

"You did very well." The OSP detective leaned forward to turn off his machine.

"There's something else," Angel heard herself saying.

Detective Riley waited for her to continue.

"Just make sure you have your facts straight," Eric had told her when she'd mentioned firing one shot. She still couldn't be sure. If she hadn't fired those three shots, someone else had been in the building with her, but that made no sense at all. Eric had explained how a person could fire multiple bullets in a deadly force situation and think they'd only fired once. Why had she opened her mouth? If she said anything, she'd look like an idiot. She

154

took another drink of water to cover the silence. Finally, she put the glass down. "I know this is going to sound strange, but I . . ."

Forget it, Angel. Let it go.

"If you'd rather wait . . ." Riley said.

"No. I'm all right. I was told that I fired three shots. I guess I must have — there's really no other explanation. Eric and Nick came in while I was kneeling next to the kid, trying to stop the bleeding. Bo was there too, and Mike, but I'm not sure of the order. I didn't want him to die." Angel bit her lip and closed her eyes, fighting back a surge of tears. *God, please don't let me fall apart now. I have to stay strong and at least look confident.* Forcing Billy's image from her mind, she let her gaze move to Joe. Then to the detective, she said, "I heard three shots, but I think I only fired once."

"Who told you you'd fired three shots?" The detective seemed annoyed.

"Um . . . I'm not sure. I don't think they actually told me that; they said they heard three shots and so did I. I guess everyone assumed I'd fired all three."

"Did you see or hear anyone else in the warehouse while you were there?" Detective Riley asked.

"No. I looked around and didn't see anyone. It was dark, but I'm sure Billy and I were alone."

"There were three gunshot wounds in the victim." Joe pushed away from the wall and placed his hands on the table. "You're saying only one of them was yours?"

Angel ran a hand through her hair, hitting several snarls.

"We'll know soon enough." Detective Riley focused back on her. "It's all right. No need to feel embarrassed. You may remember things more clearly in a few days. That's why we like to wait before getting a formal statement."

"So do I." Joe straightened. "I told you about the situation with the mayor."

"Hang the mayor." Riley tossed the recorder back in his briefcase and snapped it shut. "Since when does politics come before an officer's well-being? And while we're on the subject, who leaked Angel's name to the media?"

"I did," Joe admitted. Turning to Angel he said, "It was a mistake, and I'm sorry."

Angel didn't know what to make of the three men. Joe was acting true to form, but Detective Riley seemed to be more of an advocate for her than her lawyer.

Riley turned back to her, and his demeanor softened. "Unless you have something more to add, we're through for now. I'd like to talk with you when I've had a chance to go over the evidence. For now though, I'd suggest you get some rest. Do something good for yourself." He reached into his left jacket pocket and retrieved a card. "Call me anytime you want to talk."

She pocketed the card and mumbled her thanks.

"Angel," Joe said as he opened the door, "thanks for coming in."

"I'd say my pleasure, but that would be a lie." Angel stepped into the hall.

Joe smiled. "Glad to see you still have a sense of humor."

Sense of humor? Hardly.

Randy Grover shook Joe's hand and walked with Angel to the main door. "I'm sorry we couldn't meet yesterday. We should've gone over your case before you made your statement."

"It's not a problem."

"We really do need to talk." He handed her a card. "My cell phone is on there too."

Angel smiled politely and thanked him again. "Um, I need to go. I have an appointment with the psychologist this afternoon."

"Good. That's good." He held the heavy glass door open for her. "You know, a lot of officers think they don't need help or don't need to see a professional, but they do. You don't go through what you have and not suffer emotionally. This one is especially tough, since it was a kid."

Angel didn't respond, just nodded her head.

"Uh, would you call me later?" Randy asked. "So we can set up a time we can get together."

"Sure."

Randy walked away, and Angel heaved a sigh of relief. Maybe it was her imagination, but he didn't seem too competent. She'd have to deal with that later; right now she had to do something to relieve her stress. Detective Riley had told her to do something good for herself, and she knew just the thing.

She drove home, determined not to think about Billy or the shooting. Once there, she changed into shorts and a T-shirt and hit the deck running. She raced down the stairs to the path that led to the beach.

Callen told Joe he'd see him later and watched the petite female officer walk down the hall with her lawyer — if that's what you could call him. Where were the guy's brains? He should have contacted her yesterday — at least by phone. And the Delaney woman worried him. She was taking this thing harder than she wanted them to believe.

And that political garbage about wanting her statement right away made him want to slam Joe against the wall. Joe was usually a good man to work with, but he was obviously afraid of what the shooting incident would do to his career. Tough. Officer Delaney should never have been asked to come in today. *Coerced* might have been a better word. A blind man could see how affected she was. He glared at Grover's back and clenched his fists.

Get a grip, Riley. He liked to consider himself an easygoing kind of guy, so why was he getting so worked up about this? *Because Angel Delaney isn't just another cop.* Callen stopped the thought midstream, mentally backing away from the emotions she had evoked in him. In his line of work, he needed objectivity and a cool head. And right now he had a whole lot of work to do.

He stopped at the water cooler and lifted the blue spout, watching the small stream fill the flimsy paper cup. He downed the water and got a refill. He drank it in two gulps and tossed the cup in the trash receptacle beside the cooler.

That business about her only firing one of the shots had taken him by surprise. All the officers at the scene had indicated that Officer Delaney had fired all three. But none of them had been in the warehouse at the time, and none had actually seen her shoot. If the three bullets hadn't come from her gun, he had to figure out who else had fired at the kid and why. He was glad he'd had the foresight to do the gunshot residue test. That would at least tell him if another officer had fired the shots.

FIFTEEN

A fine mist swirled around Angel and pelted her face as she ran into the wind. A flock of seagulls feasting on the carcass of a fish cawed raucously when she came near, frantically flapping their wings and flying to safety. She turned and ran backwards, watching them drift back down to their find, picking at each other in an effort to get the choicest morsels.

"Greedy bunch of scavengers, aren't you?" She turned back and kept running, darting in and out of the waves as they pushed farther and farther into the dry sand. When the waves receded, they left lines resembling a mountain range. As a child, Angel had watched the formation of the magical mountains and imagined fantasy worlds where fairies and ogres lived. Times had changed, but the ocean never had.

And neither have I. The voice seemed almost audible. She recognized it, or thought she did. She had once thought of it as God's voice.

The temperature had dropped at least twenty degrees from yesterday, and her thin jacket offered minimal protection, but by the time she reached her turnaround point at two and a half miles, she was almost ready to take it off.

Angel paused to stretch her leg muscles, and before heading back she scoured the beach for agates among the rocks. She picked up two small ones and a piece of smooth green glass, settling them deep into her pocket. When the rocks gave way to fine sand, she started running again.

After the hour-long run, she drove straight to the health club for forty-five minutes of weight training. By the time she finished her workout, it was noon.

The beach run and exercise regimen had helped her to relax. Callen Riley was a smart man. And a very nice one. She'd have to remember to thank him.

After showering, she put on a pair of khaki slacks and a blue sleeveless sweater with a mock turtleneck. Slipping into her semidressy ivory windbreaker, she stuffed her feet into a pair of leather clogs and grabbed her purse and keys off the counter.

She still had forty minutes before her appointment with Dr. Campbell. The thought didn't bode well and almost erased the high exercising had given her. If someone had asked her what she was so afraid of, she wouldn't have been able to answer, at least not truthfully. The truth lay in some obscure pit of past hurts she'd long since buried, or had at least tried to. Her stomach pitched and rolled then growled, partly from nerves and partly as a reminder to Angel to feed it.

She stopped at the Burger Shed on the way to Dr. Campbell's office. The small restaurant was located near the wharf, only three blocks from the old cannery. It had been there for as long as she could remember and still served up the biggest, juiciest burgers in town. Living up to its name, the restaurant looked like a shed with weathered gray siding. A sign, made of the same gray wood, had been sloppily painted in red letters and hung haphazardly near the entrance. In the center of the door at eye level was a porthole.

In the summer months, people could eat outside on the dock at one of the half dozen picnic tables. With dark clouds threatening, Angel chose to sit inside. The place smelled like french fries and charred meat and made her stomach growl even louder. The owner, Jack Cole, and his wife, Minnie, greeted her with their usual smiles. Jack did most of the cooking and looked it, while Minnie waited tables and took orders.

"What'll it be, sweetie?" Minnie rested her thin freckled arms on the counter.

Without hesitation, Angel ordered a Monster Burger with bacon, cheese, onions, lettuce, tomato, mayo, relish, and catsup, with fries and a milkshake. She waited while Jack tossed the half pound of raw ground sirloin on the grill and fished the fresh golden fries out of the hot oil. Minutes later, she took her feast to the far booth that offered a view of the bay. Her mother would've had a fit if she'd seen her. Ma was always harping at Angel to have a healthier diet. After setting the catsup and fries within easy reach, Angel unwrapped the hamburger and held it up, wondering how she was going to get her mouth around it.

"You're not going to eat that, are you?"

Angel snapped her head around and lifted her gaze. "Detective Riley." Her heart picked up tempo. She frowned and looked from her hamburger to his face and back again. "Is there some reason I shouldn't?"

"Yeah, if you want to live past forty." He slid into the seat across from her. "That stuff will kill you."

She shook her head and stretched open her mouth, ready to take a bite.

"Seriously." He rested his arms on the table and looked straight into her eyes.

"I disagree." She lowered the burger and tipped her head from side to side as if examining it. "What could be healthier than a hamburger, fries, and a shake?" She grinned at him. "You got your protein with 30 percent less fat than regular ground beef. Says so right on the menu. There's lettuce, two tomato slices, onions, and relish — and of course the fries, made from Idaho potatoes — that's got to be good for at least two servings of veggies. And then there's the dairy." She pointed to her milkshake. "Two servings. You know what they always say, 'Milk — it does a body good.' And it has Marionberries in it, so there's my serving of fruit." She leaned back with a satisfied grin.

He raised an eyebrow and chuckled. "Sounds like you've rehearsed that spiel a few times."

"For my mother."

"Ahh." A look of understanding crossed his handsome features.

For the first time, she noticed a ragged two-inch-long scar running from his left ear along his jaw.

"If this stuff is so bad for you, why are you here?" Angel chomped down on the burger while she waited for an answer.

"They serve a mean veggie burger and decent salads."

"Here you go, big guy." Minnie brought his food and placed it in front of him. The bun looked like whole wheat, and off to the side was a pile of sprouts, two large slices of tomato, and onion. A small dinner salad topped with cherry tomatoes, carrots, and purple cabbage took up the rest of the space on his plate.

Angel chewed and swallowed, trying to ignore him as he spread some sort of yellow grainy stuff on his bun. Her curiosity got the better of her. "What is that?"

"Hummus. It's a mix of garbanzo beans, garlic, tahini —"

She wrinkled her nose. "Never mind. You're actually going to eat that?"

"Ever try it?"

She shook her head. "No, and I don't intend to."

"Then don't knock it." He bit into his veggie burger. "Mmm." He closed his eyes, acting as though he'd just bitten into a chocolate truffle.

Angel rolled her eyes and attacked her meal, determined to enjoy every bite. "Detective," she said when she was down to her last two fries, "did you just happen to come in here, or did you want to talk to me?"

He shrugged. "Both. I saw you drive in and thought it might be a good opportunity to touch base. You look a lot more relaxed than when I saw you earlier today."

"I am. I took your advice and did something good for myself."

"Which was?"

"Running — and pigging out on a burger, fries, and a shake." In an all-out act of rebellion, Angel slurped up the last of the Marionberry milkshake then stuffed the last two fries into her mouth.

"Running is good. The rest we'll have to differ on."

Angel scooted out of the booth. "Hate to eat and run, but I have an appointment with a shrink, and goodness knows I shouldn't miss that."

"Officer Delaney." He grabbed her wrist, effectively halting her progress. His green gaze bore into hers. "Seeing the psychiatrist is nothing to be flippant about. A counselor can help you through the trauma. And it is a trauma — a huge one. They can help you deal with the grief, but it's going to take a lot more than one session."

What, are you psychic or something? A wild mix of emotions crashed around inside her. She swallowed hard, staring down at the hand still resting on her forearm. He let her go, but she found it hard to move away.

While he hadn't said as much, she suspected he was speaking out of experience. Not trusting herself to respond, she turned and walked out to her car. How could he have known how she felt about the shrink, or that she'd only planned on one visit?

Getting into her car, she caught a glimpse of him through the window — still sitting in the booth, still eating his health food. He'd been meaning to talk to her about something but hadn't. She wondered what it could be.

With a shaky hand she forced the key into the ignition and turned it. The food that had tasted so good going down now rolled around in her stomach and threatened to come back up. She drew in several

168

deep breaths. The courage she'd gathered during her workout had drained away, leaving her empty as a leaky cup.

Callen forced himself to eat the rest of his meal, but only because he needed it. The stuff tasted like cardboard now. His fault, not the proprietors. He'd been out of line grabbing hold of Angel like that. His action had surprised him as much as it had her. He'd have to watch his step in the future. He couldn't afford to get too close to her, not if he wanted to keep his job.

She'd gotten to him with her negative attitude toward counseling. Too many cops had the idea that seeking counseling made them appear weak.

You should talk. Look at how you fought it.

He stuffed a mouthful of salad greens into his mouth. He'd waited almost too long to get help, thinking he'd be able to handle everything on his own. He remembered all too clearly how he'd fallen apart after his wife's death. He'd stopped eating and started drinking. He turned away from his family and friends and nearly got fired from his job for using excessive force on an alleged child abuser.

Alleged, nothing. The guy deserved more than a bloodied nose. Still, he'd been wrong and out of control. His supervisor had strongly urged him to get help if he wanted to keep his job. Kathleen came at him from the family side and even made an appointment for him. After the first session with the grief counselor, he realized how important it was to get some guidance and learn about healthy ways to deal with his grief and all the emotional garbage that came with it. He wanted the same chance for Angel. But Angel's psyche wasn't his problem or his business.

When had he started thinking of her as Angel rather than Officer Delaney?

Pushing his plate aside, he threw down a two-dollar tip, waved to Jack and Minnie as he left, and dodged pelting rain as he hurried to his car. His notepad, which he'd left on the seat, reminded him of why he had gone into the restaurant in the first place. He'd wanted to ask her about the casings that should've been at the scene where she shot the boy. There should have been three, or if she was right about firing once, there should have been one. The lab guys hadn't seen them, and they'd covered a substantial area around the boy's body. Callen had asked the other officers, but they denied seeing anything. Nick had suggested that Angel might've automatically picked them up without thinking. Many officers did.

Callen backed out of the parking lot and headed south on Main toward the boat docks. He'd been meaning to get back out to talk to the guy who lived on his sailboat. He wanted to follow through on his suspicion that the perps who'd pulled off the Bergman robbery might've escaped by boat. Now he had even more questions. The Monroe kid had been murdered in the early morning hours. Callen figured somebody must have heard something.

He parked near the wharf and checked his notepad again, flipping back a couple pages to where he'd talked to the fisherman. *Jake Ensley — lives aboard his thirty-foot sailboat.* Callen headed down to the docks, past boats of various shapes and sizes to the berth where he'd seen the sailboat the previous morning.

The boat was gone.

Angel turned on the windshield wipers to clear off the moisture the heavy rain had left, then headed toward the Smith building, which housed Maxwell's Restaurant along with a number of offices, Dr. Campbell's being one of them.

The reception area consisted of eight

chairs and two end tables covered with magazines. The waiting room had been decorated in hues of lavender, cream, and pale green and smelled of some kind of fruit and spice potpourri that reminded Angel of her mother's bathroom. One patient, at least Angel assumed he was a patient, sat in the chair nearest the exit with his legs crossed, reading a worn copy of *People* magazine and looking like he wanted to be there about as much as she did.

Angel took a deep breath and plodded to the check-in window to introduce herself.

"Oh, hi, Ms. Delaney." The perky receptionist removed her glasses and let them drop. A funky gold and silver chain stopped them from colliding with the cluttered desktop. She reached for a clipboard and handed it to Angel. "We'd like you to fill out these forms and sign them while you're waiting. Dr. Campbell will be with you in a few minutes."

"What are these for?" Angel took the board and made a face. She hated filling out forms and was tempted to just leave. *Hold on. It's just one visit. One hour. You can do anything for one hour. Besides, it's not like you have a choice.*

"One is medical history, one is for insurance purposes, and the other is a standard form Dr. Campbell wants all of her clients to fill out."

Angel nodded and took the forms with her to the seat by the window. Three floors down, people dodged in and out of buildings and cars, trying to escape what had become a deluge. As she sat down to fill out the forms, a man in a dark blue dress shirt and black slacks opened the door to the inner sanctum. "Mr. Roberts?"

The man set down his magazine and with reluctance in every step moved through the open door.

Angel had finished the forms, turned them in, and waited for five minutes before the door opened again. A familiar-looking woman with shoulder-length blonde hair, wearing a denim dress and Birkenstocks, called her in. "Hi, Angel."

Her name and hair had changed, and she'd put on a few pounds, but her round face with its warm smile and sparkling hazel eyes hadn't. "Janet Langley?"

"One in the same. But it's Janet Campbell now." Her smile deepened. "It's good to see you again, Angel."

"You too." *I can't do this. You're supposed to be a stranger. Not an old friend.*

"Come on back to my office." Janet led

the way down the hall to the third door on the left. The room had a picture window that looked out over the water, and the mauve and mint tones had carried over from the reception room to this one. Once inside, Janet motioned her to sit in one of the plush cushioned armchairs that had been strategically placed to almost face one another. A sofa sat against one wall, and a small cabinet under the window was filled with various games, toys, and stuffed animals.

Angel eased into the chair. "I hadn't expected . . . I mean, I thought you were going to med school."

"I did. At first I thought I'd be a surgeon, but when I did my first psych rotation, I changed my mind."

"And you're married now?"

Janet flinched slightly and bit her lip before answering. "Divorced, actually." She lowered herself into the remaining chair and tucked her hair behind her ear. "But enough about me. I'm glad you called. I've been reading about the shooting."

"You and everyone else in the state."

Janet leaned back and crossed her legs, her hazel eyes fixed on Angel's, assessing, judging. No, not judging. Questioning, maybe.

"Should I be here — I mean, seeing you about this? Since we know each other . . . ?" Angel picked a piece of lint from the hem of her sweater.

"It's fine, unless you feel uncomfortable. I can set you up to see my colleague Dr. Kelly if you'd rather . . ."

"No, no. I'd rather see you. If you're sure it's okay." Angel glanced at the window. *Just get it over with. One visit.*

"This must be terribly hard for you. I wish I could say I understand what you're going through, but I can't imagine. But I have worked with other officers, though, who've been through similar crises." She tucked her hair back again. "Angel, before we officially get started, I need to go over some things with you. You know that anything you say here is strictly between us. I'd like you to feel safe."

Safe? I don't think so. "Don't you have to tell Joe about my visit?"

"Only to report that you've come."

Angel nodded. They hadn't been best friends in high school, but then, Angel hadn't really had anyone she considered a best friend. She didn't do a lot of girl things, preferring instead to hang out with her brothers when they let her. But she remembered that even back in high school,

Janet'd had a way of making people feel comfortable.

"I may take notes from time to time, but those are just to help me remember what we talked about. I'll keep a chart on your visits, and you're welcome to read them anytime."

"I don't think there'll be another visit." Angel glanced down at her hands. She clasped them together and put them between her knees.

"Hmm." Janet pursed her lips. "It's true you're only required to come once. I hope you'll change your mind. I won't push you, of course, but I will be glad to see you whenever you want."

"I appreciate that." *"Seeing a psychiatrist is nothing to be flippant about."* Angel could almost hear Detective Riley's admonishment, could almost feel his hand on her wrist. "I'll see how it goes."

"Well, if you only plan on coming once, what do you think would be most helpful to you?"

"Um . . ." Angel paused to lick her dry lips and rubbed a damp palm across her slacks. "I don't know." She stared at a spot on the carpet. "I never had to shoot a person before."

"And how are you feeling about that?"

How do I feel? Lousy, guilty, sick. Angry. "I feel like I did what I thought was right."

"But that doesn't make it any easier, does it." Janet leaned forward. "How are you sleeping, Angel?"

"Fine." She rubbed at her wrist and thumb. "Well, that's not quite true. I had a hard time getting to sleep last night."

Janet nodded. "I can give you something for that."

"I don't need meds. I just need a few days to . . ." Her argument drifted off.

"I'll write you a prescription. It's up to you, of course, but I strongly suggest you take them." Janet pulled a prescription pad out of her pocket and scribbled on it. "It's one of the better sleep aids and shouldn't make you feel hungover in the morning."

Angel reached for the script. "Thanks."

"Are you eating?"

Angel smiled. "My mother is seeing to that."

"Good." Janet grinned. "Knowing your family I imagine you have a good support system."

"Are you kidding? Too good."

"Lean on them; let them take care of you. And feel free to call me anytime." Janet paused. "What would you like to talk about today?"

Nothing. Everything. "I don't know." Angel folded then unfolded her arms.

"You could start by telling me what's the hardest part of all this."

Angel thought about that for a while before answering. "Feeling like I committed a crime when I didn't. I hate having people think of me as a racist and implying that I shot Billy on purpose. And having the media pick me apart." She frowned. "Being placed on leave. That's hard. I'm supposed to just sit back and leave the investigation up to strangers. I understand the rationale, I just don't like it."

"All those things would be difficult to deal with. What are you doing now to cope?"

"I'm ignoring the press." Angel glanced at her watch, glad the session was almost over. "I'm trying not to think about what people are saying. I'm adjusting."

Janet nodded. "Are you?"

"What do you mean?" Angel lifted her head and answered in a defensive tone. "What else can I do but adjust? It's not like I can fight back."

"Do you remember the words to the Serenity Prayer?"

"You mean the one that goes: 'God, grant me the serenity to accept the things I cannot change, the courage to change the things I can, and the wisdom to know the difference'?"

"That's the one."

"I haven't thought of that for a long time." Angel let the words play through her head again.

"You may want to repeat those words from time to time. Might help."

Angel doubted it but promised to keep it in mind.

Janet uncrossed her legs. "Our time is almost up. Are you sure you don't want to come in again?"

"I don't know. Let me think about it."

When the session was over, Angel thanked Janet and hurried out to her Corvette. Ten minutes later, she turned onto her street. She sucked in her breath and made a quick U-turn. The dead-end street had turned into a parking lot with media vans and reporters swarming all over the place. She had a feeling most of them had come to see her.

Sudden tears heated her eyes. Now what? She drove to Joanie's Place, her favorite espresso shop, and went inside. After ordering an eight-ounce mocha latte from Joanie's assistant, Angel plopped onto one of the sofas in front of the fireplace. Leaning back, she closed her eyes. She could go to her parents' house, but how long before the vultures found her there? If the members of the press had done their homework, they'd be able to track her down no matter where she went — unless she called Brandon and got a key to his new house.

No way. How could you even think such a thing? Besides, you've never been a coward, and this isn't the time to start. You have to go back.

God, grant me the serenity to accept the things I cannot change, the courage to change the things I can, and the wisdom to know the difference.

Angel sipped at her coffee, letting its warmth seep into her bones before heading back to the apartment. She couldn't change the media, but she could refuse to let them get to her.

She released a grateful sigh when she approached the apartments and saw two black-and-whites with their lights flashing. Nick Caldwell was talking to the apartment manager, who looked none too happy. Mike Rawlings stopped her as she turned into the apartment complex.

Angel greeted him. "Hey, Mike, what's up?"

"Wondered when you'd show up." He offered her a sympathetic smile. "You've become quite a celebrity."

"Not by choice." Angel ran a hand through her hair. "Look, Mike, I just want to go home. Is there any way you can get these people to leave me alone?"

"We're working on it. In the meantime, I can escort you in."

"Thanks, I'd appreciate it."

"Give me a sec, and I'll tell Nick." He went over to where Nick and the manager were talking. Nick glanced over and waved at her.

Mike jogged back, looked at the crowd, and said, "Are you sure you want to go in there?"

"No, but I'm not going to let them run me out of my own place."

Reporters fired questions at her as she drove into the crowd, but Angel ignored them. Mike went ahead on foot, clearing the way through the crowd to give Angel access to a parking spot. Once she'd parked, he escorted her upstairs to her door. "Yell if you need someone to run interference when you leave."

"Thanks, but I think I'll hibernate until they find someone else to pick on."

"That could take a while." Mike hurried

down the stairs, and Angel heard him use his lapel mike to call in another officer.

She briefly considered holding a press conference and telling her side of the story, but what would that accomplish? Besides, she was bone weary and close to tears. She turned around to slip the key into the lock and found that someone had already unlocked it.

SIXTEEN

The hair on the back of Angel's neck rose. Her throat constricted. She reached for the gun that wasn't there, remembering she'd left it in the holster hanging in her bedroom closet. The door had been locked when she left; she was sure of it.

"Okay," she murmured to herself, "don't panic. It could be Ma." She moved to the side and eased the door open with her foot. "Ma? You in there?"

No one answered. Angel cautiously stepped inside.

The sight that greeted her made her feel as if she'd been kicked in the stomach. Someone had been there all right, and it hadn't been a social call. Her furniture had been overturned and slashed, and it looked as though the intruders had mopped the floor with everything she owned.

She didn't hear anything and suspected

the vandals were long gone, but she wasn't taking any chances. She backed out of the apartment and started to yell for Mike. Her fellow officer had already gone, and though she could see him pushing through the crowd toward his patrol car, she didn't want to attract attention by calling him back. Instead she knocked on her neighbors' door.

Rob had clothes on this time, jeans and a green-and-gold Oregon Ducks T-shirt. "Angel, how's it going? You see all those people? Man, must be weird getting all that attention."

"Yeah, weird. I —"

"Guess what?" he interrupted. "I'm gonna be on the news tonight. They said they wanted to interview some of your neighbors." He shrugged. "I told them you were a really nice kid."

"Thanks, Rob. I appreciate it, but I have a problem and I could use your help."

"You name it."

"Someone trashed my place while I was gone." She cleared her throat. "Can I use your phone? I don't want to touch anything in there, and to be honest, they may still be there."

"Yeah." He stepped back, motioning her in. "Why didn't you say so? Trashed it, huh? Are you sure? I mean, I guess you are. Funny, I didn't hear a thing."

I wonder why. Angel glanced at the blaring television. She asked Rob to turn the volume down, then reported the break-in to the dispatch operator. After the call, she thanked Rob and went back outside to wait.

As she suspected, Mike and Nick responded immediately. From her vantage point on the second floor, she could see them elbow their way through the crowd, dodging the media and all their paraphernalia. When they reached her building, they took the stairs two at a time. Nick got to her first. "What's this about a break-in?" he panted.

"See for yourself. I went to unlock the door and realized someone had already done it. Thought at first it might be my mother, but no way would she leave a mess like this."

"Sorry, Angel," Mike said. "I should have gone in with you."

"Don't be. It's not like we expected it." She stepped aside while Mike and Nick pulled their weapons and cautiously moved inside.

A few minutes later, the men came back into the hall. "Something tells me this wasn't a simple robbery." Nick holstered his gun.

"No kidding." Angel released the breath she'd been holding.

"We'll get the crime lab guys in here to process it."

She nodded her head. "I want to look around."

"Shouldn't hurt; just leave stuff as it is," Nick cautioned.

"I know the routine." Stepping carefully to preserve evidence, Angel picked her way from room to room, swallowing hard to keep from dropping to her knees and sobbing. Nothing was as it had been when she left. Her cupboards had been stripped bare, contents scattered all over the floor and counters. The furniture had never been in the best shape, but now all of the cushions had been slashed and the stuffing spilled out of them. Even her clothes had been torn off their hangers and lay on the floor in shreds. And the gun was gone. No surprise there.

"Can you tell if anything is missing?" Mike asked.

"The gun Nick gave me. Otherwise, I have no idea."

She needed to get away from Nick and Mike for a minute, so she went into the bathroom and closed the door. She flicked on the light and caught sight of the mirror. The intruders had written "Racist Pig" with red lipstick across the mirror. She clenched her stomach and turned away from the mirror, swallowing back the bile rising to her throat.

"Angel?" Mike knocked on the door. "You okay in there?"

He and Nick were both standing outside when she opened the door and pointed to the mirror.

"Did you see this?"

Mike stepped into the tiny room and froze, his big hands making tight fists at his side. His Adam's apple moved up and down, and for a long time he didn't speak. Then he pushed past them. "I need some air."

Nick swore and rubbed the top of his head.

Angel felt numb and nauseous and hot and cold all at the same time. Her knees buckled, and Nick caught her on the way down. He eased her onto the rim of the bathtub.

"Stay put," he ordered when she tried to push herself up. He wet a washcloth with cool water and placed it on the back of her neck. "Keep your head down."

She offered a mild objection but did as she was told.

"Your dad's on his way," Nick said. "He'll take you home."

Angel felt too sick to argue. By the time the dizziness had passed, her father had arrived and with him, her partner, Eric Mason.

Eric looked around and whistled. "Looks like someone's trying to get even." His concerned blue eyes met Angel's. "You okay?"

She sighed. "I'll manage."

Frank Delaney's angry gaze traveled around the apartment, finally settling on her. "Come on, little girl. Let these guys do their job. I'm taking you home."

Little girl. He hadn't called her that in a long time. But she didn't argue. Like a robot, she walked outside with Frank on one side, Eric on the other.

"Don't worry, Angel," Eric said. "We'll find out who did this. I promise."

"Darn right, we will," Frank added. Then he suggested they go around to the back of the apartments to escape the reporters. At the moment, Angel didn't care about the reporters or anything else. She just wanted to get as far away as possible. When she and her dad reached his patrol car, which was parked about a block and a half away, Eric went back to her apartment.

"I can't believe this," Frank grumbled as he pulled his keys out of his pocket and unlocked the car. "Revenge, that's what it is, pure and simple. Probably that Broadman fella. He as much as said he planned to get even."

Angel started to go around to the passenger side and stopped. "Dad, wait. I can't leave."

"Of course, you can." He took hold of her arm, guiding her as though she were a child. Angel pulled away. "I'm not going anywhere. I need to stay here and clean up this mess."

He huffed. "What's the matter with you? The boys won't be done sifting through the evidence for hours yet. You need to be someplace safe. You need to come home."

"No. You go ahead, Dad. Tell Ma I'm okay. I'll stay a while and maybe come to the house later."

Frank shook his head. "Angel . . ."

"Don't. The last thing I need is a lecture on how stubborn and mule headed I am."

Her father looked stricken. His ruddy complexion took on an ashen tone.

"Dad?" Her refusal to go with him

couldn't have caused the change. What was the matter with him?

Frank took a step back, connecting with another patrol car. He gasped for air, grabbing at his chest as his knees buckled. His face contorted in pain as he dropped to the blacktop.

She dropped down beside him. "Dad, what is it?"

He gasped and pressed a hand to his chest.

Angel's heart skidded to a stop. She'd been on enough emergency calls to know he was having a heart attack; she just couldn't bring herself to believe it was happening to him. "Where's your phone?" She reached around to his right side, pulled his cell phone from his belt, and punched in 911.

She knelt beside him as he twisted around and tried to sit up. "I'm okay," he gasped. "Just a twinge." He unbuttoned the top button of his shirt then pulled out a small vial of nitroglycerin tablets and fumbled with the cap. "Need to take one of these."

Angel pushed his hand away. "Let me get it." With shaky hands she removed a tiny tablet and gave it to him. He placed it under his tongue.

"How long have you had nitroglycerin tablets?" she asked as she replaced the top.

"Couple . . . of . . . months."

"You got heart trouble and didn't tell me. I suppose you haven't told Ma either."

"Didn't want to worry her. You know how she is. . . . Besides, it's nothing." He winced again as he tried to stand.

"Don't move. You know better than to —"

Her lecture was interrupted by screaming sirens as the ambulance careened toward them. A few media people, curious about the sirens, began showing up but had the good sense not to interfere.

Minutes later Frank was hooked to an IV and he and Angel were heading for the hospital in the back of the ambulance. The EMTs verified her suspicions — her dad was having a heart attack. But they wouldn't know for certain how bad it was until the doctor ran some tests.

Angel gripped the gurney. *He's not going to die.*

Frank placed a beefy hand on top of hers. "If . . . if I don't make it . . ."

"Don't talk like that. You aren't going to die. Since when did a little thing like a heart problem stop a Delaney, huh?" She wanted to yell at him for not telling the family about it and for continuing to work when he had a life-threatening condition. She shook her head. "What were you thinking?" she whispered as she placed her free hand over his.

God, please let him be okay.

When they arrived at the hospital, several of the emergency room staff met them at the door, and while they whisked her father inside, they left Angel to answer questions and fill out papers.

Her father had been taken to a room and was already hooked up to a monitor when she was finally able to see him. An army of attendants in scrubs, masks, and gloves surrounded him. Someone broke the pack — a lab tech carrying a tray and vials of blood. The monitor showed an erratic heart rhythm, but the beep reassured her that he was alive.

Suddenly, the blips gave way to a long steady beep. He'd flatlined. Angel felt as if her own heart had stopped as well. A guy in a white jacket and black slacks began barking orders while grabbing paddles off the cart. The paddles connected with her father's chest, and the jolt raised him off the table.

"We're losing him, people!" someone shouted.

She wanted to turn and run but couldn't move. She bit into her fist. *Don't let him die. Just please don't let him die.*

A woman in a white lab coat, holding a chart, approached her. "You're his daughter?"

Angel managed a nod.

"I'm Marley Dale." Her name tag identified her as a nursing coordinator, whatever that was. "Let's go out to the waiting room."

"Can't I stay here?"

"It's better that you don't."

Angel let herself be ushered out of the room. "Is he going to make it?"

"I don't know." Marley adjusted her glasses. "Dr. Larson is one of our best cardiologists. He'll do what he can."

Angel followed the woman into a room equipped with numerous chairs and love seats. Dozens of magazines were scattered on several tables. A coffee station had been set up in the far corner.

"We need a medical history on Mr. Delaney."

"I already filled out some forms."

"I know, but unfortunately we'll need more than what you gave us."

Angel had done the best she could with what she remembered, but there were too many questions she'd had to leave unanswered. She glanced around for a phone. "I need to call my mother. She'll be able to give you the information you need."

The woman touched her arm. "There's a phone over here." She pointed to a cubicle in the corner to their right.

Angel punched the numbers in and waited. No answer. She was just hanging up when she heard her mother's voice in the hallway. "Where is he?"

"Take it easy, Mrs. Delaney. I'll find out." The masculine voice belonged to Eric.

"Where's Angel? She should be here." Her mother sounded almost frantic.

"I'm here, Ma." Angel stepped into the hall. "I was just trying to call you."

"Well, thank the good Lord I didn't have to wait that long. Eric came to get me."

Angel gave him an awkward glance. "Thanks." He and the others would have heard dispatch and known the ambulance was bringing them in.

"What happened?" Eric and her mother asked together.

"He's had a heart attack." She didn't add the fact that he'd been angry with her. Why couldn't she have just gone along? She tried to tell herself that her compli-

194

ance wouldn't have made a difference, but she couldn't quite convince herself.

"Oh, Angel." Ma wrapped her arms around her daughter. "And right after having your apartment broken into. You must've been scared to death."

Terrified. "I'm okay."

"It's a good thing you were there with him." Turning from Angel, Anna headed for the door. The frightened look was gone, replaced by sheer determination. "I want to see him."

"He's being worked on right now. They might not let you go in."

"Let them try and stop me."

"Ma. Wait." Angel hurried after her.

Being a volunteer at the hospital twice a week, her mother didn't need to be shown where anything was. She stopped a nurse coming out of her husband's room. "Frank Delaney, he's my husband and —"

"Oh, Mrs. Delaney, I'm glad you're here. He's asking for you." The nurse placed her hand on Anna's shoulder. "You can go in, but only for a minute. He needs to rest."

"He's okay then?" Anna clutched her purse to her chest.

"He's stabilized for now. Dr. Larson will give you more details later."

Angel leaned against the wall outside the

room while her mother went inside. *Come on, Angel, pull yourself together.* She'd dealt with plenty of emergencies and had managed just fine. But this was her father.

She sucked in a long breath. She knew she should walk to the phone and call Tim and Susan, but her knees had turned to mush. If she moved away from the wall, she'd slide to the floor.

Eric came up beside her. "You don't look so good."

She straightened and took a wobbly step. When he grabbed hold of her elbow to steady her, she bristled. "I have to call Tim and —"

"I already did. He and Susan are on their way over."

"Efficient, aren't you?" She glanced up at him. She hadn't meant to sound so cranky. "I'm sorry."

"Hey, no problem. I wouldn't be in the greatest mood either. And it wasn't my efficiency — it was your mom's. She asked me to call while we were in the car. They should be here any minute. In the meantime, maybe we should wait in the waiting room. You look like you could use a chair. I'll buy you a cup of coffee."

"The coffee's free."

He grinned. "I know."

Somehow she managed to walk without Eric's help, and plopped down in the first chair she came to. Eric headed straight for the coffee machine, pulled a cup from the stack, and pushed down the black lever. He came back with two cups and handed one to Angel. "Here you go, straight up. Looks strong enough to eat with a fork."

"Thanks." Angel took the cup, staring into it for a long time before bringing it to her lips. It was bitter, but she hoped it would give her the jolt she needed.

Seconds later, Tim and Susan came in. "Sorry to take so long," Tim said as he leaned down to give Angel a hug.

"We had to find a sitter for the kids." Susan clasped Angel's hand and took the chair next to her.

"We heard what happened at the apartment," Tim said. "And then Dad having this heart attack. Seems like everything is hitting all at once."

Angel frowned. "Ma's with him."

Susan nodded. "I'll go see what I can find out. Can I get you anything?"

Ever the nurse. Angel shook her head and blinked back tears.

Susan squeezed her hand. "I'll be back in a few minutes."

Tim started to sit beside Angel and

changed his mind, going to the coffeepot instead. "Thanks for bringing Mom," he said to Eric.

"No problem. I figured I'd save you some time." He took a sip of his coffee, made a face, and tossed it into the trash. "I'd better be getting back to work."

Tim thanked him again. "Appreciate your help, Eric."

Eric nodded and turned to Tim. "Don't let Angel go home tonight, okay? The apartment isn't livable, and the crime lab guys are still working on it."

Angel started to protest, but the words caught in her throat. She sipped at the bitter coffee. In the distance she heard the elevator ding and the door swish open. Tim set his coffee on the table and lowered himself into the chair.

"You look exhausted, sis. Why don't you go to the house and get some rest? There isn't much you can do here and —"

"Ma won't leave. She'd be upset if I did."

"She'll understand — what with all you've been through."

Tim was right. Ma probably would understand. But Angel wasn't going anywhere — not until her father was stable.

SEVENTEEN

"What do you mean the evidence isn't there?" Callen cradled the phone between his jaw and shoulder and settled his elbows on Joe Brady's desk. Joe had gone out and offered to let Callen use his office for a couple hours. "I left written instructions for the clerk here to send it out first thing Monday morning with specific orders to get your people on it right away."

He rubbed his forehead. This was not the time to be losing evidence. As the investigating officer, he had the responsibility of gathering the evidence and making certain it got to the crime lab in Portland. Before he'd gone home Sunday evening, he'd pulled everything together in the officer-involved shooting: Angel's gun and magazine from Nick, her uniform, her urine sample, the swabs he'd done for the GSR test, the stuff that had been in the

Hartwell kid's pockets, along with his clothes. He'd even included the hollow point bullets the medical examiner had recovered during the autopsy. Callen had packaged it all up himself and put it in the temporary evidence locker, leaving explicit instructions with the clerk that it be sent via UPS Monday morning so it would arrive in Portland on Tuesday. He should have double-checked with the clerk yesterday to make certain it had actually gone out.

"I'm sorry, Detective Riley, we've looked everywhere. It was never logged in to our department. UPS is saying they have no record of a package being sent. Best we can figure is that the clerk in Sunset Cove never sent it."

"All right, I'll check with the clerk here. Call me if it shows up."

"Will do."

After disconnecting, he went down to the basement to the evidence lockers. The temporary lockers were like those in a gym, and they served as a place where evidence could be signed in and stored if there was no clerk available, which often happened in a small town. That was what he'd done on Sunday night. When a clerk became available, the evidence was supposed to be placed into the permanent lockers, to which only the clerk and supervisor had keys. With the temp lockers, all of the officers had keys and ready access — he himself had gotten a key from Joe on Sunday.

When he'd checked the locker Monday morning and found it empty, he assumed the clerk had found his message and taken care of it. Big mistake.

"Sorry, Detective," said the clerk, lifting her hands in a shrug. "I didn't see your note and haven't seen the evidence. I don't know what to tell you."

"Are you suggesting one of the officers stole it?" Callen didn't even attempt to hide his annoyance. "Or maybe I didn't put it there?"

She was a short woman, maybe five-one, but hefty with dark, short hair that had been heavily moussed to stand on end. She straightened and put her hands on her hips.

"Young man, I understand why you would be upset, but you have no reason to take out your frustrations on me. If I had seen your note, I'd have followed your instructions to the letter. I check these temporary lockers as soon as I come in and transfer the evidence to the permanent lockers. When I came in on Monday morning, there was no evidence in that locker and no note. Now if that means another officer took it, which I sincerely doubt, then I guess your job is to find out who."

Her tirade had calmed him down as much as it was possible to calm down. Unfortunately, he couldn't ignore the fact that every piece of evidence in a very high-profile case was missing, and he was going to cook for it.

"You're right." Callen frowned. "I'm sorry."

Having made her point, the woman backed down. "This is a secure area, Detective Riley. People aren't just going to walk in off the street. Still, it is possible that someone could've gotten hold of the key. I know this is serious business, and I wish I could help you. But somewhere between the time you packaged up that evidence and I came to work Monday morning, it disappeared and so did your note."

At Callen's insistence, they looked in all of the lockers, both temp and permanent. The package and the note he had written were gone.

Having no other option, he went back up

to Joe's office to call his supervisor in Portland to tell him the bad news. He winced as his boss lit into him.

"You should have brought it in yourself, Riley. You know how important this case is."

"You're right. I'm kicking myself about it."

"The governor called me again this morning. We're even getting pressure from the U.S. Attorney's Office."

"You're kidding." Callen released a long sigh.

"I wish I was. If we're not careful, we'll have the Feds on us. We don't want the FBI called in for a civil rights investigation. From what I hear, the ACLU is already on the move. Brady's not the only one whose job is on the line here."

He didn't have to elaborate. They could all be in trouble if they didn't clear up the delicate matter soon. The public was outraged and wanted answers; they wanted the matter settled once and for all. They wanted Angel Delaney's head or a good reason why she blew away a twelve-year-old kid with a toy gun.

After getting explicit orders in not the most delicate language to find out what was happening, Callen hung up and leaned back in the chair. As he put his feet up on the desk, he wondered what had possessed him to get into this business. It was funny, though; he'd never imagined himself doing anything else since he was a kid playing cops and robbers with the Nelson boys down the block. He was always the cop. He wondered briefly what had happened to the Nelson boys.

His gaze went back to the picture on Joe's desk. Joe, his wife, and probably a daughter smiled broadly into the camera. Nice-looking family. The girl had blond hair and a wide smile. She reminded him of Karen. An old ache burrowed its way into his heart, and to ease it he went into the break room and poured himself a cup of coffee.

"Hi, Detective." Brandy Owens and another officer were sitting at one of the tables. "We're signing cards and collecting money for a gift for Frank Delaney. We were also wanting to raise some money to help Angel out. You want in on it?"

He took his coffee over to the table. "What's going on?"

"You mean you haven't heard?" Brandy asked. "Frank had a heart attack yesterday afternoon. And Angel's apartment was vandalized. It was all over the news."

He hadn't heard. He'd spent most of the afternoon tracking down potential witnesses to the shooting death out on the wharf. Never had been able to find the guy with the sailboat. He opened his wallet and took out a couple twenties, then signed the card for Frank. When he finished, he pulled up a chair and told them about the missing evidence. "Has anyone in the department mentioned losing a key?"

Both checked their key chains and responded in the negative. He excused himself and went back to Joe's office, stopping at the secretary's desk on his way in. Leaning on the counter, he said, "Rosie, I have a problem. Can you get me a complete list of all of the officers who work here — anyone who'd have a key to the temporary evidence lockers?"

"Um — I suppose so." Rosie Gonzalez had a smooth southern drawl that went down like honey and butter on a cornbread muffin. "Am I allowed to ask why?"

He told her about the missing evidence.

Rosie frowned. "Oh, Detective, you can't be thinking any of our officers would take it."

"Believe me, that's the last thing I want to be thinking, which is why I need to account for all the keys in the department.

Make sure none are missing."

"I'll check my files and make a list. I should talk to Joe before I give it to you though. I mean, I'm sure he won't mind — just don't want to do anything without his say-so."

"I understand."

Callen went home then for a number of reasons — to feed Mutt and to eat lunch himself. Primarily though, he needed to think, and he did his best thinking running on the beach or cooking up some exotic dish in his state-of-the-art kitchen.

Why would someone steal evidence in a deadly force investigation, and who would benefit? The questions burrowed like a tick in his brain while he fed and played with Mutt, ran on the beach, and rearranged his kitchen to where everything was within easy reach.

Once his kitchen was in working order, he sliced and sautéed onions, mushrooms, and garlic, then tossed in freshly cut tomatoes with the seeds removed. Into that he poured three beaten eggs and stirred, adding cilantro, salt and pepper, and shredded Tillamook cheese. With skills he'd mastered watching various chefs at work in restaurants and on television, he lifted the pan and flipped the omelet into the air, catching it easily as it fell. Too bad no one was there to see his performance. He grinned. "Hey, Mutt, did you see that?"

Mutt danced around his master's legs, barking his approval.

Callen enjoyed showing off his culinary skills and even more enjoyed watching people eat his meals. Angel Delaney came to mind. He thought he wouldn't mind sharing one of his gourmet meals with her. Maybe he'd invite her over sometime. He shook his head, erasing the thought. There would be no dinner with Officer Delaney or any other woman anytime soon. His heart still ached over losing Karen. He had loved her more than he'd thought possible. In their wedding vows they'd spoken the words "Till death do us part." He'd just never expected it to happen.

He tucked away the memories, as he always did when they emerged. Time had taken away the raw edges of his wounds, but he doubted he'd ever heal completely.

He took his feast out on the deck, where he'd set out a place mat, napkins, silverware, and a tall, cold glass of iced tea. Mutt kept him company by sitting at his feet, inclining his head every now and then for a handout.

Somewhere between the first delicious bite and the last savory morsel, Callen had answered his question about the evidence, but he didn't like the answer one bit.

EIGHTEEN

Thirty-six hours had passed since her father's heart attack. It was Wednesday morning, and Angel had spent most of that time in the hospital with her parents. She seemed to have drifted into a fog, her mind refusing or unable to deal with the reality of the past few days. Those times when she did attempt to think about the shooting or her apartment, she'd feel as though she'd been dumped into the ocean with only a piece of cork to hold on to.

Frank was doing better. His color had returned, and there was talk of him going home in a day or two. He'd been placed on medical leave and wasn't too happy about it. Angel doubted they'd let him come back to work at all.

Most of the guys she and her dad worked with had come in at least once, bringing cards, balloons, and flowers and trying to lift his spirits. Detective Riley had been in once as well. He'd told her he had some questions but that they could wait until things settled down. Then in an act of supreme kindness, he'd driven her to her apartment to get her car and had gone in with her. He'd offered to help her clean up, and they spent the better part of two hours picking through the mess. There were a few salvageable items they were able to put away, but most of it would have to be dumped — something she set aside for another day.

The media had picked up the story about Angel's father, and for a while at least, not one of them had bothered her, not even when she'd gone to her parents' place to shower and wash her clothes. They had taken to reporting other events, other tragedies, but every day the newspaper managed to run an article about some aspect of the case.

In the latest, the one she'd thrown to the floor only minutes before, the writer had titled his piece "Angel Gone Bad?" He'd cited Angel's exemplary work with the police force, how as a woman officer she had beaten the odds, and how she often came into domestic violence situations and helped abuse victims find a way out. "Will one black mark destroy her career?" he had asked. Although most of the article had put her in a positive light, the title more than hinted at her guilt.

Susan picked up the paper Angel had dropped.

Angel glanced up at her sister-in-law. Sweet and attractive, Susan had been married to Tim for thirteen years now. They had two girls and one on the way. Susan placed a hand on her slightly rounded tummy as she straightened.

"You didn't have to pick that up. I'm sorry."

Susan shrugged and grinned. "Habit. Tim is always leaving newspapers lying around, and I'm always picking them up."

"Make him pick up after himself. He always was a slob. First Ma and now you." She sighed.

"Angel." Susan reached for her hand. "I'm so sorry this is happening to you. I really wish I could help."

"There's nothing anyone can do now but wait until the investigation is over."

"And that could take a while." Detective Riley sauntered up to them, looking like he wished he were anywhere else. He rubbed his eyes and lowered himself into the chair across from Angel. "I know this is a bad time, but we need to talk."

"Right. You had some questions, and I'm sorry I haven't gotten back to you. I haven't been avoiding you, it's just . . ."

"I know. You've been through more than your share." His green gaze locked on hers. "We have a problem with the investigation involving you and the Hartwell kid."

Susan patted her hand. "I'll leave you two alone," she said as she headed for the doorway.

Angel sat up straighter. "What's the problem?" From the look on the detective's face, she could tell the news wasn't good.

"The evidence is missing."

"What evidence? What are you talking about?"

"Your duty gun and magazine, clothes, and everything else that was collected in regard to the shooting. I put it in one of the temporary evidence lockers at the station on Sunday night with instructions that it be sent to Portland first thing Monday morning. The clerk says she never saw the note or the evidence, which means someone took it." The detective leaned forward, placing his elbows on his knees, his eyes assessing hers.

"Took it? But that doesn't make sense."

"That's what I thought at first."

Angel stared at the painting on the wall, a copy of Monet's "Waterlillies," barely able to assemble the unsettling news. "But why? Who would do such a thing?"

Riley leaned back, his gaze never leaving her face. "You."

Angel bounced out of her seat and went to stand by the window. "You can't be serious. What reason would I have? The evidence would just tell you whether or not the bullets that killed Billy came from my gun. It's not like I'm a suspect in a murder investigation."

"Think about it. You'd be the only one to benefit from the missing evidence."

Angel folded her arms, refusing to look at him or into his accusing eyes. "I'm not sure what you're getting at."

He got up and came to stand beside her. She found his closeness intimidating and unnerving. "Without your gun and magazine, we can't prove the bullets that killed that boy came from your gun. All we have is circumstantial evidence."

"And my testimony. I admitted to shooting him. I'm not trying to get away with anything here."

His eyes bored into hers. "And that would be the testimony where you said you'd fired only one of the three shots?"

Angel tore her gaze from his and, wrapping her arms around herself, turned back toward the window, which offered a view of the parking lot and a tree-lined sidewalk. Several hospital workers in colorful scrubs stood near a tree, smoking.

Riley was waiting for an answer, arms folded, looking frustrated and angry. She didn't blame him. Vital evidence was missing, and he'd been responsible for it. She couldn't think clearly, couldn't put the pieces together. Who would have stolen the evidence? Did the detective really believe her capable of doing such a thing? The thought made her nauseous.

"What do you want me to do?" she finally asked. "I could tell you I fired all three shots, but I honestly don't remember doing that." She frowned. "What I can tell you for certain is that I did fire at Billy, but I didn't intend to kill him, and I certainly didn't steal any evidence."

Angel looked so cold and lost, her arms folded close to her chest. Callen wanted to believe her. While part of him said to keep badgering her for answers, another part yearned to pull her into his arms. Unwilling to do either, he went to the

214

coffeemaker and poured himself a cup then stirred in sugar and cream. Distancing himself from Angel and taking a couple sips of the brew brought things back into balance.

"When you fired at the kid, did you pick up your casings?" he asked.

She swung toward him, apparently confused by the sudden change of direction. "What?"

"The casings. You know, the shell that flies out of the chamber when you fire."

She looked horrified that he had even asked. "No, of course not. All I could think about was Billy and trying to stop the bleeding."

"There were no casings found around the body." He peered at her over his cup. "Any idea where they ended up?"

"Maybe someone kicked them away when they came in." Angel turned away from him as tears rose in her eyes and threatened to spill. "I don't remember seeing them."

"Do you still have your key to the evidence locker?"

She closed her eyes and bit her lip. "No. I turned it over to Joe the day of the shooting."

Her name was on the list as still having

it. But although he had to consider her a suspect in the theft of the evidence, he doubted she had done it. Seeing her reaction confirmed his gut feelings. If she had turned in the key as she'd said, there had to be another player. "Who besides you wouldn't want the crime lab technicians sorting through the evidence?"

"I have no idea, unless . . ." He noted a change in her when she came toward him. Her eyes seemed brighter. "Unless there was another shooter."

Callen had to admit that Angel's first mention of having fired only one shot had left him full of doubts. Now, in light of the missing evidence, the second shooter theory was beginning to make sense.

If there had been another shooter, that person wouldn't want Angel's gun examined, because that would prove she had indeed fired only once. He thought of the Monroe kid, whose body he'd found on the wharf, and wondered if by some strange coincidence there might be a connection. Callen had worked on complex investigations before, but this one had more twists and turns and dead ends than a maze.

Angel placed a hand on his arm, her eyes moving up to meet his. "Please believe me. The last thing I'd want to do is compromise this investigation."

The look in her eyes was almost his undoing. His arms ached with the desire to hold her, but he couldn't — for way too many reasons. He was supposed to be an objective investigator. He had to remember that. He straightened, and in a voice that sounded harsh even to his own ears, he said, "For your sake, I hope not."

Her arms fell to her side and her shoulders slumped. Callen could only imagine the depth of her despair. He cleared his throat. "Joe Brady asked me to tell you to come in."

"Now?"

"As soon as possible." He hated doing this to her. She'd been through so much already. He thought back to the conversation he'd had with Joe, just before coming to the hospital, and could barely conceal his anger.

Angel went back to the chair she'd been sitting in to retrieve her bag. Her heart raced for fear he'd read her thoughts. That he'd see she was holding back information that could be vital to the case. She didn't want to tell him the name that had popped into her head when she'd talked again about the second shooter. She couldn't tell him about the one man who would do anything to protect his little girl. The man who had been at the scene and left.

"You should call your lawyer. Have him meet you there," Detective Riley said.

"You're right." She dug into her bag for Randy Grover's number, then pulled out her cell phone. "I'll call, though I'm not sure it'll do any good. He lives in Portland, and I doubt he'll be able to get here soon enough."

"Wait for him." He made it sound like an order.

"I thought you said Joe wanted to see me right away."

"He can wait."

"What aren't you telling me?" Angel didn't like the worried look on his face.

"Anything I tell you would be speculation on my part. I'm just saying that you need your lawyer there just in case . . ."

"In case?" Fear gripped her, turning her stomach inside out. "In case they arrest me? Could they do that?"

He hesitated a few seconds too long.

"They're going to arrest me?" Angel couldn't seem to stop the panic rising up inside her like bubbles in a shaken-up can of soda.

"Angel, stop." The detective guided her to a chair. "Sit down."

She sat, her hands gripping the wooden arms.

"First of all, I don't think you're going to be arrested." His voice was firm and strangely reassuring. "I doubt Joe would go that far. There's a lot of political garbage going on here, and the district attorney is talking about charging you with man one."

Angel sat straight and stiff. She didn't want to believe that Joe would let this happen. Man one, manslaughter first degree, was the taking of a human life while displaying extreme indifference. "How could he do that? The last thing I feel toward that kid is indifference. I've never felt so terrible about anything in my life."

NINETEEN

Two hours later, Angel parked near the entrance of the Sunset Cove Police Station and went inside. She had taken Detective Riley's advice about calling Randy, who had promised to meet her at the station at 12:30. She had spent two hours shopping for clothes and had gone back to her parents' house to shower and change. She'd found a sale at the outlet stores in Lincoln City and purchased jeans, slacks, and three tops. She had thought about going home but couldn't bear facing the huge pile of garbage. Tomorrow, she promised herself. She'd go home and finish cleaning up things tomorrow. Provided she wasn't sitting in jail.

Rosie Gonzalez, the receptionist and Joe's assistant, glanced up from her computer when Angel walked in. "Hey, doll," she said in that mellow southern drawl of hers. "How are you doin'?" Rosie buzzed

Angel in, and while she waited for Angel to come through the security door, she swiveled around in her chair, preparing to give her a hug.

Usually, Rosie's hugs were wonderful. But this particular one was Angel's undoing. Her throat clogged, and she couldn't answer.

"It's okay, sugar." Rosie handed her a tissue. "Bet you haven't had a good cry since all this started."

Angel dabbed at the corners of her eyes and blew her nose. "Thanks. I'm trying not to."

Rosie shook her head, giving Angel a look of concern. "Cryin' is good for the soul. Lets all that poison out of your system."

"You're probably right." Angel grabbed a tissue from her bag and blew her nose. "Just not right now." She needed to rein in her emotions before talking to Joe.

"How about I buy a half gallon of chocolate-chip mint ice cream and you come to my place tonight. We can eat and talk and cry and have ourselves a great time."

"Thanks." Angel chuckled. "Sounds like fun, but I'll have to take a rain check."

"Sure, honey. Say, how's your daddy doing?"

"Better." Angel frowned as her suspicions surfaced again. And with the suspicions came guilt. How could she suspect her own father? He was an honest man. She refused to entertain the idea that he could have been there, backing her up and later stealing the evidence.

"We sure do miss him around here." Rosie tapped her artificial pink nails on the counter before going around to the office side.

Angel had known Rosie since tenth grade, when Rosie and her parents had moved up from Texas. Rosie had immediately fallen in love with Angel's brothers — all of them. In high school, she'd swooned over Luke. After he left, she turned her attention to Tim and actually cried at his wedding. The last Angel had heard, Rosie was ready to settle for either of her twin brothers, Peter and Paul. In fact, only last month she'd taken Angel aside. "If those bachelor brothers of yours ever get serious and start looking for a wife, tell them I'm still available."

Rosie hadn't mentioned Peter or Paul lately, and Angel soon discovered why. Nick Caldwell ambled in, and Rosie's cheeks flushed.

"Hey, Angel." Nick Caldwell leaned on

the counter. "How's it going?"

She shrugged. "All right, considering."

"Good." Nick turned to Rosie and winked before heading out the door.

Just then, Angel's attorney came in. "Hello, Angel. Hope I'm not too late."

"No, I haven't talked to Joe yet."

"I'll let him know you're here," Rosie offered. She spoke on the phone for a moment with Joe, then buzzed Randy in.

Joe was leaning against his desk when they walked into his office. "Have a seat," he said.

Angel sank onto one of the straight-backed wooden chairs. Randy took the one beside her.

"Detective Riley said you wanted to see me."

"Yeah." He hitched a leg up on the corner of his desk. "I'm not going to beat around the bush here, Delaney. The DA is getting pressure from the mayor and the governor's office to press charges against you. If they go ahead with the arrest, you'll be brought up on charges of manslaughter first degree." He stood and went around to his chair, putting his desk between them. "It isn't formal yet, so we won't be arresting you."

"Why? Giving me a chance to skip

town?" Sarcasm dripped from every word; anger was quickly replacing fear. How dare they even think about charging her with anything?

Randy cleared his throat. "That's not something to joke about, Angel."

Joe glared at her. "Don't even think about going anywhere." He sat in his chair and sighed. His shoulders sagged as he clasped his hands on his desk.

Randy tapped his pen on his pad. "I'll talk to the DA and see what's going on. Maybe we can get him to go for criminally negligent homicide. In any case, you won't do jail time. Just turn yourself in and pay your bail, which would be one hundred thousand dollars with 10 percent acceptable —"

"And get printed and mugged like a criminal. But I haven't done anything wrong!" Angel clamped her mouth shut before she said something she'd regret.

"Listen, Delaney, I wish we could make this business go away," Joe said. "I think eventually it will. In the meantime, all we can do is appease the public and let justice take its course."

"I'm not sure I trust the system," she retorted.

Joe's frown told her he didn't either.

"Detective Riley told me about the missing evidence," she said. "I told him I'd turned my key over to you."

Joe frowned. "Did you? I don't recall."

"How can you not remember? Detective Riley thinks I took the evidence. Now you're saying you lost the key?" She should have watched him log it in and gotten a receipt.

"Hold on, here. What evidence? Care to enlighten me?" Randy leaned forward.

Joe filled him in on the details while Randy drew boxes in the margins of his legal pad.

"Without evidence, the DA doesn't have a case." Randy put his pad into his briefcase.

"We have witnesses and Angel's testimony." Joe rubbed a hand over his bald spot and turned to Angel. "There's something else. Even if the DA decides not to charge you, it isn't over. The kid's family has talked to an attorney. They want to bring a civil suit against you and the city for fifty million dollars."

"Fifty million." She closed her eyes, trying to catch her breath. Then she turned to Randy and asked, "Did you know about the civil suit?"

"Yes. I got a call this morning. I was

225

planning to talk to you about it. Maybe we could have coffee." He looked uncomfortable and probably didn't want to talk in front of Joe.

Joe pushed his chair back and got to his feet, apparently ready for them to leave. She stood as well. Randy leaned across the desk to shake hands with Joe. "We'll be in touch."

"Oh, and Angel," Joe said, calling her back. "I talked to Dr. Campbell this morning. Says you weren't planning on going back in. Not a good idea. I think you should sign on for a six-week stint."

She nodded. With all that had gone on in the last few days, she was ready to admit she might need a good shrink after all.

"Listen," Joe added, "when you see Frank, tell him hello from me. I thought I might go up and see him sometime tomorrow."

"I'm sure he'd appreciate that."

Joe went back to his desk, head bent over some paperwork. She could see no hint of empathy or compassion now. No "I'm sorry this is happening to you" or "We're behind you on this." He clearly wanted to be rid of the entire incident — and the woman who'd created it. She felt as though she'd been cut off, left to drift in a raging ocean with nothing to hold on to.

Minutes later, Angel and Randy stepped outside into bright sunshine.

Randy glanced at his watch. "I have to be back in Portland before dinner. Is there a place close by where we can get some lunch? There are some things I'd like to go over with you."

"Um, sure." Angel led the way, walking a block toward the water to Earth's Bounty. "This place serves mostly vegetarian, but they have wild fish and organic chicken."

"Sounds good to me." Randy reached into his suit pocket and pulled out a white cloth hanky and, leaving it folded, wiped his brow. "Organic chicken?"

"That's what I call it. It's like free range or something. They raise them in big pens where they can roam free and eat natural grains. There aren't any chemicals in their food."

"So are you a vegetarian?"

"Me? Hardly. I just like their food."

"Hmm."

Angel had to hurry to keep up with his long, determined strides. "Can I ask you something?"

"Sure." Randy slowed his pace.

"You don't seem too interested in this

case. In fact, both times we've met you acted like you'd rather have been somewhere else."

He ducked his head, looking sheepish. "Sorry you feel that way. I apologize if I've given you that impression."

"So you are interested?"

"In representing you? Sure." They walked several minutes before he spoke again. "Look, I need to be honest with you. My wife is having a baby soon and . . . well, she was going in for an ultrasound today. Guess my mind has been more with her than with you. I'm sorry."

Angel grinned. "Why didn't you say so? We don't need to talk now."

"Thanks, but I have to eat lunch anyway, and there are a couple of things we need to go over."

They reached the restaurant, a grayish tan two-story house with green and purple trim. The Victorian showplace had been built in 1910, and with the remodeling it looked as elegant now as it must have back then. It sat up from the water about fifty feet and had a deck out the back where customers could eat if the weather cooperated. Angel and Randy sat on the deck. A light breeze ducked in and out between the umbrellas.

"This is a nice spot. Do you come here a lot?"

"About once a week." She picked up her menu and spotted Brandon sitting inside with his father and his brother, Carl. They hadn't seen her, or at least they gave no indication that they had. Brandon didn't look too pleased about being there. His father leaned forward and said something, causing Brandon to put down his napkin. He pushed back his chair, then got up and walked out. Carl started to get up as well, but his father laid a restraining hand on his arm. Mr. Lafferty rubbed the back of his neck and took a drink. She'd have to remember to ask Brandon about it later. That is, if she saw him later.

Angel turned back to Randy, who was still studying the menu. A waitress came by with their water. "What can I get you?"

Randy ordered a turkey sandwich with salad on the side. Angel ordered a chicken salad, and, since they didn't serve Coke, an iced tea.

"Would you like something to drink?" the waitress asked Randy.

"Yeah. Do you serve fresh vegetable juice?"

"Sure do. There's a list on the back. We can put anything in it. Carrot, celery, spinach, chard . . ."

"I'll have the carrot with ginger and a little celery."

Angel made a face. "You actually drink that stuff?"

"My wife converted me. It's really pretty good."

"If you say so. You should get together with Detective Riley. He's into health food too."

"A lot of people are." Randy pulled up his briefcase and studied some documents. "We need to talk about the charges being brought against you."

Angel's stomach knotted again. "I don't understand why this is happening. I mean . . . I do, but it isn't right. That kid represented a clear and present danger."

"Yes, but there's more at stake here. We've got an African-American child who, as it turns out, had no affiliation with the gang members who robbed the store. We've got the kid's family ready to take you to court. No matter what the DA or the grand jury decides, we have that to contend with."

"I feel like I'm being thrown to the wolves."

"Well, I guess in a way, you are. So I think it'll be best all around if we just put a lid on everything right now. We'll plea bargain for a lesser charge, and with the civil suit we can settle out of court."

"And where does that put me?" Angel picked up her water glass.

"You'll be terminated from your position in the police department. You'll get a sentence of maybe five years but won't have to serve any time."

"I'd be on probation for five years? No way."

"I don't like it either, but you'd be better off if we don't end up in court. Let's face it, you're not exactly coming off as a saint here."

"There hasn't even been a grand jury hearing yet. They probably won't let this go to trial."

"The DA thinks otherwise. He's certain that because of the high-profile aspect of the case, it will go to trial and you will lose."

Their lunches came. Angel picked at her salad, and when she finally put a bite into her mouth, she wished she hadn't. She set her fork down and sipped at her tea. "I don't want to plea bargain or settle out of court."

He grimaced. "I was afraid of that."

"I can't just walk away from my job. I

didn't do anything wrong." She twisted the napkin on her lap.

Randy took a drink of his carrot juice. It left an orange smile on his lips like he'd been drinking orange Kool-Aid. "Fair enough. If you don't settle, this is going to drag on for a long time, and I may not be able to represent you."

"Because of the baby?"

"Partly. I'm resigning my position with the union and going into private practice so I can stay in Portland. Just traveling down here and back takes a five-hour chunk out of my day."

"So you want me to accept the charges, hope for a plea bargain, and get it over with."

"That's about it. I think you should settle out of court on the civil suit as well."

"I can't believe this."

"A trial of any kind won't be good for you or for the department. There's too much bad press. If you decide not to settle, I'll have to turn your case over to one of the other lawyers."

Angel watched him finish his juice. He wiped his mouth with the napkin, but the orange stain remained. Angel decided not to tell him. She understood his dilemma but didn't like his advice.

"Who would represent me?"

"One of the other lawyers from the firm. Um — everyone is pretty busy at the moment. I'll have to check. I think I can have someone down here tomorrow."

"Forget it." Angel picked up her bag and pulled out her wallet. "I'll find my own lawyer."

"As a union member, you're entitled to representation, but it's your prerogative."

She pulled a ten out of her wallet and set it on the table. "I hope everything is okay with the ultrasound."

"Angel, I'm sorry."

"Hey, I understand. You guys are busy, so I'll find someone who . . ." *Someone who gives a rip.* "Who's local." Angel smiled at him to show there were no hard feelings. "I need to get back to the hospital to see my dad. Can you find your way back to your car?"

"Sure. No problem. If you change your mind, give me a call."

While she walked back to her car, she wondered at the wisdom of firing her lawyer. She'd have to use her own money to pay for one. Maybe Brandon would help — he'd told her he would the night of the shooting.

But things had changed radically since then.

TWENTY

On the way to the hospital, Angel called Janet's office and made another appointment. She was surprised when the receptionist told her to come in that afternoon.

When she arrived back at the hospital, she found Brandon in the waiting room, talking to her brothers Peter and Paul, who had been at their resort in the Caribbean. She felt a rush of guilt when she realized she hadn't called Brandon to tell him about her father.

Brandon flashed her a hurt look. "I came by to see your dad and see how you were doing."

Angel found it hard to meet his eyes. "Thanks for coming." Not certain what to say next, she turned to greet her brothers.

Peter set down his cup and captured her in an exuberant hug. Paul gave her shoulders a squeeze. Physically the twins were identical, but Angel never had trouble telling them apart. They were both tall, tan, and rich. Both were thirty-two years old, just under six feet, with thick dark hair and dark chocolate eyes. But Peter, the extrovert, acted as if he didn't have a care in the world, while Paul worried too much — a little something he picked up from his mother. He was the introvert — analytical and detail oriented. Peter handled the public relations side of their business. Paul did all the accounting.

"What are you guys doing here? I thought you weren't due back for another month." She frowned. "Dad's okay, isn't he?"

"He's okay — better in fact. We thought we should come home to give you some moral support."

"Me?"

"Tim told us what's been going on," Paul said.

Angel stared at a dust bunny skittering across the polished floor. "And you two thought you'd come to my rescue?"

Peter handed her a cup of coffee. "Sounds like someone has to."

"The truth is," Paul said, "Mom told us if we didn't haul ourselves out here, she'd come get us."

"Yeah, like you were worried." Angel grinned. Somehow being around Peter and Paul always raised her spirits. Being six years older and closest in age they were usually the ones who'd ended up baby-sitting her when she was little. "How's the resort business going?" she asked.

The twins owned several resorts — in the Caribbean, France, and Mexico — all located on the most beautiful beaches in the world. Which accounted for their bronzed Mediterranean looks. Of course, being part Italian helped. They had recently built a new resort just a few miles north of Sunset Cove, their first venture in the Northwest. "How's the Bay Village Resort doing?"

"Business is great," Peter responded. "We've been having to turn people away, especially on the weekends."

Paul nodded. "They like having another five-star resort in the area."

Peter nudged her arm. "So when are you going to come see it?" he asked. "We'll let you stay in one of our best suites."

"That's sweet, guys, but this isn't a good time."

"Seems to me it's a perfect time." Paul scrutinized her. "You can soak up some rays, swim, hot tub, play volleyball on the beach. Think about it, okay?"

"Okay." Angel had to admit it sounded wonderful.

Brandon tossed his empty cup in the wastebasket, looking uncomfortable and unhappy at being left out.

She turned to him. "I'm glad you're here. I need to talk to you about something." Glancing back at her brothers, she said, "It's private."

They gave her a knowing look. "Maybe we should come along as chaperones," Peter said with a grin.

"Not that kind of private." She rolled her eyes at them and slipped her hand into the crook of Brandon's arm.

"Want to go somewhere to eat?" Brandon asked. "I could use a sandwich."

She didn't mention seeing him at the restaurant. Apparently he'd left before finishing his meal. "I've eaten, but I can sit with you."

They didn't speak until they reached the elevator. "Why didn't you tell me about your dad?" Brandon asked. "I shouldn't have to read about something like that in the paper."

"It all happened so fast. I'm sorry."

"You didn't tell me about your apartment either. Angel, we may have had a disagreement, but I still care about you."

"There was nothing you could've done about the apartment. It happened. It's over."

"So what did you want to talk to me about?" Brandon held the elevator door open as she stepped inside.

"It's the legal mud hole I seem to have fallen into," she said. "I've been told the DA is going to bring charges against me, and that there's going to be a civil suit."

"I heard." Brandon looked at the elevator buttons, then at the door.

Angel found a table and waited for Brandon to go through the cafeteria line. When he got to the table, she picked up the conversation where they'd left off. "I fired the lawyer the union sent to represent me."

"Why?" He picked up his sandwich and took a bite.

"He wanted me to admit I was wrong. He said we should try for a lesser charge and settle with Billy's family."

"Maybe you should." Brandon kept his eyes focused on his plate.

"No way." She brushed some crumbs from the table. "That would mean losing my job and being sentenced and put on probation. What kind of settlement is that?" She went on to tell him about Randy's personal situation.

"Can't you get another union lawyer?"

"Yeah, but I'm not sure I want one. I thought maybe you could . . ." Something in his expression stopped her. "What?"

He glanced around the room, still not meeting her eyes. "I can't. We're too close. It would be unethical."

"That didn't seem to bother you the other night when you offered to help."

He set his sandwich down and wiped his hands on a napkin. "You're going to hear about it eventually anyway, so I might as well tell you."

"Tell me what?"

"I can't represent you because it would be a conflict of interest."

"I don't see how. It's not like we're married or even engaged. We're friends."

Angel watched his Adam's apple move up and down as he swallowed. He turned to look out the window. His gaze finally met hers but only briefly. "There's no easy way to tell you this. Dad informed Carl and me about it this morning. I tried to talk him out of it, but he's not budging."

"Talk him out of what? What are you saying?"

He licked his lips. "Our firm is representing Ray Broadman in the civil suit against you."

"Ray Broadman." A lump the size of a soccer ball sat in the pit of her stomach. "That's Billy's uncle."

"He's filing on behalf of Billy's mother."

Angel rubbed her arms, hoping the friction of skin against fabric would warm her. She had felt adrift in Joe's office; now she felt as if she was going down for the third time. One by one she felt the supports slip out from under her.

"I'm sorry." Brandon reached for her hand.

Angel moved out of his reach, pulling together what little resources she had left. "I'm going up to see my dad."

He got up and followed her out of the cafeteria. "Angel, wait!"

She swung around when he grabbed her arm. "I don't think we have anything more to talk about."

She pulled her arm out of his grasp and left him standing there. Beneath the anger, though, she felt sad. She understood that his father had put him in a no-win situation. That must've been what they were arguing about at the restaurant earlier. But the knowledge did little to ease the pain of betrayal.

When she got to the door of her father's room, she hesitated and took a deep breath before going inside. "Hi, Dad. How's it going?"

"I'd do better if I could get out of this place," Frank grumbled.

"You need to stay a few more days. Hearts take time to heal."

Hearts take time to heal. Angel wondered if hers ever would.

"I saw the news last night." Frank scooted himself up in bed. "Those vultures just won't let it go."

"The press is always blowing things out of proportion. You know that."

He nodded and closed his eyes. When he didn't open them again and his breathing deepened, Angel kissed his cheek then whispered good-bye and left. *Were you there, Dad? Did you shoot at Billy? Did you steal the evidence?* No, she wouldn't ask. Not now. Maybe never.

When she joined her brothers in the waiting room, she avoided their questioning gazes. "What happened to Brandon?" Peter asked.

"He had to go back to the office." She dropped into the nearest chair. "Where's Ma?"

"Tim took her down to the cafeteria."

241

Paul shook his head. "I don't think she's had anything decent to eat since she got here Monday night."

Angel nodded. "Do you guys know a good lawyer?"

They eyed each other then turned their gazes back to her. "Didn't the union provide one for you?"

"I fired him."

"What about Brandon?" Paul asked.

"Brandon is sleeping with the enemy." Angel went on to explain the situation.

"How could they do that to you?" Peter scowled.

"You can't really blame Brandon, though," Paul said, obviously trying to be rational. "He'd have to quit the firm in order to represent you. Besides, he's not a criminal lawyer."

"I'm not a criminal!"

"That's beside the point, and you know it."

"Okay, okay. I need someone who'll work cheap."

Peter chuckled. "Somehow I don't think we should be using the words *lawyer* and *cheap* in the same sentence."

"Well, with things going the way they are, I need someone fast."

"How about Rachael?" Paul pursed his lips.

"Good idea, bro." Peter patted his brother's back.

"Who's Rachael?"

"You don't know Rachael?" they asked at the same time.

Angel frowned. "Should I?"

"Duh. Rachael Rastovski is the babe renting an office at Tim's church."

"She's more than a babe," Paul said, rolling his eyes at his brother. "She's a lawyer, and I've heard she's very good."

"I haven't met her," Angel said, "but then, I haven't been to church lately. Let me guess. She's new and working on charity cases."

"Not new exactly. She was working with some big firm in L.A. Don't know the specifics — just that she's starting over. Talk to Tim about her."

Angel hesitated. Maybe she could check Rachael out. First, though, she wanted to know why someone would leave a cushy job in L.A. to work out of a church in Sunset Cove. "Thanks for the tip." She sighed and pushed herself to her feet. "I'd better get going."

"Have dinner with us tonight," Peter said. "We're taking Mom out. She needs a diversion."

"I don't know."

"We can do Asian. That Vietnamese place you like."

Paul glanced up at her. "Come on, Ange. You have to eat."

"Our treat," Peter added.

"All right. I'll meet you there. What time?"

"How's 6:30?"

"Good." Angel turned to leave and nearly ran down the hall to the elevator, though she wasn't sure why. She still had thirty minutes before her appointment with Janet.

Going out the hospital's revolving front entrance, she spotted the headlines on the *Oregonian*, Oregon's primary newspaper, announcing that Billy Dean Hartwell's funeral would be held the next afternoon. She bought the paper and tucked it under her arm.

Angel wanted to attend the funeral and yet she didn't. She felt an obligation but at the same time worried that her appearance might cause more trouble. She would go, she decided, but she'd disguise her appearance and bring a camera so she'd fit in with the media that would undoubtedly be there.

Angel parked near Janet's office and spent fifteen minutes walking through the nearby park. Five minutes before her appointment, she went inside the building.

She didn't have to wait long; Janet met her as she came in and ushered her to her office. "I'm glad you decided to come back."

"I don't need psychoanalysis," Angel said after they were seated. "Just let me come in here and talk to you once or twice a week to satisfy my boss."

"That's fine with me." Janet leaned back in her chair and put her feet on the coffee table. "So talk."

"About what?"

"Whatever you want. I'm here to listen."

"Right." Angel settled herself into the cushioned chair and tipped her head back. Closing her eyes, she waited. The silence built to deafening proportions, and she finally had to break it. "You want to hear about the shooting?"

"If you want to tell me."

"I don't really. Besides, you know about it."

"Not from your perspective."

"Yeah, I guess not." So Angel told her what had happened that day. From the call to investigate the robbery at the drugstore to finding Billy Dean and pulling the trigger.

"The papers said you shot him three times. You only mentioned shooting him once."

Angel opened her eyes. "I only remember shooting once. The guys told me it happens like that sometimes. You get so caught up in an adrenaline rush and can fire off an entire magazine without realizing it. I wish I could remember for sure. I mean, obviously I shot him, but . . ."

"I may be able to help you remember for sure." Janet lowered her feet and leaned forward.

"How?"

"Hypnotherapy."

Angel shook her head. "You'd hypnotize me? I don't think so."

Janet smiled. "It's not what you think. A lot of people freak out about the idea of hypnosis, but it's a valid tool. I don't put you under or anything like that. It's really all about relaxation."

"I don't know."

"No pressure, Angel. Just think about it. Sometimes after a traumatic experience like yours, the memory does odd things. You may remember what happened at any time — or you might not remember at all. Do you still have my card?"

Angel nodded.

"How are those sleeping pills working for you?"

"I haven't gotten the prescription filled yet. I just haven't had time. I mean, first there was the break-in, and then my father's heart attack."

"I understand that," Janet said. "But I have a feeling that isn't what's kept you from getting the medication. It's okay to take something, you know. And you can quit acting like everything is fine. We're old friends, remember? I know you like to stay in control, but you also need your rest."

"Humph. I'm not sure I know what control is anymore." Angel's lips curved in a half smile. "I know. I'm defensive, but I can't afford to let this get to me. I have to stay on top of things."

"I understand. But not getting enough sleep will wear you down faster than dealing with this situation. A good night's sleep will help you cope much better with everything."

Later in their conversation, Angel brought Janet up-to-date on her dad's condition and told her about the latest bombshell, being brought up on charges. Janet was easy to talk to, and pretty soon Angel was thinking counseling might actually do some good.

When their time was up, Janet walked her to the door. "I meant what I said, Angel. Call me anytime. And why don't you come in Friday at 11:00, and we'll try the hypnosis? Sooner if you want."

"Thanks, Janet. And thanks for taking me on as a patient. I know it's unusual to take on a friend as a client, but I just don't think I could trust anyone else."

On the way home, Angel struggled with her anger toward Brandon, or more specifically, Brandon's father. How could he do something like that? It was a slap in the face, and she was furious with Brandon for not standing up to his father. If he really cared about her, wouldn't he just leave the firm? But maybe Brandon didn't have the backbone for it. After mulling it over, though, she decided she was more disappointed than angry — at least with Brandon. Michael Lafferty was another story.

When she pulled into the parking lot of her apartment complex, she was surprised to find the place clear of reporters. She eased into her regular spot and hurried up the stairs.

Angel paused at the landing and cautiously slipped her key into the lock. She held her breath. Would the intruders be back? At Callen's insistence, she had gotten the locks changed after they'd cleaned the place up, but she doubted if it would make a difference. If the vandals wanted to get in, they could. Angel hauled in a deep breath as she let the door swing open. She doubted coming home would ever be the simple act it had once been.

She stepped inside. Her breath caught. Someone had been there, only this time was far different from the last.

Whoever it was had left the place im-maculate. Someone had cleared out all the garbage. In place of the old sofa and chair were a matching set with a soft floral print. Her slashed mattress had been replaced, and the bed made with a new comforter set in her favorite pastel colors. Though she hadn't checked the cupboards or the linen closet, she had a feeling nearly every-thing she'd lost had been replaced.

Tears gathered in her eyes at the unex-pected act of kindness. She didn't even know who to thank but suspected Tim and Susan had instigated the project. She opened the cupboards and shook her head. Whoever her benefactor was had stocked her kitchen with everything that had been destroyed, and more. In one cupboard she found a new set of pottery mugs, a set of dishes for six, and glasses in all shapes and sizes. Canned goods, flour and sugar, spices, and all kinds of stuff kitchens were supposed to be stocked with filled the pantry. If her mother hadn't been spending most of her time at the hospital with her father, Angel would've suspected her of masterminding the cleanup effort.

After pulling down one of the mugs, Angel heated water in the microwave and fixed some herbal tea. She carried the mug over to the new stereo. Propped up against it were three CDs, *Celtic Romance*, *Classics*, and *Quietude*. Angel put them in the CD player, thinking she'd get an idea of who to thank by listening to their choice of music. It wasn't the type of music she usually listened to, but it soothed her, and by the time the changer had gone through one of the disks, she had fallen asleep on her new sofa.

TWENTY-ONE

Angel awoke to the ringing of the doorbell and peered through the peephole. Tim.

"Hope I'm not disturbing anything." His questioning gaze took in her disheveled appearance as she opened the door.

"I was taking a nap." She yawned. "What do you want?"

"Is that anyway to treat your favorite brother?"

Angel rolled her eyes and gestured him inside. Instead of entering, he stepped aside and ushered in an attractive brunette with eyes that sparkled like aquamarine gemstones. She wore jeans and a classic white shirt topped with a navy jacket, and carried a black leather briefcase.

"Angel, meet Rachael Rastovski."

The woman grinned, revealing a deep set of dimples, and extended her hand. She shook Angel's with a firm grip. "Nice to meet you, Angel. I've heard a lot about you. I hear you're looking for an attorney."

"Peter and Paul told me you needed one," Tim offered. "Um — I mentioned your dilemma to Rachael, and she's agreed to represent you."

"Did they also tell you I couldn't afford to pay you much?"

"Hey, it's not a problem, honest. Tim and Susan and I have a great working relationship. He provides the space, Susan feeds me, and on occasion I get a paying client so I can actually pay the rent." She chuckled. "Don't worry about it. We'll work it out."

Angel rubbed her forehead. "Tim, I wish you'd called me first."

"Hey, if you've found someone else, no problem." Rachael waved her hand.

"It isn't that, Rachael; it's just that my brothers tend to take over, and I really like to make my own decisions."

"We just want to help," Tim said. "Is that so bad?"

"I understand totally." Rachael's dimples appeared again. "I have two older brothers. They can be incredibly bossy. Listen, we can send Tim away and you and I can talk. If you don't like me and decide not to hire me, it's okay. I can take it."

Tim started backing away. "I'll wait in the car." He turned toward the door then turned back. "Hey, your place is all fixed up. Looks great."

"Like you didn't know. Come on, fess up, you got your congregation working on the place, didn't you?"

He looked surprised. "I didn't. I'd planned to ask for donations, but with Dad sick and all, I didn't get around to it. I'll ask around, though. Maybe my team went on ahead of me." He grinned at her then turned to Rachael. "Just come down to the car when you're ready."

"Why don't you go back to the office?" Rachael suggested. "I know you have a lot to do. I can take a cab back."

Tim was reluctant at first then acquiesced. "All right. If you're sure."

"I am."

When Tim had gone, Angel offered Rachael coffee then set about making it.

Rachael wandered over to the sliding glass door. "I assume you want to know something about me."

Angel nodded. "I heard you'd worked in L.A."

"Yeah. Criminal law. I didn't much care for living in L.A. though. It was about as appealing as going to the dentist every day.

I'd visited the Northwest a few years ago and fell in love with it. So I quit my job and moved."

"Where do you live?"

"I bought a little house on Cliff Road. It's only two blocks from the beach, and I love it."

"This must be quite a change for you. Do you work alone?"

"Yeah. Except for Sherlock."

"Sherlock?"

Rachael laughed. "My cat." She turned to look out at the ocean. "I had a chance to work for a prestigious law firm here in town but decided not to."

"Which firm is that?"

"Michael Lafferty's."

"Really. And you turned them down?"

"I've had my fill of the big guns," Rachael went on. "Too restrictive. I want to be able to handle any case I want, regardless of whether or not they can afford to pay the big bucks. I like working for myself."

"You're hired. When can you start?" Angel poured coffee into two mugs and handed one to Rachael.

"Thanks. How about now?"

"Great."

"Let me get a pad and we can get

started." Rachael retrieved a legal pad and pen from her briefcase, and the two of them settled on the couch. Rachael asked questions, and Angel answered the best she could, relating the shooting incident and everything that had happened in the aftermath.

"Angel," Rachael said, picking up her half empty cup. "If you don't remember shooting more than once, then maybe you didn't. I'll get the autopsy report and talk to Callen."

"You mean Detective Riley? Do you know him?"

"We've met."

Angel got up and took her cup to the kitchen and rinsed it out. "I don't think it'll do much good. Someone made off with the evidence."

"Yeah, but he should have something." Rachael chewed her lower lip. "In the meantime, get some rest. You look terrible."

"Gee, thanks."

Rachael waved her hand. "Don't mention it." She glanced at her watch. "Oh, wow. It's almost 6:00. Want to catch a bite to eat? I'll buy if you take me home after."

"Sounds good, but I'm having dinner with my family." She paused. "Why don't you come along? You'd fit right in."

"Really? Hey, I'd love to if you're sure it's okay."

"More than okay. You already know Tim and Susan. And you must know the twins — Peter and Paul. They told me about you."

"Oh yes. The twins." She smiled. "I met them once. They'll be there?"

"Uh-huh. I take it you approve."

Rachael placed a hand over her heart. "Approve? Angel, I have died and gone to heaven."

Angel shook her head. "Sounds like you have it bad. Which one are you in love with?"

"In love?" Rachael chuckled. "I don't know either of them well enough for that. I only saw them once, and that was very brief. But the memory is definitely lasting."

"Hmm. I think you had the same effect on them. Especially Paul."

"No kidding. Which one is Paul, the fast talker or the quiet one?"

"The quiet one."

"Mmm. Things are looking up." Rachael set her briefcase on the coffee table. "Um . . . did you want to take a shower or something before we go?"

"I guess I should. You'll be okay out here?"

"Go ahead. I want to make some more notes." Rachael went back to her pad and began writing.

Angel showered and dressed in fresh jeans and a pale blue T-shirt, then pulled a bulky sweater over it.

"Ready?" Angel took a jacket out of her closet and draped it over her arm.

"More than."

They left the apartment and were halfway down the stairs when Angel noticed several members of the press back on duty. "Oh no. I thought they'd given up."

"Are you kidding? You're a big news item. They'll never give up. Want to talk to them?"

"No."

"Then let's go. Just keep moving. They tried to talk to Tim and me on the way up."

Angel and Rachael reached the car at about the same time as the members of the press. Angel ducked into the driver's side and shut the door. Several cameras flashed. Bodies pressed against her car. She honked her horn and shifted into reverse. One reporter tapped on her windshield. Another went around to the passenger side, intent on talking to Rachael.

"I can't believe this. They won't even let me back up!"

"Just do it."

Rachael rolled down the window a crack and pulled out her cell phone. "I suggest you all move out of the way. I'm calling the police. I'll have you all arrested for harassment."

"Angel!" one of the reporters shouted. "We've heard rumors that the DA is about to bring formal charges against you. How do you feel about that?"

"She has no comment!" Rachael yelled back.

A tall angular man leaned over and peered into the passenger side window. "Rachael Rastovski, is that you?"

"Last time I checked. Hi, Sam."

"You representing Angel?" Sam asked.

"Maybe."

"Talk to me."

"Hey, Sam, do me a favor. Clear these guys out of here, and I'll give you an exclusive interview in my office tomorrow."

Sam grinned. "Yeah? Is that a promise?"

"Word of honor. Tomorrow at . . ." Rachael glanced at Angel, giving her a play-along-with-me look. "What time can you be at my office?"

Angel shrugged. "Ten, I guess, but . . ."

Turning back to the reporter, Rachael repeated the time and rolled up the window.

Angel blew out a frustrated sigh. "What did you do that for? I don't want to talk to these guys!"

"Of course, you don't. And you don't have to. I'll talk to him."

"But you told him I'd be there."

"Uh-uh. I asked what time you could be there — not that you would be. And I promised him an exclusive. He'll get that." She grinned. "From me. It's better if you don't say anything anyway. Could cause problems down the road."

As she backed the car out, Angel decided that she liked Rachael. She inched her car forward as the reluctant news crews stepped out of the way, and a smile crept to her mouth. Maybe, just maybe, things were beginning to turn around.

TWENTY-TWO

A few minutes later, Angel and Rachael pulled into the restaurant parking lot. Her brothers were already there and had secured a large table in the banquet room. Angel couldn't help but notice Paul's approving gaze as it settled on Rachael.

Taking the seat beside her, Paul reached out his hand.

"You're Paul, right?" Rachael said before he could open his mouth. Her dimples deepened as she shook his hand. "I'm Rachael Rastovski."

"Right. We met about four months ago. I didn't think you'd remember."

"I'm good with names." She cleared her throat. "And faces."

"Glad you could join us, Rach." Tim looked from Angel to Rachael. "You two strike a deal?"

Rachael nodded. "She's agreed to let

me represent her."

"Listen," Paul said. "Pete and I talked about it, and we'll cover the attorney fees."

"You will not," Angel insisted. "I'm perfectly capable —"

"Come on, Angel. This is no time to get all weird on us. We have the money. You want Rachael to get paid, don't you?"

They had her there. "Okay, you can pay up front, but I'll pay you back."

"Fine."

Angel wondered if the twins had anything to do with fixing up her apartment, so she asked them. They both denied it, and Tim told her no one on his board had done it either. So who had? Angel couldn't stand not knowing and had to get to the bottom of it.

"Where's Ma?"

"Susan's bringing her from the hospital." Tim glanced at his watch. "They should be here any minute."

"What about the girls? Aren't they eating with us?"

"They're with Susan. There's a day care at the hospital now, so she picks them up when she gets off work. Very handy."

Angel nodded. The girls would prove a sunny diversion from the black cloud that had been following her of late.

"I wish more workplaces would offer child care," Rachael said. "Takes the stress level down for kids and their parents to be at the same place."

"Susan worries less — I do too. The care is excellent."

The restaurant door opened, and two adorable girls rushed in ahead of Susan and Angel's mother. "Girls," Anna scolded, "behave yourselves. Remember what your mother told you in the car."

"Yes, Nana." Heidi, the oldest, glanced back over her shoulder as she slowed to a jog.

Abby, the four-year-old, made a beeline for Angel. "I get to sit next to Auntie Angel." She squealed as Heidi pulled out the chair.

"No, I do. It's my turn."

"Hey," Tim said, getting to his feet. "No arguing."

Abby climbed onto Angel's lap, her lower lip protruding. "I said so first."

"You can both sit beside me. Heidi, scoot over one." Angel set Abby on her chair then waited while Heidi moved into the next spot. "There." She squeezed each girl's hand and turned to Heidi. "How's school?"

"Good." Heidi beamed. "My teacher

told me I could help her teach some of the other kids to read. She said I had to wait until the other kids had a chance to answer questions before I did, cause I always know the answer. I can read the Bible already."

"I can read too." Abby got to her knees and leaned into Angel.

"Already?" Angel gave the girl a hug. "You'll both have to read something to me next time I come over."

Susan and Anna had been seated during Angel's interchange with the girls. Anna looked pale and glanced at Angel as if to say, *I don't want to be here.*

"How's Dad this afternoon?" Tim asked.

Anna filled them in on Frank's condition then picked up her menu. "I promised we'd stop to see him after we ate."

The waitress arrived with water and tea then began taking orders. After much ado, they settled on family style with salad, rolls, appetizers, soups, chicken with peanut sauce, game hens cooked in clay pots with coconut milk, and sticky rice.

Probably because of the girls, the conversation stayed away from talk of the shooting, for which Angel was thankful. If not for her father's absence, it would've seemed like a normal family gathering. Even Rachael seemed at ease and talked freely with everyone. Angel already felt like she'd known her a lifetime.

After dinner, they stopped at the hospital to check on Frank. He looked better and was delighted when the nurse let Susan bring the girls in. But by the time Heidi and Abby had taken their turns, he looked tired and pale.

"I hope we didn't tire you out too much," Angel said.

"Never." He held her hand in his, reluctant to let go. "Angel, I told the boys, but I need to tell you too. If anything happens to me, you take care of your mother."

"Don't talk like that." The words caught in her throat. "Nothing's going to happen."

He tightened his grip when she tried to pull away. "I didn't think so either. But I was wrong. I have to go in for a triple bypass. Doc says it's pretty common these days, but nothing is a sure thing."

"Surgery? When did you find this out?"

"They've been doing all kinds of tests since I came in here. The doctor told me about it just before supper. I told the boys, and now I'm telling you."

"What about Ma?"

"I haven't told her about it; don't want her to worry. I'll tell her in the morning."

His voice had a rough edge to it.

"Dad . . ."

"Don't argue. She's tired. Been here day and night. I finally talked her into going home tonight. If I tell her about the surgery, she'll insist on staying here. She's a good woman, Angel, but she's wearing herself out." His features softened. "Do this for me. Bring her in first thing in the morning. That's soon enough for her to know."

Angel disagreed but didn't say so. "What time is your surgery?"

"Eight."

Angel sighed. "I don't know." She eased her hand out of his grasp. "It's a cruel thing you're doing, not telling her."

"Why's it cruel? I'm doing her a favor. She'll get a good night's sleep. She'll be able to handle things better tomorrow."

"Okay. It's your call. I'll get her here before you go in." She leaned over and kissed his cheek, wondering what other secrets her father had. *Did you try to protect me too? Were you at the warehouse, Dad? Did you shoot Billy?* She chided herself for thinking it. There was no reason to suspect him. No reason at all.

Angel left her father's side and went to the waiting room. As the rest of the family gathered there, Anna invited everyone over to the house for ice cream and cookies. Angel, feeling overwhelmed and tired, declined. Minutes later, she and Rachael were headed for the car. Once they were buckled in, Rachael sighed heavily.

"What?" Angel gave her a sidelong glance.

"I was hoping you'd want dessert."

"Why didn't you say so? Are you hungry?"

"Not for food."

Angel almost choked. "Let me guess. You have a thing for Paul?"

Rachael shrugged. "He's so cute and sweet, and I was hoping to spend a little more time with him."

"You could've gone with them. I'm sure Paul would've been happy to take you home."

Rachael winced. "I didn't want to come off as being too forward."

"Okay, you win. We'll go to the house. Only I'm not staying long."

Rachael grinned. "Maybe you won't have to. Hmm, you could ask Paul to take me home. I wouldn't mind."

Angel laughed and shook her head. "Ask him yourself."

"Maybe I will."

★ ★ ★

Angel ended up spending the night. Not because she wanted to, but because she'd fallen asleep on the sofa and no one had bothered to wake her.

She awoke the next morning to the smells and sounds of bacon sizzling. Light filtered through the lace curtains in the living room window. She yawned and rubbed her eyes. It took her a few seconds to get her bearings. The night before, she'd eaten the ice cream and cookies with a cup of tea. The fire in the fireplace had made her sleepy, and she'd closed her eyes, intending to rest for a minute.

Angel tossed off the quilt someone had put over her and sat up. She rubbed her eyes again and ran fingers through her mop of thick curls. Someone, probably her mother, had placed a pillow under her head and taken off her shoes.

Angel padded to the kitchen. "Morning."

"Hi, sleepyhead." Anna turned and pointed her fork toward the already set table. "Help yourself to some juice. I'll have your French toast ready in a minute."

The table seated twelve and sat in the center of the kitchen, which seemed almost empty now with just her and Anna. The kitchen had always been a family gathering place, full of warm memories. Angel loved the room with its tile floors and high ceilings, and it was her mother's pride and joy. "The kitchen is the most important part of the house," Anna had said when the house was built. She'd wanted an Italian kitchen like her mother's in Italy.

Anna had a huge gas range and oven that were almost always in use. Most days savory aromas filled the kitchen and wafted into every room of the house. Two large windows faced southwest, letting in lots of light. On nice days, the sun streamed into the room to bless the flowers and herbs that grew on the counter. A wide archway led from the kitchen to the living room. Anna had more cupboard space than could be found in most mansions, and every inch was filled with dishes, utensils, pots and pans, and equipment that allowed her to create anything she wanted.

"You didn't have to make me breakfast." Angel felt a smidgeon of guilt, but she didn't offer to help. The kitchen was her mother's domain. Besides, her culinary skills were practically nonexistent.

"Of course, I did. You need to eat — we both do."

"Why didn't you wake me last night?"

Angel rubbed the back of her neck and sat down.

"I didn't have the heart. You were sleeping so soundly."

"What happened to Rachael?"

"Paul took her home. Neither of them seemed to mind." Anna wiped her hands on her apron and pulled down two melon-colored plates and covered each of them with two slices of French toast and two pieces of bacon. She smiled. "Nice girl, that Rachael. Paul could do worse."

"Ma, they just met." But she had to admit they did make a nice couple.

"Honey, the minute I laid eyes on your father, I knew I was going to marry him." Anna set one plate on the place mat in front of Angel and set hers down as well. Then she sat down, folded her hands, and said the familiar table grace.

When she'd finished, Angel reached for the strawberry freezer jam and spread some on one slice of French toast; on the other she drizzled maple syrup. She sliced off a bite of the one with jam and put it in her mouth. "Mmm." For a moment she lost herself in the delicate taste of berries and the hint of the cinnamon her mother always sprinkled into the batter. She missed her mother's breakfasts. Her own usually consisted of cold cereal — when she had milk. Or maybe a cinnamon roll from Brainard's bakery. But she wouldn't tell her mother that. Knowing Ma, she'd be over every morning to cook breakfast.

Wouldn't be such a bad thing. She missed the food and the conversation. Meals at the Delaney house had always been pretty rowdy, but in a good way.

Angel stuffed a bite of the syrupy French toast into her mouth. *You're a grown woman,* she reminded herself again. *You're living on your own. You don't need your mother to cook for you.*

Her father's words leaped into her mind. *"If anything happens to me, take care of your mother."* Her fork clattered to the table.

"Goodness, Angel, what's wrong?"

"What time is it?" Her gaze shot to the clock on the stove.

"Six."

"Oh." Angel picked up her fork and took several long breaths.

"What's wrong?"

"I just — I need to be somewhere by 7:00, that's all."

"So do I."

"You do? Where?" Angel frowned. She had to get her mother to the hospital.

"Your father is having surgery. I want to

270

get there before they take him in."

Angel coughed. "You knew?"

"Of course." She leaned over and placed a hand on Angel's arm. "How could you think I wouldn't know something that important? I talk to the doctors and the nurses." She drew her hand back. "Susan gave me the details."

"So you've known all along?"

"I knew before your father did."

"You two are something else. Dad didn't think you knew. He didn't want to worry you."

"Like he could stop me."

Angel finished the last bite of French toast and drank the rest of her juice. She took her dishes to the sink and refilled her coffee cup, then brought the carafe to the table, refilling her mother's as well.

"I should shower." Angel sipped at her coffee.

"Go ahead."

She carried her cup with her as she made her way through the living room and down the hall to what used to be her room. It was just as she'd left it, only cleaner. Having limited closet space in her apartment, Angel had stored clothes here that she seldom wore. When she opened the closet she noticed that her things had been moved to the far side to make room for shelves that stored plastic containers of blankets, pillows, and winter clothes. She sorted through the hangers and pulled out a pair of gray slacks and a white blouse. Anna had given them to her for Christmas last year. She had worn them once. Mostly, she wore jeans, rarely dressing up except for those few times she needed to. Those times were rare, since jeans were acceptable almost anytime, anywhere in the Northwest. She found some extra underwear in the dresser and headed for the bathroom.

Within twenty minutes she was ready to go. When she emerged from the bathroom, her mother was in the bedroom, setting a picture of herself and Frank on the dresser. Tears dripped down her cheeks. She brushed them away with the back of her hand.

"Ma?" Angel glanced around the room, grabbed a tissue from the box on the bedside table, and handed it to her mother.

"I . . ." Anna stopped to blow her nose. "I feel so foolish. I didn't want to cry."

"It's okay. You've been through a lot. Dad having a heart attack is pretty scary stuff."

Angel sat on the bed and pulled her

mother into her arms. She had never in all her twenty-six years seen her mother cry. Oh, maybe at weddings, but not like this. She hadn't even cried when Tim had his accident, unless she'd done it alone.

"Oh, Angel!" Anna tightened her grip on Angel's shoulders. "What if he doesn't make it? What am I going to do without my Frank?"

TWENTY-THREE

Anna Delaney was a strong woman; somehow Angel had always known that. But she hadn't really considered just how strong her mother was until she saw her that morning in pre-op. The earlier tears had dried, and she showed no signs of her former distress. But Angel knew how she must have felt inside; her own stomach felt as though vines had grown up overnight, curling and twisting her insides into a painful mass.

Anna leaned over Frank, holding his hand, reassuring him that he was healthy and strong and would make it through just fine.

Their former pastor, Dan Carmichael, who'd served at St. Matthew's until his retirement two years ago, came into the room. Anna stepped into his embrace. "Reverend Carmichael, thank you for coming."

"I'm happy to, Anna." He hugged her, then Angel, then shook Frank's hand. "I understand you're having a bypass. I came not only to pray with you but to offer hope. Had the same thing done two years ago, and I'm still going strong."

"Did you now?" Frank smiled broadly. "That's good to hear."

"I'm much healthier these days. Eating the right foods and exercising. I've even taken to working out at the gym. In fact, I run nearly every day. When you're ready to get back into your normal routine, you give me a call. We'll do some things together."

Frank nodded. "You really think I'll be able to run?"

"Oh, for certain. It'll take some time, mind you, but you'll be up and around before you know it."

"I hope so." Her father wove his thick fingers together and rested them on his stomach.

"See, honey." Anna squeezed his hand. "I told you there was nothing to worry about."

Angel wished she could be half as confident.

"They'll take good care of you here," Reverend Carmichael said. The pastor then offered to pray, so Angel bowed her head and listened. While he spoke, she hoped with all her heart that God was listening.

Tim arrived as Rev. Carmichael was getting ready to leave. The two priests greeted each other as old friends. Rev. Carmichael had been instrumental in helping Tim with his decision to become a pastor and getting him appointed to the church he was vacating.

When the doctor came in, the reverend said his good-byes. Tim walked out with him and came back a few minutes later. From there on things moved quickly. A woman in scrubs came in to administer some medication through Frank's IV that would relax him. Several minutes later, he was wheeled out.

Angel, Tim, and Anna went to the waiting room. Time seemed to stand still while they waited. Anna, far calmer than Angel thought she should be, picked up her bag and pulled out a fluffy pink bundle of yarn resembling cotton candy and began knitting. Probably something for one of Tim's girls. Tim left several times to visit other hospitalized parishioners.

Angel thumbed through old magazines. And paced, went to the cafeteria for a latte, came back, read some more, and paced.

"Sit with me for a few minutes, Angel." Her mother patted the chair beside her. "Tell me how things are going between you and Brandon."

"They're not really. He asked me to marry him and I said no."

"Hmm."

"What? You're not going to tell me what a fool I am for letting him slip away?"

Anna smiled. "He called your father and me a few weeks ago."

"He did?" Angel lowered herself into the chair her mother had indicated. "Why?"

"Wanted to know what we thought about his asking you to marry him."

"And you said?" Brandon hadn't said anything about talking to her parents.

"We told him that if and when you accepted his proposal, we'd welcome him into the family. I'm just curious about what happened."

"Nothing happened. Like I said, he asked me, and I said no."

Ma nodded, a knowing Mona Lisa smile curving her lips.

"What?"

"Nothing. I had a feeling you'd turn him down."

Angel picked up an old *People* magazine. "You don't seem disappointed. Where's the lecture you're always giving me about marrying Brandon and settling down?"

"I was wrong. For a while I thought you'd eventually marry him, but I can see now that Brandon isn't the man for you."

"Humph." Angel flipped the pages and tossed the magazine back down. "Why would you say that?"

"Because you aren't in love with him. If you were, you'd have married him months ago. He's more like your safety net."

Angel rolled her eyes and slumped in the chair until her neck rested on the back cushion. *My safety net?* "What do you mean by that?"

"Having Brandon around is a perfect excuse for you not to get involved with anyone else."

"You make it sound like I'm using him."

Anna peered over the half glasses she used for handwork. "Aren't you?"

Angel hadn't thought about it like that before.

When she didn't answer, Anna lowered her knitting. "Brandon loves you, or he thinks he does. All I'm saying is that if you have no intention of getting married, maybe you should break it off. Give him a chance to find someone who's right for him."

"I care about Brandon. He's a good friend."

"He's a sweet boy, and friendship is important in a marriage, but there is so much more." Anna set her knitting aside. "I don't expect you to take my advice, Angel. You seldom do, but just think about what I said."

"Okay." Angel sucked in a deep breath and got up, making the excuse that she had to use the rest room. She had to admit her mother had some valid points, and she would think about them. Just not right now.

When she came back to the waiting area, her mother had replaced the knitting with a devotional book called *Riding the Waves*. Angel was tempted to read it. She certainly could use some help staying afloat.

"How do you do it, Ma?" she finally asked. "How can you stay so calm when Dad's in there . . ." Her words were swallowed by a sob.

"Oh, honey." Anna put down the book and settled a hand on Angel's arm. "I'm only calm because God is giving me the strength and peace I need."

"But what if Dad dies? He could, you know."

"I know." Anna patted Angel's arm. "I

have thought of practically nothing else since the heart attack." She sighed, tears gathering in her eyes. "If he dies, and I pray he doesn't, we will grieve and we will go on as he would want us to. God will see us through this, Angel, just as he has everything else."

Angel covered her face. "If it were only that simple."

"It is that simple, honey. You trust God, and no matter what happens, you refuse to let your faith be shaken."

"Easy enough for you to say." Was that what had happened to her? Her faith certainly had been shaken more than once. She thought of Dani. Dani's faith had been like her mother's. The last words Angel had heard her say were in the form of a prayer. *"Heavenly Father, don't let any of those children be harmed."*

"Oh, Angel. What happened to you?"

Angel closed her eyes and began to tell her mother about Dani. She could still hear the sirens and feel the tightness in her chest as they entered the day care through the back door, hoping to surprise the man who'd taken a worker and six children hostage. Two other police officers were supposed to come in from the front. The man must've heard them as he stepped into the hallway at the same moment Dani did. He fired twice and ducked back into the room with the children and their caregiver, shouting at the police to stay away or he'd kill them all.

Angel saw one of the bullets rip into Dani's forehead, the other into her neck, hitting the carotid artery. Dani staggered back and fell into Angel's arms. She heard another shot and dragged Dani into one of the empty rooms. Blood oozed out of the neck wound, and Angel pressed her hands against the wound to try to stop it.

"Don't die. Please don't die. God, help her. Why don't you help her?" Her prayers were as futile as her efforts to stop the bleeding. Dani had died the moment the bullet entered her skull.

"It's too late, Angel." Another officer pulled her away from Dani's body.

"So that's it, Ma." Angel wiped away her tears with her hand. "When the shooter went back into the room, a member of the S.W.A.T. team got a clear shot and killed him. The ordeal was over, and Dani was dead."

"My poor baby." Anna slipped an arm around Angel's shoulders. "So that's why you left Florida. Why didn't you ever tell us?"

"I couldn't." She looked at her mother through tear-glazed eyes. "Why couldn't it have been me? Why Dani? She believed in God, and he let her die."

"Oh, honey. Such a terrible thing. But God didn't pull the trigger, that horrid man did. Dani sounds like a wonderful woman."

"She was."

"I'll bet she's in heaven right now wishing you could see this as she does."

"What do you mean?" Angel took the tissue her mother handed her and blew her nose.

"You and Dani distracted that man and gave the other officers an opening. Dani prayed for the children, and her prayer was answered. None of the children was injured, you said. Think of how happy that must've made Dani."

"But why her? Why Dani?"

"I don't know. Why is one life taken and another spared? Look at Tim's accident. He lived, his friends died." Anna shrugged. "All I can say is that God sees the whole. We only see a small part. I've learned not to ask so many questions of God. It's hard sometimes, but there's a Bible verse that helps me sort it through. 'God works all things for good . . .'"

" 'For those who love and serve the Lord.' " Angel sighed. "I know. I just wish . . ." She pinched the bridge of her nose. "Why does life have to be so complicated?"

Anna rubbed her daughter's neck and back. "Thank you for telling me about her."

Angel didn't respond. What more could she say? She wasn't sure why she'd confided in her mother, but as painful as the telling had been, she felt better knowing her mother shared the burden. God *had* answered Dani's prayer to save the children. And thinking of Dani being in heaven gave Angel a better perspective. She determined she would use that image when she thought of her friend, not the one where Dani lay dead in her arms.

Tim came back at 1:00, and at about the same time the doctor emerged from the operating room to tell them everything had gone well with the surgery. "We'll keep him in recovery for an hour or two then transfer him to his room."

When he'd gone, Tim turned to them. "Have you eaten?"

"No," Angel answered, "but you two go ahead. I need to get home."

Her mother looked disappointed. "What's

going on that you can't stay here a little longer?"

"I have something important to do." Angel didn't think it would be a good idea to tell them what she was really doing. They might try to talk her out of it, and they would probably succeed. A funeral was the last place she wanted to be. But she had to say good-bye to the boy whose life she'd so tragically ended.

At her apartment, Angel pulled her hair into a tight bun, wrapped her head in a black silk scarf, and slipped on a pair of dark sunglasses. Fortunately the sun was out, so the glasses wouldn't draw attention. She figured no one would notice her, since the place would be crawling with media people. Before leaving, she took a long look at herself in the mirror, pleased with the transformation.

Angel parked nearly a block away and got to the cemetery just as the graveside service began. The cemetery was located on a hilly area at the northeast corner of Sunset Cove. She stayed at the back of the crowd on a knoll where she could see the proceedings clearly, placing herself near a thin, gray-haired man who wore a long, straggly ponytail and beard and carried a camera.

Her heart did a little flip when she spied a familiar face. Detective Riley stood off to one side, leaning against a tree, his arms folded, his gaze scanning the crowd. That cool gaze landed on Angel, lingered a moment, then moved away. Had he recognized her?

She turned back to the green canvas awning stretched over the stands of flowers, the shiny blue casket, and the gaping hole where the casket would be lowered at the end of the service. Her heart ached for the family as they huddled together near the grave. The mother and several other women sat in folding chairs. Grandmothers, aunts, cousins, uncles, she supposed. And friends. There had to be a hundred people there, along with members of the press who'd come to gather more grist for their gossip mills.

I'm sorry, Billy. More than anything I wish I could change the past and fix it so Sunday had never happened.

A woman wailed. Billy's mother? Angel needed to visit the woman to apologize in person. Not today. Probably not tomorrow but someday.

A short stout man wearing a clerical shirt and collar and a black suit stood on a platform behind a lectern. His powerful voice began expounding on Billy Dean Hartwell's virtues.

Hallelujahs and amens rose from the crowd.

"It is hard to see a child die, and when that death is a violent death — a death that could have been avoided — well, sisters and brothers, that's even harder. It's natural to want to seek revenge, but I'll tell you, revenge is not the answer. It breaks my heart to hear that the officer responsible for Billy's death has been targeted — her home torn apart. I pray that none of you fine people was responsible. I would remind you that the place to fight injustice and racism is in the courts, not on the streets."

Angel felt the hairs rise up on the back of her neck and arms. She had the feeling someone was watching her, but she looked around and didn't see anyone suspicious.

"Brothers and sisters," the reverend continued, "we must not repay evil for evil. Our job is not to hate, not to do harm. Our job is to love and forgive. When a wrong is done to us, we must let the Lord punish the wrongdoer. Vengeance is mine, saith the Lord."

A small scattering of amens told Angel many of them didn't agree. She knew the minister was right. They shouldn't be going after her. But she disagreed with his implication that what she had done was evil.

The reverend spoke a little more about Billy and his life and how he had died serving others, citing that Billy's reason for being in the pharmacy that day was to pick up a prescription of insulin for his diabetic grandmother.

Angel tuned him out, wondering again how she could have misread Billy's intentions. Had she misjudged him? How would she ever be able to trust her judgment again?

At the end of the service, Billy's mother tossed a yellow rose onto the casket as it was lowered into the ground. Angel's vision blurred with the onset of tears. When the pastor began a final prayer, she walked back to her car. As she pulled out of the parking place, she heard someone shouting. Glancing back toward the cemetery, she saw several men running toward her, and behind them, the media. Were they after her? How could they have known?

The car. They recognize my car. How could I have been so stupid? She hit the steering wheel with the palm of her hand. Heart hammering, she locked her doors and drove into the street.

Shouting obscenities, one of the men jumped on the hood of the car and hammered at the windshield with his fists. Angel's foot hit the brake. The car lurched and died. Bodies slammed against the car on all sides. One man had somehow gotten hold of a rock and slammed it against the passenger side window. Angel screamed and ducked.

They were going to kill her — drag her out of the car and beat her to death.

TWENTY-FOUR

Angel heard the screams and shouts of the onlookers, then the distant sounds of sirens. The voices faded as the sirens screamed with increasing intensity. *Thank you, God.*

Angel screamed again when a hand shot through the broken window and grabbed at her hair. He pulled off her scarf, taking a handful of hair with it. Tears stung her eyes. She clutched at her head and sank her teeth into his arm. He growled obscenities, and with his teeth bared, he reached for her again. Angel moved as far away from him as she could.

Her assailant's features went from rage to surprise when someone yanked him backwards. Eric flattened him against the car and snapped on cuffs, then read him his rights.

On the passenger side, Bo grabbed the man with a tire iron and spun him around.

The guy turned and swung. Bo ducked and shoved a fist into his face, then brought his arm down on the man's wrist, disarming him.

An officer yelled above the chaos, "Put down your weapons and step away from the car!" Angel recognized the voice as Nick's.

One by one the attackers raised their hands. Angel gripped the steering wheel and leaned her forehead on her fists.

"Angel?" Detective Riley leaned in the driver's side window, releasing the lock and opening the door.

Angel tumbled out and flew into his arms, burying her face in his chest. She wanted to thank him, but nothing came out except for the choking sobs.

"Are you hurt?"

"I . . . I don't think so."

Detective Riley led her away from her battered Corvette to his unmarked Crown Victoria and helped her into the passenger side. "Stay here. I need to help round these guys up. I'll be right back."

Angel had no intention of moving. She held her fist to her mouth, afraid to take it away. She tried to slow her breathing down and look at the incident objectively, as if someone other than herself had been the victim. Her fellow officers were still making arrests. Most of the crowd had backed away and stood on the sidelines.

The media, of course, had their microphones hot and their cameras rolling. For once she was almost glad to see them. Their photos would document the assault. Angel wondered if it would change the public's opinion of her. On the other hand, the media had a way of making the police look bad. She adjusted her sunglasses and lifted her right hand to her brow to block a photographer's shot.

She heard the driver's side door open, and Detective Riley folded himself into the seat. Her hands shook as she ran them through her hair.

"You okay?" he asked. "Should I call an ambulance?"

"No. I'm just shook up." *Shook up? I'm terrified.*

"Our guys will haul these creeps down to the station. I assume you're going to press charges?"

"Of course." She reached for her seat belt. "They were going to kill me."

"And might have, too, if I hadn't been there to call for backup." The detective turned the key in the ignition and turned around to check for traffic. "You're lucky

I recognized you."

Angel frowned. "You did?"

"You'd have to do a lot more than wrap your hair in a scarf and wear glasses to fool me."

"Then I'm glad you were here."

"You shouldn't have come." He seemed angry, and Angel couldn't tell if his anger was directed at her, her attackers, or himself.

But she bristled at his parental tone. "You're probably right, but I had to. I don't expect you to understand."

"What's not to understand? You wanted to pay your respects. I might've done the same thing."

Angel gasped as they drove past her Corvette. "My car looks like it's been in a demolition derby."

"Nick is calling a tow truck to haul your car into the impound lot. We'll need it for evidence."

A man from the crowd shouted at them as Riley started to pull out. "Racist pigs!" He came into the street and slammed his fist against the passenger side window. "Killer cop!"

Detective Riley was out of the car and on him before he could finish the sentence. He whipped the guy around, slamming

292

him against the car. Not an easy feat, since the guy must've weighed close to three hundred pounds.

The man cried out as the detective yanked his wrist around and pulled it sharp against his back. "Do that again and I might forget I'm a cop!" Riley then shoved him in Bo's direction. "You'd better take this scumbag before I do something I'll regret."

"I hear you, man." Bo slapped the cuffs on the guy, mirandized him, and put him into his patrol car. "I'll take it from here."

Detective Riley got back into the car. His hands gripped the steering wheel as he stared straight ahead. After a few seconds and several calming breaths, he drove out onto the main road.

"You were a little rough on him," Angel said.

"Don't remind me."

Callen wasn't certain what had happened in those few minutes. Seeing those guys on Angel's car had turned his blood hot. He very seldom got riled to the point where he'd manhandle anyone. But he'd been blindsided, and all he could think of was protecting her. He glanced at Angel, angry with himself for caring and angry with her for being there.

He'd gone to the cemetery to observe the crowd and maybe get some clue as to what was going on. He'd asked both Nick Caldwell and Mike Rawlings to come too. He'd wanted them to look around and see if they spotted any of the gang members who had hit the pharmacy. He hadn't gotten a chance to ask them. He'd do that later. Right now his biggest problem was sitting beside him.

She was safe — at least for the time being. There was something a lot bigger than a burglary and the deadly force situation going on here. Angel's apartment had been vandalized, and she'd just escaped being beaten to death. Callen had no doubt they would've killed her if they hadn't been stopped when they were. He thanked God he and the other officers had been close by.

Angel tipped her head back against the headrest and looked at him. "Thanks."

He nodded. "Just doing my job."

Angel sighed. "I . . . I'm not sure I want to press charges. It'll just make the situation worse. They already hate me. Maybe they have nothing to do with the gang. Maybe they're just family members trying to get revenge." She remembered the pastor's sermon cautioning them against the use of violence.

"I don't think loss is a factor. I doubt these guys were even part of the family. They're more than likely opportunists, taking advantage of the situation."

Angel turned to look out the window.

"You can't let them get away with this, Angel. I'll take you down to the station. You can give your statement and take a look at the guys who attacked you."

The idea made her stomach ache. She changed the subject. "I have to get another car."

"You can call a rental agency. My truck is in the shop, otherwise I'd loan it to you."

"Thanks, but it's my problem. I'll take care of it."

"You shouldn't be alone, you know." Callen frowned. "These guys will probably be out by tomorrow. Do you have any place you could hide out for a few days?"

"You may be right. Maybe I'll take the twins up on their offer and stay at their resort."

Callen raised his eyebrows. "Twins? Resort?"

Angel told him about her brothers and their new resort.

"Sounds like a nice place. Don't suppose

they'd have an extra room for a worn-out cop."

She smiled as though she might not mind his company. "We could ask."

The thought of staying at the same resort with her was far too appealing. And far too impossible. He had to change the subject, and fast. "How did things go with Joe yesterday?"

She turned slightly in her seat. "Not good. They want me up on man one."

"No way." Callen couldn't believe they'd actually go that far.

Angel leaned back and stared out the window.

"Guess I shouldn't be surprised," he said. "The public has been leaning pretty hard on us lately. Every time we have to use deadly force, they turn against us. Look at the incident last month when that psycho kidnapped his son and threatened to kill him. Officers shot the guy, and his family threw a fit. He wasn't armed, but our guys didn't know that."

"Yeah, we do our job and then have to take the criticism. It's not fair." Angel sighed then looked over at him again. "I should've waited — with Billy, I mean. I should've tried to talk to him first. Maybe then I would've seen that his gun wasn't real."

"You indicated that he was a threat. The gun could have been real. Then it would've been your funeral. I can't say what I would've done in the same situation, but from what you said in your testimony, I doubt that any police officer would've acted differently."

"I appreciate that, Detective."

Callen pulled up in front of the police station. "Good, now do the right thing and file charges against the hoods who messed up that great car of yours."

He waited until she stepped inside before driving off. He was beginning to feel like a hooked fish on a line. The more he fought, the more securely the hook embedded itself. Angel was reeling him in bit by bit, and Callen was willing to bet that she had no idea she was holding the pole.

At the station, Angel gave her account of the attack. By the time she'd finished, anger had replaced the fear. How dare they ruin her car? She loved that car. And what would Luke say? It would cost a fortune to have it fixed. People could be mad at her, but they had no business breaking into her home or destroying her property — and they had no business threatening her life. She wasn't certain what had prompted her to consider not taking action against the men who'd attacked her. Nerves, maybe. Or fear that they'd come after her again.

Well, let them. She'd go after them until they either killed her or were put away for a long time. Callen had been right in advising her to press charges. He had been right about a lot of things. She thought back to his remark about coming to the resort with her and wondered what it would be like to spend some time with him without the pressures of the criminal investigation.

Since Eric was on his way out when Angel left, she asked him to drop her off at the hospital. Her father was doing well. His color looked good, in spite of all the tubes and wires. Still, her mother insisted on spending the night and insisted Angel go home and get a good night's rest.

For once she obeyed her mother.

Brandon dropped by Angel's apartment at 6:00 that night, bringing another bouquet of roses.

"What's this, a peace offering?" Angel asked.

"I figured you needed some new ones." He leaned down and kissed her cheek as though nothing had changed between them. "How are you?"

"Things could be better." She stepped

aside to let him in.

"I heard about your run-in at the cemetery today." His brow furrowed and worry lit his blue eyes. "When I saw that footage I couldn't believe it. I . . . I should have been there with you."

Angel went to him, and they held each other for a long time. It felt good to be held and comforted, but her mother's words drifted around in her head. *You don't love him. You're using him.*

Brandon took a step back. "Does this mean I'm forgiven?"

She looked at him and raised up on her toes to kiss his cheek. "You haven't done anything wrong, and I don't blame you for your father's decision." She was feeling magnanimous in light of the fact that she now had a terrific lawyer.

"I just wish there was something I could do." Brandon sighed.

"You can. Just be a friend."

"I can handle that." He settled on the couch. "Where did all this furniture come from? I thought your stuff got trashed."

"It did. I have no clue who did this. I came home the other day, and it was all here. There was no note or anything. My family denies having anything to do with it. Was it you?"

A blush crept up Brandon's neck. "I wish it had been. I'm sorry, I didn't even think about you having to replace everything."

"Don't worry about it." Angel stood with her hands on her hips, looking around the room again. There were things she hadn't noticed before, like the blue marbled glass ball that sat on the end table. "I'll figure it out."

"What are you going to do about a car?" Brandon asked.

"Rent one, I guess."

"You can borrow one of ours. Or I can lend you our limo driver. Dad and I never use him unless it's to impress some wealthy client. Mom uses him a lot, but I'm sure she won't mind."

"I don't want a limo driver." Angel shook her head. "I can see it now. I'm shopping at Goodwill and telling him to wait outside." She chuckled at the thought. "But thanks. I'll get a rental. My insurance will cover it — I hope."

"Then use my car."

"No, it's fine. I'll figure out something."

Brandon sighed. "Okay, you don't want to talk about it. I can take a hint."

Angel sat down beside him. "Tell me about the Kelsey case. How's it going?"

"Not good. Kelsey's body turned up today."

"Really? Where?"

"A tourist spotted him at the bottom of a ravine up toward Cannon Beach. Saw the body through binoculars." Brandon settled an arm on the back of the sofa, his hand touching Angel's hair.

Angel moved forward slightly, and Brandon's arm dropped to his side.

"He'd been shot, and he either fell over the cliff or someone pushed him."

"Michelle?"

"I don't know. She still claims she didn't kill him. The guys from the crime lab are going over the area, so we should have some answers before long."

"Are you still going to represent her?" Angel asked.

"Yeah. I just hope she's leveling with me."

The phone rang, and Angel got up to answer it. Big mistake. The caller issued forth an assortment of vile names, some of which she had never heard before. As a police officer, she was used to hearing vulgarities, and at times even had them directed at her, but it wasn't his words that twisted her stomach. It was the threats that went with them. Her hand shook as she slammed the receiver down.

Brandon stood up and came toward her. "What's wrong?"

She could almost feel the blood drain out of her face. "It was an obscene caller," she managed to say. "He threatened to kill me."

TWENTY-FIVE

Angel wasn't used to being the victim, and she didn't like it. *God, what's happening to me? I'm a police officer. I shouldn't be letting these guys upset me like this.*

"I'm scared, Brandon," Angel admitted. "These guys mean business. I pressed charges against them. I don't know, they . . . they're like the mafia and I . . . well, I guess I don't know how to fight back."

"You don't have to. The police are supposed to do that."

But I am a cop! Or was.

"Let's get out of here." Brandon took her hand and pulled her down the hallway toward the door.

"Where to?"

"I don't know. We'll drive up to the house. I want your opinion on something. Maybe we can get something to eat after and walk on the beach."

Angel grabbed her jacket. Getting out seemed like a good idea, regardless of where they ended up. "I'm not changing my mind. About the house, I mean."

"I'm not asking you to."

Brandon had parked at the north end of the parking lot, so by walking along the upper deck to the stairs at the far end of the building, they were able to escape the press and quite possibly the caller.

Once on the road, she breathed a little easier. Several times she checked to see if they were being followed, but in the darkness it was hard to tell. For a long stretch, there was no one behind them — at least as far as she could see. She probably should have reported the call, but what good would that have done? She'd tell Detective Riley about it in the morning. Besides, she and Brandon would be safe out at the house.

That's not quite true, is it? You're really not safe anywhere. Angel shook her head, refusing to give in to her fears and choosing instead to keep her mind on Brandon and the house.

Brandon's place was as magnificent as she remembered and looked even better now that he had started furnishing it.

"What do you think?" He nodded toward the leather sofa and chairs. "My mom helped me pick them out."

"They're very nice. Earthy. You'll need more color though." He'd brought a watercolor from his collection at home and placed it on one wall. Soft rose tones and lavenders depicted a horse and rider at sunset. "I'd probably pick up some pillows that match the colors in the painting."

He nodded. "Good idea. I got some rattan furniture for the solarium." They walked through the great room to the solarium. The room was shadowed by plants, the only light coming from a spotlight that lighted the area around the Jacuzzi. Just before Brandon put on overhead lights, Angel thought she saw a shadow moving away from the shrubbery.

Probably an animal. A panel of spotlights lined one of the frames in the ceiling. Except for the back wall, the entire room was made up of glass panels and doors. Angel imagined the room in daylight with sun streaming in. Colorful tropical print cushions accented the white rattan furniture. Two chairs and two chaises.

"I love it." The room was elegant yet practical and made a wonderful greenhouse. The ceiling fan with its wide, leaflike arms would cool the room when the sun overheated it. She lowered herself onto the chaise lounge and put her feet up, luxuriating in the feel of the thick cushions beneath her. "Nice." She leaned back and closed her eyes.

Angel almost wished she could say yes to Brandon's proposal. If he asked her now, she might. It was tempting to let herself flow with the tide — to get married and have children. *But you don't love him, Angel.*

Of course I do. He's kind and decent and loyal.

So is a pet.

"I have a feeling I'll be spending a lot of time out here," Brandon said.

You're using him. Angel felt a flash of annoyance at her mother. Why did she have to poke her nose into something that was none of her business?

"It's relaxing and lets in a lot of light," Brandon went on. "I have air-conditioning to keep it cool even with the hot afternoon sun."

"I'm glad you bought the house. It suits you." Reluctantly, Angel got to her feet, afraid that if she didn't she might never want to leave.

"Where are you going?" He got up as well.

"Um — nowhere. I'm just feeling restless."

Angel flipped off the lights and stood at the sliding glass doors, letting her eyes adjust to the darkness, admiring the sparkling lights of Sunset Cove. Above them, the moon showed its brilliant face in a cool white, with shadows of a smile. "You have a spectacular view."

He draped an arm around her shoulder and drew her close. For a moment she thought he was going to kiss her. She thought about letting him. He didn't. Nor did he remind her that she could have the view and everything that went with it if she changed her mind. And as much as Angel wanted the security Brandon offered, she couldn't bring herself to alter the course she'd taken. Turning him down had been the right choice. She loved Brandon as a friend, and she doubted it would ever be anything more.

Looks like you were right, Ma. She smiled, realizing she'd acknowledged that more than once in the past couple days.

Brandon moved away. "I have some drinks in the fridge. Want anything?"

"Just some water, thanks." She stayed where she was a few moments longer, wishing Brandon would come back and wondering why she insisted on torturing herself like this. Wavering wasn't usually part of her game plan. But the shooting and everything associated with it had set her reeling, and she couldn't seem to find her footing.

Angel took a long drink of the water he handed her. "So when are you moving in?"

He shrugged. "I'm in no hurry."

She yawned. "Oh, sorry."

"Tired?" Brandon guided her back into the great room.

"Exhausted."

"It's no wonder with all you've been through lately. I'm not too excited about you staying alone though — not while the creep who called you is on the loose."

"I'll keep my gun under my pillow." No, she wouldn't. Her gun had been stolen out of the evidence locker. And the goons that had vandalized her apartment had Nick's.

"Not good enough. What if there's more than one? I'll stay. I'll sleep out on your couch. And if you won't let me do that, I'll camp outside your door all night."

Angel grinned at the thought of Brandon Lafferty sitting on her doorstep in his polo shirt and his designer jeans and leather jacket.

"You can have the couch." She didn't

have the heart or the strength to argue. Besides, the thought of Brandon being there gave her a measure of comfort.

You're using him, Angel.

Angel ignored the pestering voice. She'd been going with Brandon for a long time and wasn't about to break it off now — not until she felt certain it was the right thing to do.

When Angel got up the next morning, Brandon was gone. He'd made coffee for her and set the newspaper on the table beside his car keys and a note.

Angel, I had Carl pick me up this morning. Use my car. That's an order. And be careful. I'll call you later. Love, Brandon.

She poured her coffee and picked up the paper. The headlines bore her name again. Someone had snapped a photo of her at the funeral and in the car with the gang of thugs pummeling it. While the photo of her car being beaten up might've brought a shred of sympathy for her in the public eye, the article below would nullify it.

A well-known white supremacist had called Angel's actions "commendable." The article quoted the man as saying, "The world will be better off with one less street kid who would (if he wasn't one already) become a gang member."

Angel groaned. "Great. This is all I need." She rolled up the paper and threw it against the wall. Then she poured mini shredded wheat into a bowl with milk, peeled a banana, and sliced it over the top. As she ate her breakfast and tried to calm down, she realized she was looking forward to seeing her shrink. Janet had penciled her in for Friday at 11:00, and she intended to go. Today was the day, she decided. This time she'd let Janet do her hypnosis thing. Maybe she'd remember details about the shooting. She had to try.

Too early for her appointment, Angel drove to the beach and parked Brandon's Lexus at an angle that gave her a clear view of the coastline north and south. Another sunny day. She'd worn a white sweater with jeans and Reeboks. She removed the sweater and tossed it into the backseat, then locked the car and headed toward the water. The tide was out, leaving the sand firm and perfect for exploring.

Angel walked for about a mile, stopping to pick up agates and looking for shells. When she returned to the car, she realized she still had a thirty-minute wait. After watching a couple with a kid and a kite exit their van, she leaned back against the headrest and closed her eyes.

In the distance a dog barked. A child laughed. Angel's eyes drifted open, and she stared at the beach beyond the windshield. The child laughed again, running with a kite twice his size. A young couple, probably his parents, urged him on.

Did Billy ever fly a kite?

The wind lifted the rainbow-colored kite out of the boy's hands and carried it several yards before depositing it in the sand. Undaunted, the child tried again. This time the kite sailed higher and higher until it danced in the air currents, bound only by an invisible thread.

Angel rubbed her eyes with her palms and dragged her hands down her face. The clock on the dash read 10:45. She had an appointment with Janet at 11:00. She started her car and backed out of the parking space.

Minutes later she was lying on a couch under a blanket, listening to quiet music with the sound of rain. Janet's soft voice guided her into a relaxed state.

Her eyelids felt heavy — too heavy to open. The past few days began playing in her mind like scenes from a movie, the images as vivid as they had been on Sunday morning. She saw herself following Billy into the warehouse and saw him raise his weapon. She brought up her gun and took aim.

In an instant the scene changed.

Angel was twelve. Billy's age. Tears streamed down her face as she held the rifle across her lap. She didn't want to learn to shoot anymore — didn't want to use a gun ever again.

Angel sat up and pushed the blanket aside.

"It's not helping. I remembered everything except the shooting."

"It takes time. And you did remember some things."

"I'm sorry. I feel like I'm wasting your time and mine. I thought it was going to happen. I remembered seeing Billy and raising my gun — then all of a sudden I'm a kid and I'm crying and I'm scared. I don't understand what it's all about. It's almost like I'm afraid of guns, but I'm not. How crazy is that? I'm a police officer."

Janet nodded. "Being a police officer doesn't mean you can't be afraid."

"I don't *want* to remember my childhood. I just want to remember the shooting."

"Maybe the memories are somehow linked."

"How?"

Janet shrugged. "We won't know that until you remember them. Don't try to force the memories or stop them. Let yourself drift through them."

Angel fell back against the cushions. She hadn't been truthful with Janet. She did have a fear of guns — maybe not a fear exactly, more like an aversion. But she had forced herself to use them. "This isn't getting me anywhere."

"Give it time. Would you like to make another appointment?"

Angel sighed. "I'll think about it."

On the drive home, Angel thought about her first encounter with a gun. She'd been ten years old when her father had finally taught her to shoot. She'd gotten a hunting rifle for her birthday, and she remembered being thrilled, thinking that now she and her father would have something they could do together. Frank had been happy for her; he'd wanted to go out right away and teach her how to shoot. Her excitement hadn't lasted very long though. He helped her hold the heavy weapon up, placed the butt against her shoulder. When it went off, she screamed. It kicked hard enough to knock her down. Anna had said she was too small for a gun that size, but Frank insisted that if she was going to shoot, she'd do it right. He wiped her tears then made her pick up the rifle and fire again and again.

Angel hated the gun and the noise but determined then and there she would not complain. Her father didn't want a cry-baby. He wanted his kids to be tough.

Now she wondered if the pain of firing the rifle could have been enough to cause her stomach to tighten in knots whenever she had to shoot. She tried to remember more details about the shooting but couldn't. Janet had told her to be patient — easier said than done. The OSP crime lab should've been able to determine exactly what had happened, but now with the stolen evidence, all she had was her memory — an apparently faulty one at that.

Angel bypassed her apartment when she saw the mob waiting in the parking lot and headed for the hospital. Peter and Paul accosted her in the waiting room. "We're taking you to the resort," Paul said. "No argument."

"You need a break from all of this." Peter hooked an arm around her neck.

"We all think it's a great idea." Paul seemed more animated than usual. Angel suspected it was because of a certain lawyer.

"We'll even kidnap Brandon if you want." Peter chuckled and released her.

"Don't you dare."

Paul shook his head in disgust. "We're supposed to protect our little sister, not lead her astray."

Peter grinned and shrugged. "Just trying to help."

Angel surprised them by agreeing. "You're right. I do need to get away."

"Wow. That was easy. We didn't even have to bribe you with our best suite."

She hugged both of them. "I love you guys, you know that?"

"Yeah. We know. Now get in there and see Dad, then we're leaving."

At the resort, the twins treated her to a wonderful dinner of filet mignon and lobster. After dinner they escorted her to her room. "You should be safe here on the premises. We have a security guard on duty all the time." Peter opened the door and handed her the key.

"Use your safety lock though," Paul cautioned.

Peter clipped her on the chin. "The place is all yours. We'll be heading for the pool and hot tub area in an hour or so if you want to join us."

Angel yawned. "Thanks, but I think I'll just curl up on the sofa and watch television for a while, then go to bed."

She tried watching TV for about an hour, but nothing held her attention and she began pacing. Then she figured the best cure for nerves was a walk on the beach. From her window on the second floor, even the dark surf looked inviting. She slipped on her athletic shoes, pocketed her key, and stepped into the hall. When she got to the sand, she began having second thoughts about heading out alone, so she went back inside, thinking to track down Peter or Paul. Maybe one of them would run with her.

Since they'd mentioned something about swimming, she headed for the pool area. The lodge had two pools, one inside and one out on the patio area. Her brothers weren't in the indoor pool, so she headed through the lobby, past the enormous fireplace, and outside where the underwater lights and blue tiles made the water glisten.

Passing the bar, Angel noticed several couples. At a table close to the wall she spotted two African-American men. One had his back to her. The other glanced up as she walked by and nodded as if he knew her. She couldn't place him, but then again, maybe she'd never met him. He may have just recognized her from the recent television broadcasts and the papers. Then she noticed he was wearing a clerical collar, and suddenly she remembered where she knew him from. He was the minister who had officiated at Billy's funeral.

She stopped, feeling a moment's panic. What were they doing here? Had they come to confront her?

She shook her head. *You have to stop thinking that way.* The reverend didn't seem angry or out for revenge. He merely turned back to the man he'd been talking to. She relaxed. *Get a grip, Angel. Not every African-American wants you dead, for goodness sake.*

She found her brothers in the outdoor Jacuzzi.

"Hey, Angel, come join us." Peter waved her over. "We just got in."

"Thanks, but no. I was thinking about going for a run."

"Not by yourself," Paul said, taking on a parental tone.

"Sheesh, don't worry. I was hoping I could talk one or both of you into going with me." She folded herself onto the chaise.

"Count me out. I'm going to veg in the tub and head for my room." Peter leaned back, apparently enjoying the pulsing jets on his back and shoulders.

"How is your room?" Paul asked.

"Awesome. You two are spoiling me. How am I supposed to go back to my mundane apartment after all this?"

"We're here to serve," Paul said. "Speaking of service, why don't you sign up with our massage therapist? She said she could work you in tomorrow if you're interested."

"She'll whittle all your worries into toothpicks." Peter rubbed his shoulder and winced. "Wish she were here right now."

"Sounds wonderful." Angel tipped back her head to look at the clear sky. Millions of stars glittered and winked against the inky black night.

"What are brothers for?" Peter flicked water at her. "Besides, you've had a rough time of it. We want to help."

Paul ducked his head under the water and popped back up. The jets looked inviting.

"Hey, guys, if I go up and get my suit,

will you still be here when I come back?"

"Sure."

"Give me ten minutes."

Angel made her way back through the lobby. As she passed the bar, she noticed that the two men she'd seen before were gone. An odd feeling rolled around in the pit of her stomach. She put her uneasiness aside.

She hurried up to her room, changed into her swimsuit, and slipped on the thick white terry cloth robe the resort provided, then headed back out. The lobby was quiet when she went back through it, but then it was nearly 11:00. She followed the same path she'd taken before, meandering through the manicured shrubs and lawn. She had almost reached the pool area when she thought she heard something up ahead. Her heart leaped to her throat. She glanced around but saw nothing.

Angel went on, noting that one of the footlights was out. She made a mental note to tell the twins. Her foot hit something, and she pitched forward. Her arms shot out to break her fall. She expected to connect with dirt and gravel; instead, she landed on something soft and hard.

Fabric.

Flesh.

Her eyes grew more accustomed to the darkness. She pushed herself up and found herself looking into the wide, staring eyes of a dead man.

TWENTY-SIX

Angel rolled off the body and scrambled to her feet. Gasping for breath, she glanced around for the man's assailant. When she saw no one, she swallowed hard and forced herself to look at the victim.

It was the man she'd seen in the lounge earlier. His throat had been slit. The small white square of a clerical collar was now stained red. She hunkered down beside him, trying to think and act like the police officer she was — or used to be.

"What's going on?"

She looked up and saw Peter skidding to a stop. Paul nearly plowed into him. "Was that you screaming?"

Their disbelieving gazes shifted from Angel to the dead man and back again. She hadn't realized she'd screamed. "I guess it was."

Peter's mouth hung open. "Angel.

What have you done?"

"I haven't done anything." She straightened her robe and pulled the belt securely around her waist. Looking down, she could see splotches of blood on her hands and the white robe.

"You'd better call the police," she said in as calm a voice as she could manage. "He's been murdered."

She started to reach inside the victim's jacket for ID, then stopped. She had been relieved of her duties. The wise thing would be to wait and let the responding officer deal with it.

Brandy and Mike responded first; seconds later, Callen showed up. His hard gaze swept over the scene and caught Angel's eye for just a moment. Then he took charge, asking Mike to begin the questioning process and Brandy to take the photographs. After securing the crime scene and ordering a crew from the crime lab, Callen drew Angel aside.

He glanced toward the body and the officer taking photos. "What happened?"

She stared at the darkening stains on her robe. "I'd just gone up to my room to change around 10:45 — he wasn't here then, but when I came out to join my brothers in the Jacuzzi, I, um . . . I tripped over him."

"Any idea who he is?"

"I saw him in the lounge earlier with another guy. He's the pastor who officiated at Billy's funeral."

Callen jotted something down in his notebook. "The victim's name is the Reverend Todd Elroy Dixon," he said. "What do you know about him?"

"Not much." Angel swallowed back the lump lodged in her throat. "I remember reading about him in the paper. He's a televangelist, well known, I guess, though I'd never heard of him before this. He flew in from Atlanta right after the, um, shooting to meet Billy's family."

"I read that too," Callen said.

"He was probably advising the family to file a civil suit against me." She glanced up to catch him studying her. Once again she looked away. She didn't like him seeing her like this. "You're probably going to want to talk to the guy I saw him with."

Callen poised his pen above his notepad. "Can you give me a name?"

"No — not for sure. But I have a hunch it was Ray Broadman."

"The Hartwell kid's uncle." Callen raised an eyebrow. "The guy who's trying to turn the shooting into a racial incident?"

"Yeah. That's him."

Callen's blue-green gaze penetrated hers, making her look away. "We need to get photos of you and take that robe and your swimsuit."

She closed her eyes and nodded. This was the second time in less than a week she'd had to turn bloody clothes over for evidence. What was Callen thinking? Did he suspect her? She couldn't blame him if he did. She had the victim's blood all over her, and worse, the man was connected to Billy's family. "Do I need to call my lawyer?" she asked.

"Have you done anything you need a lawyer for?"

"No. It's just that with the relationship between Reverend Dixon and Billy's family, I thought . . ."

He shook his head, his eyes catching hers. There was no condemnation there. Admiration, maybe.

"Hey, Riley." One of the crime lab guys signaled to Callen. "We've got a weapon."

Turning back to Angel, he said. "Hold on a sec."

"Do you mind if I take a look?"

"Be my guest." Callen took her arm and walked with her. He was strong, and though he had a kind face, she noted an edginess about him. He was a man you wouldn't want to cross no matter which side of the law you were on, she decided. Each time she saw him, she felt more drawn to him. Maybe because they were both Irish and both in law enforcement. But he didn't look Irish — except for those sea-green eyes. She looked at his back. Straight. Confident. She tried to rein in her thoughts. "I must be crazy," she murmured.

He turned and fastened his gaze on hers. Her breath caught. Did he know what she was thinking? He smiled. "We're all a little crazy. Have to be in this business."

She pursed her lips and blew out a relieved sigh. He thought she was talking about wanting to see the weapon.

"Looks like a steak knife," the tech who'd summoned Callen said.

"It is." Angel glanced at Callen. "It's the kind they use in the restaurant here."

She'd used one just like it three hours ago.

"Prints?" Callen peered at the alleged weapon.

The tech from the crime lab dropped the knife into an evidence bag. "Some smudges. Looks like the killer either wiped it off or was wearing gloves. We'll run some more tests on it at the lab."

A light flashed. Angel glanced toward the lobby entrance. A photographer had his camera aimed in her direction. She ducked her head and turned as it flashed again. "Great. Looks like I'm going to be fodder for the media again."

Callen stalked over to the periphery of the crime scene and barked at the officers maintaining security to get the onlookers and media out of the lobby area. Eric went up to the photographer, and after giving Angel a thumbs-up sign, led the guy away. They ducked under the crime scene tape and disappeared into the darkness. It was the first she'd seen of Eric tonight, and she felt a modicum of relief knowing he was here.

Angel watched Callen's demeanor change as he came back toward her. "I'm sorry," he said.

Tears gathered in her eyes as his tender gaze met hers. He motioned her away from the scene. "I hate to do this to you, but we need to get those photos of you." He called Brandy over and gave her instructions.

Angel endured several minutes of embarrassment as Brandy snapped photos that would be used as evidence. But it helped some that a friend was the designated photographer. When she'd finished, Brandy said, "Angel, we're going to need the robe and your swimsuit."

Angel nodded. "I know. I'll go to my room and change."

"I'll walk with you," Brandy said.

Angel kept her head down and ignored the members of the press who had moved out of the lobby and were milling around just outside the expanded yellow crime-scene tapes.

Callen watched the two women get into the elevator, his mind spinning in a hundred different directions. While he waited for the CSI guys to finish gathering evidence, he paced across the patio, then took the path to the beach and began walking. Three bodies in six days. All African-American, but that was as close as he could come to similarities.

John Monroe had been murdered first, obviously a drug-related incident. The investigation into J.J.'s death hadn't taken high priority. The local agency was supposed to handle the investigation, but they had their hands full with routine stuff and hadn't gotten far.

Then, in what looked like an unrelated case, two, maybe three, gangbangers hit the pharmacy, stealing all the narcotics the poor pharmacist had on hand. Drugs again. The perps had scattered, possibly abandoning the Hartwell kid, who was supposedly innocent of any wrongdoing.

According to Angel's testimony, the boy had acted as though he was giving up at the pharmacy when his buddies opened fire on her. He rubbed his forehead, wishing he had some answers. So far Bergman hadn't been able to tell them anything. The guy was barely hanging on.

Now a respected and internationally known reverend in the black community was dead, and Angel Delaney was in the middle of that one as well.

When Callen reached the end of the lighted beach area, he turned and began walking back. A fine mist had started to fall, and the wind picked up. He pulled up the collar of his OSP jacket and zipped it up.

"Detective!" Mike Rawlings hailed him and waited on the lawn while Callen slushed through the soft sand. "We're about done."

Mike fell in step beside him. "The victim was a guest here and had dinner with Ray Broadman."

"Did you talk to the servers?"

"In the cocktail lounge, but the kid from the dining room left. I've got his address. According to the bartender in the lounge, they went their separate ways around 10:30. The valet verified that Broadman drove out of the parking lot a few minutes later."

Callen listened to the report then asked, "Tell me something, Mike, have you guys got anything at all on the kid we found out on the dock Sunday?"

"Not much. I asked down at the youth center, and a couple guys admitted to knowing him. He hung out at the Dragon's Den a lot. My take is that he was bringing in ecstasy and selling it to the kids during the weekend dances."

"I thought the Dragon's Den was a no-drug/no-alcohol zone." Callen wasn't a big fan of places like that. They had to be well supervised with strict rules in order to work. Even then, kids seemed to find ways to get around the rules.

"It is, but you know how that goes. My church runs the place." Mike drew a stick of gum out of his pants pocket, unwrapped it, folded it in thirds, then popped it into his mouth. "We check people coming in, and if we catch anyone drinking or doing drugs, we boot them out, but that doesn't stop them from getting the stuff outside."

"Any idea where the drugs are coming from?"

"Yeah." Mike brushed the moisture from his coal black hair. "They're making the stuff right here on the coast. We haven't had the resources to do much more than arrest the users. We tried a sting operation, with a kid from the center who was supposedly going straight. He'd arranged to meet his dealer, but the guy never showed up. It's almost like the supplier knew ahead of time."

"You're suggesting someone in the Sunset Cove Police Department might be working both sides of the fence?"

He shook his head. "No, but whoever is working this area knows how to stay ahead of us."

Mike worked more closely with the gang members than anyone else in the department. "I heard you spend a lot of time down at the rec center, trying to rehabilitate these kids."

"A couple nights a week." Mike frowned. "You going anywhere with this?"

"I'm looking for answers." Callen could almost see Mike's defenses rising. "Officer Delaney is claiming she only fired one shot into the Hartwell kid. What do you think about that?"

Mike's eyebrows shot up. "No way, man. I heard three shots — we all did."

"Well, just for a minute let's assume she's accurate. Would you have any idea who might have fired the other two shots or why?"

Mike's dark features settled into a scowl, his jaw working up and down as he chewed his gum. The scent of wintergreen and garlic wafted into Callen's nostrils. "No idea at all. There were five people in that warehouse when I got there: Angel and the kid, Nick Caldwell, Eric Mason, and Bo Williams. Anyway, what does the Hartwell shooting have to do with J.J.? You think there's some kind of connection?"

Callen sighed. "I'm saying it looks pretty strange that we've got three bodies in six days."

The scowl deepened. "I don't see how they can be related, Detective."

"Have you done anything about notifying Dixon's family?" Callen asked.

"Dixon was staying here with his wife. She's not around, so we haven't been able to contact her to let her know about her husband's death."

"They must have family back home who knows where she is." They were back at the crime scene now, and Todd Elroy Dixon's body was being bagged and placed on the stretcher.

"Right," Mike said. "We're looking into that."

Callen stayed until the lab guys finished, then he put all of the evidence they'd gathered into the trunk of his car. Monday morning he'd take the evidence to the clerk in person. No way was he going to risk having evidence go missing again. He thought about going up to talk to Angel, but it was already after midnight. He was beat, and he imagined Angel was too.

For one brief moment he allowed himself to wonder what it would be like to be married to Angel, curled up against her, telling her he loved her. His eyes snapped open, and he shook his head to clear it. *Don't go there, Riley. The woman's nothing but trouble. And you'll be in even bigger trouble if you start acting on your feelings.*

He turned his thoughts back to the conversation he'd had with Mike regarding the drug dealing at the Dragon's Den. Mike had indicated that J.J. went there often. Mike volunteered there and was a member of the church that ran the place.

From the back of his mind, Callen drew a piece of information from another unresolved case. Jim Kelsey had been missing for weeks and presumed dead. His body had finally showed up. He had been a member of the same church as Mike. He also had volunteered at the Dragon's Den. Coincidence? Callen chewed on the inside of his cheek. *I don't think so.*

TWENTY-SEVEN

Once she had undressed and handed her clothing over to Brandy, Angel took a long shower, once again washing off the blood of a victim. First Billy's and now Dixon's.

Who had killed Dixon and why? And why was he killed here at Peter and Paul's resort, where she happened to be staying? It almost seemed as though she'd been set up. Which made no sense at all. Who would do that, and what would the motive be?

Suddenly the motive seemed simple enough — payback for shooting Billy. Ray Broadman immediately came to mind. Angel felt certain the man Dixon had been talking with in the lounge earlier that evening was Ray Broadman. She'd only seen him once on television. The haircut fit; so did the span of his shoulders. Broadman could have hired someone to tear up her apartment, and he could have instigated the attack on her at the funeral, but would he go so far as to kill a man — a reverend and member of the ACLU who was helping him with the civil suit against her?

Again, it made no sense. Broadman couldn't have known she'd be at the funeral or at the resort.

Unless he's had someone following me.

Angel stepped out of the shower and dried off. "Broadman could've set up a meeting with Dixon knowing I was here," she murmured at her reflection in the mirror.

She shook her head and sighed heavily. "There's no way he could've known I'd leave my room and go for a walk." So much for the setup idea. Maybe the Dixon murder was totally unrelated. Maybe his wife or someone close to him had done it or hired a hit. On the other hand, it could've been the white supremacist who'd applauded Angel for Billy's death. Angel shuddered.

She knew one thing for certain. She was utterly exhausted, which was probably the reason for her far-fetched scenarios. She slipped into her cotton pajamas and, after brushing her teeth, crawled into bed.

Questions continued to strobe in and out of her mind, but she managed to fall asleep only minutes after turning out the light.

On Saturday morning Angel awakened to a tap on her door. She felt disoriented and confused, and it took several seconds before she remembered where she was. Too soon, memories flooded in as she recalled falling on top of a dead man. She could still see his vacant eyes staring at her even in the semidarkness. Her stomach rolled and pitched.

"Just a minute!" she called as she got out of bed to peer out the peephole. Joe Brady stood on the other side looking as if he'd gone a round with the IRS and lost. "Give me a second to get dressed," she said through the door. She grabbed the robe from the hook behind the bathroom door, flung it on, and cinched it up, then ran an unsteady hand through her hair before opening the door.

Joe brushed past her without an invitation.

"What are you doing here so early?" She glanced at her watch at the same time he did.

"It's 10:00."

She tried without success to stifle a

yawn. "I had a late night."

"So I heard."

"What are you doing here? I thought Riley was investigating this one."

"He is." Joe handed her a copy of the newspaper.

She had expected the murder to run on the front page, but this was too much. She was wearing the bloodstained bathrobe, and blood was smeared on her hands and on her forehead where she'd brushed her hair back. "Not the most flattering pose, is it?"

"Are you trying to complicate matters? The phone's been ringing all morning — calls from people wanting to know when we're going to lock you up."

"I didn't kill that man." Angel tossed the paper on the unmade bed.

"Most people don't see it that way. You knew who he was. You saw the newscast when he was introduced, and you knew why he was in town. You must've known he was going to do a fund-raiser here in Oregon to raise money for the Hartwells, part of which would be used as legal fees in the civil suit they filed against you."

"I don't believe this. I came out here to relax and get away from the media. I didn't even know he was staying here!"

Joe rubbed a hand across his balding head and down to his neck. "The press has you tried and convicted. You had access to the steak knives. In fact, you even had steak for dinner. How do we know you didn't slip your knife into your purse and use it later on Dixon?"

"You can't be serious. You know I wouldn't —"

"Mike talked to your waiter. The guy doesn't remember if the knife was on your plate when he picked it up."

"That's ridiculous, and you know it!" Angel lowered herself to the bed, rubbing her temples.

Joe went to one of the armchairs and after sitting down blew out a long breath. He pursed his lips. "All I'm saying, Angel, is that folks out there think you did it. You not only have motive, you had the means and the opportunity."

Angel felt as if her heart had dropped into the same deep pit as her spirit. How could her own boss, a man who counted her father as a friend, level accusations like that at her? He'd practically called her a murderer. "I didn't kill him," she said when she finally found her voice, "but obviously you don't believe me."

"I don't know what to believe." Joe

stared at a spot on the wall just over her head. "Did you know Dixon was staying here?"

"No."

"Why else would you come here? You live in the same town. People who live in the area don't usually spend the night in an expensive resort."

"I already told you. To relax. My brothers own this place. They thought I could use a respite, and so did I. But they were the ones who suggested it." She got up again and paced over to the window. The mist was turning the ocean and sky into a swirling gray mass. "You know perfectly well I didn't come here to kill Dixon. Even if I had wanted to, do you seriously think I would involve my brothers?"

"Look, Angel, for what it's worth, I don't think you did it. But my job is on the line here."

Where have I heard that before?

"If we don't come up with some answers soon, it's going to be my head on the chopping block."

Angel felt the heat of her anger rise to her neck and face. "Why did you come here, Joe? Are you going to arrest me to appease the masses?" She held out her arms, wrists together. "Go ahead. Take me in and while you're at it, call the media to make sure they get pictures."

Joe pushed out of the chair and brushed past her. "Give me a break, Angel. I told the press we didn't have enough evidence to arrest anybody." With his hand on the doorknob he turned back. "I also told them that if you are guilty, you'll be treated like anyone else."

"Thanks a bunch."

Callen came as Joe was leaving. Angel could feel the antagonism between the two men. When the door closed, Callen leaned against the door frame, his gaze traveling from her face to her bare feet.

She pulled her robe tighter. "Are you here to rate me on a scale of one to ten or did you have something to tell me?"

"Lack of sleep does that to me too."

"What?"

"Makes me irritable." He stepped inside and glanced around the room.

"Go ahead. Say it."

"What? That you look cute in that getup or that you got trouble leaking out of your pores?"

"That I look terrible — and that things are looking bad for me."

He gave her a lopsided grin. "You already know that. You had a pretty rough night. I just came by to check up on you."

Angel tipped her head, appraising him. *What is it about you, Detective?*

She looked good. Too good. Callen knew he should've left then and there. Angel standing so close in her cotton pajamas and bathrobe, with her hair tousled, stirred up a desire he thought he'd laid to rest when he buried Karen. He was much too aware of the unmade bed and her husky morning voice. She smelled faintly of berries and spice.

He looked away, forcing himself to walk to the window and immerse his mind in the thick fog hovering on the other side. *Idiot. You're working on a murder case — make that three murder cases and one officer-involved shooting. You can't afford to let yourself think of Angel as anything more than a fellow officer. An officer who happens to be a suspect. A woman who is definitely off limits.*

Callen slipped out of his jacket and threw it on the chair near the window. She must have the heat cranked up to eighty in there. Drawing in a deep breath, he turned back to her and tried not to notice her state of dress. "Now that you've had time to sleep on it," he said, "do you have any ideas on who might've killed Dixon?"

She raised her eyebrows at his question but seemed pleased that he'd asked. "Several. I'd start with any enemies he might have. Then I'd look at Ray Broadman, and then that white supremacist group that made me out as a hero for shooting Billy. I'd look at the guys who trashed my apartment — if you can find them, though I suspect they're the same ones who attacked me after the funeral." She licked her lips and glanced at the carpet. "Why are you asking my opinion?"

"I want to know what you're thinking."

"I thought I was a suspect. Joe said everyone thinks I killed Dixon."

"Joe isn't working on this case." Callen had about had it with Joe's interference. The guy was a first-class nuisance. "He's out of line telling you anything."

Angel bristled. "He wanted me to know what was going on."

"Don't get me wrong, Angel. Joe's not a bad guy. He's just scared. He doesn't know what's going on. He didn't even bother coming to the staff meeting this morning, and I doubt he's read my report. If he had, he'd know the assailant was probably a man."

"What?" Angel placed a hand on his arm, and he felt the heat of it shoot through him. It was all he could do to stand still and not pull her into his arms and kiss her until the room swayed.

He cleared his throat. "I'm waiting for the official word from the medical examiner, but the angle of the wound indicates that Dixon was probably sliced by a man about his own height or taller."

Angel had needed some good news, and it pleased him to be able to give it to her. Seeing the change in her expression made him even more determined to find out who was responsible for the killings.

His exonerating words sank into her bones, making her weak with relief. She seriously thought of throwing herself into his arms and kissing him. Instead she wrapped her arms around herself and sank into the empty armchair. "Why didn't Joe tell me that?"

"Like I said, he probably hadn't read my report. He's too concerned about what people think. You don't deserve that kind of treatment, Angel."

"Thank you."

He hunkered down in front of her. "How are you holding up? With the shooting and now this?"

Angel almost reached out to draw her

hand down his face and trace the scar that rested along his jaw. *Not a good idea, Angel.* "I'm okay. I took your advice and decided to keep seeing the counselor."

The warmth of his smile reached his eyes. "I'm glad to hear that."

He was too close and too nice and all she had to do was lean forward just a few inches and their lips would meet. For one brief instant she imagined them kissing. Her heart quickened, and she could hardly breathe. She straightened at the same time he stood up.

"I'd better be getting back to work." He sounded almost as breathless as she was.

Good idea. She pushed herself out of the chair and walked him to the door. He paused briefly in the hallway, gracing her with a smile that nearly melted her insides. She bit her lower lip. Callen Riley scared her, but at the same time she felt as though some sort of invisible magnet was pulling them together. She ducked back inside before she acted on her emotions.

Hurrying to the bathroom, she showered the night's grogginess away and got dressed in a clean top and the same jeans she'd worn the day before. She'd just finished brushing her teeth when someone knocked on the door.

"You again?" Her gaze traveled over Callen's ruggedly handsome face and lingered on his somber eyes.

"You haven't eaten yet, have you?"

"No, why?"

"Good. You can eat with me while I ask you some more questions."

"And tell me what you've learned so far?" She grabbed her handbag, stepped out beside him, and closed the door.

Once they were seated and had given their orders, he leaned back, assessing her again.

She placed the paper napkin on her lap. "You were going to ask me some questions?"

Callen moved forward, arms resting on the table. "Oh, right. Are you seeing anyone?"

She frowned. "You're the detective. I'd think you'd know all about me by now."

"I know you hang out with an old school chum named Brandon Lafferty." He grinned. "I also heard you turned down his marriage proposal."

"That's not common knowledge."

He shrugged, apparently not willing to reveal his sources. Not that he had to. Callen would have been interviewing a lot of people about her; he must have talked to Brandon.

Angel didn't like the way he was looking at her. Actually, she did, but it screwed up her insides. In an almost desperate attempt to change the subject, she asked, "Have you questioned Ray Broadman?"

Callen sipped at his coffee, set the cup down, and rubbed his chin. "Do I look as bad as I feel?"

"You look like you've pulled an all-nighter, but I guess that's the look girls like these days — guys who are a little rough around the edges."

"How about you — what sort of guy do you like?"

Guys like you. "I don't think that's any of your business."

His crooked smile indicated he'd read her thoughts. "Yes. I talked to Broadman. The guy's a piece of work."

"So was I right? Was he with Dixon last night?"

"He was."

"And?"

"You could watch the news tonight."

"I'd rather not wait." Angel clasped her hands. She didn't appreciate the way he switched topics and kept her on edge.

"He's afraid you'll come after him next.

You and your henchmen."

"Henchmen?" Angel almost choked on her coffee.

"That's the word he used. He told me that he and Dixon were talking strategy. They'd had dinner and drinks, and he left around 10:30. They were concerned about pushing ahead on the civil suit they were filing against you and were worried about repercussions from you. He said he was afraid something like this would happen. He's worried you'll come after him next."

"He's afraid of me? If this wasn't so scary, it would be funny."

"It isn't just you he's afraid of, Angel. It's that white supremacist group you're so buddy-buddy with."

Angel groaned. "You can't be serious. He actually said that?"

"He did." The corner of Callen's mouth twitched slightly. Apparently he wasn't taking the comments too seriously.

Their breakfasts came. Angel busied herself with smashing her eggs into her hash browns and sprinkling on salt and pepper. "Broadman is covering his bases, isn't he?" She set her fork down without taking a bite.

"I don't trust him." Callen spoke between bites. "He's an opportunist, but I doubt he killed Dixon. The reverend was helping Billy's family raise money for legal expenses."

Angel pushed her plate to the side. With the way her stomach was feeling at the moment, eating eggs would not be a good idea.

"I hate to break it to you, Angel, but Broadman had no reason to want Dixon dead." He paused to take a drink of coffee, then leveled his green gaze on her.

"Joe seems to think I have motive. Do you think so too?"

"What I *think* doesn't matter. Truth is, I can't rule anyone out at this point. The crime lab hasn't sorted through all the evidence yet."

Angel felt herself pale under his scrutiny. She had seriously underestimated Callen Riley. He wasn't only someone to be reckoned with, he was just plain dangerous. She twisted the napkin still lying on her lap. How far would the authorities go to find the real killer? Maybe not far enough. She made a good scapegoat and was getting a reputation for being a renegade cop with an attitude, one whose courage was being touted by white supremacists. As if she didn't have enough trouble already with the shooting incident.

Callen was under the same pressure as Joe to settle things quickly. The detective had encouraged her, said he believed her — but could she trust him?

TWENTY-EIGHT

Callen set down his coffee. "Angel, relax." His gaze softened as he spoke. "We'll get to the bottom of this, and I have no doubt your name will be cleared on all fronts."

Angel wished she could believe him.

She turned when she heard a familiar voice behind her. "Look who's here!" Tim patted her shoulder and kissed her cheek.

"Morning, Angel." Rachael scooted into the seat next to her. "I thought you might need me." Glancing at Callen she added, "You haven't been telling this guy anything that might be incriminating, have you?" She grinned at him, dimples sinking deeper than usual.

"I take it you two know each other," Angel said, trying to ignore a twinge of jealousy.

"Unfortunately," they answered in unison.

Rachael laughed again. "Tim, this is Callen Riley with the Oregon State Police. Tim is Angel's brother."

The two men shook hands. Tim settled into one of the empty chairs.

"Callen and I met a few months ago in court," Rachael said. "So, Riley, what brings you to Sunset Cove?"

"I just moved here."

"Really?" Rachael beamed at him.

"Yep."

"Hmm." Rachael nodded. "And did you sell your house in Portland?"

Callen went quiet, and Angel thought she saw a flash of pain in his eyes.

"I'm sorry." Rachael pinched her lips together. "I shouldn't have said anything."

"No — I'm being overly sensitive." Looking at Angel and then Tim, he said, "My wife died a couple years ago, and selling the house has been hard."

"I'm sorry." Angel could almost feel the depth of his grief. More than anything she wanted to offer comfort, but didn't.

"Yeah." His lips formed a thin line. "Me too."

Rachael must have felt their discomfort; she changed the subject. "Are they keeping you busy down here?" she asked.

"Are you kidding? Besides all the stuff

going on in Sunset Cove, I've been working the Kelsey case."

Angel stared at him. "I didn't know that."

He shrugged. "There's a lot you don't know about me, Angel."

She almost expected him to say something about remedying that, but he didn't.

Peter and Paul came in then and pulled up chairs. Before sitting down, Paul asked, "Anyone want anything?"

"Yeah," Angel said. "A ticket to South America."

"I could probably arrange that." Paul glanced at Callen and added, "But under the circumstances, I don't think it's a good idea."

Callen chuckled. "Oh, I don't know. If you left the country, Angel, I'd just have to follow you." His grin told her he wouldn't mind that at all.

Paul caught a waitress who took the newcomers' orders and brought coffees.

"What's going on?" Angel asked. "Have you all decided to do an intervention and put me out of my misery?"

Peter chuckled. "In a sense. We decided you needed some support. We're here to do that."

"We know you're innocent," Tim said.

"According to the autopsy report, Dixon was probably cut by someone as tall as he was, and because of the pressure and depth of the cut, they figure it was a guy."

"So I heard." Callen had said the same thing earlier.

Callen sighed. "And you have access to the autopsy report because . . . ?"

"Friends." Tim grinned. "Don't worry, we won't say anything outside this group."

"It's a small town," Rachael reminded him. "Almost impossible to keep a secret."

Callen shook his head.

"I don't know." Rachael picked up her coffee and took a sip. "The DA might argue that Angel could've dropped the guy then cut his throat."

"Gee, thanks. I thought you were on my side." Angel set her lukewarm coffee aside.

"I am. Just being practical." Rachael turned to look at her. "You're a police officer and you're in great shape. I bet you've taken down more than one guy."

Angel shrugged, her gaze darting to Callen's again. He was looking at something outside, obviously deep in thought. He glanced at his watch and shoved his chair back. "Much as I'd like to stay and chat, I have a commitment in Portland this afternoon."

Angel watched him go, not quite sure what to think. Her reverie was interrupted a moment later when the waitress came and set the new orders on the table.

"What's wrong, Angel?" Rachael slathered Marionberry jam on her toast.

"Nothing, it's just that I don't know how to read that guy."

"Callen?" Rachael tipped her head. "Why?"

"He says he thinks I'm innocent, then he says he can't rule out anyone. He confuses me."

"You haven't said anything that might be incriminating, have you?"

"I don't think so."

Rachael took hold of Angel's arm. "There is something you should know about Callen."

"What's that?"

"Well, I'm not saying he isn't a nice guy, but you need to watch what you say around him. He can be very charming, and he's good at getting people to talk to him, which makes him a very good cop."

"Did you ever go out with him?" Angel drew a circle in the condensation on the side of her glass.

"No, we're just friends." Rachael took another sip of coffee. "He's still grieving over his wife. He told me he wasn't interested in getting involved with anyone." She chewed on her lip for a moment. "I talked to the medical examiner this morning about Billy's autopsy."

"You did?"

"Yes. I told him what you'd said about firing only one of the shots. And I asked him about the possibility of a second shooter."

Angel leaned forward. "And . . . ?"

"He agreed that might be possible because of the trajectory of the bullets. One shot went into Billy's right shoulder." She held her arm up and crooked her elbow, making a gun out of her thumb and forefinger. "And it came from this angle." She pointed down.

"That's right." Angel moved her hand slightly. "I was four, maybe five steps above him — six feet away at the most."

"Another shot went into his stomach. And a third into his chest. That's the bullet that actually killed him. The shots to his chest and stomach were fired from more than ten feet away and went in at a different angle."

"Are they sure?"

"That's what I was told."

Angel watched the waitress fill their coffees. Relief washed through her. "I was right, then?"

"It looks that way." But Rachael didn't look as thrilled as she should have.

"That's good news, isn't it?" Tim asked.

"Well, maybe," Rachael hedged. "Unfortunately, it doesn't prove she didn't fire all three shots. She could have fired as she came down the steps toward him."

"But I didn't." She felt her hope sink. Without any concrete evidence, there would be no proof of her story.

Rachael nodded. "The medical examiner says it's possible that Billy was shot by two different people, but without the actual bullets and Angel's duty gun and magazine, there's no way of knowing for sure."

"Say there was another shooter," Tim said. "It stands to reason that whoever it was would want to get rid of any evidence that implicated him."

"Yes, but who?" Angel asked. "Billy and I were the only ones in the building until the other officers got there." Once again the image of her father emerged, and again she shook off the thought.

"Maybe you weren't. It's a big place. Suppose someone was there, like one of the gang members?" Tim pressed back in his chair to let the waitress take his empty plate. Before it disappeared, Angel snagged a slice of toast.

"You may have something there, big brother." She felt the fog lifting for the first time in days. The possibility of Billy being shot by a gang member seemed plausible. "Maybe when he saw that Billy had been caught, he killed him to keep him from talking."

"Wouldn't you have known if someone was there?" Rachael patted her lips with the napkin.

"I don't know. I was too intent on Billy. I remember being so shocked. I mean . . . his eyes and all the blood. I was too focused on him to notice anything else." Angel spread the toast with jam and took a bite.

Rachael studied the notepad she'd been writing on. "If Billy was shot by one of his buddies, wouldn't someone close to the gang know about it?"

"They probably do, but getting them to narc on a buddy is not going to happen." Angel rubbed her neck to ease some of the stiffness. "I'll mention that to Detective Riley. Also, Mike Rawlings has been working with some of the kids down at the youth center. He might have some contacts there."

Angel polished off the piece of toast, suddenly feeling ravenous. She was beginning to think that maybe there might be hope after all. She had been right all along about firing only once. Angel knew for certain she had been looking down at Billy and hadn't moved until he went down — until all three shots had been fired. If someone had fired at him from more than ten feet, it hadn't been her.

Angel hadn't fired the bullet that killed Billy. Someone else had — someone she needed to find in order to prove her innocence.

Angel hitched a ride with Rachael to the hospital, where she had left Brandon's car. From there she drove home and put in a call to Janet. She got an answering machine and realized the office was probably closed for the weekend. Disappointed, she hung up without leaving a message. Janet had told her to call anytime, but Angel didn't want to bother her on her days off. Besides, this wasn't exactly an emergency.

Still, Angel wanted to undergo hypnosis again and let the memories come without restraint. Maybe she would remember the details more clearly. Had she heard someone in the warehouse? Had she sensed someone lurking in the shadows? Janet had told her that there was no guarantee she'd ever remember exactly what had taken place, but if there was a chance, she wanted to take it.

She paced around her apartment for a while, feeling anxious. Maybe a run on the beach would help her relax. She always felt more at peace there than anywhere. Determined to do just that, she dressed in water-resistant sweats, went down the back steps of her apartment, and hurried along the path leading to the beach. The fog had lifted some, revealing thick, soppy clouds that leaked a steady mist. Her hair was already forming into damp ringlets.

She ran her usual route and paused briefly to admire one of the houses that was being remodeled. She had enjoyed watching the restoration process of the aging beach house, glad someone had chosen to salvage it rather than tear it down. The house wasn't elegant but looked homey and inviting. The exterior was a weathered gray, and the trim a spectacular shade of blue. The owner had good taste.

Angel hoped to buy a house on the beach one day. She frowned, realizing she could have that and more with Brandon.

But she wasn't ready for a commitment now and wasn't sure she ever would be.

She sat down on a large piece of driftwood near the remodeled house. The beach was quiet here. No public access, and the misty fog kept tourists inside visiting galleries and gift shops. Letting her arms support her, she tipped her head back, shaking out the excess moisture in her hair.

Dropping to the sand, she used the driftwood as a backrest, then closed her eyes and listened to the waves. "God, please help me to remember what really happened." She focused on her breathing, like Janet had taught her, letting her mind drift to where it wanted.

Images of the pharmacy came into focus — the quiet street, then the shattered window. She and Eric calling for backup and going inside, finding Mr. Bergman lying in a pool of blood. Spotting Billy, ordering him to drop his gun. Billy looking frightened and pretending like he was going to give up. He put his gun down. Two gang members rushed out and fired, pinning her down.

Even in her relaxed state, Angel could feel the terror of those awful moments seep back into her bones. She wanted to stop.

Go on.

She took several deep breaths.

You can do this, Angel. Keep going.

She focused on relaxing the muscles in her neck and shoulders and breathing away the tightness in her chest. The three of them had escaped through the back of the pharmacy. Several minutes later Billy had ducked into the abandoned warehouse. She followed him and called out, looking around for the other gang members. The rear of the building was in shadows. She heard footsteps on the second floor and started up the steps. Billy barreled down them as though he were being chased. Had he seen something or someone who'd frightened him? Billy's family had insisted he hadn't been a gang member. Had the thieves found him in the pharmacy and forced him to go along with them? Had they been on the second floor waiting for her?

Angel had yelled for him to stop, and he did, but then he raised his gun. She remembered hesitating. "I didn't want to shoot," she murmured. "But I had to." She fired once, hitting him in the shoulder. "I was lowering my arm when the second two shots went off."

I lowered the gun. If she had fired those last two shots, wouldn't they have been lower — to his legs?

Angel opened her eyes. She hadn't killed Billy, but who had? She stood and dusted off her backside, then started running back toward the apartment.

Both times she'd confronted Billy, he'd acted frightened. She had assumed he was afraid of her — of being caught. But maybe that wasn't it at all. Billy must've seen something or someone who had frightened him more than she had. Someone else must've been in that building, someone who had shot Billy and stolen the evidence to keep anyone from finding out.

Angel paused at the base of the back stairs leading to her apartment and placed her hands on her knees to catch her breath. *What did you see, Billy? What frightened you? Did the gang recruit you or just use you as a decoy?*

Angel pondered those questions while she showered, dried her hair, and got dressed. Sitting down with a cup of tea, she tried to assimilate the information she'd gotten from Rachael and from her own memories. Who had been in that building? Why would that person shoot Billy? She grabbed a pen and pad and began making notes.

Why shoot Billy?

Because he could ID the gang members, and they were afraid he'd talk.

Angel frowned, remembering the body Callen had found behind the warehouse. J.J. Monroe had been shot at around 3:00 a.m., but his body hadn't been found until later, after the incident with Billy. The body was still on the dock when Angel shot at Billy. Was there a connection?

Had the gang members shot Billy and escaped through a rear entrance? As much as she wanted to believe that scenario, she didn't think it likely. Angel doubted any of the gang members had access to the evidence locker keys — which left one of her coworkers as the suspect. Her father?

"No way." She tossed her pen and pad on the table. Maybe she could clarify matters by talking to Billy's mother. She'd been wanting to offer her condolences, and this was as good a time as any.

Fifteen minutes later she arrived at Mavis Hartwell's home, an older two-story badly in need of paint. The yard, however, had been nicely maintained. Impatiens lined both sides of the walk that led from the sidewalk to the porch. Two huge rhododendrons flanked the front steps, and buds were already opening to reveal deep red blossoms. A small boy who'd been sitting on the top step jumped up and ran into the house.

Mavis Hartwell came to the door, eyeing Angel warily.

"Mrs. Hartwell, I'm Angel Delaney."

"I know who you are." She glared at Angel. "I'd like you to leave."

"Please, ma'am, I'd like to talk with you. I wanted to tell you how sorry I am about Billy."

"A little late for that, isn't it?"

"Mavis?" a gravelly voice called from inside. "Where are your manners, girl? Invite the woman in."

Mavis stepped back, her chest rose and fell in resignation. "Come on in, then." She opened the door. "I'm sorry for being rude. Isn't the least bit Christian, is it?"

Angel stepped inside. The living room was neat and tidy despite the shabby furniture. An older woman, most likely the owner of the voice she'd heard earlier, sat in a rocker, a shawl over her shoulders and a crochet hook and yarn in her arthritic hands. The woman's handiwork was evident in the many afghans and doilies lying about the room.

"That's my mother, Emmie Broadman.

Mama, this is the woman who shot Billy." Mavis said it like she was introducing the Avon lady.

Angel's mouth opened. She wanted to refute the statement, but it didn't seem right. Even though her shot wasn't the one that killed him, she was in part responsible for his death. If she hadn't fired the first time, maybe he'd have gotten away.

"I'm going to fix me a cup of coffee." Mavis nodded toward the older woman. "You want something?"

"Tea." Emmie went back to whatever she was working on. "Some of that passion fruit stuff you brought home the other day."

"How about you?" Mavis fixed her dark gaze on Angel.

"Coffee would be fine, thanks."

"If you're fixing to stay a while, you might as well have a seat," Mavis called out as she walked into the kitchen.

Angel settled on the end cushion of the sofa. The original green fabric showed definite signs of wear, but it had been covered with a pale pink chenille bedspread. The little boy she'd seen on the porch peeked out from behind his grandmother's chair. His dark eyes seemed to take up a quarter of his face. Angel offered a tentative smile, but he ducked out of sight.

"Angel." Emmie sucked in her lower lip and released it several times. She had a round face that was drawn in at the mouth. "That's a good name."

"Thank you." Angel glanced toward the kitchen and could see Mavis pulling down three cups. She wondered at the wisdom of coming here.

"Your mama have a reason for calling you Angel?" Emmie asked.

Angel snapped her head in the woman's direction, caught off guard by the question. "I . . . I was born on Christmas Eve, and my mother heard the carolers singing 'Angels We Have Heard on High.' "

Emmie chuckled. "Good a reason as any. You a Christian then?"

"I was raised a Christian." Angel rubbed the thumb of her right hand.

"Now, that isn't exactly what I asked you, is it?" Emmie lowered her crocheting and leveled a long, hard look at Angel.

"I'm not sure I know what you mean."

"Oh, I think you do. You got a lost look about you. I've seen it too many times. You've lost your way, honey. But don't you worry. The Lord'll bring you back to the fold."

Mavis came back into the living room

with a tray. "Mama, are you preaching again?"

"Just making an observation."

After handing Angel a cup, Mavis set the tray down on an end table beside her mother.

"She's come to say she's sorry," Emmie said.

"I heard." Mavis peered over at Angel and set her cup on the scarred coffee table atop a crocheted coaster. "I know the right thing would be to forgive you, but I'm not ready to do that just now."

"I don't expect you to." Angel bit her lip. "I'm not going to make excuses, but I'd like you to know what happened. I . . . I thought he was one of the gang members who broke into Bergman's Pharmacy. He'd been in trouble before. I thought your son had a real gun."

"He wasn't a gang member," Mavis insisted loudly, then fell silent for a moment. "I guess I can understand how you might have thought that, though. Billy was heading down the wrong road for a while. But lately he'd been doing real good. Partly because of that police officer who's been working with some of the neighborhood boys. Bo Williams, I think Billy said his name was."

"Bo was working with Billy?"

Mavis nodded and took a sip of her coffee. "Truth be told, I blame myself for that morning more than I blame you. I never should have sent him out alone."

Emmie set her handiwork aside and began stirring sugar into her tea.

"It doesn't help to blame yourself," Angel said. "You couldn't have known about the robbery. If what you say is true, then Billy was at the wrong place at the wrong time."

Emmie shook her head. "I think it's us who ought to be apologizing to you," she said. "Them boys who vandalized your place and busted up your car — and this lawsuit business. We didn't want any part of that."

"That's right." Mavis nodded. "We had nothing to do with that. We didn't know half the people at my boy's funeral. My brother decided to file the lawsuit. I told him not to, but he wouldn't listen. He's got this idea in his head that you're a racist and got to be punished."

Angel took a sip of coffee. "If you feel that way, why not drop the case?"

"It's not that simple." Mavis sighed. "It's not our fight anymore, and besides, when Ray decides to do something, there's no stopping him."

Angel rubbed the back of her neck. "I see. Do you think it would help if I talked to him?" She blew out a long breath. She shouldn't even be here talking to these people. Rachael would have a fit. *Not the smartest thing you've ever done. Too late to think about that now, though. You're here.*

"You could try, but he's not the type to listen."

The room was silent for an awkward moment. Then Emmie piped up. "Why did you come to the funeral?" she asked. "You sure managed to stir up a hornet's nest."

Sudden tears filled Angel's eyes, and she blotted them with her fingers. "I wanted to say good-bye to Billy. I've never had to shoot anyone before, and believe me, I never wanted to hurt your son."

Angel thought about telling them that she had fired only one of the shots, but would they believe her? She doubted it. It would be best to wait until she had proof.

As she put her coffee cup down and got ready to leave, the door flew open. A large shadow filled the doorway. Ray Broadman's furious gaze flitted to her then fastened on Mavis. "What's she doing here?" His voice was deep and threatening as thunder.

Angel had heard that voice before. Ray

Broadman had been the obscene caller.

"She came to offer her condolences and say she was sorry about what happened." Mavis leaned back, looking almost as frightened as Angel felt.

"And you believe her." Teeth clamped, he snarled at Angel. "Get out. You got no business being here."

"Ray, this is my home." Mavis stood up and took a step toward him. "I have —"

Ray pushed her aside.

Angel didn't want to cause Mavis any harm, so she moved toward the door. "It's all right, Mrs. Hartwell, I should be going anyway. Thanks for the coffee."

"I'll be praying for you, child," Emmie called after her. "Lord knows you need all the prayers you can get."

"Ain't nobody going to pray for that killer." Ray raised his fist and shook it in Angel's face. "Get out!" He swung at her and would've hit her jaw if she hadn't turned away from him. His fist connected with her shoulder, sending her out the door and onto her knees. His eyes flashed as he stood over her, poised to strike again.

TWENTY-NINE

Angel scrambled to her feet. The door slammed shut, but not before she heard Broadman turn his rage on Mavis and Emmie. It would serve him right if she had him arrested for assaulting her, but she doubted the charges would stick. Likewise on the obscene phone call.

She limped back to Brandon's car. At least no one had bashed the Lexus in. She drove to the beach and sat there looking out at the water for several minutes, wondering what to do next. She called Callen's cell phone and got his voice mail. On the message she told him about Broadman. As soon as she got another dial tone, she punched in her partner's phone number.

He answered on the second ring.

"Are you on duty?" Angel asked.

"Yeah. What do you need?"

"I'm going back to the old cannery

where I found Billy."

"Why?"

"Meet me there."

"Okay, but why?" Eric didn't sound too pleased.

"I'll tell you when you get there." Angel tossed her bag into the backseat and jammed the key into the ignition.

Eric hesitated. "I wish you wouldn't. It's not safe."

"That's why I called you. If you'd rather not go, I'll go in alone."

"I'll be there."

She hung up and arrived at the cannery five minutes later. While she waited for Eric, she let her gaze roam over the brick exterior. The building was awaiting its final sentence — be destroyed or be remodeled. Plans had been put before the city council to turn it into a unique waterfront shopping mall. The contractor wanted matching funds from the city. The city in return would get 50 percent of the rent. Not a bad deal for all concerned, if the venture was successful. In light of what had happened there, Angel doubted she'd ever frequent the place. Even remodeled, it would always be the dark, dank warehouse where Billy Dean Hartwell had died in her arms.

Eric pulled up beside her. Jumping out of his car, he looked over at her and frowned.

"Brandon's car?"

She nodded. "He's letting me borrow it."

"Nice." He walked with her to the entrance and paused. "It's not too late to change your mind."

"I want to have a look around."

He opened the door and peered inside. "Why?"

"I just do."

"I don't understand why you keep punishing yourself like this, Angel. It happened. Let it go."

"I can't." Inside, the floor still bore dark brown stains of Billy's blood. The memory and the stench almost made her vomit. She pressed a hand to her stomach and ducked back outside. She gulped in fresh air and leaned against the building, letting it support her rubbery legs.

"You don't have to do this. Coming here isn't going to prove or disprove anything. Why don't you let me buy you a cup of coffee instead?"

"No. I want to go through the place, see if I can piece together what really happened."

"He threatened you. You shot him in

self-defense. Don't forget that. It doesn't do any good to go back over it. It happened. At some point you have to accept that and move on. Besides, the grand jury will never indict you on this. They'll clear you, and you'll go back to work."

Angel raised her head and looked into Eric's eyes. "I wish I could be as sure of that as you are." She took a deep breath and went back inside to the stairs, where she had been standing when Billy brushed past her. Eric followed her.

She envisioned the scene again, going through the motions. "I heard him go upstairs and started to follow him. All of a sudden he's tearing back down, he pushes past me, and I yell for him to stop. He turns around to face me, raises his gun . . ."

"And you shot him," Eric finished.

"He raised his hands, but what if he wasn't going to shoot? What if he was giving himself up? He was terrified, Eric. I remember that."

"You said he had the gun in his hands," he reminded her. "If he were giving up, he'd have put the gun on the floor."

"An adult would have. But he was a scared and confused kid." Shoving a hand through her hair, she closed her eyes. She'd fired once and hit him in the shoulder. She clearly remembered the look on Billy's face. His eyes were not focused on her but on something or someone behind her.

She turned around, peering into the dimly lit structure. She'd been facing the door. "He must've been standing at the back of the warehouse, in the shadows."

"Who?" Eric rested his hands on his hips.

"The other shooter."

"Are you back on that again?" He shook his head.

"I know for certain now that I fired one shot — the medical examiner's report confirms it." Angel told him about the medical examiner's findings. "My shot went into his shoulder. The second two shots went into his chest and stomach at a different angle. There had to be someone behind me."

"Okay, suppose there was another shooter. What happened to him? How did he get away? We had this area pretty well covered."

"I don't know. Do me a favor. Stand here. I want to check something."

He shrugged. "Whatever you say."

Angel went under the stairs and walked a straight path back to the wall. She turned around to face the stairs then moved to the left until she had a clear view of Eric and the place where Billy had been standing. She raised her hand and pointed her finger in Eric's direction. From that position the shooter would have a straight shot at Billy.

Or at me.

A strangled sound escaped her lips.

Eric started back toward her. "What's wrong?"

"I've been trying to come up with an explanation as to why someone would fire at Billy. I've been thinking that maybe one of the gang members shot him to keep him quiet."

"That's possible."

"But what if the shots weren't meant for Billy at all? What if they were meant for me?"

"Whoa, partner. That's a pretty big leap." Eric rubbed his chin. "But you might have something there. Say there was someone here — one of the gangbangers we were after. Either scenario would work. Kill Billy to keep him from talking, or kill you because you're a cop."

"But how could he have gotten by me?"

"Well, there are several possibilities." Eric pointed to a door to her right. "He could've waited in the back, knowing that the shots would bring most of the officers in the area in here with you. We all thought you shot the kid, so there wouldn't have been any reason for us to look for another shooter."

"So he waits until everyone is here and sneaks out the back?" She started to open the door and stopped. Fingerprints. She doubted the crime lab guys had bothered checking the area back here. Like Eric said, they had no reason to, since the shooting had happened up front. "Do you know where this goes?"

"To the receiving area. The place used to be a processing plant. Boats would come right up to the dock. They'd empty their holds into bins and the fish would be sorted, cleaned, and packaged." His beeper went off. He looked down at it then called dispatch.

"Sorry, Angel, I have to go." He started to leave. "You coming?"

"I thought I'd take a look at the second floor."

"You won't be able to see much. The place is boarded up tight. There's no electricity. And in case you hadn't noticed, it's getting dark outside."

Angel glanced up at the windows. The sky had gone from a cornflower blue to a hazy gray. She could barely make out the stairs and the exit beyond. Whatever exploring she wanted to do would have to wait until tomorrow. Besides, she wasn't crazy about wandering through the place on her own.

They walked out together. Once inside her car, Angel rolled down the window. "Thanks for coming with me."

"No problem." Eric climbed into his car, backed out, and headed south.

There were no reporters at her apartment, so she parked in her usual spot. But when she got to her door, she stopped cold. It was slightly ajar. "Oh no," she moaned. "Not again."

THIRTY

Angel heard voices inside the apartment. Whoever had broken in was still there. She backed away from the door and pulled the cell phone from her bag.

"That has got to be the most delicious pasta sauce I've ever tasted." The voice was a man's and sounded vaguely familiar.

Angel frowned. Since when did crooks break in to eat pasta?

A woman laughed. "Yes, but making it was the best part." That voice belonged to her mother.

"Glad to oblige. We work well together."

A strange man in my apartment with my mother?

Angel slipped out of her jacket and hung it in the closet.

"Angel, is that you?" Anna asked.

The man who stepped into the hallway took Angel's breath away. Callen had traded his suit for a teal shirt with long sleeves, folded to three-quarter length, and khaki slacks. She told herself the reaction was just one of surprise, nothing more. "What are you doing here?"

"Came to see you. Your mother was kind enough to let me wait." He winked in Anna's direction. "She even invited me to dinner."

"How could I not? He brought dessert," Anna chuckled. "Come in and sit down, honey. You're just in time." She waved a spoon in her direction. "Callen has been helping me cook."

Angel must have looked as confused as she felt.

"It's all right," her mother explained. "I wouldn't let just anyone into your apartment. Callen is a police officer."

"A detective," Callen corrected.

"Whatever." Anna waved her hand.

"I know who he is." Angel frowned. "But what are you two doing here? Cooking. Together."

"I think I can explain." Callen pulled a chair out for Angel and guided her to it. "As I said, I came to see you."

"He brought food, Angel. Wasn't that nice?"

Angel rubbed her eyes. "Wait. I'm having some kind of weird dream, aren't I?"

"No dream." Callen leaned down and whispered, "If it was, your mother wouldn't be here."

Her stomach fluttered. *From hunger,* she told herself.

Yeah, right. Who am I kidding?

She jerked away, ignoring the teasing look on his face. "Why did you bring food? And Ma, why are you here?"

"I brought groceries."

"Why? Do I look malnourished?"

"Honey, I know how you are when you're worried. You don't eat. You don't take care of yourself."

Angel gave up and let her mother do what she did best — feed her. But once she'd dished up plates for Angel and Callen and set them on the place mats she'd put on the dining room table, Anna said her good-byes. "I have to get back to the hospital. Your father will be waiting."

"Are you sure you don't want to eat with us?" Angel's tone was almost pleading. She couldn't explain it, but the thought of being alone with Callen Riley was scarier than catering a dinner at the country club — well, almost. He seemed different than before, more relaxed and less reserved.

"I'm taking some with me to share with your father."

Callen opened his arms for a hug. "It was a pleasure meeting you, Mrs. Delaney." He kissed her cheek and in Italian said, *"Buon giorno."*

She waved her hand. "Call me Anna. Soon you'll have to come to my house for dinner. I have a real kitchen. With fresh herbs from my garden."

"Fresh herbs! My dear lady, you have stolen my heart." He looked genuinely pleased. "Cooking with you again would be a pleasure."

"Come Monday night." Anna grinned, her voice high with excitement. Angel hadn't seen her mother so animated since Christmas. "We'll have a welcome home dinner for Frank."

Callen glanced in Angel's direction as he walked her mother to the door. "It's a date."

"Ciao!" Anna called to them as she closed the door.

"You really won her over," Angel said when Callen returned and sat down at the table.

"Your mom is fantastic. She's everything . . ." He stopped. His smile melted into a scowl and without another word, he attacked the pasta like a man on a mission.

Angel wanted to ask him what had upset him, but she doubted he'd welcome her intrusion. No doubt about it, Callen Riley was a complicated man. A man she wanted to know better. A man she didn't want to know at all.

She tried to focus on her dinner, long golden strands of pasta covered with a rich, red sauce and topped with a sprinkling of freshly grated Parmesan. Her mother would never use anything but fresh Parmesan. The thick sauce was a mixture of tomatoes, onion, garlic, ground beef, sliced olives, mushrooms, and a blend of basil, oregano, cilantro, and other spices.

Angel picked up two strands of spaghetti with her fork and twisted them around and around, then scooped up more sauce. Once in her mouth the flavors exploded. "Mmm." She closed her eyes. "Mmm, this is so good."

Callen didn't respond. She opened her eyes to find him studying her again. She set her fork down. "Why do you do that?"

"What?"

"Look at me like that."

His mouth curved in a warm smile. "I like looking at you."

"Well, don't." His gaze disturbed her,

383

frightened her, sent shivers through her. Under his scrutiny she felt exposed, guilty, afraid of what he might find if he looked too closely.

He obliged, turning his attention back to his food.

She finished chewing a piece of garlic bread and took a sip of water. "Um, I thought you had to be in Portland today."

"I did." He reached for his napkin. "Needed to pick up my computer equipment and visit my sister and her family."

Angel leaned forward. "Tell me about them."

Callen complied, giving her a brief synopsis of his family — sister, Kathleen, her husband, Stan, and their two girls. When he finished, they sat in silence for a while. He stared into the glowing gas fireplace and seemed a million miles away. He hadn't mentioned his parents, and Angel thought it better not to ask.

"I realized something today," Angel said, breaking the silence. She told him about her visit to the cannery with Eric. "I want to go back."

He shook his head. "Not you. I'll go in and take another look around."

Angel started to argue but thought better of it. "Did you get my message about the obscene caller? I think it was Ray Broadman."

"It'll be tough to prove that. Too bad you didn't get a tape." He picked up their empty plates and took them to the sink. "Want dessert?"

"No. I'm stuffed." She hadn't meant to eat it all, but she had. Every delectable bite.

"Coffee?"

She nodded. She should've been the one offering him coffee. Instead she watched him move around her kitchen like a pro. "You really cook, don't you? I mean, all that with my mother wasn't an act."

"Cooking is a hobby."

"The sauce was wonderful."

"A joint effort."

"You and my mother . . . I'm amazed. She doesn't like to share her kitchen."

He grinned. "Maybe she's never found someone to share her enthusiasm for food."

"Huh. And you do. You actually *enjoy* cooking."

"Yeah. I didn't at first, though. But then it was either make it myself or go hungry." He glanced over at her. "My mother deserted Kath and me when I was twelve. Left us with an alcoholic father."

"I'm sorry."

"We adjusted. After a while I got to where I enjoyed cooking — even took some classes in college. I'll have to show you my collection of cookbooks someday."

"I don't cook."

He chuckled. "No kidding."

"What's that supposed to mean?"

"Some people cook, some don't. Your mother told me you don't have a domestic bone in your body." He set two cups and saucers on the counter and poured the coffee.

Angel bristled. "She said that?"

"She told me a lot of things about you." Instead of handing one to her, he took both to the coffee table in front of the sofa.

"Didn't anyone ever tell you that it's rude to talk about somebody behind their back?"

He sat down on the sofa and rested an ankle across his knee. "Your mother likes to talk about you. Only good stuff, I promise. And I enjoyed listening."

She crossed the room and picked up her cup, then sat in the chair farthest away from him. His presence took up too much space in the room — and in her heart. Besides, hadn't Rachael said he was still grieving?

She watched him for a long moment as

he picked up the glass globe and examined it, his long fingers moving over the smooth glass as if he'd done it before. She had an inkling then. "It was you, wasn't it?" She got to her feet and waved an arm around the room. "You did this — the furniture, the cupboards."

Callen didn't deny it. "You don't like it?"

Angel wasn't certain how she felt about it — thankful, yes, but at the same time annoyed. She doubted he could afford to furnish her entire apartment any more than she could. "I love it, but you shouldn't have done this. How did you get in? Where did you get the money? I mean, I may not have much, but I'm not a charity case."

"It wasn't just me, Angel. Granted, it was my idea, but everyone in the Sunset Cove P.D. and the sheriff's department chipped in. Other officers around did too. I just put it all together, bought it, and had Brandy and a couple of the guys come in and help me set everything up."

Tears formed in her eyes. "Oh." She sat back down, embarrassed at her tirade. "Why didn't anyone tell me? I should write thank-you notes."

"We wanted to surprise you. I suppose you could just write a note to each of the

P.D.s — Lincoln City and Newport, and to the county sheriff's department. That would about do it." Callen set the glass globe down and placed an arm across the back of the sofa.

"And to you." Angel looked around the room. "Thank you." The words seemed insignificant and conveyed so little of what she really felt. She wanted to cross the room and settle down beside him, feel his arms slide around her.

Not a good idea. Angel blinked away the image and picked up her coffee. "Before dinner, you . . . um . . . said you came to see me. Have you learned anything more about Dixon's death?"

"I didn't come here to talk about Dixon."

"What then?"

"You. I want to know more about the shooting you were involved in."

"I told you everything."

"Right, but I have some questions." Callen leaned back, resting his feet on the coffee table. "You said you were on the stairs and less than six feet from the boy when you fired."

"Right. I shot him in the shoulder. I remember."

"The medical examiner tells me that two

of the shots went in at a lower angle and from farther out."

"Which proves I didn't kill him." Angel set her cup down. "Rachael told me about the report."

"It proves someone shot him from different angles, once at close range, less than six feet, and twice at probably more than ten feet. That could've been done by the same person. Which brings us back to the missing evidence."

Angel bounced to her feet and began pacing. "We've been over this ground before. I didn't take it. I don't know who did. Despite Joe's faulty memory, I didn't have a key. The only thing that makes sense to me is that whoever fired those last two bullets didn't want anyone to know that he — or she — was there."

"Would you like to walk?"

"What?" Callen had a knack for throwing her off balance, and he was doing it again.

"Walking is good for clearing the head and working off a heavy meal."

"It's raining."

"So?"

"Yeah." Angel smiled. "While we walk, you can fill me in on Dixon."

Callen pulled on the Aran sweater he'd

shed earlier and slipped on an olive-drab rain jacket. Angel put on a sweatshirt and her oversized rain gear. Once outside, she led the way over the rocks and onto the shoreline. It was dark, but lights from the apartment and nearby hotels gave them adequate visibility.

Callen held out his hand to help her over the driftwood.

"Thanks. Now, tell me about Dixon."

"Can we talk about something else? I'm off duty."

"Like what?"

"Us."

He was still holding her hand, and Angel didn't think it should feel quite so comfortable or make her feel so safe. She pulled her hand away. "There is no us."

"That's what I keep telling myself, but when I'm with you . . ." He brushed rainwater from his hair. "I can't stop thinking about you. I'm losing my perspective." He tipped his head back. "I even like your mother."

Angel couldn't help but laugh. She liked him too, but would it be wise to tell him that? "I'm — I have a boyfriend."

"I know. Brandon. Do you love him?"

She didn't respond. How could she? She didn't love Brandon except as a friend, but she wasn't ready to give him up. She closed her eyes for a moment, wishing things were different, wishing she could trust Callen.

He stopped and turned her to face him. "There's something going on between us, Angel. I can't explain it, and I'm not even sure I want to. I just know it's there. I don't want to lose it."

Angel didn't either.

"We're both in a tough place right now." He traced her jawline with his finger. "We have some important issues to work out."

Like my guilt or innocence? She reached up and wrapped her arms around him and rested her head on his chest where his jacket hung open. His arms went around her, and he laid his cheek on her head.

But he was right; this wasn't the time for either of them to pursue a romantic relationship. She stepped back and took his hand again, then began walking back to the apartment. "Then what do you suggest we do about 'us'?"

"Well, we can be acquaintances." He squeezed her hand.

"Meaning?"

"I can help your mom cook dinner for you, get to know you and your family. And you can get to know me . . ."

"I can handle that."

They walked a while in silence. "So tell me about Dixon," she finally asked again.

"Not so fast. Since you're on leave, you're only going to get what's been released to the press."

"That's not fair. I was there. I found the body and —"

"Rules are rules."

"Do you always play by the rules?"

"When I can."

It was too dark to see his face now. She missed reading his expressive eyes. "Then tell me what you can."

"Someone slashed his throat with a steak knife."

"I knew that."

"There were no signs of a struggle."

"Do you think he was surprised by the attack or that he knew his killer?"

"Could've been either — or both. He'd been knocked down or had fallen. The killer slashed him when he was on the ground."

Angel sighed. "I guess that blows the theory about the killer being a man."

"And there were samples of your hair on his jacket."

"Of course there were. I fell on him." She looked up. "What about Broadman?"

"So far we have no evidence connecting

Broadman to the crime, except that he was there earlier. Like I mentioned before, he was seen leaving the resort within minutes of the time he and Dixon left the lounge."

"How much time would he need to follow Dixon into the shadows, trip him, and slice his throat?" Angel was grasping at straws, and she knew it. As Callen had already told her, Broadman had no reason to kill Dixon.

"Not a lot," Callen replied, "but more time than he had."

"He could've driven out of the parking lot and parked on the street and come back," Angel suggested. She wasn't being logical in pressing her case against Broadman, but she was angry with him and wanted some kind of retribution.

"He could have, but why would he do that? You don't kill your benefactor."

They had reached her apartment, and Angel put the key in the lock. "I'm your only real suspect, aren't I?"

"The crime lab seems to think so." Callen slipped his hands into his pockets, looking troubled.

Angel put a hand on his chest to keep him from following her inside. Rachael had said he was slick. Had his friendly attitude been a ploy to get her to reveal something incriminating? It hurt to think so. "What do you think?"

"I think I need to dig a little deeper. I also think I'd better get home." He leaned down and brushed his lips against her cheek. "Good night."

She watched him hurry down the stairs and climb into his car, then she closed and locked the door. After removing her coat and wet shoes, she hung the coat in the bathroom and set the shoes on the balcony out of the rain. Back inside she turned on the gas fireplace and watched the flames curl around the fake wood. She pulled the burgundy velour throw from the basket beside the sofa and wrapped it around her shoulders. Another gift from Callen. Why hadn't she noticed before? The afghan had the faint scent of his cologne.

She felt confused and unsure of herself. Did Callen really believe she was innocent? He had intimated that he felt something special for her. Then wham, he had to go and remind her again that she was a suspect in a murder investigation.

Well, he told you the truth, didn't he? It wasn't his fault Dixon was dead or that she had fallen over the body. It wasn't her fault either. Deep down, she knew he was doing his job and that he was being sincere in the way he felt about her. Maybe it was his honesty that frightened her the most, not what the investigation might turn up. Still, no matter how much he cared about her, Detective Riley was a cop and he needed to look at the facts, not be swayed by feelings. She just hoped the facts sorted themselves out and that the evidence eventually pointed away from her.

THIRTY-ONE

On Sunday morning Angel woke up to the bells ringing in the distance — bells from St. Matthew's Church. She had a strong urge to go to church that morning, for the first time in years. She tossed the covers aside and went into the living room to turn on the fireplace and watch the waves.

What had changed? Angel wasn't sure; maybe it had something to do with her mother's wise counsel and her advice to imagine Dani in heaven. Dani would want her to go back to church. Dani would tell her to get her act together.

Angel showered, dressed in black slacks and a white blouse, and showed up at St. Matthew's at 10:00 a.m. Tim greeted her as she came in and wrapped his arms around her. "Welcome back, sis."

Welcome back. Even though she hadn't attended church services since her return from Florida, she felt a deep sense of belonging — almost like she had as a child when her faith had been young and unblemished.

Angel slipped into the pew her family always occupied, next to her mother. Anna murmured a thank you and embraced her daughter. When Angel turned back, she realized someone had just come into the pew. Callen. He smiled down at her. "Your mother invited me."

Angel glanced back at Anna, who gave her a knowing smile and picked up a hymnal.

Callen handed Angel his open hymnal as the music began, indicating they could share. Standing there beside him, their arms touching, felt frighteningly normal. Angel felt herself relaxing and enjoying the service, the singing, the prayers, and especially Tim's sermon.

The day was one of the most pleasant respites Angel had experienced in years. After the service, Peter, Paul, Tim and Susan and the girls, Angel, and her mother gathered at the hospital to visit her father, then converged on the Delaney house to eat. Her mother had already prepared most of the meal — roasted game hens, herb-roasted potatoes, and salads — before church and asked Susan and Angel to set the table. Following dinner they all pitched in to clean up then headed for the beach to play volleyball.

When she headed back to her apartment later that day, Angel felt better than she had in a long time. Maybe her shift in attitude was due to the fact that she now knew she hadn't killed Billy; or maybe it was going to church and finding that God was the same as he had ever been.

The one thing that would've made the family gathering perfect was her father and Luke. And Callen. He'd been invited, but he declined, saying he had to get his computer set up and look through some police records.

Monday morning brought back the rain and the darkness — and the reality of the trouble Angel found herself in. She was afraid to trust Detective Riley and afraid to leave the investigation up to the police. What she should have done and would do in the future was to have Rachael with her whenever she spoke to an officer — regardless of how green his eyes were. She had to remember she had no friends on the force now.

To make matters worse, Callen had a

huge caseload, and now with Dixon's murder, he'd likely be pulled in too many directions. With budget cuts and with herself and her father off work, the police department was operating with a skeleton crew. The shooting incident would be dealt with as quickly as possible to appease the masses and that worried her. Would they rush to judgment? Saturday night Callen had agreed to go back to the warehouse with her. Well, not exactly with her. He only said that he would go. Could she count on him to do that? She decided to call him later and remind him.

First, though, she needed to pay a visit to her lawyer. Rachael had called earlier to say they needed to prepare for the grand jury hearing. Not something she was looking forward to.

Angel ate leftover spaghetti for breakfast, trying not to think about how natural and right it had been to have Callen in her kitchen or standing beside her in church. After eating, she rinsed the dishes and left them in the sink. Then she studied her pitifully sparse wardrobe, thinking she probably should wear something other than the jeans and T-shirts she'd been living in.

She ended up wearing a white cable-knit

sweater and a pair of black jeans. Her hair put up its usual resistance to any kind of order, and she finally gave up on it. The damp air would have its way, and within an hour she'd look like Shirley Temple.

She eased out of her apartment, hoping to avoid the press, and was surprised at their absence. Maybe they'd found someone else to hassle. One could only hope. Relieved, she hurried to the end of the lot, where she'd parked Brandon's car. The Lexus was gone.

Angel felt a moment's panic. Had someone stolen it? Brandon could have picked it up, but knowing him, he'd have called or dropped by to let her know. Then again, maybe he had. She didn't remember checking her messages the night before. She hurried back inside and saw that the answering machine light was blinking. When she hit the play button, the mechanical voice indicated the call had come in on Sunday at 5:45 p.m. "I'm back in town," Brandon said. "I haven't been able to get away. Dad's got all of us working on an important case. Anyway, I'm sending my secretary over to pick up my car. Don't worry, you'll find a replacement — my sister's Blazer. I told her to park it close to your apartment. The key is under the mat in the front. I'll call you tonight." He paused. "Love you."

She blinked back tears as she heard the last part of his message. She was going to have to tell him she didn't love him. It wasn't fair to keep him dangling like that. *I will tell him,* she promised herself. *Today.*

Angel found the Blazer and the keys and headed over to Tim's church. She parked on the street in front and started up the sidewalk and around to the side, where an addition had been built to accommodate the offices, classrooms, and fellowship hall. Tim greeted her with a hug and pointed her toward Rachael's office.

Rachael was looking at some files. Her office, if you could call it that, was a small cubicle that looked as if it had once been a storage room. There was barely enough space for a desk, let alone for the file cabinet, bookshelves, and a chair. Perched on the top shelf of a bookcase was a huge white cat. When Angel spoke, the cat assessed her with wide blue eyes then stretched, turned around in a circle, and curled back into a ball.

"Hi, Angel. Welcome." Rachael greeted her with a wide, dimpled smile. "Hang on a sec. I want to file these."

"Is that Sherlock?" Angel nodded toward the purring feline.

"Yeah. He's resting. Poor baby, he had a late night."

Since the room had no client chair and obviously no room for one, Angel waited in the hall. On the opposite wall a door stood open, revealing colorful banners, paintings, and drawings that were prominently displayed; she guessed the artwork came from the preschool children. She smiled at their efforts to re-create the world around them.

"Aren't they wonderful?" Rachael closed her door and started back the way Angel had come. "I love being here and watching them."

"It's a wonder you get any work done."

She shrugged. "I don't have that many clients. I help Angie when I can — makes me feel like I'm contributing something for my office space. Besides, I love kids."

They wove past Tim's office, veered left, then right again, finally reaching the sanctuary. Rachael slid into one of the stained wood pews. "I hope you don't mind. There's no room in my office to talk."

"So I noticed." Their voices echoed in the high-ceilinged chamber.

"But isn't this great? All this space and a stained glass window. I'll bet even the Laffertys would envy this."

Angel chuckled. "I doubt it, but I like your enthusiasm and your taste."

With a pen and legal pad in hand, Rachael said, "You told me on the phone this morning that you have some new information."

Angel filled her in on her trip to the warehouse and her talk with Callen. "I think he believes I didn't kill Dixon, but I imagine he's being pressured to get the case wrapped up. I know how these things go."

"Let's not worry too much about that right now. We need to concentrate on your case specifically, your part in Billy's death. The hardest thing we have to face here is the missing evidence."

"I think I've convinced Callen that there was another shooter, but what if I'm not able to prove it?"

"Well, don't give up yet. We've still got your reputation. And we can probably fault Billy's mother for her less-than-adequate parenting skills."

"No." The objection came out rather harshly.

Rachael gave her an odd look. "Well, we need something."

"I don't want her character brought into question. She's a single parent and is already feeling guilty. I don't want anything we do to add to that guilt."

"Okay." Rachael sighed. "We'll just have to hope the missing evidence turns up or the crime lab guys find something at the warehouse to prove you didn't fire those last two shots." Rachael picked up her briefcase and rested it on her lap. Opening it, she drew out some notes.

Angel's stomach knotted up. "Is that my file?"

"Uh-huh. Relax, Angel. I have a good feeling about all this. The grand jury rarely indicts a police officer."

"Yes, but how many of them have shot a kid with a toy gun?"

"There have been a few." Rachael tipped her head. "I know it looks scary."

"What if they decide against me? I'll be charged with man one and —"

"And we'll cross that bridge when we get there. In the meantime, we need to make sure you have your story straight."

Angel wished she could relax, but she wouldn't, not until it was all over — maybe not even then.

"I have some good news — at least I hope it's good." Rachael opened her appointment book. "I've been doing some investigative work on my own. I found Dixon's wife."

"In Atlanta? You talked to her?"

"She isn't in Atlanta. She came with him. She's been visiting friends in Newport, and I have an appointment with her in an hour. Want to come?"

"Sure." Angel wasn't sure what good it would do to talk with the woman. She suspected someone from Sunset Cove P.D. already had. Maybe Callen. She tried not to picture him standing in her kitchen or walking with her on the beach. She tried and failed.

Rachael glanced at her watch again. "Do you have something to do between now and then?"

"No. Want to get a cup of coffee?"

"I like the way you think. Let's go to Joanie's, and I'll buy you a latte."

"Perfect, I love that place." The coffee shop was located downtown in the refurbished area, sandwiched between two shops, one that carried every gift and souvenir known to humankind, the other an upscale art gallery.

A bell tinkled when Angel and Rachael entered the shop.

"Hi, girls." Joanie poked her head up from behind the counter. She spoke with an English accent, despite having come to the States fifteen years ago. "Be with you in a moment."

Angel and Rachael chose one of several thick-cushioned armchairs by the fireplace, where they could enjoy the view of the ocean as it collided with the rocks below. Beside the chairs and sofas were white metal patio tables with matching chairs. The scent of delicate potpourri wafted through the room, along with the scent of coffee and fresh-baked pastries. Shelves were filled with treasures from Joanie's native England, as well as an ample supply of coffees, teas, kitchen supplies, and candles.

"Sorry about that," Joanie said as she headed toward their table, wiping her hands on a towel. "Just had a supply of ice cream come in, and I had to get it put away. Now then, what can I get for you?"

"One of your anise and orange biscotti — chocolate dipped." Rachael studied the menu. "And a twelve-ounce mocha cappuccino."

"I'll have a . . ." Angel drummed her fingers on the table. "An amaretto latte. And do you still make those yummy chocolate-chip hazelnut scones?"

"I do. Do you want it with lemon curd or preserves and clotted cream?"

"Mmm. All of the above." She tossed Joanie and Rachael a guilty look. "I'm drowning my sorrows in fat. Can you tell?"

"Like you need to worry," Rachael chuckled. "Better that than booze."

"Don't worry," Joanie teased, "I'll stop serving you when I think you've had enough."

Angel laughed. "Actually, I think I'm doing it because my mother thinks I don't eat well."

"I have news for you," Rachael said. "This may be eating well, but it isn't eating healthy."

"How can you say that? Joanie told me herself that she takes all the calories out. Don't you, Joanie?"

"Well, of course," she said with a giggle. "Is that it, then? Want some soup or a sandwich with that?"

Angel hadn't eaten since breakfast. "Thanks for reminding me. I'll have a bowl of clam chowder."

"Me too." Turning to Angel, Rachael asked, "Want to split a chicken salad sandwich?"

Angel nodded. "Sounds good."

As Joanie prepared their food, Angel listened to Rachael extol Paul's virtues. After delivering the order and bringing them waters, Joanie sat in a nearby chair. "How are you doing then, Angel? If you don't want to talk, that's fine, but I've been worried about you. All that awful stuff they're saying."

"I'm okay. I'm sure it'll blow over soon. At least I hope so."

"Most of the locals are on your side, luv." Joanie got to her feet. "There now. That's all I'm going to say on the subject. I imagine you get your fill of it elsewhere. You two relax and enjoy yourselves."

"We will, thanks." Rachael turned to Angel. "It was nice of her to say something. I know it must seem like everyone is against you — especially when you watch the news."

"Or listen to certain cops."

They both concentrated on eating, and it didn't take long for Angel to realize she'd ordered far more than she could eat. She asked Joanie for a bag for her scone.

Rachael glanced at her watch. "We'd better take off. Mrs. Dixon will be waiting."

Fifteen minutes later, they were standing in the doorway of Alicia Dixon's hotel room, introducing themselves.

If Alicia Dixon were to audition for the role of a grieving widow, she'd never get the part. There was no sign of smeared mascara, no telltale redness around her eyes. Her hair had been brushed up and teased to perfection, and it framed her oval face and accentuated expertly applied makeup. She was dressed in an elegant pantsuit of soft, draping fabric.

"Some people are accusing you of killing my husband."

Angel forced her gaze to meet Alicia Dixon's eyes. "I didn't kill your husband, ma'am. I didn't even know him."

"Why are you here?" She pursed her lips and folded her arms, looking as though she was going to make them stay in the hallway.

"Mrs. Dixon," Rachael said, "we'd like to find out who did kill him."

The woman's skeptical gaze caught Angel's. "I'll talk to you, but I doubt I can be of any help." She opened the door wider and motioned them inside. She indicated a table with four chairs and took one of them herself.

"Did your husband have any enemies?" Angel asked once they were seated.

"Not that I know of. He was a kind man, and everyone looked up to him. I've already told the police all of this."

Angel wondered if Callen had questioned her, but didn't ask.

"Yes," Rachael said, "I figured as much.

We're just following up."

"Why was your husband here?" Angel asked.

"Mr. Broadman asked him to come. He insisted that the Hartwell boy's shooting was a racial incident. Broadman told Todd that he was filing a civil suit and needed his help." She sat stiff and poised, her words sharp and to the point. "He wanted my husband to help him raise money to cover legal expenses."

"You don't like Ray Broadman much, do you?" Angel asked.

Mrs. Dixon raised a perfectly formed eyebrow. "Neither Todd nor I particularly cared for the man."

"Why was that?" Angel picked a piece of lint from her pants.

"My husband doesn't like being pressured. And Mr. Broadman was putting a lot of pressure on him to make a public statement to the effect that the police department here was prejudiced and would likely sweep the boy's death under the carpet. He was concerned you would be exonerated and wanted to make certain the public knew the truth."

"Was Broadman angry with your husband?" Rachael asked.

"Not angry." She frowned, then added,

"I'd say impatient. Todd likes to take his time and get all the facts. I think Mr. Broadman wanted things handled more expediently."

Angel pressed on. "Can you tell us what happened the day your husband was murdered?"

"As I told the police, Todd had meetings all day. I left around 10:00 to go to Newport. I was meeting my sister and a friend at the aquarium there. We'd arranged to spend a couple days together." She covered her eyes, showing grief for the first time. "I shouldn't have left him alone."

"We're terribly sorry for your loss, Mrs. Dixon," Rachael said. "The reverend sounds like a fine man."

Alicia nodded, her lips pinched.

"We won't take any more of your time." Rachael stood. "We appreciate your help."

Angel stopped at the door. "Do you by any chance have Mr. Broadman's address?"

She shook her head then touched her hand to her mouth. "Wait. He called here the morning after we arrived. Todd jotted something down on a pad by the phone. It's gone now, but maybe there's an indentation." She looked embarrassed. "Um — I read mysteries and, well, I don't know if

411

police officers ever do this, but can't you tell what was written by doing a pencil rub?"

"It's not very sophisticated, but it works." Angel lightly rubbed the pad's surface with a pencil she'd pulled out of the desk and jotted down the revealed address. She and Rachael then thanked Mrs. Dixon and left.

"That was interesting," Angel mused as they walked down the hall to the elevators. "It looks like Ray Broadman may have had a motive after all."

"Because Dixon was taking his time?"

"No, but if Dixon refused to cooperate, if they argued over it . . ."

"That's a lot of ifs, but I agree. I wish we had a tape of the conversation those two had Friday night." Rachael punched the down arrow and waited for the doors to slide open.

"We don't have a tape," Angel said, "but we could talk to the person who waited on them. I think waiters and waitresses hear a lot more than they let on."

"Hmm. You have a point."

They stopped at the resort and were surprised to find Callen's unmarked Crown Victoria parked in the circular drive under the wide and brightly lit canopy. Had he come back to look over the crime scene and question more people?

As they walked into the restaurant, Angel and Rachael stopped one of the servers and asked to speak with the manager. She led them to a room in the office complex. "Mr. Sykes is with someone right now, but you could wait over there," she said and gestured toward a small waiting area that looked much like that of a doctor's office. Rachael seated herself and began looking through a *Coastal Living* magazine. Angel paced up and down the hall, noting that her brothers had offices in this section of the resort as well.

The door of the restaurant manager's office opened, and Callen stepped out. His surprised gaze met Angel's and moved to Rachael. "What are you two doing here?"

"I was hoping to talk to the manager to find out who was serving Dixon and Broadman Friday night."

"And you were going to do what with that information?"

Angel licked her lips. Callen didn't have to say it. She knew what he was thinking.

"I know, I'm on leave, but I thought it might be helpful to find the server and see if he'd overheard anything . . ."

The pained look in his eyes stopped her.

"It's too late, Angel. The kid's name was Alex Carlson."

"Was?"

"He's dead."

THIRTY-TWO

"Where are we going?" Rachael asked when Angel turned off the highway onto Sixth Street, away from the ocean.

"I thought we might pay Ray Broadman a visit."

"Why would we want to do that?"

Angel chewed on the inside of her cheek. "Alex served Broadman and Dixon last night in the restaurant. Dixon was murdered and Alex is dead. Tell me that's a coincidence."

"Maybe it is. Callen said the kid apparently died from a drug overdose."

"But Alex waited on Broadman and Dixon. He might've heard something."

"He may not have," Rachael argued. "Seeing Broadman isn't a good idea, Angel. The man threatened to kill you."

"I just want to ask him some questions."

Rachael shook her head. "You're treading on thin ice, kiddo. It sounds as though you're doing your own investigating, and that's definitely taboo."

"All right. I'll stay in the car while you ask him questions."

Rachael rolled her eyes. "Like what? Did you murder the Reverend Todd Elroy Dixon and Alex Carlson?"

"That'll do for a start." Angel wondered at the wisdom of coming here herself, but she had to do something.

Broadman lived in a ten-year-old subdivision filled with expensive homes. The yards, his included, were neatly maintained. Broadman was obviously better off than his sister and mother.

"I'm not really worried about it," Angel went on. "You're with me, so I doubt he'll try anything, and if he does, I'll have a witness. Anyway, let him try. I'd take great pleasure in seeing him arrested."

Rachael folded her arms. "Humph. I just hope he's the one who ends up getting arrested and not you."

There was no car in the driveway, and no one answered the door. Disappointed, Angel started back to the Blazer. "We might as well go."

They were just getting into the car when

Callen drove up. He didn't look happy to see them. "Would you two mind telling me what you're doing here? In case you've forgotten, Delaney, you're on leave."

"I haven't forgotten." Angel lifted her gaze to his face.

"And you're here because . . . ?"

"We came out to talk to Broadman."

"Any particular reason?"

"I know Broadman is guilty."

"You know nothing of the kind." Callen rubbed his jaw. "Look, I know you believe he's the one who threatened you, but again, you have no proof."

"Well, not proof exactly. But listen to this. Rachael and I talked to Alicia Dixon, and she indicated that all was not well between Broadman and her husband." Angel frowned. "Why are *you* here?"

"I talked to Mrs. Dixon on Saturday, and based on her testimony and the alleged animosity between the two men, I was able to obtain a search warrant. I was just about to go in."

Angel nodded her approval. Not that he needed it or wanted it. "Do you mind if we stay to see if you turn up anything?"

"Suit yourself." He still sounded angry. "You can come in with me if you want. I'll do a walk through, and if we find anything,

I'll get the lab people out here to take samples."

The house was a single story home in which all the walls were painted white. Except for a few breakfast dishes in the sink, it looked spotless. In the office they found notes and papers pertaining to the lawsuit, and correspondence to Dixon, but nothing to indicate Broadman might've killed the man.

Angel and Rachael followed Callen through the house and yard. After checking the garbage can, Callen brushed his hair back and straightened. "Place looks clean on the surface."

"If he did kill Dixon," Angel said, "he wouldn't be stupid enough to leave any evidence laying around."

Callen placed both hands on her shoulders and looked into her eyes. "I know this is important to you, but we're on it, okay? Why don't you go home and let me handle the investigation?"

"I am letting you handle it; it's just that I need to know what's happening."

"I'm telling you what I can." Callen dropped his arms.

That isn't good enough. She heaved a sigh. "All right, you win. I'm going now." She'd gone a few steps when she stopped and turned around. "Callen, about Alex Carlson. Call me when you get the medical examiner's report, okay?"

"Yeah."

Once in the Blazer, Angel cranked the key. In her rearview mirror, she saw Callen get into his car and ease away from the curb. She fell in place behind him.

"You know, Angel, Broadman may not have killed Dixon." Rachael gave her a sidelong look. "Maybe you have the wrong person."

"Yeah, maybe." She chewed on her lip as she maneuvered around a garbage truck. "But then who did it?" She had to admit there were other possibilities, but none so compelling as Broadman. The man was a menace, and she had no problem imagining him as a killer.

Rachael shrugged. "Maybe you need to step back and —"

"Hold on." Angel made a sharp right.

Rachael yelped and grabbed for the dashboard. "Where are you going?"

"Broadman wouldn't leave any evidence around for anyone to see it." Angel drummed her fingers on the steering wheel, turning right again. "He'd get rid of it."

"I'm not following you."

Angel pulled up on the opposite side of the street from Broadman's house and stopped. "Dixon's throat was slit. If Broadman did it, he would've gotten blood on his clothes and maybe on his shoes. He'd need to get rid of the evidence as soon as possible."

"So?"

"So he gets into his car and drives home."

"But we didn't see any blood in the house."

"Because he would've cleaned it up. Put yourself in his place. You've just killed a man and have blood all over yourself."

Rachael made a face. "Okay. First I wouldn't want to get in my car because I'd get blood on the seat and the floor mats."

"But you have no choice."

"Okay." Rachael frowned. "I can clean it up later, especially if I have vinyl seats. I need to get home fast so I can shower and change."

"But you can't go inside — there's blood on your shoes," Angel reminded her.

Rachael glanced at the house. "I could drive into the garage, take off my clothes and shoes, put them in a garbage bag, then go inside."

"And what would you do with the garbage?"

Rachael thought for a moment. "I couldn't put it in my own garbage can. The police might check that."

"Exactly. Which we did and found it empty. In fact, that empty can is what got my attention. The garbage truck we saw was heading toward Broadman's house, not away from it. So where is Broadman's garbage?"

"Maybe he took it to a dumpster somewhere."

"Or maybe he used a neighbor's can, knowing that the garbage truck would be coming today." Her hands gripped the steering wheel. "Let's take a look."

"I don't know, Angel. Maybe you should call Callen back."

"I will if we find anything." Angel drove around to the alley and parked behind the house. All of the garbage cans except for Broadman's were out at the curb awaiting pickup. Angel checked the cans on either side of Broadman's house while Rachael went to the other side of the alley.

Angel proceeded to the right to the end of the block and came back to the can two doors down. After she carefully lifted the lid to preserve fingerprints, she noticed a black plastic bag, layered between two white bags.

Rachael came up behind her. "What've you got there?"

"I don't know. Let's open them and find out." The top white bag contained the usual kitchen garbage. She pulled out the black one and untwisted the tie. Inside she could see a bundle of clothing and a pair of men's shoes. "Rachael, I think we may have our evidence." Angel turned around.

A large hand covered Rachael's mouth. Ray Broadman stood there even bigger than Angel remembered him, holding a .38 snub-nosed revolver to Rachael's temple.

THIRTY-THREE

Angel dropped the lid and stepped away from the can. "Let her go."

Ray Broadman dragged Rachael backward toward his house. "Make a sound and she dies."

"You're not going to get away with this." Angel took another step toward them.

"Stay back." He waved the gun at her, then directed it back to Rachael. His left arm was hooked around her throat.

Rachael's gaze caught Angel's. Angel sent her a silent message. *Don't try anything foolish.*

But in a sudden movement, Rachael raised her hands and grabbed Broadman's arm. Then in a maneuver any karate instructor would've been proud of, she jabbed her heel into his instep and slipped her head free.

Angel took advantage of his surprise and

made a dash for him. She kicked his right hand, sending the .38 to the ground. Rachael got around behind him and pushed while Angel slammed the back of his neck with her fist, sending him to the ground. She scooped up the revolver and held it on him.

She had Rachael go to the car for the cell phone to put a call in to dispatch. Five minutes later a police car pulled up. Nick climbed out of his vehicle. "What's going on?"

"These perverts were poking around in the garbage cans," Broadman spat out. "Arrest them."

"Garbage cans? What the . . . ?"

"He's the one you need to arrest." Rachael leaned against the garage door. "He pulled a gun on me. He was going to kill me."

"They attacked me!" Broadman countered. "They're the ones with the gun."

Another police car pulled up, this one unmarked but all too recognizable. Callen stepped out, his gaze sweeping over them and landing on the gun Angel was holding. Nick briefed him on what he knew about the situation, which wasn't much.

"I thought you went home." Callen looked directly at Angel.

"I was going to and then I spotted the garbage truck. But Broadman's garbage can was empty. I got to thinking that if Broadman did kill Dixon, he'd have gotten blood all over himself. He couldn't use his own can, but I thought he might use a neighbor's." Angel pointed to the black bag she'd dropped. "I think he did. I have a hunch you'll find more than enough evidence here to charge him."

Broadman glared at her. "She framed me. I got a right to protect my own property. Those aren't even my clothes."

Angel folded her arms across her chest. "I'm sure the crime lab will determine that they are and that the blood is Mr. Dixon's."

"She's right. It won't take the crime lab long to find out." Nick mirandized and cuffed him. "In the meantime, we'll be taking you in for questioning."

"This is police brutality!" Broadman yelled. "Can't you see what they did to me?" He turned to Nick. "They kicked me. I got the bruises to prove it."

"You creep." Rachael pushed off from the garage door. "You had a gun in my face. Don't preach to me about brutality. Sheesh."

But when Nick left with Broadman,

Rachael started to shake, her face going pale. "I'm going to the car. I'm not feeling so good."

Angel started to follow, but Callen grabbed her arm and swung her around. His green eyes bore into her. "How could you do something so stupid? You not only risked your life, you risked Rachael's, and you may have damaged the credibility of the evidence."

Angel stepped back as though he'd slapped her. But she knew he was right; she should've called him with her suspicions right away instead of looking through the garbage cans on her own. "I just wanted to —"

"Smart thinking," he interrupted, "but your follow-through was lousy. What I should do is arrest you for obstructing justice. This isn't your investigation! You . . . are . . . on . . . leave."

Angel wasn't about to let him have the last word. "If I hadn't found that evidence —"

"We'd have found it sooner or later."

"Right. And just how long do you think that garbage would be there?"

"Long enough. I saw the garbage truck too, Angel, and realized his can shouldn't have been empty. I'd already called the lab

426

guys to come out and do a more thorough search. Besides, if we hadn't had the clothes, we had his car." He dragged a hand through his hair and heaved an exasperated sigh. "Go home and stay there. Let me do my job."

Angel spun around and headed for the car. Without a backward glance she climbed in behind the wheel, revved up the engine, and drove away. She had made him angry, and she couldn't afford to do that. If he filed a complaint against her, she'd probably be out of a job for good.

Callen watched her leave, then jogged to the alley where he had instructed the garbage collectors to bypass the block. He went back out to his car to wait for his lab team and thought again about Angel. What was he going to do with her? She frustrated him to no end, and at the same time he admired her spunk. She had the tenacity of a bull rider in a rodeo. She'd been thrown more times than he could count, yet she kept coming back, refusing to stay out of the saddle.

She was understandably concerned, but in trying to conduct her own investigation, she was getting in over her head. She hadn't been trained as a detective and wasn't aware how delicately a crime scene needed to be handled.

Callen's phone rang, and he flipped it on. "Detective Riley here."

"Riley, this is Dr. Murrey. You wanted me to call when I got something on the Carlson boy."

"Right, what do you have?" Callen had seen the boy's body and had a hunch what the findings would be.

"Looks as though the boy's mother might be right about Alex not being a drug user. The kid had drugs in his system, but he also had trauma to the mouth and throat that indicates he may have been force-fed. I should have a preliminary report to you in a day or two."

Callen thanked him and hung up. When the lab techs showed up, he gave them instructions to go over the entire house to look for blood evidence. They found traces in the shower and in the garage, as well as in his car. That along with his discarded clothing should put him away for a long time — if the blood matched Dixon's.

By the time they'd finished, it was 5:00 p.m. and time for Callen to call it a day. He had dinner to make for a very special lady.

Later that evening Angel brought

Rachael along to dinner at her parents' home. Paul put an arm around Rachael's waist the minute she stepped inside. "Miss me?" he asked in a low voice.

"Like crazy," Rachael whispered back.

Angel squeezed around the two lovebirds blocking the door and followed the wonderful aromas coming from the kitchen. She stopped just short of the wide arch, suddenly wishing she hadn't come. She could hear Callen's rich baritone voice and her mother's soprano; she had forgotten that her mother had invited Callen to join them.

He was the last person Angel wanted to see, especially after the way he had confronted her at Broadman's place. She was surprised he'd come at all. She started to back out when Peter came up behind her.

"Something sure smells good." Peter ruffled her hair before making a beeline to Anna.

"Peter, you made it." Anna reached up for a hug. Gesturing toward Callen, she said, "Look who's come to dinner."

Peter looked from his mother to Callen and then to the white apron Callen wore over his polo shirt and slacks. "What gives?"

"He cooks," Angel offered. "Our mother

429

has found her soul mate."

Callen ignored her tone and grinned at her. "Wondered when you'd show up."

"If I'd known you were coming, I wouldn't have."

"Angel Delaney," Anna scolded. "That's no way to talk to our guest."

"*Your* guest." She glanced around. "Where's Dad?"

"Right behind you." Frank squeezed her shoulders and took his regular place at the large wooden table.

Angel looked at Callen again. For some reason, seeing her mother cook with him stirred up a fierce jealousy. Anna looked vibrant and happy as she showed Callen where to find utensils. Somehow Angel had gotten the idea that her mother didn't like anyone helping in the kitchen. But thinking back, she realized the opposite was true. Her mother had invited her to help make a meal many times. Why hadn't she?

Because I was too busy trying to please Dad.

Angel tossed the idea aside, focusing again on Callen. No one else seemed to notice his intrusive presence. Peter sat down next to their father. Paul and Rachael squeezed past, followed by Tim,

Susan, and the girls. Angel remained in the doorway.

You can still leave, she told herself. Instead, she watched as Callen sampled a dish he'd been working on. He tossed the contents of the pan into the air and caught it all in the pan again, then repeated the move several times without spilling a drop.

"Where did you learn to do that?" Angel asked.

He grinned over at her. "Practice. I'll teach you sometime."

"I don't cook, remember?"

"It's not too late to learn." Callen slid the contents of the frying pan onto a serving platter. Anna placed a bowl of steaming, oven-browned vegetables in the center of the table on one of the brightly designed trivets. Callen helped her bring the rest of the food to the table, and while she took her place beside Frank, he sat down in one of the two end places.

"Angel, come sit down," her mother urged.

Angel shrugged and slipped into the only empty chair, next to Callen. She was hungry, and the food looked great. Her feelings for Callen would have to take a backseat to her rumbling stomach.

For the next few minutes they all focused their attention on the succulent Marsala chicken, gnocchi made with potatoes, cream cheese, and herbs, and the large tray of oven-browned vegetables — broccoli, asparagus, squash, cauliflower, onion, and mushrooms.

"I could get used to this." Rachael set her fork down to pick up her drink. "It's decadent."

Anna grinned and with the pride of a mother announced, "Callen made the chicken."

Angel didn't comment as the compliments flew. But she had to admit the chicken was tender and moist, and its delectable sauce was smooth and almost as good as dessert.

Paul asked Rachael how her day went, and to Angel's chagrin, she went into the entire spiel about how she and Angel had single-handedly captured Dixon's killer.

"Ahem." Callen cleared his throat. "His alleged killer. We're still testing blood samples."

"Whatever." Rachael shrugged her shoulders.

Paul turned to Angel. "How could you take a chance like that?"

"Don't blame Angel, Paul." Rachael came to her defense. "We both went. The creep snuck up on us and caught me by surprise."

"It's a good thing you know self-defense." Paul's reaction was a lot like Callen's had been.

Rachael rolled her eyes. "Are you kidding? These days women are foolish not to."

"You two were lucky," Frank barked. "You could've gotten yourselves killed. What were you thinking, going to the man's house?"

"Shush, Frank," Anna said. "Don't be getting yourself all upset. You know it's not good for your heart." She got up from the table, poured him a cup of hot water, and handed him a tea bag. "Here, have some chamomile tea."

"I'm not drinking anything made from weeds. Give me some coffee."

"No," Anna said firmly.

He muttered something unintelligible and took a deep breath. "I think I'll have a talk with Joe tomorrow, Angel. Maybe he can spare one of the guys. Now that I'm out of commission, you need someone else to look after you."

"Look after me?" A raw ache started in her midsection. All these years and he still didn't think she could take care of herself.

She still wasn't good enough. As much as she wanted to confront him, she wouldn't. It wouldn't do any good, and she wasn't about to make a scene in front of everyone. She shot a look at Rachael. "Maybe we'd better go. We've had a full day."

Paul slipped an arm around Rachael's shoulders. "I can take Rachael home."

Angel shrugged and pushed back her chair. "Okay by me."

Anna hurried after her, catching her at the door. "Your father loves you, honey. You know that. He didn't mean anything bad by what he said. You're still his little girl, and he wants to protect you."

"I know, Ma. I know." Angel slipped on her jacket.

Her mother always seemed to know how she felt. *Am I that transparent?* She let her mother hug her then stepped outside, closing the door behind her.

She sighed loudly when she got within sight of the driveway. Peter had parked his Jag behind the Blazer, blocking her in. She didn't want to go back inside — at least not yet.

"I'm not going to let him get to me." She tipped her head back, speaking into the wind. "I'm not."

She heard someone come up behind her.

"Do you always talk to yourself?" Callen's voice was tender and full of understanding.

"Doesn't everyone?" She should've been annoyed that he'd followed her, but she wasn't.

Callen tucked his hands into his pockets. "Want me to have your brother move his car?" He grinned. "Actually, I wouldn't mind moving it myself, maybe take it around the block."

"That's not necessary. I just need some air."

"Want to walk?"

He held his hand out to her, and she took it. "I'm sorry about this afternoon," she said. "I overstepped my boundaries. It's hard to just sit by. I'm not used to being a civilian."

"I'm sorry too. I was rougher on you than I should've been."

"Yeah, you were."

"I was so mad at you, Angel. Not so much because of what you did, but because of the danger you put yourself in. Sometimes it's hard for me to be objective where you're concerned."

"Let me guess — you reacted because you care."

"More than I should."

"Well, you know what? I'm not some hothouse orchid. I don't need to be protected. I can take care of myself. I'm a cop, for Pete's sake."

"Of course you can take care of yourself. It's just that people come with a built-in mechanism that springs into action when someone is in danger. Especially someone they love."

She guessed he was talking about her father. "I know my father loves me in his own way. But there's more to it than that. He wants to make sure I don't fail." Tears stung her eyes. "I keep telling myself that I'm a grown woman and I don't need his help or his approval."

Callen stopped and drew her into the circle of his arms. "I know how you feel. But sometimes we never get that approval."

She looked up at him. "Your father?"

"And my mother." His eyes held a distant pain.

Angel nodded. "I'm trying not to let it upset me."

"If it's any consolation, you made a good call today. We hadn't gotten that far, and you were right. By the time my guys got there, all the trash in the neighborhood might've been picked up."

"You still would've had his car."

"Mmm. We found traces of blood in the garage and his shower. There was a smudge in the kitchen where it got into the grout on the tile floor. He cleaned things up pretty well, but with the tests we have today, blood evidence is impossible to hide. We'll run DNA tests."

"It'll match Dixon's."

"I'm sure it will."

"What about Alex Carlson?"

Callen told her what the medical examiner had said.

"Poor kid. I wonder how much he really knew."

Callen shook his head. "We'll never know. His shift was over at 10:30 — somewhere between then and midnight, he was murdered."

"Maybe he saw Broadman kill Dixon, and Broadman went after him."

"I don't see where he would've had time."

"Well, suppose you were killing someone, and you looked up and there's a kid watching you, what do you do?"

Callen smiled down at her. "Ever thought about becoming a detective?"

"As a matter of fact, I have."

"Good. Now to answer your question,

I'd take out the kid and leave the scene. Which would leave two bodies."

"What if Alex ran?" Angel persisted.

"I'd go after him."

They walked for several minutes without speaking. Then Callen stopped and drew her to him. He wove his fingers into her hair and lowered his lips to hers.

Angel gave herself up to it. She forgot to breathe, forgot to think. But too soon, all the reasons she shouldn't be kissing Callen drifted into her consciousness.

Maybe he was getting the same message. He stroked his thumb across her cheek. "You're driving me crazy, you know."

"I am?" She closed her eyes and leaned into him. His arms wrapped around her, and he kissed the top of her head. She put her arms around his waist.

"I'm losing my objectivity, Angel. I think it would be best if we didn't see each other until all this has been settled. I may have to hand over the investigation you're involved in to someone else."

Angel didn't know what to say. She didn't want him off the case. He was one of the few who believed in her. And she didn't want to stop seeing him either.

"Please don't." Angel squeezed his hand. "Give it a few more days."

He held her for a long time without speaking, and when he did say something, it was to tell her he had to go. Peter's Jag was gone by the time they got back. She avoided looking at Callen as she got into the Blazer and backed down the drive. He didn't kiss her or say good-bye. He just stood there with his hands in his pockets, leaning against his car, looking as though he'd lost his best friend.

As she turned onto the main road, a car moved out of its parking place and seemed to be tailing her. It stayed behind her as she entered the freeway. When she slowed, it slowed; when she sped up, it sped up. Her heart leaped to her throat as she thought about her trashed apartment and the thugs who had attacked her after the funeral.

"Who are you?" She glanced in the rearview mirror, wishing she could see something more than headlights. "Why are you following me?"

THIRTY-FOUR

"Maybe it's a coincidence," Angel told herself as she watched the headlights bob up and down after going over a speed bump. The vehicle was dark in color, and the driver hung back far enough so that she couldn't get a good look at it. When she turned into the apartment parking lot, the car stayed behind her, closing the gap. Angel pulled into a spot, hoping the driver would move past. Instead, he stopped behind her, blocking her in.

Angel let out a long sigh. Her fears subsided as the parking lot lights illuminated the familiar green sports utility vehicle and its driver.

She got out and stood there with her hands on her hips, waiting for her partner to step out of the car. "Eric Mason, what do you think you're doing, following me like that? You scared me half to death."

He raised both hands in surrender. "I'm sorry, Angel. I didn't mean to scare you."

"Why were you following me?"

"To make sure you got home safe." He was out of uniform, and she had a hunch someone had asked him for a favor.

"Did my father put you up to this?" she pressed.

He hesitated a bit too long.

"He did, didn't he?"

"You don't need to get so bent out of shape. After what's happened with your apartment being broken into and those guys smashing up your car, you need —"

"What, a keeper?" She clamped her lips together. It wasn't Eric's fault. If she were going to yell at someone, she should go directly to the source. "Okay, I give up. You can tell Dad I made it home safely. But in the future, would you please ask me if I need protection before you start following me?"

"If you say so." His perfect white teeth glistened in the light. "Hey, I heard how you nailed Broadman today. Good call."

"Thanks."

"Sure hope everything works out for you in that shooting situation. I miss working with you."

Angel smiled up at him. "I miss working

with you too, Eric. We made a pretty good team."

After an awkward silence, he said, "Well, I guess I'll be going. Uh, do you want me to check out your apartment? I can follow you inside."

"No, that's okay."

"I'll see you later then."

Angel took a step toward him. "Eric, I'm sorry if I sounded ungrateful. It's just that my dad — well, he still sees me as his little girl. You don't have to keep an eye on me."

He grinned. "It's always a pleasure to keep an eye on you."

"Go away, Eric." She chuckled as she headed for the stairs.

He waved. "Call if you need me."

Unlocking the door, she let it swing open then stepped inside. She listened intently but heard only the soft purring of the heater. The room was dark except for an illuminated clock on the microwave door. There were no strange smells — just a hint of vanilla room deodorizer her mother had left for her.

The apartment seemed safe enough. She closed the door and locked it. Weariness overtook her as she moved through the rooms, turning on lights. She changed into pajamas then went into the kitchen to put a cup of water into the microwave.

Angel needed to have a long talk with her father. Though she hated to admit it, even to herself, she was glad that Eric had followed her home. She should've let him see her inside as well. She used to look forward to coming home after a long day. Now every time she opened the door, she half expected someone to be waiting for her.

You'll get over it, she assured herself.

I hope so.

After putting a tea bag in her mug of hot water, she turned on the television and watched the last part of a movie. At 11:00 she turned to the news. As expected, the feature news story focused on Ray Broadman's arrest for the murder of Reverend Todd Elroy Dixon. There was no mention of her involvement, but then, she hadn't expected there to be. Hopefully, there would be plenty of evidence linking Broadman to the crime.

The bad news was that even with Broadman arrested, the civil lawsuit against her would go on as planned. Apparently Michael Lafferty had no qualms about continuing to represent a murderer. She shouldn't be surprised.

Angel briefly considered talking to Mavis and Emmie again. Now that Broadman was in jail he wouldn't be able to intimidate them.

She picked up the phone and dialed and was greeted with a chilly and indignant Mavis. "You'll have to talk to Mr. Lafferty. He told us we shouldn't be talking to you." She hung up. The woman had apparently changed her mind. Probably their lawyer's influence.

The creep. Justice shmustice. Brandon's father would do everything in his power to extract as much money as possible from the city and from her.

The phone rang, and Angel let the answering machine pick up.

"Angel. Are you there?"

She grabbed the receiver. "Brandon, hi. I was just watching your father on television."

"Yeah. That's one of the reasons I called. I'm sorry you had to see that. I've tried talking to him, but he's convinced that representing Mrs. Hartwell is a good political move."

"Hmm." She couldn't help wondering how Brandon would feel if she weren't involved. "Well, he can forget it if he thinks he'll get any money out of me."

"Don't worry about it, Angel. I doubt it will get that far."

"I hope you're right." She kicked off her slippers and flopped onto the sofa. She felt a tug on her conscience to break it off with him completely, but she didn't. *Not over the phone,* she told herself.

"Angel, there's something I need to talk to you about. Remember I said I was representing Michelle Kelsey?"

"Right, the woman who killed her husband."

"That's hearsay," Brandon was quick to say. "Well, she found something today that made me wonder if her husband's death might have something to do with the drug activity that's been on the rise down here."

"What's that?" Angel muted the television set so she could hear better.

"She was cleaning out the garage — Jim's workshop, actually — and came across a stash of cocaine. She says she'd suspected he was a user but didn't have any proof."

"Interesting." Angel leaned forward and picked up her tea. "How do you know it isn't hers?"

He sighed. "I just do. But I'm afraid if I turn this evidence over to the police, they'll think the same thing."

"You haven't called the authorities?" Angel set the mug down so hard the hot liquid splashed on her hand and the table. "Brandon, what are you thinking?" She padded to the kitchen to retrieve a towel.

"She's scared, and I don't blame her. The authorities haven't exactly been kind toward her."

"Call them, Brandon. Better yet, call Detective Riley. He's investigating that case. You can trust him to do the right thing."

"I don't know . . ."

"Brandon, what's the matter with you?" She mopped up the spilled tea and went to the closet to get her handbag. After rummaging through it for a moment, she came up with the business card Callen had given her. He'd written his cell phone number on the back. She read the number off to Brandon and insisted he make the call. "It'll be best if you call. I'm going to give you thirty minutes, then I'll call Callen myself. This is important evidence, Brandon, you know that. Besides, it might be just what you need to get Mrs. Kelsey off."

"I'll think about it."

After saying good-bye, Angel turned off the television and got ready for bed. As she brushed her teeth, Brandon's phone call nagged at her. Callen was working on the

Kelsey murder, and now it looked like there might be drug involvement. J.J., a known dealer, had been shot, and hours later the pharmacy had been stripped of narcotics. Alex Carlson was dead, with drugs found in his system. Then there was Billy's death, in which someone other than herself had fired the two fatal shots. Finally, she thought about Dixon's murder. So far there didn't seem to be any indication of drug involvement, unless you added Alex's death to the equation.

She grabbed a pen and paper out of the kitchen drawer and drew a circle. In it she wrote "drugs." She drew lines from the circle like spokes, then at the end of each she made a circle. In each circle she wrote the names of the victims.

Broadman had killed Dixon, she felt certain of that, and he may have killed Alex. Could he be the head of the drug ring she'd heard about? She'd heard the narcotics officers talking about some guy whom they thought oversaw the drug operations along the coast. So far no one had been able to get a handle on him. But they did know he did most of his dealings on the phone and went by the name of Duke. Suppose Duke was actually Ray Broadman, and Ray was behind all of the murders?

She couldn't wait to talk to Callen about her ideas. She glanced at her watch. Thirty minutes had passed since she had talked to Brandon, so she picked up the receiver and punched in Callen's number.

He answered on the first ring.

"Did Brandon call you?"

"Yeah. I'm meeting him and Mrs. Kelsey right now." He hesitated. "Thanks. You did the right thing."

"Callen, I've been thinking. Is there a possibility that all of these murders, including Billy's, are drug related?"

"I've considered that. Now I'll be looking at it even more closely."

"Do you think Broadman is behind it all — like could he be the kingpin or something?"

"I doubt it. The guy's too hot tempered to head a successful operation like that."

"I just wondered — I mean, he's got a nice house and car, and it takes a fair amount of money to retain Michael Lafferty as an attorney."

He sighed. "Angel, I do notice these things. I already have people trying to pinpoint Broadman's location to find out where he was and what he was doing at the time of the deaths."

She should have known Callen would already have it covered. He wanted her to butt out, and she should.

He cleared his throat. "I just pulled up at the Kelsey place so I have to go."

"Let me know how things turn out, okay?"

"I'll tell you what I can. And thanks, Angel. This might be the break we've been looking for."

Angel thought seriously about getting dressed and going to the Kelsey place but finally decided that her being there would serve no purpose except to make Callen angry with her again. Besides, she was exhausted.

When she finally got into bed, she did something she hadn't done in a long time. She prayed.

Morning came too quickly, but instead of dawdling in bed, Angel got up and stumbled to the kitchen to make coffee. At 8:00 she called Janet's office for another appointment. Just before falling asleep the night before, she'd realized that she needed to come to terms with the conflicting and destructive patterns that had developed between her and her parents — especially her father. Angel hoped Janet could help her work through the problems.

"I'm sorry, Angel, Janet is all booked up. Hang on a second though, she'll want to talk to you." The secretary put Angel through, and Janet told her to come in at 11:30.

"You don't have to skip lunch for me," Angel said.

"Don't worry about it. I'll grab a bite after your appointment."

After hanging up with Janet, Angel called her parents.

"Angel, what a surprise," her mother chirped.

"How's Dad this morning?" Angel pulled down a mug and poured a cup of coffee — inhaling the freshly brewed Italian blend. Callen had thought of everything.

"He's an ornery old coot, complaining about everything — which means he's getting better."

"I'm glad it's you taking care of him and not me. I'd never be able to tolerate him for that long." Of course, as a kid she'd wanted to be with him constantly.

"We do what we have to do, you know that. If I wasn't here to care for him, you'd do it, and without complaining, I'll bet. Family is family."

Angel let the subject drop and took a sip

of coffee. Nothing like a fresh cup of joe in the morning.

"Come by and have lunch with us, Angel. Your father would love you to visit."

"He's bored, right?"

"Yes. I thought maybe you could get him interested in a Scrabble game or something."

"I have an appointment with Janet at 11:30. I'll come over later." *After I'm armed with ways to deal with him — and with you.*

Angel hung up, skimmed the paper, and went for a run. By the time she'd come back and taken a shower it was 10:00. She didn't have to leave for another hour.

She wandered around the apartment, feeling at odds. She still couldn't get used to not working. Angel poured herself another cup of coffee and settled down on the sofa to read the paper. For once she wasn't on the front page. But Alex Carlson's obituary was, and next to his story was an article about the increase in gang activity and the use of drugs among teenagers. The article mentioned a group from a local church who had developed a teen club called the Dragon's Den to give kids something to do on weekends other than having parties where there was drinking and drugs. Angel knew of the place and had worked with some of the other officers to deal with disturbances. The Friday and Saturday dances were well attended and the security tight. "Still," the reporter wrote, "the drugs, primarily ecstasy, were easily accessible to anyone who wanted them." Authorities and the club's managers had no idea who was supplying the drugs or how they were being smuggled in.

Angel's boss, Joe Brady, was quoted as saying, "We want kids to have fun, and we had hoped a club like this would offer an alternative. Now it looks like we may be forced to close the place down."

The writer claimed the drug operation was all part of a Portland-based mob organization that had set up shop along the Oregon coast and other small communities, recruiting local kids to peddle their wares. The reporter went on to ask, "Had Alex Carlson been one of them?"

So far law enforcement agencies hadn't been able to connect the dots. The writer went on to criticize the police but neglected to mention that they were severely shorthanded because of budget cuts.

Angel tossed the paper aside, wondering what Callen would think of it. Though she'd promised herself she wouldn't think about the handsome OSP detective, she couldn't get him out of her mind. She missed him, and the fact that she did irritated her. She thought about calling him to ask what, if anything, he'd determined about the Kelsey murder. She also wanted to know if he'd gone to the cannery with the lab techs to search the rest of the building. She had planned to go back, but too many things had gotten in the way.

At 11:15 she slipped into her black windbreaker, grabbed her bag, and headed out the door. Janet was waiting for her when she got to the office. "How's it going, Angel?"

"Good. Like a huge load has been lifted off. I still have to deal with Billy's death, but at least I'm off the hook where Dixon is concerned, and I know I only fired that first shot. The hard part is waiting for the authorities to find out who the second shooter was."

Janet nodded. "I bet it's hard to stand by and let someone else investigate."

"More than I can handle at times." She told her about the encounter with Broadman the day before. "I shouldn't have interfered, but it's almost impossible not to."

"That's understandable with you being a

police officer. You can't just stop being who you are."

Angel nodded. "So true."

Janet smiled. "What would you like to work on today?"

Angel frowned and explained what her father had done the night before and how his intrusion had made her feel angry and inadequate. "I used to adore my father, but now I feel uncomfortable around him. I mean, I love him and everything, but most of the time I feel like he's disappointed in me."

"It's not unusual for daughters to adore their fathers as children. Sometimes it's just a matter of growing up and realizing that Daddy isn't the hero you once imagined him to be. Was your father ever abusive?"

Angel rubbed her forehead. "I never thought so. He was stern and expected a lot — especially from the boys. But there is something I can't quite get a handle on."

"Go on," Janet urged when Angel hesitated.

"This feeling I have about guns. I'm not exactly afraid of them, it's more of a dislike. I think it's worse now, after shooting Billy."

Janet raised an eyebrow. "That's quite an

admission — especially for a police officer."

"Most of the officers I work with have several guns in their personal collection. All I have is my duty weapon — well, before it got taken away from me." She sighed. "I know it sounds crazy. Like why would anyone who hates guns want to be in law enforcement? I forced myself not to think about it, and when I'd go out on the practice range, I found I could handle guns well. Maybe that's because there was no threat to myself or anyone else. I was okay until Dani . . ." Her eyes flooded with tears, and she brushed them away with the back of her hand.

"Dani?"

Angel told her about the day care center incident and how seeing Dani die had changed everything.

"How awful," Janet murmured. "Of course it would change everything. No wonder you hate guns."

"But that's just it. I don't think that's the source of the gun thing. When I was in the drugstore during the robbery, my chest got tight and I could hardly breathe. I remember thinking how much I hated guns. The incident with Dani came to mind, but so did something else, something deeper.

I'm sure it has something to do with my father, because whenever I had to go out to the shooting range, I'd hear his voice in my head telling me to stop being such a baby. I'd like to know what's behind all of that."

"You think maybe something that happened in your childhood brought this on?"

Angel nodded. "Can you help me sort it out?"

"I can help you relax. The answers may come or they may not. That's up to you. Let yourself go."

After a moment of silence Angel said, "I need to confront him about something today, and I thought maybe if I could figure out . . . This is stupid, isn't it?"

"Not at all. Going back and remembering childhood events can help us understand why we act and feel the way we do around our parents. Tell your mind you need to know what happened to turn you against guns."

"And against my father."

Angel dropped onto the couch and fluffed the pillows. Lying down, she closed her eyes. Janet's gentle music filtered into the room. Angel focused on the colors behind her closed eyelids, wondering how they came to be. Like rainbows. Her mother used to say rainbows were God's gift and that they allowed us to see beauty after a storm. She'd always been fascinated by rainbows. Before long, she felt the anxiety drain from her body, and she said a prayer to God to help her remember.

Janet's voice was gentle and rhythmic, and Angel drifted, letting herself float back into her childhood.

She'd never been her mother's little girl. Always hanging out with the boys and her father. While other girls wore pretty dresses, hers hung unused in the closet. Dolls she'd gotten for Christmas and birthdays laid in their boxes while the catcher's mitt she'd inherited from Luke had worn thin in spots and looked as though it had seen a few dozen years of hard labor.

How she used to love playing ball with the boys. Her brothers had been good to her, involving her in their games, except when they played with friends who tended to get too rough.

Anna didn't like her propensity for boyish stuff much. She was always trying to get Angel to do things with her. Poor Anna. She'd finally gotten the baby girl she'd always wanted, and Angel had turned out to be a rough-and-tumble tomboy.

Though Anna had encouraged her to

learn to cook and clean, sew and knit, she never forced Angel to do these things. Not that Angel didn't have her share of chores — but if she preferred mowing the lawn to vacuuming, that was okay. Angel learned early on that her mother was easy to please. All she had to do was compliment her on her cooking, hug her a few times a day, and say her prayers, and Anna was happy. Or so Angel had thought.

Pleasing her father was much more difficult. He could rarely get the boys to go hunting with him. They had other interests. Angel would volunteer to go, but he always put her off. She was too small, too weak, too fragile. But he finally gave in and taught her how to shoot. They started with a .30/.30. After firing the weapon, she hurt her shoulder from the kick and started to cry. Dad had no use for her tears, telling her that if she was going to make it in the world, she had to be tough. Her shoulder had turned bluish purple by the time she got home that day. Anna was furious. She wanted to put ice on it, but Angel, not wanting to be a sissy, shrugged it away. She wanted her dad to be proud of her, and he was — or seemed to be — telling people how she had hit her target after only a few practice shots.

One weekend in the fall Frank announced that he was taking her hunting in the mountains. They would camp out in the wilderness and bring home a buck; the trip was all Angel could think or talk about for days. The first day was more fun than she could have imagined — they drove into the mountains, then hiked into the woods and set up camp. They'd laughed and talked and roasted hot dogs and marshmallows over an open fire.

The next day everything changed. Toward afternoon her father became grumpy — so far he hadn't even seen a buck. They'd seen several does though — beautiful deer that looked at them in surprise then scampered away. Twice her father had raised his gun then lowered it, saying he couldn't shoot a doe. Angel was relieved; she didn't want to shoot the beautiful animals. She began to worry about finding the kind with antlers. Then on Sunday they stumbled upon a magnificent buck with a full rack.

Knots formed in Angel's stomach. "Don't shoot him, Daddy, please," she begged. The buck heard her and disappeared into the thicket.

Frank shoved her aside and lowered his gun. "Don't you ever do that again or you can forget about ever going anywhere with me."

Angel didn't know what horrified her more, the thought of never going anywhere with her father or shooting the deer. She prayed that the bucks would stay away so Frank wouldn't shoot them, but her pleas went unanswered. Later on that day, he stopped and pointed to a buck standing in a clearing. The wind was blowing toward them. "You wanted to go hunting. Here's your chance." His voice was hard and angry as he told Angel to take aim and shoot.

Angel's heart raced, and her breathing came in quick gasps. She started shaking. But she forced herself to do as her father said. She ignored the warm liquid flowing down her legs and soaking her thermal underwear. She ignored the tears welling up in her eyes.

"Come on, Angel," Frank urged. "He won't stay there forever."

Angel settled the rifle butt to her shoulder and looked through the scope. *I have to do this. He won't love me anymore if I mess up.*

"That's my girl," he whispered. "Aim for body mass."

No, Daddy, no. Please don't make me shoot.

Please! But she couldn't say the words out loud. She couldn't take the chance for fear her father would hate her.

She got the buck in her sights and moved the gun slightly, aiming at a spot of sky above his head. She closed her eyes and fired. Lowering her gun, she felt movement behind her. She turned around and watched in horror as her father took aim and fired. The buck reared and took several wobbly steps and stumbled. The animal she'd been so careful to miss now lay wounded, his back leg twitching as his lifeblood poured onto the ground.

"That was a good try, Angel." Her father patted her on the back. "We'll have plenty of venison for the winter."

Angel opened her eyes and stared at the ceiling of Janet's office. She sat there for a moment, quiet, then told Janet what she'd remembered. "I was just a kid. He didn't even know." She frowned. "I should've been furious with him for what he did. But I never stopped trying to please him. In some ways I'm still trying."

"I may be wrong," Janet ventured, "but I think that little girl who adored her father and would do anything for him was outraged. The anger you had toward your father had to go somewhere. You couldn't let

461

those feelings turn toward him. So you put them into the guns."

Angel nodded. "Odd as it seems, you might be right. I couldn't be mad at Dad. I guess I've been holding all that anger inside all this time. I loved him too much."

Angel thought again about the way her father had shot the buck. No wonder she'd been imagining him in the background shooting at Billy.

Her father had been on duty that morning, and he could have been in the building when she shot Billy. Last night at dinner he'd said something about watching out for her. He'd asked Eric to see that she got home safely. How many times had he felt the need to back her up and make sure she didn't get hurt? She'd never thought much about it before, but officers seldom had partners anymore. Had her father insisted Joe put Eric and Angel together to protect her?

Had he been the second shooter?

THIRTY-FIVE

As Angel drove away from Janet's office, she wondered how she would go about asking her father if he'd been at the cannery the morning she shot Billy. He'd been in the area; she was certain of that, since she'd seen his patrol car.

She could clearly imagine him standing behind her, firing the second two shots. But if he'd done that, why not tell the truth about it?

Because he knew how I'd react.

Angel mulled over what she would say to her father. Should she work up to it or come right out and ask?

When she got to her parents' house, she walked in without knocking. As usual, she could smell something yummy cooking in the kitchen.

Frank was sitting in the recliner, his feet up, his eyes closed, the television on. A sports announcer sounded excited. "Mariners get the Yankees to hit into a rare triple play. Mariners win three to two over the Yankees!"

"Dad?" she said softly. He didn't stir. His mouth hung open as he snuffled on an exhale. She decided not to disturb him and wondered if it would be wise to confront him at all.

She wandered into the kitchen and lifted the lid on a simmering pot of what looked like a cauliflower and tomato stew. She inhaled deeply, reminding her stomach it hadn't eaten anything substantial all morning. Off to the left of the stove sat a basket of freshly baked scones. Angel snatched one and headed out to the backyard, where her mother was pulling weeds from her neatly manicured garden.

The house was well back from the ocean. Still, sitting on a hill as it did, it offered a magnificent view of the coastline. She stood there for a while, eating the cranberry scone and watching the water roll in and out. Up near the high tide line she could see the ringed form of a crab pot. A group of seagulls congregated together, looking as if they were having some important meeting.

Her mother had her back to the house

and couldn't see Angel. She stood and lifted her knee pad, placing it a couple feet from where it had been. Anna dropped onto the pad again and started digging around one of her lavender plants.

When Angel finished the scone, she hunkered down beside her mother and pulled up a clump of grass.

"You should be wearing gloves." Anna shoved her spade into the soil and uprooted a dandelion. "You'll ruin your nails."

Angel ignored the comment. She'd never worried much about manicures or nail polish. She kept her nails trimmed short and tidy. "You've gotten a lot done. Looks like you've been out here a while."

"Mmm. It was either come out here and yank weeds or murder your father."

"That bad, huh?"

Anna sat back on her ankles. "He's at that stage where he's feeling better but still restricted. It's frustrating for him."

"This is the first time he's ever been really sick." Angel found herself defending him. "Must be scary."

"For both of us." Anna stood, moved her knee pad over to the next section, and began digging again. "I suppose I should get lunch together. How was he when you came through?"

"Sleeping. Snoring. He's okay."

Moisture seeped into Angel's jeans where her knees sank into the deep, lush grass.

"There's another pad in the shed." Her mother nodded toward the small building that housed the miscellaneous garden tools and supplies.

"I know." Angel rose and dutifully made her way up the path to the shed. The pad was hanging on a peg. She grabbed a pair of gloves from the basket on one of the shelves. Looking around the well-organized room, she couldn't help but smile. Martha Stewart had nothing on Anna Delaney.

When she set the pad down near some weeds, Anna looked up and smiled. Angel half expected her to ask why she'd come, but she didn't. Angel decided to tell her. "I had a session with Janet this morning."

"And how did that go?"

"She's been helping me to remember things."

"About the shooting?"

"Yes, but other stuff too." Angel grunted as she pulled out a dandelion with an especially long root. She set it on the pile her mother had started. The dandelion greens would be saved and mixed with other greens for salads. "Do you remember the first time Dad took me hunting? None of the boys wanted to go. I waited for him to ask me, but he didn't."

"I remember. You cried yourself to sleep that night."

"The next day he asked me to go. You told him to ask me, didn't you?"

Anna wiped her shirtsleeve across her brow to catch the perspiration forming there. "I reminded him he had a daughter who would love to spend time with her father." She looked out over the ocean. "But you were different when you came back. I wondered if it had been a good idea."

"Yeah, I guess I wonder that too." Angel then told her what she remembered of the trip.

When she was done, Anna placed a hand on her arm. "I had no idea. He was so used to the boys and . . ."

"What would it matter if I was a boy or girl? He was mean and demanding. No wonder the boys didn't want to go with him."

"Don't be too hard on him, Angel."

"I can forgive him for that. There's one thing I may not be able to forgive. If he followed me into that warehouse — if he shot Billy."

"Angel!" Anna sat back on her heels. "What are you saying?"

"He stood behind me that day and shot the deer I missed. Maybe he was the one who shot Billy."

"That's nonsense."

"Is it? He's never really trusted me to do anything. There have been rumors that I got to where I am in the department because of Dad. I have a partner — none of the other officers do. I never really thought about that before."

"What are you going to do?" Anna yanked up another weed and tossed it onto the growing pile beside her.

"Talk to him. Ask him straight out."

She shook her head. "That doesn't sound like your father, Angel. For one thing, he'd never allow you to suffer for something he did."

"Maybe he doesn't believe it'll go to trial."

"No. He's not sneaky. At the first hint of trouble he would have come forward."

"How can you be sure?"

"Oh, honey, your father would do anything for you. Besides, you told me the evidence disappeared."

"Dad could've taken it to compromise the case."

"Steal?" She shook her head. "Frank may not have been a perfect father, but he is not a thief. He's an honorable man. Yes, he looks out for his family, but . . ." She leveled a pleading gaze on Angel. "I don't want you to ask him. An accusation like that — who knows what it could do to his heart? And coming from you . . . no. Please, Angel. Don't talk to him about it."

"I have to know what happened." Angel yanked another dandelion out and tossed it in with the others.

"I know your father, and I know he wouldn't do such a deceitful thing. Now promise me you won't talk to him about it."

"I won't accuse him." Angel realized that even if her father had been in that warehouse, even if he had shot Billy, she wouldn't let him take the blame. She'd recant the story about the second shooter and take full responsibility. *And you would be protecting a killer.*

No, not a killer, an officer — an old man, a heart attack victim, a father trying to protect his child.

But the last two shots weren't necessary.

He wouldn't have known that.

"But I am going to talk to him. He was there that day. I want to know if he saw anything."

"I suppose there's no harm in that." Anna stood and removed her gloves, laying them neatly on her knee pad. "Do you want to stay for lunch?" She picked up the pile of dandelions and set them near the back door.

"Sure." Angel cleaned up and helped her mother make grilled turkey sandwiches to go along with the cauliflower and tomato soup.

Her father had awakened by the time they'd finished. "Don't fix me a tray. Doc said I should walk more."

"Suit yourself." Ma set the kettle on a trivet and began ladling soup into bowls.

Frank shuffled out to the kitchen and sat down in his usual place at the table.

Angel brought the plates with sandwiches and sat down. She waited while her father asked the blessing, then said, "Can I talk to you about something, Dad?"

"What — you need money?"

"I don't need money. I need information."

He smiled. "Information, huh. Well, not sure I can help, but I'll try."

"I saw your car parked by the pharmacy the day of the robbery. I didn't see you, though, and wondered what happened to you."

He shrugged. "I wasn't there very long. Another call came in from dispatch, so I took it." He bit into his sandwich.

"Did you see anything that might be helpful? Were you near the warehouse?"

"No. I didn't say anything because I had nothing to add." Frank patted his heart. "Started after the others, but I had to stop because I was having chest pains. Took some nitro and went back to the car."

"I'm sorry."

He blew on the soup to cool it then dipped his spoon in. "What's with all the questions?"

Angel got a warning look from her mother. "Nothing. I just wanted to talk to everyone who was out there. I'm trying to piece together where everyone was."

"You still thinking you weren't the only shooter?"

"I'm certain of it. I just can't seem to figure out who fired the extra shots and why."

"And you thought maybe it was me?"

"I didn't say that."

"You didn't have to." He shoved a spoonful of soup into his mouth. "Guess I can't blame you for wondering. You have to look at every angle. But you got to remember one thing, Angel: If I had been there and seen you were in trouble, I'd have fired without a moment's hesitation. I wouldn't have split though. I'd have stood right there with you. I'd bet any of the other guys would say the same thing."

He had a point. There would have been no reason for any of the officers to back her up and not take credit for it. They'd have had no way of knowing the kind of trouble shooting Billy would bring. But none of them had done it.

"If you didn't fire those shots, then the person who did has something to hide." Frank went on. "My guess would be one of the gang members. They wanted to make sure the boy couldn't ID them."

Angel picked up her sandwich. "I'm sure you're right, Dad."

"One more thing. Do you really think if I shot the kid, I'd let you take the rap?"

Angel took hold of his free hand. "No. I guess I hadn't really thought it through. I just remembered the time you took me hunting and —"

"I shot the buck you missed." He became more animated. "He was a beaut, wasn't he? We got a lot of good meals from him."

"Yeah, we did." Angel had hated those meals. But she'd eaten the meat along with everyone else, not daring to object.

"I took credit for it, didn't I?" Frank asked.

"Yes, you did." She smiled. "Every time we ate it."

The phone rang, and Angel pushed her chair back and went into the living room to answer it. She picked up on the fourth ring.

"Oh, good. It's you." Eric sounded tense. "Listen, there's been an accident — no, scratch that. Accident isn't the right word."

"What is it?" Angel held her breath.

"It's Brandon. His car's been bombed."

THIRTY-SIX

Angel sank into the nearest chair. She felt sweaty and cold at the same time. *Oh no. No!* "Is he . . . ?"

"We don't know. There are body parts . . ."

Angel's stomach tightened, threatening to release the food she'd just eaten.

"What's wrong, Angel?" Anna came into the room, wiping her hands on a towel.

Angel raised her hand. "Okay," she managed to say to Eric. "I'll be there right away."

"You don't want to see this, Angel. Trust me. I'll let you know as soon as I hear anything."

"I'll be there. Thanks for calling me."

She heard a click as Eric hung up. She stared at the phone in her hand for a moment, then looked up at her mother's fading form as shock gave way to weeping.

Anna sat down and wrapped her arms around her. "What is it, honey? What's happened?"

Angel told her between sobs. "They did it because of me." She pulled out of her mother's embrace. "They're still trying to get back at me because of Billy." She folded her arms and rocked back against the seat cushions. "When is it going to end, Ma. When? How could God let this happen?"

"I don't know, honey," her mother said, stroking her hand, her eyes filling with tears. "But I think we need to put the blame where it belongs, on whoever did it."

Frank came in and settled a hand on her shoulder. "Would you like me to go downtown with you?"

"No, I'm okay." Angel sniffled and blew her nose in the tissue her mother handed her. She clutched the tissue, suddenly frozen in fear, not so much for herself but for her family. She pictured the men who had surrounded her car. Had they done this? Had their anger driven them to extract the worst kind of revenge?

She couldn't let fear get the better of her. She stood up, determined to walk out to the Blazer and drive downtown. "I have to go. I need to find out who did this, before they kill someone else."

"You let the authorities handle this, Angel," her father called after her. "You hear me?"

She was halfway to the Lafferty offices when her cell phone rang. She picked up. "Angel?"

Angel slammed on her brakes just in time to avoid hitting the car in front of her that had stopped for a red light. The caller sounded like Brandon.

She threw the phone onto the seat. *That's it. I've gone over the edge. Now I'm hearing things.* Her hands shook as she pulled over to the curb and picked up the phone again. Whoever it was had hung up. She turned the phone off, but it rang again. Drawing a deep breath, she told herself to ignore it, but in the end, she had to pick up.

The voice said her name again, but she stopped him. "Who — who is this? What kind of sick joke are you playing?"

"Angel, please don't hang up. It's me — Brandon."

Relief mingled with disbelief. "Are you sure? Eric told me you were dead." Or had he? He'd said there'd been body parts, and she had assumed they belonged to Brandon.

"It was my car. I was hoping to get to you before you found out." His voice cracked. "I loaned my car to my secretary. She had a doctor's appointment and hers was in the shop. I still can't believe it."

"Where are you?"

"At the office. The police won't let me leave."

"I'll be there in a few minutes." She hung up and glanced upward. "Thank you. Thank you, thank you, thank you!"

But her joy was short-lived as she thought about Brandon's secretary. Muriel had children and grandchildren. They would be devastated.

Just concentrate on Brandon for now. He's alive, and somehow I have to keep him that way.

Angel parked her car in the lot about two blocks away from Brandon's office building. Most of the block was taped off, and the street had been closed. Several officers were already on the scene taking pictures and evaluating the debris. Bo and Mike were talking to Callen. Eric and Nick were interviewing people outside the crime scene, probably looking for potential witnesses.

She could see the bombed-out car and the shattered glass in the nearby buildings but had no desire to get a closer look. She went in the back entrance and was immediately stopped by a sheriff's deputy. She told him who she was and waited while he called Brandon to verify whether or not he should let her into the building.

Apparently satisfied, the deputy walked her down the short hall into the lobby, where she took the elevator to the third floor. Brandon was waiting for her when she stepped off the elevator. His eyes were red rimmed, and his expression one of disbelief and horror. He swept her up into a bear hug.

Angel couldn't have spoken if she'd wanted to — tears clogged her throat and eyes. He was safe. For now.

Brandon finally pulled her arms from around his neck. "Let's go into my office."

The office was elegantly appointed, as one might expect, with an executive desk and two walls of bookshelves made with a dark, expensive-looking wood. Brandon's father stood by the window, looking out over the water. He turned as they entered, his cool gaze assessing Angel and finding her lacking. She lifted her chin as though his opinion of her didn't matter.

"Why you, Brandon?" Angel lowered herself into one of the chairs in front of

Brandon's desk. "I don't understand why they would go after you."

"They?" Brandon's father turned back from the window. "Are you saying you know who did this?"

"Not really, but it might've been the guys who attacked me when I went to the Hartwell boy's funeral. They're probably the same ones who wrecked my apartment. Maybe they decided to hurt me by going after people I care about."

"Seems pretty far-fetched." Brandon's father took his usual condescending tone with her. "I doubt they'd harm Brandon since I'm representing the Hartwells in the civil suit." He rubbed a hand over his nearly bald head. "I'm afraid this is rather uncomfortable for you. With us representing the other side. It isn't personal, you understand."

"I understand." She didn't, of course. To her, the decision to represent Broadman had been a slap in the face.

"My guess," the older Lafferty said, "is that this bomb wasn't meant for Brandon at all. I think it was meant for you."

"Me?"

"Brandon said you borrowed his car."

Angel gulped. She hadn't even considered that possibility. "I haven't driven it since Sunday night." But Broadman had seen her with the Lexus. Even though he was in jail now, he could've arranged the whole thing.

"Well, it's something to consider." Michael Lafferty walked from the window to the door. "I'm waiting for a call. If you need me, I'll be in my office."

Angel watched his retreating back. *And I thought my father was bad.* She felt sorry for Brandon, but as she turned back to him, he seemed unfazed by his father's behavior. He was focusing on a spot on the floor, apparently deep in thought.

"What are you going to do?" Angel asked.

"What do you mean?" He lifted his gaze to hers.

"Whoever tried to kill you failed. I'm worried they'll try again."

"So am I. So is everyone else. Dad thinks the bomb was meant for you, but he isn't taking any chances. He's hiring a bodyguard for me." He straightened and went around to his black leather executive chair. "I won't be going home for a few days. I'll stay in a hotel — undisclosed location."

"That's wise."

Someone knocked on the door, then

opened it. Brandon's father poked his head in and frowned disapprovingly. "There are a couple of police officers here. They want to talk with you. If you'd rather wait, I can tell them to come back."

"No." Brandon got up again and walked to the door. "I'll talk to them. We need to get to the bottom of this as soon as possible."

Eric and Nick came in.

"Angel. I've been trying to call you," Eric said. "But I see you already know Brandon wasn't in his car."

"Yeah. He called me while I was on the way over here."

"Good. I'm sorry I scared you like that. Guess I should've waited for a positive ID."

"I appreciate you letting me know."

Nick turned to Brandon. "We need to ask you some questions."

"Go ahead." Brandon sat in the client chair next to Angel and clasped her hand.

"Do you know of anyone who might want to kill you? Any enemies that you know of?"

"Anyone who'd want me dead? I have no idea."

"Any angry husbands?"

"That's an odd question." Brandon

tightened his hold on Angel's hand.

"Not really. You handle divorce cases. Some husbands get pretty upset with their wife's lawyer, especially when the lawyer takes them to the cleaners."

"Now that I think about it, I suppose that's possible." He released Angel's hand and went back to his chair and opened a drawer. "There is one, a new client who wants out of an abusive relationship."

"Can you give us a name?" Eric had pulled out a notepad and pen.

"I'd rather not — client confidentiality."

"We can get a warrant." Nick pursed his lips.

"I can talk to her and see if she'll let me release the information. I'll get back to you on it."

"Sounds fair enough." Nick turned to Eric. "Can you think of anything else?"

"That should do it for now." Eric's gaze wandered around the room. "Um, work up a list of possible suspects for us, and we'll check them out."

"Will do." Brandon picked up a pen and tapped it against the desk blotter. "Before you go, there's something you should know."

"Yeah?" Eric took a step back toward them.

"Angel thinks the guys that have been harassing her might've come after me."

Eric squinted at Angel. "I doubt they'd hit Brandon. It's you they want."

"Yes, and as Brandon's dad just pointed out, I'd been driving Brandon's car. Maybe they didn't realize we'd switched." She rose and walked to the wide bank of windows. "I wish I had been. Then Muriel would still be alive."

"But you wouldn't." Nick came over and settled an arm across her shoulders. "Don't beat yourself up over this, Angel. You have to learn to let things go — especially the things that are out of your control." He gave her neck a squeeze.

They started to leave when Nick leaned back in. "Angel, that second shooter theory of yours. Mike did some research for you. He found a guy who's got some pretty good connections. I'm thinking that if any of the gang members wasted Billy, he'd know. Mike is meeting him down on the docks at 6:30 tonight, said you could show up if you wanted to talk to him."

"Thanks, Nick, I'll be there."

After Nick left, Angel wondered why Mike had extended the invitation. Probably because she had been the one to ask him, or maybe it was their way of keeping her in the loop. Whatever the reason, she appreciated it.

Brandon came to stand beside her, his gaze roaming across the water. "I don't like the sound of that."

"I'll be fine. Mike will be with me."

"Can you trust him?"

"Of course." She leaned down to pick up her handbag, thinking she should break things off with him right then and there. But how could she do that now? He'd just been through a terrible ordeal.

How can I not? His association with me could kill him. Next time he might not be so lucky.

"Brandon, I . . ." She stopped when Brandon's gaze jerked from her to the door and remained fastened there. She turned around to see what had captivated him.

A petite woman with streaked blond hair knocked on the open door. She held on to her black bag with both hands and stepped over the threshold. Angel scrutinized her, recognition finally dawning. Michelle Kelsey looked younger than she remembered, perhaps because she was wearing makeup and not bruises.

"Brandon?" Michelle's voice wavered as she looked from Brandon to Angel. Brandon beckoned her in and introduced them. The flush on his neck and cheeks indicated much more than a lawyer-client relationship.

"I know Angel," Michelle said in a soft, feminine voice.

Angel reached out to shake her hand. "You look great, Michelle."

"Thanks. I hope I'm not interrupting anything." She glanced at Brandon. "I heard about the explosion on the news."

No wonder Brandon was so obsessed about handling the Kelsey case and so insistent about her innocence. One look into her sad blue eyes would bring any man to his knees.

"I was just leaving," Angel said.

Brandon walked with her to the elevator. "It's not what it looks like."

Angel laid a hand on his arm. "Yes, it is, but that's okay. You and I are friends, Brandon. I think we've always known that. I just hope she's as innocent as you seem to think."

She left Brandon standing in the hallway looking guilty and perplexed.

As she drove back to her apartment, she thought about her meeting with Mike and his informant. Could she trust Mike? He was a police officer, and she'd worked with him for a year. Still, how well did she know him? Or the others for that matter. The brainstorm she'd had about her father backing her up could pertain to any of the guys. Nick, who was like a brother; Eric, her partner; even Bo. She reined in her wild thoughts with a reminder that, like her father, if any of them had fired at Billy, they'd have stayed with her and taken responsibility.

What if one of them was dirty? The evidence had been stolen out of a police locker, so someone with a key had done it. The first one to come to mind was Bo Williams, the sheriff's deputy. Billy's mother had said Bo had worked with Billy. He didn't socialize much with the other law enforcement officers in town. In fact, he pretty much stayed to himself. She'd heard about his work with troubled youth. Was it more than that? Could he be involved with the gang, turning a blind eye on their illegal activities? Could he be the head of the drug operation in Sunset Cove?

And what about Mike? He worked with troubled youths as well.

Angel gripped the steering wheel more tightly, annoyed at where her thoughts had taken her. She shouldn't be making an assumption like that. Still, she couldn't help but wonder how the gang seemed able to operate as freely as they did and not get caught.

Angel put her mutinous thoughts aside. The guys she worked with were clean. She'd know if they weren't. Bo had been on the scene when she'd been attacked at Billy's funeral. He'd pulled the men off and made arrests like the others had. He'd been professional — more so than Callen.

Of course, Callen was a different matter. He loved her. She flushed at the thought. He'd never actually said that he loved her, and it was far too soon to be thinking about love. But Angel felt something special in the way he talked to her and held her. Her heart skittered just thinking about him.

But then again, Rachael had warned her about him. Maybe he made every woman feel that way.

Callen saw Angel go into the building where the law offices were. Her face was ashen, and he wished he could've gone to her. No doubt she'd come to comfort Brandon. Not that it mattered. He'd promised himself he wouldn't get involved again. With Angel around, it was getting harder and harder to maintain his focus.

He wondered if she knew about Brandon's relationship with the Kelsey woman. Of course, he may have read it wrong; Michelle seemed the vulnerable sort, and maybe Brandon was just caught up in being the hero. Regardless, Callen was glad she had someone on her side. At first he'd thought her guilty of murdering her husband, but now that Kelsey's body had been found and the autopsy done, he knew that wasn't the case. Michelle could not have killed her husband and pushed the car off the cliff — it was not physically possible. On the other hand, she may have had an accomplice. She'd been seeking a divorce at the time, which meant she knew Brandon before her husband's death. She had a good-sized insurance policy and was attractive and sweet. It wouldn't be the first time a man fell for a woman and helped her escape a brutal lifestyle.

With the cocaine find, though, Callen was having to rethink the situation. While he mulled over the various aspects of the murders, he decided to go back to the warehouse where Billy had been killed. Angel had described the events in detail, and he had listened to the tape so many times he knew it by heart.

Just as he was getting into his car, he saw

Angel leaving. He almost went after her but held back. He couldn't afford to be anywhere near her right now. What he needed to do was settle matters in the deadly force situation so he could conclude at least one case.

Angel had intimated that Billy's death might be drug related as well. Callen had at first seen it as a separate entity. Maybe one of the gang members had fired those last two shots; if so, it would have been to silence him.

When he saw that he was no longer needed at the scene of the car bombing, Callen headed out to the warehouse to have another look around. He parked in front of the cannery and ducked under the crime scene tape. Inside, his stomach rebelled at the stench. Light filtered in through the filthy windows. He found the staircase and began to climb. Angel had suggested the possibility that Billy had seen something on the second floor that frightened him. His head cleared the floor, and he looked around. The floor was bare wood planking and looked solid.

There were windows on this level as well. At the west end was the viewing window where, as a kid, he'd watched the boats being unloaded. From the window he had a clear view of the dock where he had discovered J.J.'s body. The body would have been there when Billy came in. Had he seen the body? Was that what had frightened him and caused him to run back down the stairs? Near the window was another set of stairs that went down to the docking area. Why wouldn't he have come down this way? He'd have been home free. Unless someone was there.

Callen descended the stairs and found that there was a wall separating this part of the warehouse from the front area where the fish used to be stored. He was in the cannery itself. He tried shoving back a large sliding door that would access the area where Angel had been, but it wouldn't budge. On inspection he realized it had been nailed shut. He tried another door and found that it opened readily and led from there to a small room. That space used to be an office, and it led him straight back to where he'd started.

Callen wandered around to where he thought the second shooter might have been. Light glinted off an object about thirty feet away, and he went to check it out. Bending down, he shined his flashlight on a .40-caliber shell casing.

He wished now he'd had the crime scene

investigators comb the entire area instead of just the area around the shooting. At the time he thought the case was isolated and there was no need to scour the entire building. He'd have to put a call in and get someone out first thing in the morning.

Callen thought he heard a soft shuffle, but before he could turn around, something hit him on the back of the head.

THIRTY-SEVEN

At 6:20 Angel parked the Blazer at the south end of the parking lot near the wharf, next to Mike's white Bonneville. The streetlights in the parking lot were dull from the shrouds of mist. The businesses lining the street were all closed now. Like a lot of beach towns, most of Sunset Cove folded up the sidewalks by 5:00 p.m.

Mike nodded at her. "Are you ready?"

She nodded and zipped up her jacket. The wind had shifted, bringing a sharp, cold wind from the north.

"Let me handle the questions, okay? This guy's still squeamish. He just came forward, and I have a feeling he'll be a good contact for us. J.J. was a friend of his, and he's eager to find the guy who shot him." Mike blew on his cupped hands, his breath coming out in white puffs and flying into the wind.

Angel tucked her hands in her pockets. "Ask him if Billy was involved with the gang members — or even a wannabe. I want to know if one of them killed Billy to keep him from talking."

"You still claiming you didn't pull the trigger more than once?"

"I've been over and over it in my mind, Mike. I'm sure."

He shrugged. "If you say so."

As they approached the docks, Angel could see a bulky figure, probably one of the boat owners, standing near a sailboat. Down the pier from the boat owner, three ships away, a yacht sparkled with bright white lights. A song from a Kenny G album drifted up to them. The area looked like something out of a scary movie, the fog creeping in and out and settling in the places where the wind didn't whip it away. She burrowed deeper into her coat. Several boats docked in the marina were lighted. A number of people lived aboard their crafts, moving from port to port. There weren't many here right now; it was just too cold. Come summer the marina would be full.

Instead of going down the dock where she'd seen the man a few seconds earlier, Mike led her down the one running parallel to it. As they came closer, Angel could make out the contact's features, even though he stood in the shadow of one of the large pilings. He looked to be about five-eight with spiked black hair that had been bleached at the ends. They were about ten feet away when he stepped on to the center of the dock. His hands were in his pockets, and the right side of the jacket sagged.

From the weight of a gun? Angel's heart raced, and she could hardly breathe. Had she walked into a trap? Had Mike brought her out here to have her killed? She made a sudden turn and started to run back up the dock when she heard the distinctive click of a gun being cocked.

The world stopped, and Angel waited for the inevitable. She heard the gun go off just as she dropped to the deck, fully expecting a bullet to catch her in the back. Two shots along with a *thunk thunk* as they hit their target. She heard a groan and scurried to the nearest piling about five feet away.

Her heart hammered as she peered around the piling. Mike was sprawled on the dock. At first she thought he'd been hurt, but he scrambled to his feet. Their contact, blood covering his face, staggered across the dock and plunged into the water.

"Call it in!" Mike yelled then tore back down the dock to where the contact had fallen in. Angel went after him, putting in a call to the dispatch operator and asking for backup. They fished the contact out but there was nothing they could do. Half of his skull had been blown away.

Angel covered her mouth to suppress an anguished cry. The kid couldn't have been more than sixteen. Mike swore loudly, berating himself for arranging the meeting. She waited for the nausea to pass and got off her knees. Mike swore again and wiped blood from the corner of his mouth.

Angel touched his arm. "Did you get hit?"

"No. I bit my tongue when I went down." He spat a mixture of blood and saliva into the water. "We'd better get these people back on their boats."

She and Mike spent the next few minutes talking to the curious onlookers who had left the safety of their boats to see what was going on. It didn't take much to convince them to go back to their boats.

All too soon the adrenaline rush dissipated, leaving Angel shaking and cold. Nick had responded to her call, and she and Mike filled him in on the shooting.

"The shooter," Mike said, "was on the

dock parallel to the one we were on."

Angel remembered seeing the shadowy figure there and told Nick. "I wish I'd paid more attention."

"We were set up." Mike glanced at her. "Did you tell anyone you were coming down here?"

"No."

"Nick?"

"I just told Angel." He frowned. "Come to think of it, Brandon was in the room."

"Brandon had nothing to do with this," Angel said.

Nick nodded. "Maybe. We'll have to look into it. In the meantime, you should go home."

Angel didn't argue, but she wasn't ready to leave just yet. She did leave the dock area. When she reached her car she climbed in and turned the heater on full blast. Only when the medical examiner and the medics arrived, with a couple reporters close behind, did Angel decide to leave. She drove down Main Street, past the old cannery, and pulled over when she saw a vehicle that shouldn't have been there. It looked like Callen's unmarked car. Was he at the other end of the wharf with the others? Come to think of it, she hadn't seen him there at all. She called dispatch to put her through to Detective Riley.

"He's not answering his cell phone or his pager," the dispatcher told her. "We haven't been in contact with him for over an hour. I thought maybe he'd gone to Portland."

"He wouldn't have done that without letting someone know."

"Well, I did think it odd, but things have been so crazy."

"His car is parked at the old cannery on Main. Can someone meet me there?"

"I'll put out the call."

Angel found a flashlight in the back of the Blazer and walked the width of the building, looking down the streets on both sides. She hoped Callen would be outside looking around, but she decided he must've gone in. She held her breath as she stepped inside, her flashlight making a wide sweep across the huge expanse.

"Callen?" She called his name several times, and her voice echoed off the concrete walls. She walked slowly, her gaze following the narrow beam. Toward the back of the building she saw a crumpled form.

Her heart leaped to her throat. *No, please, no. Not Callen!* She ran to his side and shone the flashlight more fully on him. Her heart racing, she set the light down and began to examine him. At first she thought he'd been shot, but there was no blood except for the stuff matted in his hair at the back of his head. She checked his carotid, letting out a long breath when she felt a pulse.

"Callen?"

He groaned and rolled onto his back.

"Callen, talk to me, please."

He groaned again and lifted his right arm to his forehead. "What? Angel?" He tried to lift his head and winced in pain.

"Lay still. I'm calling for an ambulance." She called dispatch and gave them the location. Then she took off her jacket and bunched it up, laying it under Callen's head.

"I . . ." Callen opened his eyes, then closed them again. He reached for her, and she took his hand. Clasped in his fist was a .40 cartridge. "Found it . . ." He dropped it on the concrete and pinched his eyes shut. "Might be your second shooter."

Angel picked up the casing and slipped it into her jacket pocket. "Did you see who hit you?"

"No." He tried to sit up again, but Angel restrained him. She could hear the sirens approaching, and seconds later the warehouse door opened.

She told the paramedics about the head injury and stepped away to give them room. They checked vitals, supported his neck, and got him onto a stretcher. Within minutes they were on their way to the hospital. Angel followed in the Blazer, thanking God and praying that Callen would be all right.

At the hospital, while she waited for Callen to be admitted to the ER, she examined the casing. A .40. She thought again about the missing evidence. Most of the officers she worked with used a .40 Glock. Of course, it was possible that the shell casing Callen had found had nothing to do with Billy's death.

But then what had Callen walked into?

When she finally got to see Callen in the ER, he was more fully awake. He grinned at her when she came in to the cubicle.

"Hey, how are you feeling?" Angel crossed the room and took the hand he offered.

"Good for someone who got hit in the head with a baseball bat."

Angel frowned. "Is that what it was?"

"I have no idea. Sure felt like it though." He closed his eyes, and Angel sat down on the chair beside him. With his eyes still closed he said, "I talked the doctor into letting me go home, but I need a favor."

"Are you sure? Shouldn't you stay overnight at least?"

He gave her a sour look. "I need a ride home. My dog hasn't eaten since this morning."

"I can feed your dog for you."

He moved his head side to side and winced. "I'm going home. Would you be willing to stay at my house overnight? Doc says I need someone to check on me every couple of hours."

Angel chewed on her lower lip, unwilling to admit how frightened she'd been when she'd found him and how relieved she was that he was alive and how reluctant she was to leave his side again.

"I have an extra bedroom."

She found herself agreeing, and minutes later an orderly was wheeling him to the entrance of the hospital, where Angel picked him up. Callen gave her directions as they drove. When they turned into his driveway, Angel was surprised to see that his was the house she admired so much during her daily jogs.

A beautiful bichon frise met them at the door, bouncing like Tigger on the tiled entry. Angel's gaze quickly scanned the living room and kitchen. His kitchen was huge — almost like her mother's. That shouldn't have surprised her. What did surprise her was how nicely decorated it all was. But with the dog demanding attention, she didn't have much time to think about the decor.

"Hey, Mutt." Callen hunkered down to pet him, then lifted him into his arms, introducing the wiggling mass of fur to Angel.

"Mutt?" Angel rubbed between his ears while he licked her hand. "He's adorable." A watchdog, he was not. She was surprised at the breed — not the type of dog most police officers had. They often went for the bigger, more masculine dogs like German shepherds, Dobermans, or Labs.

"He was my wife's dog," Callen explained as he set the animal down to remove his jacket. "I didn't like him much at first. I called him Mutt. She called him Punky. My name stuck."

Callen put a leash on Mutt and handed the dog off to her. "He needs to go out, and I don't think I'm quite up to it."

Angel took the leash. "On one condition — that you lie down and let me wait on you."

He leaned down and kissed her cheek. "I

think I can handle that."

Angel stepped out the patio doors into the cold night air. She hadn't walked a dog in years, not since Bailey, the family's golden retriever, was alive. Bailey had been hit by a car when Angel was fourteen, and they hadn't had a dog since.

Mutt strained at the leash, urging Angel to run across the sand toward the ocean. The mist was still as thick as it had been earlier in the evening when she'd gone down to the docks. Another shooting. And the attack on Callen. What did it all mean?

Mutt did his business and hightailed it for the house. Angel wondered if Callen would feel up to talking about the investigation tonight. Then she thought about curling up next to him on the couch and resting her head on his shoulder. She smiled. The snuggling would have to wait, as would the talking. Callen needed rest, and she would see that he got it.

The next afternoon, Angel sat in the hard wooden pew of her lawyer's office, staring at the brilliant colors of stained glass. Rachael was supposed to join her soon to talk about strategy.

What strategy? She had exhausted her

resources. If a gang member had been responsible for Billy's death, there was no evidence to support the theory. The casing Callen had found in the warehouse led them exactly nowhere. He had ordered all of the law enforcement officers in the area to turn in their weapons to be checked against the casing primer. None were a match. Divers found two more casings, both .45 caliber, one in the water near where J.J. had been shot and one under the dock where Angel had seen the mysterious figure.

According to the manufacturer's batch number, the bullets apparently had all been hollow point — police issue. Three casings, coming from two guns, and no viable suspect. They still had no real evidence to support the theory that she had only fired one shot, only her word and the casing Callen had found.

The grand jury hearing was scheduled for the following morning. Angel's chest tightened at the thought. A trial could lead to conviction and possibly to prison. The idea terrified her. Even in this room of color and light, she felt as though she'd been covered in a dark impenetrable cloud from which she couldn't escape. She'd never been one to give up, but what more could she do? Her life was no longer in her hands.

"Bad things happen." Angel remembered her mother's comments at the hospital while they had waited for her father to come out of surgery. *"God never promised us they wouldn't. In fact, the Bible tells us they will. Pain and suffering are all part of life. God only promises to be with us, to uplift and encourage. To carry us to the other side."*

An odd sense of peace flowed through her, drawing her gaze upward. She closed her eyes. "Okay, God, I could use some of that guidance right about now."

Angel heard a rustling noise and glanced back. Rachael scooted into the pew beside her.

"Well, tomorrow's the day."

Angel sighed. "Rachael, I want you to know that I won't blame you if we lose and end up going to trial. The other day I was so sure I had only fired the one shot. Now, I'm wondering if it was just wishful thinking. Maybe it's one of those weird tricks the mind plays when it can't face the reality of what actually happened."

"We're not going to lose. Especially now. The owner of the pharmacy died."

"Mr. Bergman? When? No one told me."

"I just got a call from the DA. As terrible

as that is, it strengthens our case."

"How? Billy wasn't a gang member."

"We don't know that for certain. The important thing for you to remember is that you are innocent. It doesn't matter if you fired one shot or three, you are not guilty of any wrongdoing."

"But if I'm indicted, I'll be up on manslaughter charges," Angel murmured, more to herself than to Rachael. "I wish I had some answers. Callen said he thinks Billy saw J.J.'s body when he was up on the second floor of the warehouse. He thinks maybe the back stairs were blocked by someone and that person is what made Billy turn around and come back down the stairs. I wish I had waited. I made the wrong call, Rachael."

"You did what you felt was right at the time."

Angel moved her head from side to side, studying the hand that had held the gun. "We're going to need a miracle."

"Then we'll just have to pray for one."

THIRTY-EIGHT

On Thursday morning at twelve noon, Angel walked out of the courthouse in a daze. In the end, the lack of evidence had worked to her benefit. The members of the jury had found the shooting justifiable. They believed she had acted in accordance with police procedure. The number of shots didn't matter.

Eric, who'd been one of the witnesses, was the first to congratulate her. "I knew it wouldn't go to trial. I knew it. Didn't I tell you?" He pulled her into an exuberant hug. The grand jury hearing had been held in private chambers, and Eric had waited with her through the entire process.

"Yes, you told me. But I'm still in shock."

"Nice job, Rachael." Eric shook the lawyer's hand, then turned back to Angel. "I wish I could hang around, but I have to get back to work. I'll see you later, partner."

"Thanks, Eric." Angel watched him walk out the door, his large form nearly filling the doorway.

"He seems nice," Rachael said.

"He's been really supportive through this whole thing."

"Well, you should be getting clearance to go back to work soon."

Angel sighed. "I know, but I'm not sure I'm ready. I'm working through some rough spots with my counselor." *And getting things settled with Callen.* Angel kept that thought to herself. Her relationship with Callen was so new and fragile; she wasn't certain where she stood. He hadn't been the least bit affectionate while she'd been at his house and had almost seemed anxious for her to leave. She'd told herself it was because of the bump on the head and the never-ending investigations with a string of deaths and very little substantive evidence.

Angel and Rachael talked briefly with reporters then escaped to lunch at Tidal Raves in Depoe Bay to celebrate Angel's freedom. After lunch, Angel dropped Rachael off and headed for her parents' place. She wished she could stop and tell Callen the good news, but he wasn't home.

He should have been there recuperating from his head wound, but he was as stubborn a man as her father. He'd told her the night before that he wanted to be with her during the hearing but had to go to the crime lab in Portland after giving his testimony.

Her father greeted her with a hug. "You see, Angel, I told you all along the grand jury would find for you."

"I know you did, Dad." Angel hugged him back.

"Come in and have a cup of coffee," her mother called from the kitchen. "I'm making your favorite pastries."

Angel kissed her cheek, poured herself a cup of the Italian blend, and picked up the flaky turnover filled with raspberries and cream cheese.

"I'm glad for you, honey," Anna said.

Angel sat on the bar stool at the counter. She thought of Callen and envisioned him standing in her mother's kitchen. Had he heard the grand jury results yet?

"It isn't over, you know." Angel bit into the delicate, flaky crust and filling. "I still have the civil suit." And she still had to deal with her own guilt. Nothing would ever change the fact that she had raised her gun and put a bullet into a twelve-year-old boy. Maybe her bullet hadn't killed him, but she'd given the other shooter ample opportunity.

Angel spent the next couple hours running along the beach and working out. She'd just gotten home when Brandon called.

"Hey, I heard. Congratulations."

"Thanks."

"Want to have dinner with me tonight?"

"That's not a good idea."

"Please. I'm in seclusion and incredibly lonely. I have a suite at the best resort on the Oregon coast. There's a Jacuzzi in my room, and I have an awesome view."

Angel smiled. "Sounds nice, but . . . Brandon, we have to talk."

"That sounds ominous."

"Not really. We've been friends for a long time, and I just think we need to be honest with each other."

"Meaning?"

"Come on, Brandon, I saw the way you and Michelle Kelsey were looking at each other. You're in love with her, aren't you?"

He didn't answer right away. "Angel, it isn't what you think."

"Don't lie to me." She smiled and shook her head. "If you love her, call her and invite her to dinner."

"It isn't that easy. She's a client. I need to at least wait . . ."

"Brandon, I know a great attorney who would be thrilled to take over the Kelsey case for you."

"Rachael?"

Had she heard a thread of relief in his voice? "Recuse yourself."

"What about you? Will you be okay? I feel like an idiot proposing to you. I was trying not to let myself get involved with Michelle."

"I know the feeling."

After wishing Brandon well, she hung up and went to her refrigerator to get something to eat. Thanks to Callen and her mother, her cupboards were anything but bare. But making a meal required putting some of the basics together — not something she was ready to attempt alone.

She thought about going to her parents' place, but they would've eaten already. Knowing her mother, there would be plenty of leftovers, but hanging out with her parents was not the way she wanted to spend the evening.

Maybe she'd call Callen and invite herself over. As she'd seen on her visit, he had a well-stocked refrigerator and pantry and knew how to use everything in it. He'd most likely be back from Portland by now.

Angel dialed his number and hung up, thinking a visit might be better. She wanted to tell him about the grand jury decision in person. She wanted to see his face light up. She wanted to feel his arms around her. All of a sudden calling first wasn't an option. She shrugged into her jacket, her heart already speeding up in anticipation of seeing him.

She pulled up in front of the house on the opposite side of the street. Callen's car wasn't there. Disappointed, she started to drive on then changed her mind. Using her cell phone she dialed his number.

Callen answered on the second ring.

"Hi."

"Angel." Callen chuckled. "I just called your place."

"Well, I'm sitting in front of your house, waiting to be fed." Suddenly Angel thought that sounded terribly forward and wished she could take the words back. "Um, where are you?"

"Just east of Lincoln City. I should be home in about twenty minutes." He told her where to find an extra key. "Feed Mutt for me, will you? When I get there, I'll fix us one of my specialties."

Angel found the key in the mouth of an ornamental frog on the back porch and let herself in. She waited for Mutt to bark and race across the floor to greet her. No bark. No toenails clipping across the floor at fifty miles per hour.

The hairs on the back of her neck and arms stood on end as she slipped inside and looked around. The dining room curtains fluttered as the wind blew through the open window.

THIRTY-NINE

Duke sat in his car, contemplating his next move. Everything that could have gone wrong had. He thought he'd found what promised to be the perfect dealer in Broadman. The guy had connections, and he was slick and needed money. Duke had warned Broadman against getting involved in the Delaney shooting, but the guy was greedy and saw the lawsuit as a way to make some extra bucks. Like he needed more.

Then the idiot had gone berserk and killed Dixon. Broadman had called him, frantic, saying Dixon was threatening to walk away and tell the media there was no case. "What else was I supposed to do?" Broadman asked. "I couldn't let him go to the media; he'd have destroyed any chance I had to get money out of the city."

Duke had told him to calm down. He'd asked all the right questions and told

Broadman exactly what to do to keep from getting caught. Then he himself went to the resort, not as Duke, of course, but in uniform. He'd talked to the kid who had waited on Dixon and Broadman, and when the kid had told him he'd heard them arguing, Duke said they should go down to the department to get his testimony on tape. The kid was excited about helping out.

Duke felt bad about wasting that one, but what choice did he have? He couldn't afford to let Broadman get arrested.

He had run into the biggest snag with the bloody clothes and shoes. If it hadn't been for Angel and her lawyer snooping around, everything would've been fine. He'd personally gone to Broadman's house to get the bloody clothes out of the neighbor's can like he'd promised, only to find the women digging through the garbage. He'd taken off then, figuring Broadman was on his own. Fortunately, he'd done all his negotiating on the phone, so Broadman couldn't ID him. Duke doubted he'd talk anyway — no sense implicating himself further — and if he did, he'd never be able to finger Duke.

Now he was faced with another problem. He had no one to pick up and distribute the drugs to his dealers. The pickup was supposed to be simple. Jake Ensley would bring the shipment in on his boat and call him. At a prearranged time, he'd bring the drugs into the abandoned warehouse office, then go back to his boat, where his money would be waiting for him. All of that would've gone off just fine if Detective Riley hadn't been snooping around. Duke had caught him in the warehouse and had no choice but to whack him and get the drugs to a safe location. He'd never killed a cop except for his old man, and that didn't count. But he had to do something about Riley. The guy was too persistent for his own good.

Duke rubbed a hand down his face, hoping the evidence-planting would work. If all went according to plan, Detective Riley would be out of commission for a long time. Of course, Delaney was another problem. It would've been easier if she had died in the car bomb. Not that he'd wanted her dead. Broadman was obsessive in his revenge, and Duke suspected he'd contracted a hit from jail. Duke had nothing against Angel, just wished she'd stay out of things. He didn't want to kill either of them, just get them out of the way for a while so he could regroup and maybe move on.

He had it timed perfectly. According to dispatch, Detective Riley would be in Sunset Cove in twenty minutes. He didn't like cutting things so close, but he had to wait until after the sun set. He'd take the beach access out to the sand dunes and walk south to Riley's house, place the package under the deck, and leave the same way. Then he'd make his anonymous phone call.

Angel closed the window that Mutt had somehow opened and darted outside, shutting the patio door behind her. "Come on, Mutt. Come here, boy." She circled the house, calling his name and whistling. When he didn't show, she headed for the beach. She heard his playful bark at about the same time she saw a white blur streaking up and down the beach, scampering in and out of the waves about a quarter of a mile south of where she was standing. Mutt stopped and growled at a clump of seaweed and then raced down the beach. She called to him again, and he skidded to a stop, flipped around, and ran toward her, then stopped just a few feet from her, jumped in the air, and took off.

He clearly wanted to play, but it was getting too dark. Angel kept calling him, then picked up a stick and threw it. "Get the stick, Mutt. Come on." When he finally brought it back, she scooped him up.

"You're a little dickens, do you know that?" She laughed as Mutt slobbered kisses all over her face. She muzzled her nose in his wet fur. He smelled of salt water and dog and was getting her jacket all wet and sandy. "Come on. Let's go back to the house and get you cleaned up."

The wind was blowing steadily from the north, blowing into her face as she trudged through the soft sand. She came up over the sand dune and stopped cold. Someone was kneeling beside Callen's porch and placing a package there. The large bulky figure looked all too familiar. She'd seen him on the dock the night Mike's contact was killed, but he'd been too far away for her to recognize him.

But no. She had to be mistaken.

Mutt whined and barked and squirmed out of her arms, racing toward the dark figure. Mutt circled the man's legs, barking. The man swore and kicked the dog into the air.

"No!" Angel screamed and started toward Mutt, who'd wriggled to his feet and was staggering toward her.

"Don't move." The man whirled around and pulled a gun.

Angel froze. "Eric, what are you doing here?"

She took a step closer, unable to assimilate her runaway thoughts. Maybe she was wrong. Maybe he was here on a call. Maybe one of the neighbors had called the police when they saw her going into Callen's house. But why the package, and why would he be out of uniform?

He backed away, his white teeth glistening in the dim light. "Stop right there, Angel. Don't make me shoot you."

"Why would you do that? I don't understand." She didn't, but was beginning to.

"This isn't the way it was supposed to happen." His voice held a hint of regret.

Her gaze darted to the package he'd put under the deck. "What's that?"

His jaw worked back and forth. "Evidence that'll put your detective on ice." He shook his head. "Why are you here? You aren't supposed to be here. I didn't want to hurt you, Angel. Now I have no choice."

"You did it, didn't you? You shot J.J. and the street contact. You knew Mike and I were meeting him on the docks that night. Did you shoot Billy too?"

"Shut up."

"You did. And the evidence. You had to steal it because of the GSR test." She lifted her gaze to his face then looked away. How could she have misjudged him? She'd trusted him. "Was it drugs? Are you on drugs or . . . dealing?"

He pinched his lips together. "You're so smart, Angel. You tell me."

"Did you vandalize my apartment too?" Mutt put his front legs on her pants, wanting to be picked up.

"No. I wouldn't have hurt you like that. I warned Broadman — told him to leave you alone."

"What about Brandon's car . . ." When their gazes met, she shivered.

"I had nothing to do with the car."

Angel looked around for a weapon — a piece of driftwood, anything. "What are you going to do?"

His face had become a hardened mask. "You'll find out soon enough. Now move." He grabbed her arm and hauled her onto the deck, pushing her in front of him. "Inside."

Angel thought briefly about running, but Eric would have a bullet into her back before she got two feet. So she entered the house. Mutt squeezed in ahead of her, almost making her trip. He raced down the hall, apparently trying to get to a safe haven. Angel wished she could go with him.

"Eric, don't do this. You need help."

"What, now you're telling me I'm nuts?" The back of his hand flashed across her field of vision, connecting with her cheek and nose before she had time to react. She staggered back, hitting the wall. Her knees collapsed, and she sank to the floor. Blood streamed out of her right nostril and followed a path to her mouth and onto her shirt.

Looking up, she thought she saw a flicker of compassion in his eyes. "I need to use the bathroom," she said. Maybe she could climb through a window and go for help.

"Forget it."

"Please. My nose. I need to stop the bleeding. Please."

He glanced around, then grabbed the box of tissues on the counter and threw them at her. Angel mopped up the worst of the blood and set the box aside. She heard a car drive up. Callen.

Eric straightened and looked toward the door. "Looks like we have company."

Angel had no doubt Eric would shoot Callen the minute he came in the front door. She had to do something, but what? For a split second Eric's attention would be divided; that's when she had to make her move.

Callen tried the knob then inserted his key in the door. Eric glanced away from her.

"Stay out!" she screamed, and at the same time threw herself into Eric, hitting him in the side. He staggered and slammed her in the stomach with his elbow.

She doubled over and grabbed his leg, throwing him off balance. He fell forward, landing heavily on the tiled floor. His gun flew out of his hand and skittered across the room. Angel dove for it, rolled over, and staggered to her feet.

"Stop right there." She held the gun with both hands, her arms stretched out, ready to fire. Blood dripped from her nose onto the tile floor. "Move a muscle and I'll shoot."

"You won't shoot me, Angel." Eric began rising to his feet.

"You don't want to take that chance." But her mouth had gone desert dry. She licked her lips. Was he right? Would she shoot? Her hands were shaking and so wet with perspiration she was afraid the gun would slip out of her grasp.

Eric stood up, keeping his eyes fixed on her. The patio door slammed open. Callen stood with his legs apart, both hands holding his gun. "Hold it right there, Mason."

Eric ignored the order and dove at Angel. She pulled the trigger. Eric kept coming. She fell to the floor, her head connecting with the tile. The room swirled around her, and everything went black.

FORTY

Angel felt a large, warm hand wrap securely around hers. Callen's hand. Odd that she would know that. "Hi," she croaked.

"Hey." He leaned forward and brushed his hand against her cheek.

She opened her eyes and closed them again, the light too bright to tolerate. She'd seen enough to know that she was still in Callen's house. She could hear voices. EMTs, she decided, and police officers. "Eric. Is he . . . ?"

"You got him in the chest. Punctured a lung. He'll live."

"Callen, he was —"

"Shh. Don't try to talk now."

"He put something under your deck." She tried to sit up. Pain shot through the back of her head, almost taking her out again.

"Easy. Better if you don't move." Callen

eased her back down. "They'll have you on a stretcher in a minute."

Callen let go of her hand when they put her into the ambulance, and promised he'd see her at the hospital.

Somewhere on the way there, Angel disengaged. At least that's what it felt like. She was vaguely aware of being admitted and of people coming and going during the night. On Friday morning the doctor told her she could go home — not to her apartment, but to her parents' home. "Just for a few days," the doctor had said. "You need someone to watch over you."

Someone to watch over you. It sounded like the title of a thriller. Maybe it was. The doctor's words almost made her cry, because he was right. And for the first time in a long while, she was thankful to have people who were willing to care for her.

Tim drove her home, and her mother tucked her into bed in her old room, giving her a bell to ring when she needed help. "Ma," Angel said when her mother went to leave the room. "Thanks."

Tears filled Anna's eyes. "No need to thank me, honey. It's what mothers do."

Angel slept most of the day. When she awoke, it was to those familiar smells coming from the kitchen. She felt almost normal until she tossed the covers aside. Her head still throbbed, but her body hurt more. The doctor had told her she was lucky not to have broken anything.

She held her breath as she urged her muscles to comply so she could get out of bed. She wasn't sure how she did it, but she managed to take a shower and get dressed. She got as far as the living room before collapsing on the sofa. Funny how quickly the body got tired out after a trauma.

"You must be feeling better." Anna stepped through the arch from the kitchen to the living room. "What are you doing up?"

"I smelled food, and I'm starving."

She grinned. "Good. Callen and I have been cooking all day."

"Callen's here?"

"I sent him out for some ice cream."

Angel leaned her head back, closed her eyes, and smiled.

"Something came for you from Brandon." Anna picked up a card from the coffee table. "These flowers came with it."

Angel glanced at the bouquet of roses. "You should've woken me up."

"He didn't come himself." Her mother's tone indicated disapproval. "They were delivered."

Angel opened the card, and a folded note dropped out.

Dear Angel, I guess by now you've heard that all the charges have been dropped against Michelle. I just wanted to thank you for what you said the other night. I am in love with her, and she loves me as well. She's agreed to marry me. Look for a June wedding. Love, Brandon.

Angel folded the letter and inserted it and the card in the envelope.

"Is everything okay?" Anna glanced at the card, curiosity getting the best of her.

"Yeah. Everything's fine." She handed the note to her mother. "Brandon's getting married." It seemed strange to say the words aloud. After all the time they'd been going together, she'd thought she and Brandon would end up married one day. Apparently God had something else in mind.

"He is?" Anna read the letter. "What a terrible thing to do to you, and only days after proposing. Are you upset?"

"No. Relieved, actually." Angel stretched out on the couch and closed her eyes. "I'm so tired."

"Getting hit in the head does that to you. Sleep. We'll eat when you wake up."

Some time later, Angel heard the door open. Callen came in carrying a bag of groceries in one hand and a bunch of tulips in the other. He stopped when he saw her. His green gaze locked with hers. Her heart skipped like water over stones.

He closed the door with his shoulder. "Hey. Welcome back."

"Thanks." She glanced at the flowers. "Are those for me?"

"Ah . . ." He grinned. "Actually, they're for your mother, but I bet she'll share."

"Oh."

Anna hurried in from the kitchen. Taking the flowers she said, "They're perfect. Thanks. How much do I owe you?"

"Nothing." He bent down and kissed her cheek. "If anything, I owe you."

"Don't be silly. For what could you possibly owe me?"

"For treating me like family."

Anna blushed and with a wave of her hand scurried back to the kitchen. Callen winked at Angel and followed her. He set the groceries on the counter then came back into the living room. Sitting on the couch, he reached for Angel's hand. "How are you? Really."

"Better." She stared at their joined hands. "Tell me what happened. Why was

Eric at your house? What was in that package?"

"Long story."

"I have time."

He glanced toward the kitchen. "Tell you what. Let's eat dinner first, and then I'll take you for a drive."

"Deal."

After dinner, Callen drove them to one of Angel's favorite spots on the beach. The sun was making its final descent, leaving behind a hazy film of pink-tinged clouds. The horizon glowed red-orange to pale yellow above a deep blue line. They watched the brilliant sun disappear into the sea. The moment was almost too perfect to end with talk about murder.

Callen must have felt it too. He wove his fingers through hers and brought her hand to his lips.

Angel frowned. "You are going to tell me what happened, aren't you, or do I have to read about it in the papers?"

He kissed the tip of her nose. "You're a nosey little thing, aren't you?"

"Guilty as charged. Now let's have it. I figure you owe me for hauling in the big one."

He chuckled. "Okay, here goes. We're

still sorting through all the evidence, but I can pretty much tell you what went down. Eric had a big side business going in the drug trade. One of his partners was Jake Ensley, a guy who took his boat up and down the coast. About once a week, Ensley would bring ecstasy down here from Astoria and deliver it to ports up and down the coast. When he had a delivery here, he'd put it in the old warehouse, where Eric's head honcho would pick it up and sell it. He'd brought in a shipment the night I went into the warehouse. Eric had apparently gone in the back way to check on his shipment and saw me there. He whacked me with his baton. Lab guys said it still has traces of my blood on it."

Angel shivered. Temperatures had dropped, and she'd only put on a light-weight jacket. Callen pulled a blanket from the backseat and wrapped it around her. "Better?"

"Much." She rested her head on his shoulder. His arm wrapped securely around her. "What about the package?"

"Ah yes, the package. Eric was trying to hang me by planting evidence at my place but ended up hanging himself." Callen squeezed her shoulder. "Thanks to your hunger pangs and Mutt's penchant for the ocean, you caught him in the act. The package contained the stolen evidence along with the .45 used to kill J.J. and Mike's contact."

"That's pretty scary. What if I hadn't been there?"

"It wouldn't have taken long to figure it out. With the stolen evidence, I had a feeling we might be dealing with a dirty cop, so I had a couple people in the lab going over the logs for every day, pinpointing where each officer was at any given time. Eric failed the test."

"What about Billy?"

"The .40-caliber casing I found in the warehouse came from Eric's duty weapon."

"But you checked his gun right after it happened. Nick did too."

"He'd put in a new magazine."

She nodded. "And stole the evidence knowing the GSR would read positive."

"Right. There's no doubt he did it."

Relief mingled with shame that she'd doubted her father. "I feel terrible." She told Callen about her suspicions.

"I wish you'd said something earlier, Angel. I could've set your mind at ease. I knew Frank had been near the pharmacy that day. Dispatch had him on the other side of town at the time of the shooting. We checked his weapon against the .40 casing I found at the warehouse."

Angel frowned. "You checked Eric's gun against the casing too, didn't you?"

"Yeah, but Eric had three .40 Glocks. We found them in his apartment. One of them matched. That was all we needed."

"I still can't believe it. Not once in the year I worked with him did I suspect that he was dealing drugs."

"No one knew. He led two separate lives. And that matching gun had a sordid past. It once belonged to a police officer named Butch Mason. He was killed with his own gun eleven years ago, and the gun was never found until now."

"Mason? Eric killed his father?"

"Looks that way. Eric's being charged with killing J.J., Billy, Alex, and Mike's contact. There may be others. I have a feeling we've just scratched the surface."

"I still don't get it. Why would Eric kill Billy?"

"He says he was covering your back."

"What?" Angel shook her head. "No . . . he would have come forward right away."

"Not necessarily. He may not have wanted anyone to know he was in the back of the warehouse. He definitely wouldn't have wanted to draw attention to himself. He'd be questioned — especially after we found the body."

He paused and curled a strand of her hair around his finger. "I have another theory. My guess is that Billy caught him looking down at J.J. and somehow recognized him as Duke. Eric and his uncle were business partners."

"So we really don't know the true motivation." Angel hated loose ends.

"Not yet, but we will. Between Ray Broadman and Eric, we'll piece everything together eventually."

"And Kelsey?"

Callen shook his head. "We haven't found a connection there yet. Might be an unrelated case."

"Well, I'm glad I didn't kill Eric. I feel bad enough having shot him."

"You're one brave woman, Angel, taking on a guy like that." His Adam's apple moved up and down. He covered his eyes and lowered his head, and when he looked at her, tears glistened in his eyes.

"I had to do something. He was going to kill you."

"I know. You shook me up though." He looked toward the ocean. "When I pulled Eric off you and saw all that blood, I thought you were dead."

Angel turned and caressed his face. "I'm sorry."

He smiled. "Don't be. Strange as it may seem, that was when I realized how important you had become to me." He touched a finger to her lips and gently brushed across the bruise Eric had left on her cheek.

"Angel." He turned slightly, lifting her chin. "I don't want to talk about Eric anymore. I want to know where I stand with you."

Angel wanted to close her eyes and lean toward him, letting his lips cover hers. She wanted to say "I love you" but couldn't quite manage it. "Obstacles," she surprised herself by saying.

"You mean Brandon?" Callen frowned.

"Not Brandon. He's going to marry Michelle Kelsey." She twisted back around and leaned heavily into the seat.

Callen chuckled. "That's great. So what's the problem?"

"Me. I don't know how to explain it." She had so much emotional baggage to work out, it didn't seem fair to saddle Callen with it.

"Try. I really want to know."

"Well, all my life I've been doing things to please my dad. To get him to pay attention to me — to be proud of me and to love me."

"He does love you. You should've seen him when I told him what had happened to you."

"I know he does, in his own way. He just never showed it like I wanted him to." She massaged her temples. "I became a police officer because I thought it would make him proud of me. I almost quit a few times but didn't want to disappoint dear old Dad. Now I realize I don't have to please him."

"No, you don't."

"So I guess I don't know what to do. Now that the grand jury has cleared me, I can go back to work. But I don't know if I want to."

"I'm sure Joe will be disappointed, but if you want to change careers, do it."

"It's not that easy. Anyway, seeing you with my mother has made me realize how much I've missed. I cheated her out of a daughter."

"It's never too late to change."

"No, I suppose not."

"I still haven't heard a good reason for us not to be together."

Angel thought he sounded completely reasonable. "I guess that's true."

He grinned down at her, his green eyes sparkling. "Your mother is going to tell you to marry me."

"She is?"

"Mmm. She thinks I'm good husband material."

"Maybe you are." Angel forgot to breathe. "But I'm not ready to get married."

"Good. Neither am I." He brought her closer to him.

She had no idea what the future held. She didn't know if she would go back to work as a police officer. She didn't know where life would take her or where Callen would fit in. She only knew one thing. The moment Callen's lips met hers, she didn't want to be anywhere else.

About the Author

Award-winning author and speaker **Patricia H. Rushford** has book sales totaling over a million copies. She has written over forty books, including four mystery series. Patricia's most recent works include the Angel Delaney Mysteries and the McAllister Files, which she writes with a police detective. She also writes the popular Jennie McGrady Mysteries for kids and the Helen Bradley Mysteries for adults. Most of her mysteries are set in the Northwest.

Patricia holds a master's degree in counseling. In addition, she conducts writers' workshops for adults and children and is co-director of Writer's Weekend at the Beach. Patricia has appeared on numerous radio and television talk shows across the United States and Canada.